Wings

Wings

A Novel

Don L. Searle

TEMPLE HILL BOOKS

My thanks to Marie, without whose love and patience this book could never have come to be, and to Kurt and Lauren, good friends who helped.

ISBN 978-1-4341-0316-1

Published by Temple Hill Books, an imprint of The Editorium

Temple Hill Books™, the Temple Hill Books logo, and The Editorium™ are trademarks of The Editorium, LLC

The Editorium, LLC
West Valley City, UT 84128-3917
templehillbooks.com
templehill@editorium.com

Prologue

Steve wore his dark executive suit and a tasteful dark red tie. From the first time she saw him, Kate had been struck by how handsome he was. Dressed this way, he might have been a model in a men's clothing magazine or catalog. To anyone who saw him at the convention in Las Vegas, he would look just the way the president of a successful corporation ought to look.

Kate put her arms around him and kissed him tenderly. "You're going to make a great impression today." She kissed him again. "You make a great impression on me. Hurry back tonight. I've got the steaks thawing already. You'll be barbecuing."

He grinned at her. "Take good care of Junior," he said, pointing to Stevie in his high chair. "And take good care of my princess." He walked around the dinette table and kissed KatiLynn. She smiled up at him. "Bye, Daddy."

And then the scene changed. It was as though she were in the cockpit behind Steve and Gary, the pilot. She had a bad feeling about what she saw. Gary was not paying attention to his flying. His airspeed was too low, the horizon on his indicator was not level, and Gary was not watching his instruments. She tried to speak, but she couldn't. And how could they have heard her anyway? After all, she had not been in the plane. She could only imagine the way it had been.

The scene changed once more. She was looking out the front window of their home at the highway patrol cruiser parked on the street. She saw the state trooper and the police chaplain coming up the front sidewalk, and she began to murmur, "No, no, no, no," before she even heard the doorbell. Before she had to hear the trooper say, "Mrs. Warden? Mrs. Steven Warden?" Before she had to see the look in the eyes of the chaplain, knowing he was about to hurt her, wishing there were some comfort he could offer her—some comfort that no one on earth could offer now.

And then the scene changed for the last time. She saw Steve sitting in the passenger seat of the plane, looking toward the pilot's seat, where she would be sitting. He smiled that radiant smile of his and said to her, "Please don't let me go, Kate."

She woke clutching her pillow. Had she been saying, "No, no," out loud when she woke?

It was the same dream she had dreamed last night.

The pillow was soaked with her tears. She flung it angrily at the wall. She had not wanted to let him go to Las Vegas. She had tried to talk him out of it; she had said that Joe Tyler, the company vice president, could handle greeting people in the booth at the convention center. But Steve had said he wanted to make a good impression for the company on the opening day. It was just a quick flight, he had said, a day trip, and he would be home for dinner.

Her tears started again.

He would never be coming home for dinner again. Or breakfast. Or anything. She tried to tell herself she should have insisted he stay home. But it had seemed selfish at the time, and Steve had convinced her that everything would be fine.

He had always been able to make her feel that everything would be fine.

Now she would be burying him tomorrow. And now it seemed like nothing could ever be fine again. She had reached out to everyone she could think of in the past three days, and no one could show her a reason for hope.

The one person in her world who meant everything to her was gone, and that was forever, wasn't it?

1

Bill Morrow unlocked the gate to the aircraft tie-down area, then held it shut as his daughter started to walk through. "I still don't understand why you have to do this right now, Kate. Are you *sure* you're up to it?"

Kate looked into her father's eyes for several seconds, then reached out and pushed the gate open. She strode across the asphalt toward the planes with her father in step beside her. "Dad, I'm not afraid of flying just because of what happened to Steve."

"Are you trying to prove that to other people—or to yourself?"

She glanced sharply at him. "It wasn't flying that killed my husband. It was pilot error."

"You ought to be careful about assuming that, Kate—or saying it. You don't know—"

"I know Gary—*knew* Gary. He was a sloppy pilot sometimes—careless."

"And what if the investigation says you're wrong—that there was no pilot error?"

"There was nothing wrong with that plane. I flew it enough to know."

"That was the one you had to set down in the desert because of the oil pressure gauge."

"Yes, but you fixed it, and I never had any other problem with it."

Bill pursed his lips and shook his head, but his daughter was not looking at him. She stopped next to a single-engine Cessna and opened the pilot's door.

"This is the only one available right now," Bill said. "But, Honey, I wish you wouldn't do this. Your mind won't be in it completely. I haven't seen you cry once, except yesterday at the funeral. You're holding—"

"I didn't want to upset the children any more than they already are. You haven't seen me at night when I'm alone."

"But is it healthy to hold things in? Even for the children's sake? I know you. You can keep your control on the outside while it's eating—"

"Please, Dad! I *have* to do this." She put her arms around her father and leaned against his broad chest. "Please—trust me, the way you always have before."

He hesitated, then slowly wrapped his arms around her, squeezed her to him, and sighed. "My darling Kate. There's nobody I trust more. Not even myself." He stepped back and held her lightly by her arms. "But do you mind if I run through the preflight checks with you?"

"No, not if it will make you feel better."

When the plane lifted off the runway a few minutes before dawn, Kate climbed toward the northwest, away from Phoenix, following roughly the same flight path Gary and Steve would have followed on their flight to Las Vegas. It was the route they would also have followed in reverse on their return, before the plane went down.

Her father had been partly right about her feelings; she was in control only on the outside. She had spent so much time crying alone for the past three nights that she felt almost empty now.

But not completely. Something was gnawing away slowly deep inside, where she tried to keep it confined—something that wanted answers. Could she stop it from consuming her? She wasn't sure.

Her father needn't have worried about her flying. Focusing on this was one thing she could do to keep control. And if she could find her answers anywhere, it would be somewhere up here in the clear air where she had so often gone to find peace.

She had to turn east off the direct flight path to locate the crash site, but it was not hard to find. There was nothing on the side of the mountain now but a large black smudge that stood out even in the shadowed area where the sun had not yet touched the slope. What remained of the burned aircraft had been taken away. She banked the plane she was flying into a 180-degree turn, reversing her course before she reached the spot where the plane carrying Steve and Gary had gone down. She had already seen enough close-ups of boulders and charred wreckage on television and in the newspapers—usually followed by the smiling photos of the two casualties of the crash.

Kate's eyes misted over as she turned back to the west and flew above the desert landscape. Crossing over Highway 93, she banked once more, toward the south, with no particular destination in mind.

On the western horizon, the sky was still deep blue. But in the east, the sun was rising just the way God made it to do every day, day after day, for eternity.

Whatever eternity meant.

If God had answers to her questions about life and death and eternity, He wasn't sharing them with her just now, or with anyone she knew.

Since she was a little girl, she had always known that God was up there—or at least that Someone greater was watching over the world. Somehow she just *knew*. There was order in the universe, not just chance—she was sure of it. Certain principles were always at work. If you applied the principles of lift and thrust correctly, a heavier-than-air machine would rise off the ground and do what you directed it to do. If you learned the things you needed to know and worked hard enough, you'd get where you wanted to go in life. That was not chance. Men and women were in control of their own destinies, and chaos was not the rule in the universe. Of that she felt sure.

Except, maybe, in Steve's case.

Yesterday at the funeral she had overheard someone whispering the question she had not been able to get out of her mind: "Why did God take him now?" *Why?* Why would a God who was truly good take her husband, leaving her a widow at thirty with a four-year-old and an eleven-month-old? Some would say if He really existed, He wouldn't let such things happen. Not if He really loved his children. Not if He really loved *her*.

If He really loved her, Kate thought, why couldn't she feel it now?

She still knew He was there. She was tempted to deny it—but she couldn't. Even with Steve's death, things had happened to show her there was some higher power that watched over the affairs of people on earth. Five days ago, she had not understood why it seemed so important to stay at home with the children instead of making the day trip to Las Vegas with her husband. Now she knew. That decision—that *feeling*—had brought a blessing to her children.

Maybe it made her hurt more to know there was a higher power. God ought to be able to tell her why He needed Steve more than she did—if there really was reason behind it.

She had lashed out in anger at her parents when the priest from their church had not been able to give her answers. She was ashamed of that now. She had refused to let the priest officiate at Steve's funeral, but the

5

minister her parents had found, through the church of a friend, had not been able to offer her any more comfort than the priest.

This was the reason she had quit going to church when she was in college. None of these people could ever give her answers to her questions—and certainly not to the question of "Why?"

If God *is* love, as the Bible says, why would He let something so bad happen to her? The mortal father who had not wanted her to fly today would never let bad things happen to her if he could stop them. Wasn't God supposed to be a father? Wasn't He supposed to love her more than anyone else ever could?

Kate squeezed away the tears that wanted to come. She hated this battle of doubt that had gone on inside her for the past four days. She would have to teach her children now that Daddy had gone to be with God. She believed that—wanted desperately to believe it—and yet . . . what would she tell them if they wanted to know why this God of love had taken their father? *Why?*

She had been paying little attention to the landscape below, but one spot on her left seemed oddly familiar. She studied the dirt road below. Was that . . . yes, the road where she had landed the night she and Steve had spent in the plane out here—the first time he had let her know that he hoped to spend the rest of his life with her.

The rest of his life.

She banked the Cessna left into a long, slow 180-degree turn and came back toward that dirt roadway in the desert, then descended to fly along above it.

"Do you pray, Steve?" she asked.

"Ah . . . not in a while."

"Now would be a good time. Pray that there aren't any animals wandering across this road. Pray that it's in good shape."

They were silent as the plane descended. The radio crackled in her ear as the air traffic controller in Albuquerque called the number of the plane. "Radar contact lost, repeat, radar contact lost. Over."

He was asking for a response, but Kate didn't have time to answer. She slipped the plane sideways slightly to avoid the telephone lines to the right; her hands on the yoke and her feet on the pedals made constant tiny adjustments as she eased the airplane down onto the road.

Steve had been sitting tensely, one arm braced against the top of the instrument panel, watching as the airplane's landing lights reached out to light the roadway ahead. He relaxed as the aircraft touched down lightly.

The high wing of the single-engine Cessna just skimmed above the bushes that flashed by on the left side of the road. The thrumming of the wheels on hard-packed dirt gradually slowed as Kate brought the plane to a stop.

She lifted her hands from the yoke and let out a long breath. Then she keyed her microphone and called the Albuquerque Center, identifying the plane. "We are down on a dirt road about two miles south of the truck stop on I-10."

"Roger, copy you on the ground." Relief was evident in the controller's voice. "Do you require emergency vehicles or other assistance?"

"Can you notify Morrow Flight Service at Deer Valley Municipal Airport in Phoenix?" She repeated the flight service's emergency telephone number.

"Will do."

"Please tell Bill to bring an oil pressure sender for the engine in the Cessna."

Her pilot's instincts had been right; there was nothing seriously wrong with the engine that night, just a small defective part in the oil reservoir. But she could not have been sure of this at the time, and with the gauge showing loss of oil pressure, no responsible pilot would have made any choice except the one she had made—a precautionary landing.

Kate and Steve had waited out most of the night in the plane until her father arrived from Phoenix with the needed part. They had sat in the back seat of the plane to dine on granola bars and water Kate pulled from an emergency equipment compartment.

"What do you think Kenji Nakamura will do?" she asked.

Kate heard Steve shifting in the passenger seat so he could turn toward her. "I think we've got the edge with Nakamura Electronics right now— because of you."

She thought back over the events of the day. "You made the presentation. What did I—"

"Didn't you notice how he listens when you talk? I, uh . . ." She heard him shifting his long legs around again. "Ouch," he muttered, then continued his thought. "I think I convinced him we have the best equipment even if National beats our price. But he listens when you talk—you're a pilot. Did you pay attention to how he asked his questions? He checked everything out with you. Kenji respects what you have to say."

In the dim light Kate could see Steve's shoulders move as he shifted in his seat once more. She felt selfish extending her five-foot-seven frame into the empty cargo space between the seats while Steve, who was at least six-foot-one, might have to sit for hours with his knees wedged into the small space in front. "There's more leg room back here," she volunteered. "I mean, if you don't mind sharing the seat."

"Thank you, I will." He climbed out of the front seat and moved slowly through the cabin in the dark. His white shirt stood out in the faint trace of moonlight from outside.

The bench seat in the rear of the cabin was narrower than she had thought—barely wide enough even for two people who carried no extra weight—but Kate didn't really mind being close to him.

"Water?" she asked. "I didn't drink out of the bottle—just poured water into my mouth." She found his hand in the dark and pressed the bottle into it.

He fumbled with opening the spout, then raised the bottle toward his mouth. She could tell by the way his head jerked suddenly toward her that he had missed his mouth with the stream of water. She laughed. "Get it a little closer."

"How did you learn to do that?"

"I got plenty of practice camping with my father and brother."

"We didn't do a lot of camping in my family. My father was too busy building up the company."

"How old were you when you started working there?"

"Sixteen. I started on a cleanup crew. When I was eighteen, they made me a delivery driver, and then while I was in college I worked on the production line. After I had my degree in management, Dad gave me an office job."

Steve had worked nearly half his life for Warden Avionics. He had inherited the company when his parents had died in a traffic accident. He had followed his father's footsteps in building the company, insisting on the highest quality in its products. As a result, Warden had strengthened its firm hold on the top spot in the market.

It seemed that most of his time went into his job. He was known to date, but apparently there had never been a serious relationship with anyone. Traci Morgan, the company's marketing and public relations director, had been his partner several times at official functions for the company, and they had dated a few other times as well, but he seemed to feel no strong attraction. One day as Kate and Traci talked, Traci had shaken her head and wondered out loud if any woman would ever be able to occupy Steve's full attention.

He was good-looking and he was wealthy; those two things alone were enough to make most women want to get his attention. Kate had seen other things in him that impressed her—his integrity, his thoughtfulness and consideration of those around him. Stories about his generosity with employees who ran into bad times were part of the company lore. He was a man to admire and trust.

Kate was listening to him reminisce about growing up in the company when sleep began to overtake her. He stopped talking when she nodded off and went momentarily limp against his side. She felt him raise his arm and saw the faint luminescence of his wristwatch dial.

"Mmm—11:10. I'm keeping you awake. Sorry."

"No. I'm sorry. It was interesting. But this has been a long day, and a landing like that—well, there's an adrenaline high, but in the end it takes a lot out of me." She leaned toward the inside wall of the cabin on her left and closed her eyes. There was no support for her head, and her neck hurt in that position. She made tiny changes in her position several times trying to find a less awkward way to rest, but she had little room to move.

After a few minutes, Steve said, "Would you like to . . . I mean, if it would be more comfortable, you could lean your head on my shoulder. I wouldn't mind."

Would she like to? This was the only man she could remember dreaming about at night since she was in high school. Sometimes when Traci had talked casually about dating Steve, Kate had let her mind wander to thoughts of what it would be like to walk with him while he held her hand or maybe even put his arm around her. She blushed to think of it now—but he couldn't see her face in the dark. She said carefully, "Well, if you're sure it wouldn't be a problem." Slowly she tilted her head until it rested against his left shoulder. "I hope that won't crowd you."

She ignored the quiet little voice pointing out that they had just crossed a barrier separating two working professionals. She was too tired to argue with the voice, and these were not office hours. At the moment she was just Kate, who had wondered what it might be like to be this close to him. She felt secure in the warmth of him, the touch of his arm against her side. And after all, he had offered.

* * *

Lights. Flickering lights woke her. She opened her eyes to see the lights dancing off the ceiling and the walls of the cabin in the plane.

What was the weight on her left arm? Why was she leaning . . .

Kate jumped slightly as she realized that the weight was Steve's arm around her shoulders and that she was leaning against his chest. Her small movement did not disturb him; he went on breathing rhythmically, his head back against the seat in the plane. Sometime during the night, he had managed to put his suit jacket over her and his arm around her without waking her. .

Her first thought was that she should feel embarrassed about the situation. Probably she ought to apologize for inconveniencing him, and also for . . . for what—violating office protocol?

But she could not muster a sense of embarrassment at the moment. It was enjoyable to be so close to him. And she felt something more—something she would never be able to mention to him—a wish that this experience did not have to be a one-time thing.

Probably she should forget about that wish because nothing would ever come of it.

While her father was working on the plane, Steve had taken her aside to share what he had been thinking about while she slept. His words had come as a shock.

His smile seemed uncertain. She wondered what that meant; she had rarely seen Steve Warden uncertain of anything. He stood looking at her for several seconds before he spoke. "When we were coming down on this road last night, I kept thinking of things I wished I had done sooner in life. One of them was to have a talk with you."

"About what?"

He thought for a moment. "I've tried never to have, ah . . . feelings toward anybody I work with or supervise. I don't think that's a good idea, generally. But in your case, it . . . in your case, I can't help how I feel. I've wished before that I could tell you." He paused. "And I need to tell you. I'm 31 years old, and I'm running out of time to play some of the games that men and women play when they're, uh . . ."

Kate looked into his eyes waiting for him to go on. But he didn't. "What are you saying, Steve?"

"That I enjoyed having my arm around you and holding you close to me. I enjoyed it for hours, just thinking of things I ought to say to you. That I haven't been completely honest with you—or with myself. That you're more than a coworker to me, that I've been making opportunities to

be around you every day, that . . ." He paused. "That I think I'm falling in love with you."

"You're . . . you think . . ."

"I've been falling in love with you."

He looked down at the ground and scuffed at the dirt with the toe of his Bass loafer. She was startled to realize that his action reminded her of a young boy.

"I'm very good at the things I do, but the business is almost all I know of life," he said. "I was only 26 when my parents were killed, and I've spent the last five years trying to make Warden Avionics into the kind of company they—my father—wanted it to become. I'm sure you've heard people say I'm married to the company. I've never allowed myself time to be close to a woman. There's never been anyone who made me want to say things like this before. Last night, after you got us down safely, I knew I didn't want to waste any more of my life without finding out whether I might have a chance with you."

"We're being completely honest here?" she asked.

"Yes." He seemed wary of what she might say.

Kate smiled at him and took a step closer. "I liked being close to you too." She wasn't sure how much she should tell him—but he had risked disclosing his feelings. "I admire you. I trust you. I like you—a lot. I used to wish when you took Traci out that sometime you would, ah, ask . . ." She left the sentence unfinished, blushing.

Steve glanced at his watch and smiled broadly. "What about breakfast this morning? We can talk about more important things than the Nakamura deal."

Kate's smile broadened too as she glanced at her own watch. "Do you think that might be pushing things a bit? So far, we're still stranded in the desert."

"Lunch, then. I'd like to learn a lot more about you as soon as I can."

After her father had finished fixing the plane that morning, she had flown alone back to Phoenix. She had told Steve he needed to ride in the truck with her father because the takeoff from the dirt road might be risky. Her father had looked at her in disbelief because he knew it would be no problem for her, but he had said nothing.

Kate had simply wanted time alone to think about what Steve had told her. As the plane rose above the desert that morning, she wondered why she had never quite seen the real beauty of this area before. The rising sun gave a golden hue to everything it touched, driving away the shadows.

The way she had felt that long-ago morning was in stark contrast to the way she felt on this one as she flew above the dirt road in the desert.

She banked the plane ninety degrees to the right again, toward Phoenix, and called in a course change. She shielded her eyes momentarily against the morning sun as the plane came to its proper heading on the route she had flown five years ago.

She looked down as she had then on the desert with its stark beauty—the specters of the cacti stretching in shadows across flats and gullies, and the deep, deep pools of shadow behind the rocky ridges. On that other morning, she had appreciated the golden quality of the light on everything she could see. This time, it was the shadows that held her attention.

She didn't know whether she could go on without Steve. Maybe she didn't even want to go on. Several times during the past three days, she had thought that she simply couldn't handle the day-in, day-out tasks and heartaches alone. Without Steve, she didn't know whether life was worth living. Maybe that was what was gnawing away at her deep inside. Never in her life had she given up at anything. But to face forty or fifty years without Steve, the one person who had made her feel complete? She wasn't sure she could endure it.

Were people permitted to decide when they had had enough? There were times over the past few days when that thought had lingered in her mind: she could just make it all stop.

It would be so easy, Kate thought, to put the plane into a dive right into one of those dark pools of shadow on the desert below—to join Steve wherever he was right now.

She eased the yoke forward, putting the small plane into a shallow descent toward the desert floor while she thought about where Steve might be.

Nowhere.

No! That was wrong. It had to be someplace—just nowhere that she knew. But it had to be . . . something.

Somewhere. He's not gone. I know it. There's a place. If I could just . . .

Everything he was, everything he had been to her, everything they had been to each other . . . it *wasn't* gone. She did not know how she knew this—but she *knew*.

Steve was somewhere. And if this plane kept going down and down until . . . would she find him then, wherever he was?

Tears came out of her eyes, against her will, and slid down her cheeks. She was not empty after all.

Even if she knew—if she *knew*—that she would see Steve in the next few seconds, she could not let it happen yet. It would be tampering with the order of the universe somehow. It would be abandoning the course she was supposed to fly. She knew that too.

Yesterday she had been reminded that there were more people than she knew who cared about her—people who wanted to soothe her hurt.

Kenji Nakamura, the client and friend, had shown up at the funeral. She had gasped when she had seen him and his wife Lily enter the chapel. "Joe Tyler called me," Kenji had said. "I couldn't miss being here, for Steve, and for you, Kate. How can I help you?" He had offered to lend her one of his assistants for a time if she needed administrative support. He and Lily had flown from Tokyo despite that fact that Kenji had to complete a business deal in Singapore two days after the funeral. And despite the fact that they had an evening flight back to Tokyo, Lily and Kenji had lingered to help care for KatiLynn and Stevie while Kate accepted the condolences of others. When they left, Lily had whispered in Kate's ear, "I've been praying for you." She pressed a piece of paper with a telephone number on it into Kate's hand. "I know we've only met a few times, but call me if you need to talk—at my expense. I mean it." Kenji had promised to keep in touch.

And yesterday Kate had been reminded of at least two very important reasons she still needed to be here.

After everyone else but family was gone, she had walked slowly to the funeral director's limousine, assisted by her father, and sat down in the back seat. KatiLynn had trailed along behind with her grandmother, who carried Stevie. Four-year-old KatiLynn, not understanding fully what was wrong with Mommy and wanting desperately to help, had said, "Let me take Stevie, Grandma. Let me take him to Mommy." She had struggled to carry her brother the last few feet then had set him down close to the car intending to help him walk the rest of the way. Stevie had smiled at his mother and then taken a step toward her on his own. Kate had smiled back in spite of herself, had held out her arms and said, "That's good, Baby. You can do it." He had taken another step, then another to reach the safety of her arms.

13

Kate leveled the plane off and skimmed along just above the land-scape.

In those dark pools on the desert floor, there would be no answers for her.

The touchdown in Phoenix and her usual post-flight inspection of the plane all were automatic. She knew she had done them, but when she sat down in her father's office, in the chair across the desk from him, she could not remember the details.

He looked into her eyes for several seconds. "So?"

Tears started, and she could not hold them back. She sobbed—heaving sobs that shook her body—and Bill walked around the desk to sit with his arm around her shoulders.

When the sobs subsided, he held her close to him, brushing the hair away from her face the way he had when she was a girl. "Kate," he whispered, "I've never known anyone better at facing life head-on. But don't fight it by yourself. You don't have to do it all alone."

2

The half hour story time with the children seemed to go by too fast on nights like this, Kate thought as she tucked KatiLynn into bed. She sighed. There was still the report she had brought home from the office to read tonight.

By day, she ran Warden Avionics, and after work she ran her home. Life had become a blur—at the office, meetings and follow-through on different projects; at home, meeting her children's needs after hours. Each of those areas spilled over into the other at times, leaving her wondering which to handle first, and she was not sure if there was any way she could change things.

Kate had poured out her frustrations to her next-door neighbor, Evie, over coffee on a Saturday morning while their children played in the swimming pool. She had explained that she always spent the first part of the weekend just trying to overcome bone-deep tiredness. But she owed her best to the good people of Warden Avionics who had kept the company on top since Steve's death. And she owed it to Steve—or to his dream. He had planned for the company to be a legacy for his children.

"Kate," Evie had answered, "I see your light on at night when I go to bed and again in the morning when I get up. For two and a half years now, you've been trying to be Steve the chief and Kate the mom without leaving any time for Kate the person. You don't take time to relax or recharge your emotional batteries. How long do you think you can keep doing this?"

She did not have a good answer. Evie was right. But Kate saw no way out.

By the time she finished reading the quarterly earnings report for Warden Avionics this night and sat down to make her telephone call, it was after 10:00 p.m.—after 1:00 p.m. tomorrow in Tokyo, she calculated. Kenji Nakamura had called her office this afternoon while she had been away attending KatiLynn's school program. Kate knew what Kenji wanted, and she was not eager to talk to him about it again. But he was too good a friend to ignore.

"You're up late," Kenji said when she got him on the line. "Isn't it a school night?"

Kate laughed. "Yes, and I just got the children in bed about an hour ago. I'm sorry I didn't return your call earlier."

"No problem. I know you're busy." Kenji had been sent off to school in Hawaii as a boy to learn English and learn to deal with Americans—two assets he would bring into the family business. His grasp of American idiom and culture was nearly perfect. "So, how *is* KatiLynn?" he asked. Kenji had no children of his own, and he had been charmed by a shy three-year-old KatiLynn the first time he met her, on a visit to the Warden offices three and a half years ago.

"She's fine," Kate answered. "Reading now. Tonight she read *me* part of the story."

"Tell her I want her to send me another picture. And Stevie?"

"Fine too. He's talking fairly well now—enough to tell me what he wants and why I ought to give it to him."

Kenji laughed. "Negotiating already. He must take after Steve."

Kate smiled. "He's a little bit of both of us. How's Lily?"

Lily Nakamura was the *nisei* surprise Kenji had brought home to Japan after finishing a degree in business at the University of Hawaii. Kenji's Japanese-American bride had left his traditionalist father nonplussed at first, but impressed later with her intelligence and charm. "She's happy, and keeping me happy as well," Kenji answered. "I've bought us a place about an hour out of the city—our little country estate—and Lily is turning it into a piece of paradise."

So far as Kate knew, Kenji was Buddhist; when he spoke of paradise, he probably meant it the same way land developers in Hawaii used the word. "I'll give my children your good wishes, Kenji. But I'm sure you didn't call just to ask about them."

"Well, that wasn't the only reason." He paused. "I'm prepared to make you a better offer for Warden Avionics than I did six months ago, Kate. Much better. I'd like to email you the terms today if you'll consider them."

He still wanted to make Warden Avionics part of the Nakamura conglomerate. Steve had left Kate well-fixed as sole owner of the company. Now Kenji Nakamura was prepared to make her a *very* wealthy woman, able to pursue any dream she might have in this life—but at what price to others? Nakamura Industries would probably decide that many of the Warden employees, especially executives, did not fit into its plans for the future.

Kate was not prepared yet to give up Warden Avionics. Along with everything else it meant, it was a part of Steve she could hang onto. She didn't know whether she could ever let his company go—even to a good friend.

And Kenji Nakamura *was* a friend. In one way, perhaps, she owed him her marriage. Steve had told her the story after their wedding.

Kate listened with one ear as Lily Nakamura admired the large bird of paradise flowers that were centerpieces on the banquet tables. Kate's mind was on Steve, who was talking quietly in the far corner with Lily's husband. Kenji Nakamura had a reputation as a man of integrity. He also had a quiet wit and an active intellect that was sometimes masked by his soft-spoken manner. Kate wondered what his active mind was working on as he talked to Steve.

Across the room, Kenji spoke to Steve, who was looking at Kate. "Your Miss Morrow is not only intelligent, she's also very attractive. Did you think about that when you hired her?"

Steve looked at him in surprise. "No, not really—not then. But lately . . ." Steve wondered if he had let down his guard too much. He recovered quickly. "We hired her because we expected her to be good in the business. It was a bonus that she can fly too." He glanced across the room at Kate again.

Kenji smiled knowingly. "But you've never seen her quite like this before, have you?"

Nakamura was right. Steve studied Kate again. The simple, formal beige dress she wore was topped by a complementary mocha-colored jacket. Her long brown hair was done up on the top of her head tonight, and a single strand of gold chain accented her graceful neck. She looked elegant—and she probably was unaware of the impact she made on others. Steve laughed as he turned back to the other man.

Kenji's eyebrows went up questioningly.

"She told me she got the dress at J.C. Penney," Steve explained, "and the jacket came from a shop that sells clothes rich women weed out of their closets. Kate makes it all look good, doesn't she—like a $2,000 outfit from some fashion designer."

Kenji nodded. "She's a beautiful woman. Have you ever thought that you could lose her?"

Steve frowned, not sure what Kenji was trying to say. "You mean someone might hire her away? I don't think . . ."

"You don't think she'd go? Maybe not. But I wasn't talking about hiring. I'm sure other men also notice how attractive she is." Kenji paused. "But I suppose as her employer, that doesn't need to concern you." There was a slight emphasis on the word employer. *Kenji smiled again and said nothing more.*

This man must have noticed, Steve thought, that every minute or so his host's eyes went to Kate, wherever she was in the room. If so, Nakamura was smart enough to realize that Kate was more than simply an employee to him.

Had Nakamura seen some other man paying attention to her?

Kate had dated other men seriously in the past, and she wasn't a woman any man could overlook. There were other men in the company who seemed to pay a lot of attention to her—Jeff Weller, from Marketing, and Webb Nyquist, from Engineering. Both men were here tonight.

There was no reason for Jeff or Webb or any other man to suspect that he should not ask Kate out; no one in the company knew they were dating.

Kenji's question—"Have you ever thought that you could lose her?"—would not go away.

Once on their honeymoon, Kate had laid her head on Steve's chest and told him how glad she was that he had asked her to marry him. Steve had told her then about his conversation with Kenji and its effect.

He played the host perfectly during the dinner celebrating the two companies' contract. He spoke warmly of how pleased he was to be associated with Nakamura Industries, even though everyone present understood that the Japanese company had made a smart move in seeking a deal with Warden Avionics. This was Nakamura's best possible entry into the American avionics market at the moment.

Kate had been an important part of winning Kenji Nakamura's trust. That had been clear as she responded to him during the dinner.

"Mr. Nakamura, I believe we've already answered all of the questions you're asking, in the materials we prepared for you," Kate said, smiling at him. "But if you're still wondering how confident we really are about our products, I could take you for another demonstration flight in the morning."

Nakamura laughed. "Ah, the directness of American business people." He glanced at Steve, next to him, then spoke to Kate, seated at her employer's left. "Please—call me Kenji. And may I call you Kate?"

"Of course."

"Kate, it's your confidence that tells me I made the right choice with Warden Avionics. You probably know I received an offer from one of your competitors that was more attractive financially. I'll have to justify my decision to the head of my company—and my father is a very careful businessman."

Steve picked up the bottle of wine on the table and poured more into Kenji's goblet. Kenji lifted the goblet toward his hosts, then took a sip. "A very good wine—one of California's best, I believe." He glanced at Kate's empty goblet. "But you haven't tried it, Kate."

"Wine isn't one of her pleasures," Steve said.

"I rarely drink alcohol," Kate explained. "I've wondered, if it's not good for me when I'm flying, is it good at other times?" She picked up her wine goblet and held it out. "But I'll be glad to toast our association with your company."

Steve moved to pour wine into her goblet, but Kenji held up a hand to stop him. "Kate, you don't have to drink with me to wish me well. And I hope you would never compromise one of your principles for me or anyone else." He looked at Steve as he continued. "I believe you're one of the greatest assets my friend Steve has."

Steve reached for her hand under the table and gently squeezed it.

After the dinner was over and the Nakamuras had departed, Steve called a quick huddle with Traci Morgan; Joe Tyler, the company's vice president; and Kate.

"Joe, Kenji asked again about the production schedule. Can you put together an updated copy to send him?"

Joe nodded. "I'll do that tomorrow."

"Good. If there's anything else, we can talk about it next week. I probably won't be in the office tomorrow; I'm thinking of taking the day off."

Traci raised an eyebrow. Everyone in the office knew that Steve rarely missed a day at work, especially when the company was involved in a deal like this one. She wondered just how Steve Warden would spend a Friday off. But that was not the question she asked him. "Would you like me to write up a press release saying how pleased we are to be associated with Nakamura Industries?"

"Yes, for the business press. You know what to say. And I'd like to see some ideas for ads in the trade magazines."

He turned to Kate. "There are a couple of things Kenji said that I need to follow up with you. Can you stay for a few minutes longer?"

After Traci and Joe walked out of the room, Kate asked, "Was there something I missed with Kenji tonight? I thought—"

"Everything was perfect tonight, Kate." Steve took her hand. "I was wondering if you ought to take some time off too."

Her brow furrowed. "Right now? There'll be so much to do, and Joe will need me to—"

"Joe can handle it. I'd like you to spend tomorrow with me. And the weekend."

Her expression was neutral. "The weekend? What do you . . ."

"The weekend, and all of your days after that." Kate looked puzzled momentarily, then surprised as the impact of what he was saying struck her.

"Kate, I know I could have done this better—somewhere more romantic," Steve continued. "I'm asking you to marry me. I've already waited too long to do that."

She was silent for a moment, holding her breath. Then, slowly, she let it out. "Oh, Steve. You want . . ." She stepped close to him and touched his cheek with her fingertips. "You are the most surprising man sometimes. It's one of the things I love about you. It's been wonderful being close to you these past few weeks, putting all of this together, and I know you're happy about how things turned out with Nakamura. But—suddenly marriage! Are you sure?" She looked down at the empty dishes and goblets on the nearest table, then smiled uncertainly at him. "Maybe a little too much of the wine tonight? The sweet taste of success?"

Slowly he shook his head. He put her hand to his lips and kissed her fingertips. "Less than half a glass of wine. I stopped because I wanted to be completely clear-headed with you. I know exactly what I'm asking, Kate." His brow furrowed. "For me, these past few weeks have been more than just being close to you. I believe I love you with everything I have to give. You told me you love me. Have you had second thoughts about that?"

"No! Oh, no, no." She took his face between her hands and pulled him down to kiss him. "I've never felt like this about anyone before. I've never been happier."

"Then why not take the next step right now?" He put his arms around her. "You know my life so far has been mostly given to the company. I'm asking you to let me give the best of it to you from now on, and to our family, if we have kids." He paused. "I know there are other guys, nearer your age, and maybe—"

"No." She shook her head. "No one."

"And I'll have to unlearn some habits about the business, but if you could possibly see—"

She put her fingers on his lips and stopped him. "Yes." He could see tears in her eyes. "Yes, Steve. Yes!" She leaned closer so he would kiss her, and enjoyed having him hold her. She had looked forward to this several times tonight.

He let go of her and stepped back to take in the full picture of her. "Could you fly in that dress?"

Kate looked at him quizzically. "Yes, I guess I could. But why?"

"When I said this weekend, I meant it. I was thinking maybe we could fly to Las Vegas—right now. I could arrange a couple of rooms there tonight, and we could be married tomorrow. We could buy you a wedding dress tomorrow morning—anything you want—but you look gorgeous in that dress to me."

When she didn't answer, Steve's smile faded. "Of course, I know you might want a reception," he continued. "And I know it takes some time to plan those things."

"My parents . . . and my brother . . ."

"I thought about them. Your father and mother could fly up tomorrow and meet us in Las Vegas. And you said your brother probably wouldn't be able to come home again anytime soon."

Steve was right. Tom's unit was flying patrols every day in the Middle East. And her parents could fly up to Las Vegas. Still . . . "Do you—do we need time to think this over?"

"I don't. You know me, Kate; when I'm sure something is right, I go ahead. I won't push you. I know you always need to think things out." He smiled. "Right down to the last detail." He stepped close again, took her in his arms, and held her against his chest. "I wish I didn't have to wait another day to start living with you. But I'll wait if you'll just tell me I can spend all the rest of my life with you."

She never made it home that night.

Steve was right, she realized as he drove toward her apartment; this was one thing she didn't need to think through. Tomorrow night she could be the *future* Mrs. Steven Warden—or she could be Mrs. Steven Warden. There was no doubt in her mind which she would prefer. And an open house later for friends would be more enjoyable for her than a formal reception.

When they had arrived at the intersection where he would turn toward her apartment complex, she had told him to turn the other way instead. He had looked at her questioningly. Toward the airport, she had explained. Steve had smiled as he understood what she was saying and had leaned over to kiss her until someone behind them began honking.

Kate had never regretted her decision. She had never wanted a big church wedding; it was enough to have the people she cared about most with her when she was married. Her parents had been happy about it; they already treated Steve like a son.

After the wedding, Steve had bought tickets for a honeymoon in Hawaii, where he had rented an airplane so Kate could take them island hopping. On Monday, when he had called the office from Honolulu to explain why they wouldn't be at work for the next week or so, he had told Joe Tyler that there would be a new partner in the company.

And so it had been. Steve had made her a full partner in running Warden Avionics—or at least as full as she could be while being a mother. When Steve had been killed, Kate was as ready to run the company's operations as anyone could have been. But even she had not foreseen the time commitment, the physical burden that it would be.

Now Kenji was offering her an alternative. It was tempting. Maybe it would even bring greater opportunities for her children. But what would become of the legacy their father had seen for them?

She hoped Kenji could understand the reasons for her answer to his offer. "Send me your proposal, Kenji," she said into the phone. "I'll look it over. But I have two concerns. One is what will happen to the people who've built Warden into what it is. The other is more personal—about my children."

"You know I can't give you any guarantees about the jobs, Kate. But if any people are let go, they'll be treated fairly. I'll suggest how that would be handled in my proposal." He paused. "Only you can decide how Steve would have felt about letting his company go to someone besides his children. But he was my friend, and I'll make sure his children never have to want for anything."

* * *

Joe Tyler dropped his copy of the email on her desk and settled into a chair facing her. "Some people would say you'd be crazy to pass this up, Kate."

She sighed. "Yes. I know. What would *you* say, Joe?"

"No one could blame you if you accepted."

"I thought some of you who could be affected ought to have a chance to see their severance proposal."

"We could probably live with their terms." Joe gazed out the window for several seconds before looking at her again. "Kate, would you entertain a proposal from me and some of the other employees? One that would save Steve's dream and take a lot of the pressure off of you?"

Kate's eyebrows went up. "You have an idea?"

"Some of us have been talking. What we're thinking about wouldn't make you rich, like Nakamura's offer. But it would keep the company in the family."

"I'm listening."

3

Bill Morrow gazed out his window at the yellow Piper Cub sitting at the far end of the aircraft tie-down area.

"How can they charge me this much in taxes on that plane? It's an antique."

"But you're *never* going to get rid of it because it was a great plane in its day, and besides, it's the first plane you ever owned when you started this business." Kate folded her arms forcefully and scowled exactly as he did when he wanted to indicate he would tolerate no nonsense.

Bill tried to keep his stern expression, but he had never been able to resist when Kate appealed to his good humor. His frown faded into a grin. "Right. And I don't see how they can call *that* an asset."

"The point is, Dad, if you're going to keep it, you could turn it into an asset."

Bill's eyes narrowed. He had never been good at playing games with the bureaucracy, even when he was in the air force—*especially* when he was in the air force. "How?"

"At least paint 'Morrow Air Service' on it and park it out there by the gate like a sign. Or restore it. You could fly it for advertising when you go to an air show or balloon festival, or you could give lessons to people who want to learn flying in a classic like that."

Stevie tugged at the leg of her pants. "Can I play with the plane, Mommy?" He pointed at the model of a jet fighter on his grandfather's desk.

Kate remembered how carefully her father had constructed this model of his favorite fighter plane. She looked at him doubtfully. Bill smiled and nodded slightly. Kate lifted her son up onto her knee as Bill picked up the model and held it out toward Stevie.

"Dad, are you sure . . ."

Bill put the model into the boy's hands. "It just gathers dust on my desk." He smiled at Stevie. "If my grandson can get some fun out of it, let him."

Stevie took the model, slid down from his mother's knee, and walked around the desk making *whoosh* noises as he held the plane over his head.

Kate picked up the balance sheet on her father's desk and turned it so she could see it. "This looks good." She put it back in its place. "We might be able to make it look even better."

Bill raised his eyebrows. "Think so? I wondered about asking if there was any way you could help, uh . . . I mean, I got into this business because I like flying. I deal with profit and loss statements because I have to. You're better at the business part than I am." He paused. "But I didn't want to ask you to get involved if it would take you away from the kids—or anything else."

"Being on the board of directors at Warden doesn't keep me that busy, Dad." When Joe Tyler had proposed that the employees form a group to buy Warden Avionics from her, they had settled on a plan that would let employees buy forty percent of the company immediately. When KatiLynn and Stevie reached adulthood, if they had no interest in the company, its employees would have first opportunity to buy the other sixty percent. Kate was now chairing the board of directors. She had a voice in giving the company direction, but Joe was doing a good job of running day-to-day operations. Sometimes she missed helping to build the business. "I don't have any worries about the company. And with KatiLynn in school, some days I have time on my hands. If you need me, and you don't mind if I bring Stevie . . ."

Bill watched his grandson go *whoosh* around the corner of the desk again with the model plane. He smiled. "Any day."

Stevie brought the model plane in for a landing on his mother's knee. He pointed at the airplanes outside the window. "Can we go fly, Mommy? You said we could."

"After we pick up KatiLynn at the school. We'll come back."

Bill looked at his watch. "No board meeting today?"

"No, it's tomorrow afternoon."

Bill walked around the desk and sat on the corner of it to talk to his grandson. "Want to stay here with me while your mom goes to get your sister? We could go look at some of the planes."

Stevie grinned. "Yeah." He looked up at his mother. "Can I?"

"Sure." She dug her car keys out of the pocket of her jeans. "I'll be back in half an hour."

Bill leaned toward his grandson and spoke softly as though sharing a secret. "If you're really good, maybe your mother would let you and KatiLynn stay at our house again this weekend. I could take you fishing on Saturday."

"Yeah!" Stevie almost danced up and down. "Could we, Mom? Could we?"

Kate smiled at him. "We'll talk about it."

"If you want to let them stay over Sunday," Bill said, "we could take them to church with us Sunday morning and then you could . . ." His daughter's frown told him he probably should have left the idea alone. "But if you don't want us to do that . . ."

"I just want them to be able to decide about religion for themselves someday, Dad. You know that."

Bill nodded toward his grandson. "He's almost five, and KatiLynn's eight already. If you don't let them learn about God when they're little, Kate, you've already decided for them. We taught you when you were little, and you don't seem to have any trouble making your own de-cisions." He paused, wondering how far he dared push this subject. "Maybe *you're* still mad at God because He took Steve, but someone needs to teach the kids at least, uh . . ." His daughter's raised eyebrow stopped him again.

"What, Dad? Teach them what? Does the priest have some answers about God that he didn't have four years ago? Is there something new?"

Bill looked apologetic. "Kate, I'm sorry. I just thought they needed . . . I'm sorry I, uh . . . I don't want to interfere."

"I think I'm capable of deciding what they need, Dad. Please trust me. I trust you." She leaned over to give him a peck on the cheek. "This weekend is fine, if it's OK with Mom. The kids love to come to your house." She glanced down at Stevie. "Because you spoil them." She leaned down to hug her son. "Doesn't he? Grandpa spoils you, doesn't he?"

Stevie smiled and nodded his head. Kate laughed. She looked up at her father. "We'll talk about Sunday later."

It wasn't that she didn't want her children to know about God, Kate thought as she drove toward the school. It was just that she didn't know who should teach them. She could teach them—but she wasn't sure she understood Him well enough to do it. The problem was, she didn't know anyone else who did either.

And it wasn't so much that she was still mad at God. Part of her harbored anger—she had to admit it—but anger about Steve's death was not the reason she was reluctant to let her parents take her children to their church.

Her mother was dogmatic about religion. Belle Morrow insisted that her daughter needed to bring up the children in the church in which she had been reared. Belle refused to understand that Kate could not find answers there anymore. The two of them could not have a discussion about religion without reaching an angry impasse.

Actually, Kate thought, most of her old bitterness was gone—or at least what was left only came out on the bad days. She was not so much angry at God as puzzled. She still could not understand why Steve had to die—what *purpose* there was in it—and if there was no purpose, why did God let it happen? He could have stopped it, couldn't He?

She knew she needed Him. Trying to rear two children, trying to be everything two parents should be, trying to handle life alone—lately she had realized more than once that she *really* needed Him.

She had taught her children how to pray to Him—"now-I-lay-me-down-to-sleep" words she had them recite by their beds every night.

Maybe she ought to begin praying herself.

But it had been so long . . . and after Steve's death she had come to believe that she just didn't understand how God operated.

If she wanted to talk to Him now, how would she begin?

* * *

She realized she was sweating as she walked along the corridor, despite the fact that the air conditioning in the hospital seemed to be set just above refrigerator level.

Second room past the nurses' station, they had said—this one. She hesitated for a moment with her hand on the door, fearful of what she might find.

Belle turned at the sound of the door opening and smiled weakly when she saw her daughter. Belle sat beside the bed in a chair she had pulled close so she could hold her husband's hand. The overhead light in the room was turned down, making the light over the head of the bed seem like a spotlight on Bill's chalky face. "Mom!" Kate kept her voice soft. "How is . . ." Her eyes went to her father. Bill opened his own eyes when

27

he heard her. He forced a smile and raised the thumb on the hand that was gripping his wife's. Belle answered: "He's doing all right . . . now."

Kate could tell that her mother was close to tears, trying not to contradict her husband's bravado. But she was obviously frightened, and Belle Morrow did not frighten easily, so this had to be serious.

The sensors attached to Bill's chest trailed wires that led to a heart monitor. Kate watched the monitor screen for several seconds. Little electronic spikes marched across it in a regular rhythm, to the cadence of the monitor's soft beeping. That cadence had undoubtedly been stabilized by medication, Kate reflected, and it was surely slower than her own heartbeat right now.

The call had come while she was in a meeting at the Warden offices. She had gone instantly from a discussion of multiband radio receivers to her mother's sobbing: "Kate, your . . . it's your father. I'm at the hospital. Can you come?"

Kate had swiveled away from the discussion so the other people at the table could not see her face. "What is it?" she asked, trying to keep her voice low. "What's happened?"

"It's his heart. I'm not sure exactly." Belle had struggled not to give way to sobbing again. "The doctor used some term I don't understand. Your dad won't let me call it a heart attack." She paused only slightly. "Can you come now?"

"Yes—as quickly as I can find someone to take care of KatiLynn and Stevie."

She had excused herself immediately from the meeting, dashed to the school to pick up her children, and dropped them off with Evie Henderson. Then she had driven here as fast as she could, hoping not to cross the path of any policeman.

"What does the doctor say?" Kate asked her mother. Her father answered without opening his eyes. "Just a little episode with my heart. I'll be fine—be out of here in a couple of days."

Belle shook her head slightly.

Kate walked around to the other side of the bed and took hold of his left hand. There was an IV tube connected to that arm, and an oxygen tube draped across his left shoulder feeding the two small jets under his nostrils, so she tried not to disturb anything.

Bill opened his eyes to look at her. "Hon, I won't be able to be in the office for a few days. Could you see that, uh . . ."

"I'll take care of things, Dad. Don't worry about the business. I can be there most of the time, while the kids are in school. If I have to, I'll pay Trish extra to stay a little longer when I need to be with the kids." Trish, the college girl who helped out part time in the office, wouldn't mind; she could use the money.

Her father didn't answer for several seconds. When he spoke, it seemed like an effort. "It's been a big help just having you handle the books since Julia left." He paused. "Think you can handle the rest of it too?"

"If I can't, I'll call Julia to see if she can come in a few hours a week."

Bill smiled slightly. "Don't know if she will. Told me when she retired she was going to play with her grandkids, and she had enough knitting to last a couple of years."

"Don't *worry*, Dad, I'll take care of the business."

Bill didn't answer. Soon the rhythmic rising and falling of his chest told her he had gone to sleep. She sat on the edge of his bed for nearly half an hour, not wanting to let go of his hand, while her mother sat across the bed holding his other one. Neither of them spoke.

On the hour, by the clock over the bed, the door to the room swung open suddenly and authoritatively. The nurse who had opened it looked the two women over and her eyes lingered momentarily on Kate. She walked to Bill's left side, pushed back the curtain that partly separated his bed from the empty one on the other side of the room, and began what was obviously a well-practiced routine.

Bill looked at his daughter while the nurse went about her business. "Katie, I'll be all right. Why don't you go home and take care of the kids? Tell them I love them."

"They love you too. We *all* love you." She hesitated. "Please do what the doctors say. Please take care of you."

"Will you please call Tom? Tell him I'm all right."

Kate glanced at her mother. "I haven't had a chance to call," Belle said softly.

Kate kissed her father tenderly on the forehead, moved around the foot of the bed to hug and kiss her mother, and walked out of the room without looking back.

Her father hadn't called her Katie in years, she thought as she walked to her car.

Not since she was a girl, she thought again as she drove out of the parking lot.

It had been "Katie" at six or seven when she fell down while skating and skinned her knees. He had lovingly washed them and held her close, comforting her, when the alcohol he had put on them stung.

It had been "Katie" at twelve when she outshot her older brother Tom with the .22 rifle while they were hunting with their father.

It had been "Katie" at fourteen when he had tried patiently—more patiently than she had deserved—to explain why she should respond to her mother's requests for help around the house. He had not been nearly so patient with Tom three years earlier. But she had seen her father change, she had seen him learn in those three years.

"Katie" had disappeared when she was sixteen. It was the night her father had seen her in her first formal dress, the one she had bought with money she saved from what he paid her for washing and servicing airplanes. She had picked the dress out very carefully. It was conservative—modest enough not to make guys look at her in ways she didn't like—but attractive and well-fitted enough to make her feel like a woman. And that was what her father had seen—a glimpse of the future. When she had come into the living room wearing the dress, her mother had smiled proudly and exclaimed, "Oh, Kate! You look so elegant!" Her father had sucked in a breath as he looked over the dress and the way she had fixed her hair. He seemed to wonder how it all had happened. Just before she stepped out the front door with her date, her father had leaned close (she thought for a moment she saw tears in his eyes) and whispered in her ear, "You're going to knock the guys' eyes out. Have a good time . . . Kate."

Now *he* needed *her* help. He needed her to be the grownup businesswoman she had become, someone to run things while he couldn't.

And right now she felt like a little girl again, a little girl who could lose him—lose the other man in her life who had meant strength and stability.

The tears that had been trickling out of her eyes became a flood just as the stoplight turned green. She could barely read the license plate on the car in front of her. Inching carefully through the intersection, she pulled over to the curb and let the flood come while she sobbed out her fear.

When she managed to dry her tears, she drove directly home and looked up Tom's number before going to pick up KatiLynn and Stevie. She calculated that it was just after one A.M. in Germany when she reached him. "Morrow," he said crisply into the phone when he answered, evidently expecting another air force officer or noncom on the line at this time of night.

"Tom, it's Kate."

"Kate? Why . . ." Her brother went silent for a moment, and she could hear the tension in his voice when he continued. "Dad? Mom?" He had sensed that she wasn't calling in the middle of the night to chat.

"Dad. He had a heart attack." Briefly she explained everything she had learned at the hospital.

"How bad is it?"

"I'm not sure. He wanted me to tell you he's all right. Mom says it's worse than he will admit."

"Do I need to come home? I could probably be out of here in the morning."

Kate hesitated for a moment. "I don't think so."

"Are you sure? I don't want you calling me three or four days from now telling me to come home for a funeral when I could have been there."

"I can't know for sure, Tom, but the doctors don't seem to think it's that bad." She paused. "Do you remember the time when you were about twelve that Dad went up in the Cub and there was a storm?"

"Yeah. I remember."

Belle clutched Kate against her side. In the back seat, Tom gazed straight out the windshield in the direction of the runway beyond the fence. "How long has he been up there?" he asked. Kate could hear a quaver in his voice.

Belle shook her head. "I don't know." When this violent, unexpected thunderstorm had hit and she had not been able to contact her husband at the flying service, Belle had bundled her children into the car and driven to the airport to watch for him.

Kate cringed at the thunderclaps; she wondered if that's what an airplane sounded like when it crashed. At nine, her sense of time was not yet well developed, so she did not know how long they sat there before they finally saw the tiny yellow plane, buffeted by the wind, touch down on the runway and roll in their direction.

"Only God could have gotten him though that," Belle breathed.

"I'm scared like I was then, Tom. But I think it'll be like that time—Dad will come through all right."

"I remember how Dad cured your fear," Tom answered. Kate could tell he was probably smiling when he said it.

"Yours too. He took us up flying so we would know about airplanes—and we both loved it from the start. Tom, please tell Maddy I'm sorry if I woke the family."

"The kids probably haven't heard a thing. They're in our other bedroom."

"All three of them?"

"Yeah. Another year and Tommy won't be able to sleep in his sisters' room anymore. Kate, I want you to call if anything else happens—*anything*. Let me give you the number of the squadron offices on the base."

She copied it down. "You probably won't be able to reach Mom at the hospital. If you can't get her at home, call me here or at the flight service," Kate said. "I love you. Wish you all weren't so far away."

"Me too. I'm glad you can be there for Mom and Dad." He said his good-bye and hung up the phone.

Kate put down her telephone and sat with her head in her hands.

"Only God could have gotten him through that," her mother had said.

Dear God, if you're there, if you can, please help him this time too.

* * *

Her father had been right when he said he knew the flying part of the business better. Kate sighed as she examined the aircraft maintenance log. Morrow Flight Service had been doing well recently, but it was coasting. They could make it grow faster. They needed to accelerate rotation of the equipment—sell off the oldest plane in the next couple of months and invest in a new one, then set up a schedule to—

The ringing of the phone interrupted her thought. She picked up the handset on her desk. "Hello?"

"Hello, Kate," Kenji Nakamura said. "How does it feel to be able to fly away whenever you want?"

"Kenji!" Kate laughed. "I wish! I spend a lot more time behind this desk than I do in the air. How is it to run one of the world's largest electronics conglomerates?"

"I wish," Kenji replied. "I think I'd like it." He was silent for a moment, then: "I may be the CEO of record, but my father is a *very* active chairman. He's a . . . what's the expression—some kind of old horse?"

"An old war horse? Rearing to go anytime he can hear the sound of battle."

"Yeah—right." Kenji chuckled. "They'll have to carry him out of his office someday, still holding onto his antique samurai sword."

Kate voiced a thought she had avoided mentioning to Kenji in the past, but by now, she assumed, he would have certainly considered the

32

possibility. "I'm surprised your father hasn't insisted on developing an avionics line of your own for Nakamura Industries."

Kenji's answer confirmed her assumption. "I'm surprised too. I try not to discuss that with him. It would cost us millions and take years to be competitive with you outside of Japan, and your products sell well for us." He paused. "But I didn't call on business. Just checking on a friend. How *are* you, Kate?"

"I'm fine—as good as can be expected. And how are things in Tokyo? It must be . . . what time there?"

"I'm not in Tokyo—San Francisco. I had business here and thought I'd call while I was close. Things are fine in Tokyo—and I probably spend too much time there. I'd like to spend all my nights at home with Lily, but I end up staying over in the city sometimes. My father probably believes I ought to sleep at the office, the way he slept in his shop when he was starting out. How are KatiLynn and Stevie?"

"Fine. KatiLynn was the star of the third grade play, and Stevie is enjoying kindergarten." She laughed lightly. "I hope the teacher is enjoying him. He's beginning to show some of Steve's tendencies. He's not shy about telling people there's a better way to do things—including the teacher."

"And your father?"

Kate sighed. "He's . . . OK."

"Same heart problems?"

"It hasn't gotten any better. And he won't give up his cigars and get out to exercise, even though the doctor told him to. I think he doesn't feel up to it most of the time. The doctor has talked about open heart surgery if things don't change."

"Are you worried about that? No need, I think. Doctors can do wonders in surgery now. My father had it a few years ago, and he's still in good shape at 82."

"But if I lost Dad . . ." Kate left the sentence unfinished.

"Yes—the other important man in your life. How are you really, Kate? It has to be tough sometimes without Steve."

His words hit a nerve today. "Yes, it's . . . yes. I miss him so much sometimes!" She couldn't hold back the words. "It's like . . . like a part of me isn't there anymore! I can't . . . when I need someone to . . ." She stopped speaking and took two deep breaths before she continued. Tears were close. "I'm sorry, Kenji, I didn't mean to drop that on you. Yes, it's hard trying to be mom and dad and run a business." She could feel the flush in her face. "I'm sorry," she apologized again. "Really, I'm doing all right."

"Kate, you know me. I don't let my feelings out very much. Maybe it's a cultural thing, maybe it's a man thing. I don't know. I've tried to imagine how it would be for you. If I lost Lily . . . I mean, I don't know how you . . . well, this may not help much, but after you told me about your father, I thought that you've had many hard things to handle in your life. And then I realized that if I knew any woman who could handle them, it would be you."

It was kind, but he was right—it didn't help much.

"Did you know that Lily is a Christian?" he asked. "Sometimes she gets a lot of help by praying to her God. I remember when I brought her home and my father didn't know how to take her at first, she told me praying helped her. I was glad *something* could help her. *I* didn't know what to do."

I wish God would give me *a little help here.* Kate regretted the thought instantly. She was feeling sorry for herself again, and Kenji was doing what he could from a distance. "Thank you, Kenji. You're a good friend. And I know God helps some people a lot."

"But not you? Kate, are you . . ." He sounded like he wasn't sure he should ask the question. "Are you a believer? Everyone needs something to hold onto."

"Yes. Yes, I believe. But things are still very hard sometimes. And I confess I can't understand why God does some of the things He does."

Kenji was silent for a moment; she sensed that he was groping for another answer. "I don't know what to tell you there. I never went to any church while I was going to school in Hawaii—not even to the Buddhist temple. I lost religion, in a way." He paused. "But I think Oriental people accept some things better than westerners. We don't know *why* they're that way. They just *are.* We go on from there. I think you're better equipped to understand that than most westerners I've known—except maybe Steve."

He was right. Steve could take a situation that didn't look good and turn it into a win of some kind. He never saw himself as defeated—just in a different situation than he would have preferred. He never let his circumstances dictate to him. And she was, after all, in a better situation than most women who faced widowhood—comfortable financially, with children who were usually obedient and easy to love. Sometimes she forgot about those things.

"If you didn't study religion, Kenji, you've picked up wisdom some-where. You certainly sound like a believer."

"I believe in Lily, and I know that what she believes keeps her happy. I believe in hard work, and good people. You're one of them."

"Thank you. That means something coming from you. It's too bad you're not close enough to visit in person. I'd be glad to cook you dinner, and the kids would love to see you."

"Maybe next time. I hope I can bring Lily with me."

They talked briefly about his meetings in San Francisco with a group of American electronics distributors, and Kate urged him to take a little time following his meetings to enjoy the city. After they had said their good-byes, she sat thinking about his kindness to her children. The first time he had met KatiLynn she had been coloring on a piece of stationery at her mother's desk. Kenji had taken the time to talk with her, and the dark-haired, dark-eyed three-year-old had charmed him immediately. He had met Stevie under similar circumstances a couple of years ago. Kenji always inquired about them whenever he talked to their mother.

It was a shame that he and Lily had no children of their own. Maybe prayer helped Lily with that too, Kate thought.

* * *

She traced the index finger of her left hand down a column in the second quarter's financial report and the index finger of her right hand down the corresponding column in last year's report. For the past month, trying to update Morrow Air Service's records while KatiLynn and Stevie were in school had become her afternoon routine. The year was drawing to a close and she was trying to make sure everything was in order before she had to deal with the company's annual tax reports.

No one had ever kept a neater set of books than Julia, Kate thought. *It's too bad she didn't learn to do this on the computer. I'm going to have to enter these records on a spreadsheet myself. If I could spend one full day a week—or maybe a couple of mornings—if I could just do that—*

The sound of the front door opening and closing brought her back to the fact that she was alone in the office for the moment. "Trish?" she called. Trish was late today.

No answer.

"Trish, is that you?"

Again there was no answer, but there was the sound of someone clearing his throat—a male throat by the timbre. Kate got up from her desk and walked to the door of her office. Two men stood at the service counter. They were young, both wore white shirts and ties, and one carried a small backpack. She had seen these two men, or a pair like them, in her own neighborhood, she thought. "Can I help you?" she asked.

The shorter, darker one spoke. "I'm Elder Martinez, and this is Elder Swenson." He gestured to the tall blond standing next to him. "We visited with your father this morning and he said you might like to hear what we were telling him."

Kate raised an eyebrow. "Oh? And what was that?"

"How our Heavenly Father loves all of His children so much that he's made a way for them and their families to be together forever."

Kate resisted letting her impatience show. She thought she had heard this kind of thing before. "Yes, I know, together in some kind of blessed state of grace where we all do nothing but sit around God's throne and sing praises to his name forever." She didn't mean it to sound disrespectful, but this was one of those "mysteries" she had never understood: Why would God want anyone to do that?

"Not exactly," Elder Martinez said patiently. "We'll be blessed because we can go on helping Him and other people too, and because we can be linked together as families just like we are here on earth—fathers and mothers and children . . . husbands and wives."

This was something Kate *hadn't* heard before. "Husbands and . . ." We weren't going to be just some thought in God's mind, or some kind of vague presences of spirit? "You're saying *people,* like we are now?"

"But living eternally. Your father thought you might want to hear about this, Mrs. . . ." Elder Martinez consulted a small piece of paper he held in his hand. "Mrs. Warden. He said you had lost your husband." He glanced at the paper again. "Steve."

Kate felt anger rising in her. How dare her father share that kind of information with strangers! But she bit back an angry reply. It wasn't this young man's fault. She would let her father know later how she felt. Right now, could she get rid of these two quickly? "Look," she said, "my parents have asked ministers and priests to talk to me about this before. All of them tell me sure, someday I'll see my husband again, when we're all living together with Jesus and the angels—but nobody can give me any *real* answers about why Steve had to die and what it will be like when I see him again. I really don't have time for another

36

discussion right now, so if you'll excuse me . . ." She wanted them to take the hint and go away.

They didn't. The taller one—Swenson?—spoke. "Mrs. Warden, I don't think anyone on earth could tell you why your husband had to die. But we could give you a fair idea of what he will be like when you meet him again."

Kate looked at him skeptically. The other one, Elder Martinez, explained. "Everything you knew and loved about your husband he still is, Mrs. Warden. That's what he'll be like when you see him again. He could still be your husband, and you could still be his wife. When we lose someone we love, there's a reason our hearts keep holding onto them. That's because our Heavenly Father made it so we don't *ever* have to let them go. We can know that for ourselves. In here." He tapped his chest lightly over his heart.

"*You* know this?" She looked from one to the other. "You're both awfully young—maybe too young to have experience with this yourselves?"

Elder Martinez looked steadily into her eyes. "I lost my sister two years ago. In a car accident. She was sixteen. But she, uh . . ." He stopped speaking to swallow, and looked down at the floor.

Kate looked at the other man, whose face still seemed friendly even though what she had just said was not very kind. It had been a bit self-centered and thoughtless, she realized, and she felt the need to apologize. The shorter man was looking at her again. "I'm sorry, Mister, uh . . ."

"Elder Martinez."

"I'm sorry," Kate said. "I was rude. Please forgive me."

"It's OK," Elder Martinez answered. "Sometimes this is a new idea for people. The point is that my sister is not *gone*. She's not here with us right now, but I'll be together with her again, and when that happens she'll be the same person I knew and loved here. She will still be my sister, and Mom and Dad will still be our mom and dad."

This was definitely something Kate had never been taught before. The idea was stunning, in fact—so much that she forgot about her anger. People and their relationships could go on. She wasn't sure whether she liked this idea so much because of what it could mean for her and Steve or because it simply seemed to make sense. It was the way things ought to be if life in families on earth had any real meaning. A loving Father would want it to be this way for His children, wouldn't He?

Maybe she would still have to dismiss these two men in a couple of minutes, Kate thought, but it couldn't hurt to learn who they were and what they were talking about. She walked over to the counter. "You're from what church?"

"We represent The Church of Jesus Christ of Latter-day Saints," Elder Swenson answered, and then because she looked at him blankly, he added, "The Mormons."

Kate knew there *were* Mormons—but that was almost all she knew about them. She had seen the building in Mesa that they called a temple. There had been some Mormons in her high school. A couple of her classmates had laughed about them because they wouldn't drink, not even beer. One of her friends had pointed out a Mormon girl at their senior prom and had spoken disdainfully of the girl's "tacky" formal because it covered her shoulders and upper arms. At the time, Kate had wished her own narrow-strap formal covered a bit more, but it was all she had been able to find this year in the stores she knew. She had never actually been friends with a Mormon and had little idea what they believed.

"What was it you said—we don't ever have to let them go?" Why did that sound familiar?

"Our hearts don't want to let them go, and we don't have to. Our Father made a way for us to be together forever."

And then she remembered—the dream, after Steve's death. He had said to her: "Please don't let me go." She had felt anger and guilt at the time, thinking it meant she should not have let him make the flight to Las Vegas. But perhaps it meant something else—that she should never let go of him in her heart. She looked from the short man to his taller companion and back. "So you're telling me a husband and wife can still be married after they die?"

"Yes, if they take advantage of the opportunities Heavenly Father provides for us," Elder Martinez said. "He didn't mean for us to have families in this life and then give them up."

"And children are part of this too?"

Elder Martinez nodded.

Kate rested one elbow on the counter and thought for a moment before she spoke. Over the past five years, she had carefully built a shell that insulated her from any organized religion. Her head was warning her not to get involved, but something in her heart was telling her she needed to hear what these men had to say. "I don't go to church very much. I'm not sure I ever would. I don't think any religion has a corner on knowing God. But I'd like to hear a little more about what you're telling me. Will you talk to me even if I won't promise to come to your church?"

Both men smiled. "Of course," Elder Swenson said. "Could we come to your home to talk?"

"When your children are there," Elder Martinez added. "It would be a good thing for them to be part of the discussion."

4

Straightening the living room was almost an afterthought, something she did automatically every evening about this time after the children were in bed. But there really wasn't much to do. The kids didn't make messes in here, and KatiLynn had taken her schoolbooks and papers into the bedroom with her. There was nothing out of place—except, perhaps, the blue book on the coffee table.

The book was a silent challenge, a reminder of a commitment she had made. And Kate Warden was a person who kept her commitments.

She wondered now if she should have let the missionaries talk her into this. She had put them off twice, but the night before last she had finally promised them yes, she would take this seriously, she would continue reading the Book of Mormon and pray about it. And now she had to keep that promise.

Kate sat down in the easy chair in the living room, picked up the book, and turned it over in her hands. Would it be strange, maybe even a little silly, to pray to God and ask Him whether a book was "true"? She had never prayed to Him about whether the Bible was true. The entire Christian world accepted that book as truth. But then, Kate realized, she had never been impressed with the conventional wisdom of the Christian world, at least not as it was expressed by the teachers or preachers she knew.

Personally, she had always believed in the truth of the Bible—or at least of the things it taught about the way God wanted us to live. She had always believed in what Jesus taught, but she hadn't really understood why the Son of God had to be crucified or what it meant to everyone else that He had been resurrected. Didn't He have power from God before they killed Him? He *was* God—wasn't He? And He could be resurrected because He was divine, but how did that affect the rest of us?

Now, after three weeks of reading the Book of Mormon, she was beginning to understand. She was almost finished with the writings of someone named Mosiah—a prophet, the missionaries called him. Another prophet named Abinadi had gone to his death preaching about the meaning of the sacrifice and resurrection of Jesus Christ. A prophet named Alma had sprung to life spiritually because of the words of Abinadi; Alma had carried on Abinadi's teaching about our need for a Savior. In three weeks of reading, Kate had learned more about the role of the Savior of mankind than she had learned in a lifetime of hearing about God and Jesus from others. The missionaries had taught her that Jesus and our Heavenly Father are distinct beings with distinct roles. Through this book, she was beginning to understand how Heavenly Father reaches out to His children on earth. She had found nothing in the book to disagree with; it all seemed so logical.

So why was there a need to pray to find out if it was "true"?

The missionaries had talked about something called a "testimony." She had to *know* for herself, they said, or nothing they had taught her would have a lasting effect after they were gone.

Discussions with the missionaries had awakened something inside of her. She realized that at thirty-five years old, she had never had a spiritual life of her own. She had tried to live a *good* life. She believed she was a *good* person—whatever that meant. But she had never known how to be close to God. As the missionaries had talked to her this past week, she realized that she had never understood the need to nourish her own spirit. Now this need seemed to be growing in her. She thought perhaps it had been awakened by watching her children respond to the missionaries and their teachings.

Or maybe the need was fed by something else that was very important to her: she *wanted* the things the missionaries taught to be true because of their meaning for her and Steve. She was afraid of this desire in a way, because she tried not to let her decisions be governed only by emotion. She had always been the one among her friends who would not make a decision without thinking it out first, without being sure the logic of it was right. But logic simply was not enough in this situation. You could not prove by logic that their "plan of salvation," as the missionaries called it, or their Book of Mormon were true. The plan seemed like the most rational explanation for this life and its purpose that she had ever heard, but still, its logic was not *proof* that people go on just as we know them after death.

Was it right to ask God to "prove" something to you? That seemed almost blasphemous. And yet, the missionaries assured her God wanted so much for us to know the truth of what was in the Book of Mormon that He had offered to give a personal witness to those who sought Him out in prayer. She turned again to the verse the missionaries had marked near the end of the book: "Ask God, the Eternal Father, . . . ; and if ye shall ask with a sincere heart, with real intent, having faith in Christ, he will manifest the truth of it unto you, by the power of the Holy Ghost."

If ever there was a promise that was failsafe, Kate thought, it was this one. If she read the book then tried praying as the missionaries taught her and nothing happened—well, what would she have lost?

But if some kind of witness came . . . if God really told her yes, wouldn't it mean that everything else the missionaries had been teaching her was true too?

If what they had taught her about living prophets was true, then she had found a source of answers for all her questions about God's will for men and women on earth—or after this earth.

It would mean she and Steve really *could* be together again.

She settled back on the sofa and turned to the page where she had left off reading yesterday afternoon.

* * *

This way of praying was new. The prayers she had learned as a child had mostly been memorized, to be recited on certain occasions in certain ways. Any time in her life when she had prayed on her own, she had usually felt the need to recite one of those prayers first, and that recitation had been followed by some heartfelt desire spilling out in awkward words while she hoped that God would understand what she really meant.

But the missionaries had taught her that she could actually address Him as her Father, that she could put her questions or her desires to Him in her own words and He would lovingly respond according to His own wisdom.

Kneeling by her bed tonight, she had asked Him in prayer for what seemed like some standard things—first to bless KatiLynn and Stevie. She wasn't sure what she should ask Him to do for them, but she knew what she wanted for them and hoped He would understand their needs even better than she did.

She had also asked God to help her live a better life. While she had probably never done any real harm to anyone, there was undoubtedly greater good that she could do for those around her. She hoped God would show her how. She was beginning to feel a deep responsibility for what she could become spiritually.

It was time now to ask Him about what the missionaries had been teaching her.

"God . . . Heavenly Father, you know I've had questions about you many times in my life, and I didn't know what was true. I didn't think anybody really could *know*. But what the missionaries are telling me seems like the truth. When I read the Book of Mormon, it seems like the truth—I mean, it *feels* like the truth. I'm not sure if *I* can really know for myself, but if—"

She heard no voice in the room, but it was as though someone spoke deep inside her: "Yes, you can. You can know because *I* am telling you. It is true." The feeling that enveloped her was so strong that she caught her breath. She recognized it at once. It had come at times after she lost Steve, when she had in anguish appealed in her heart to God, with halting words, for help; this same feeling had brought her peace in a day full of pain, or sleep at last in a memory-stirred, solitary night. This time the feeling was so strong that no words could have measured it. But it was unmistakable—love, in as pure a form as she had ever felt, and stronger than ever before in her life. It seemed to pick her up and carry her, as though a part of her were soaring without wings, while her body, the part that knelt here by the bed, felt weak, almost as though it had no power to move on its own right now. At the rational core of her—the part that sometimes considered what God might be—Kate felt awe and a sense of wonder at what was happening to her. And yet there was complete peace. She relaxed and let this peace flow through her, cover her. She was not sure how long she knelt there feeling it, how long it stayed with her.

The feeling brought certainty: God loved Katherine Morrow Warden as His daughter, and He wanted her to know that she had found truth.

As she tried to absorb everything about the experience, Kate remembered that there was something more she needed to know—but wasn't sure she dared to ask. She thought it over, then bowed her head and closed her eyes again. "Heavenly Father, I hope you won't be upset with me for asking about this. Maybe I'm not supposed to know right now. But Elder Martinez and Elder Swenson told me Steve could learn about all this too—and maybe a lot more. If it's OK, I'd really like to be sure whether Steve knows if this is true, because if he can accept it too—"

The warm, peaceful, light feeling grew stronger in her heart again, not so breathtaking now, but still unmistakable. Tears streamed down her cheeks; there was no way to stop them.

This feeling was like basking in a warm ray of sunshine on a chilly, windy day. She soaked it up for several minutes, but finally wiped away her tears and climbed into bed, feeling like she needed to rest physically and regain her strength. She lay for a time thinking—enjoying the strong, lingering warmth—before she remembered that she had never ended her prayer. "Thank you," she breathed quietly. "Amen. In the name of Jesus Christ, amen."

As she lay staring up at the darkened ceiling, Kate realized that when morning came, she would not look at the new day the same way she had this one. Tomorrow life would have a purpose that had not been there for her before now. She knew now that there were things God wanted her to do while she was in this life—for her children, for Steve, for herself. She did not know yet what they all would be, but now she knew that she would find out if she kept on feeding the faith that was growing within her.

She would never look at life the same way again.

* * *

At first Kate had thought that she would feel out of place worshipping with the Mormons, but it had turned out to be a low-key experience compared to services in some churches. The missionaries had been there to make sure she and her children found the right classes on the first Sunday, and the people had been friendly.

Stevie was naturally outgoing, like his father, and he seemed to have no trouble getting along with the boys he met. KatiLynn was a bit more reserved, but after the second Sunday she came home talking about two new friends she had made at church. Neither of her children seemed bothered by the idea of spending part of Sunday this way.

That second Sunday had been what they called a "fast and testimony meeting." Members of the congregation had stood up and said, "I *know* this Church is true," "I *know* Jesus Christ lives," "I *know* Heavenly Father loves me." Some of them were little children. Sitting in that meeting, Kate had asked herself, "How could they all *know*?" In answer, she had felt briefly the same loving assurance that had come so strongly a few days ago when she prayed to know the truth about the Book of Mormon. That assurance told her this time: *They know. They know the same way you know.*

She believed that KatiLynn knew too, even though her daughter might not yet understand this feeling.

A week ago, KatiLynn had brought home a picture that had been given to her in Primary class—Jesus appearing to the Nephites. When she had hung the picture on their refrigerator, she had pointed to a girl holding hands with a smaller boy in the picture and said, "That could be Stevie and me."

Kate had approached the subject of baptism carefully with her daughter, wanting to be sure KatiLynn would act out of her own conviction and not simply do what her mother did. According to the elders, at nine KatiLynn was old enough to decide for herself, so three nights ago, Kate had suggested that KatiLynn pray about baptism. "I think it's important for *you* to know what you ought to do," she had explained.

The next morning, Kate had been careful not to steer her daughter's decision.

KatiLynn had stirred and opened her eyes as her mother sat down on the edge of the bed. Kate had stroked her daughter's arm gently. "Hi, Sweetheart. It's time to get up and get ready for school."

KatiLynn nodded. "Sleeping felt so good," she said, stretching. "But I think I was awake in the night."

"Bad dream? Or you didn't feel good?"

Her daughter smiled. "No, I feel good this morning. It was just . . ." She shrugged and left the sentence unfinished.

"Do you remember what we prayed about last night?" Kate asked.

KatiLynn nodded again. "About whether we should be baptized."

"And did you get an answer?"

KatiLynn's brow furrowed. "Did you, Mommy?"

Kate nodded, but she said nothing more.

"I feel just like I did last night," KatiLynn said. "If *you* want to, I will."

"But what do *you* want to do?"

KatiLynn frowned. "Well, I don't know anything different today." Then her face brightened. "But I remember why I woke up last night. I dreamed about Daddy. I liked that. I've been afraid I would forget what he was like. He was tall, wasn't he?"

Kate smiled, remembering. "Yes."

"I thought maybe it was that way just because I was so little. But he had brown hair and really blue eyes, and he was wearing his suit, just like that day when he said good-bye to me before he went flying."

Kate tried to hold her emotions in check. "What did you dream about him?"

"I was at the airport, and Daddy was in a plane. I got in with him, and he told me to fly it, the way you showed me. He said I should go on doing things just like you've taught me. He said he was looking forward to being with me again, but it would be a long time."

Barely, Kate kept tears from coming.

KatiLynn looked thoughtful for a moment, then smiled at her mother. "That's what the elders said, isn't it? We could be with Daddy again." And then KatiLynn knew what she wanted to do.

Stevie had listened to most of what the missionaries had taught, and last night he had told his mother that he wished he could be baptized too. Kate was grateful for her children's support at least. She had learned that she and her children would be alone in this as far as her family was concerned.

She had been surprised at the anger in Belle's reaction to the news that her daughter and grandchildren were listening to the Mormon missionaries.

"I *told* your father not to send those people over there! Make them go away, Kate. You've got to tell them to leave you alone!"

"But why, Mom? When it comes to religion and faith, they're the only ones I've ever heard who seem to know what it all means. It makes sense. I thought maybe you and Dad might want—"

"*No!*" Belle breathed heavily into the telephone as though she were trying to catch her breath. "Kate, you mustn't . . . I know they're fine talkers, and everything they say may sound good, but you can't let them take you in."

Kate said nothing for several seconds, trying to determine how to respond. Finally: "I think I need to hear what they have to say, Mother. You told me you want me to be happy. This may be the way. I think I'm experienced enough to know if somebody's trying to take me in."

There was silence for several seconds on the other end of the line. "You don't have any experience with *those* people," her mother said finally. "If you won't listen to me, I hope you'll listen to your father. I'm going to ask *him* to talk to you about it." And Belle had hung up.

Kate had been stunned. What had the Mormons ever done to make her mother so antagonistic? Did she have some experience with them? This was the first time Kate had ever heard her mother talk about them.

The conversation had been unsettling. For two days, Kate had stewed over whether she was making the right decision about this church; she had gone to sleep thinking about it and had wondered about it again when she awakened. Her mother's judgment had so often been an anchor that Kate felt disloyal, disobedient almost, because in her heart she was ready to go against her mother's advice this time.

And it was frightening in a way to think of the changes that might be required in her life and the lives of her children. It was obvious this would be no one-day-a-week commitment. While the elders had been teaching her and KatiLynn, it had become clear that this was not just a church, it was a way of life. Baptism was for always. Many of the people in the Sunday School class she had attended last Sunday were lifelong Mormons, thoroughly familiar with the doctrine and comfortable in their culture. She and her children would be starting from zero—and there seemed to be so much to learn!

And yet . . . yet there was no overlooking what she had felt when she had prayed. She could not deny the power, the clarity of what she had experienced. She could not go against that. Maybe later there would be other opportunities to talk with her mother about this, to try to explain her feelings. But for now she had to follow the truth she had come to know.

* * *

"Evie, do you think I'm a witch sometimes?"

Evie looked at her in surprise. "*You?* Good heavens, Kate, you're one of the best people I know. Why would you think that?"

"Gary Keeler."

Evie looked at her blankly for a moment. Then recognition dawned in her eyes. "The pilot. The pilot who was flying when Steve . . ."

Kate nodded.

"But he's dead, Kate. What could you possibly have done to him?"

"I always blamed him. It was a long time before I could let go of that—stop getting angry inside whenever I thought about him."

"Well, you had every right, didn't you? It was his fault Steve died."

Kate was silent for several seconds before she spoke. "Yes. I was sure of that from the beginning."

The plane had hit the side of a mountain in clear, calm flying weather. After an investigation, the National Transportation Safety Board had ruled that the cause was pilot error. Other experienced pilots had made the same dumb mistake, usually when they were distracted by something else. Gary had switched fuel tanks, a routine way of managing fuel, but he had inadvertently switched to an empty auxiliary tank. As soon as the engine had sucked all the fuel out of the fuel line, it had died in midair. Gary had been too close to the mountain to recover. The mystery had always been why they were in that position; it was a bit off the normal flight path. If they had been following the normal path, Gary might have been able to bring the plane down for a landing on Highway 93.

"I held onto the anger too long, Evie. It couldn't touch him. All it did was keep my pain alive. Didn't you ever get tired of hearing how I felt about him?"

"I knew you needed to talk it out, and under the circumstances I could understand your feelings."

Kate looked into her friend's eyes. "Could you? You're a better person than I am—you don't hold onto things like that."

"I don't know. If someone were responsible for Ray's death . . ." Evie reached across the table to put her hand on top of Kate's. "Anyway, it's over now—gone. You can let go. There's nothing else to do."

"Today I've been wishing there were." The elders had told her baptism was a chance to start clean. For the past several days, Kate had been thinking back on things she had done in her life that might have been wrong, hoping she could be forgiven for them if there was no way to set them right. She sighed. "It probably sounds strange to hear me say this, but if he were still here, I'd tell him I'm sorry."

Ann is still here.

The thought stunned her. Ann Keeler, Gary's wife. Kate had not thought of Ann for a couple of years, had not spoken to her in the past five—not since the funeral.

"What?" Evie asked, watching her curiously. "You look like you just thought of something worse."

"Yes—maybe."

She and Ann had never been friends before their husbands died together in the crash, and what Kate had felt for Ann afterward was more like . . . like a vague anger. Kate hadn't realized until now that she had punished Ann for something Gary had done.

You blamed Gary for the crash, and because he wasn't around anymore, you took it out on his wife.

At the end of Steve's funeral, Ann had stood there just outside the circle of supportive company employees—waiting, as though she wanted to talk. But Kate had known that she could not deal with Gary's wife just then; instead, she had turned and walked away.

She hadn't gone to Gary's funeral, and she hadn't made it a secret around the office that she believed the crash had been Gary's fault. For all she knew, someone in the company had passed her feelings on to Gary's widow. At the time, she had not cared.

She had never let herself acknowledge that Gary's death had left a void for someone. That realization saddened her now, and she felt ashamed for so callously overlooking the fact that his wife had suffered too.

The impression had come quietly to her mind, but it had been firm: *Ann is still here.* Kate understood why she had felt so uneasy about this all day.

"Evie, there's something I have to do—right now, before the baptism. Can you watch the kids a couple of hours for me?"

"Sure." She glanced at her watch. "You'll be back before it's time to leave?"

"Yes—and you're a saint to go with me. The kids and I won't have anyone else there."

Evie smiled. "You're going to be the saint, I understand. What do people wear to one of these things?"

Kate thought for a moment. "I haven't seen the women wear anything but dresses or skirts to church meetings. I guess this is one of those. I'll be back to change. But if it gets close to 3:30 and I'm not here, will you send KatiLynn and Stevie home to put on their church clothes?"

* * *

Was this the house?

She had only been here a couple of times, the last one more than six years ago. This looked like the place.

Maybe Ann Keeler didn't live here anymore. That would be a relief. But Kate couldn't drive away without knowing.

She walked slowly up to the front porch and rang the bell, then waited for what seemed like a minute or more—time enough to wonder whether anybody was home, or whether she could leave without ringing the bell again.

Before she could decide, the door opened.

The teenage girl who stood in the doorway was undeniably Gary Keeler's daughter. She said nothing, but simply looked at Kate curiously. Kate wasn't sure whether the girl recognized her; they had seen each other only once, at a company picnic more than six years ago.

"Is, uh . . . I, I'd like to . . . is your mother here?"

The girl continued to look at Kate as though she wasn't quite sure how to respond. "I'll get her," she said finally, and turned away.

When Ann Keeler came to the door, it was clear instantly that she recognized Kate. She looked at the woman on her front porch as though she were inspecting her. "What do *you* want?"

"To talk to you for a few minutes—if you'll listen to me," Kate answered.

Ann gazed at her speculatively for several seconds, then pushed open the storm door and stood back so Kate could enter.

The housedress Ann wore had seen better days, and there was a whiff of cleanser as Kate stepped past her. Kate was glad she hadn't bothered to change out of her jeans before coming.

Ann said nothing, but simply turned her back and walked into the living room. Kate followed. Ann sat down in the center of the couch. The furniture was spare and worn, but the room looked homey. There were pictures of three children on the end table next to the couch. Someone's shoes lay on the floor beneath the table. Sections of a newspaper were stacked in a pile on the far end of the couch.

Kate stood in the center of the room until Ann gestured toward the stuffed chair opposite her. Slowly, Kate sat down on the edge of the seat, without leaning back, holding her purse on her lap. The two women looked into each other's eyes for several seconds. Ann was obviously waiting for Kate to break the silence.

Kate wished for something intelligent to say. "How are you?" she asked. It sounded inane at best.

Ann's mouth turned up slightly, but there was no warmth in her smile. "Oh, we're fine. It's nice of you to think of us—after all these years."

Kate had determined that she was going to say what needed to be said, whether Ann punished her for it or not. This might be humiliating, but she would go through with it. "I came here because I owe you an apology, Ann. At the time our husbands died"—anger flared in Ann's eyes—"I was rotten to you. I know that. I'm sorry. Honestly. I refused to recognize that you'd lost just as much as I had."

"More! I lost my best friend, and the father of my *three* children." Ann pointed at the pictures on the end table. "Gary didn't leave me as well off as your husband left you. Do you have *any* idea how hard it is to try to send three children to school on what you can make at part-time bookkeeping jobs?"

"No, I'm sure I don't."

Tears glistened in Ann's eyes. "No matter whose *fault* the crash was, did you think you were the only one who felt pain?" She stared out of the window for a moment, and her voice was husky when she spoke again. "Do you have any idea how many times I wished it had been *you* flying the plane that day?"

"Not as many times as I did."

Her answer took Ann off guard. The other woman's expression softened. "But your children . . ."

Kate nodded. "They were what kept me from diving my plane into the ground when I went flying the day after the funeral."

This time Ann looked shocked.

"I wasn't very rational for a while," Kate said. "I was thinking only of myself. And I couldn't stop blaming Gary. I was wrong to hold onto that, Ann. You have every right not to like me, but I ask you please to forgive me. I'm sorry for the way I treated you."

Ann stared out the window again. She bit her lip, and tears began to roll down her cheeks. "You could have at least . . . I mean, why couldn't you, when I came to *your* husband's funeral . . ." She was silent for a moment, then looked at Kate. "I still wake up every day and notice first thing that the other side of the bed is empty and I'm alone. I stay out of my bedroom until I absolutely have to go to sleep at night because that's where we used to talk and have time just for us. I still have some of his things in the closet, but I don't look at them very often because . . ." Her tears ran freely. Slowly she bent over until her face was buried in her hands and her shoulders shook as she sobbed.

Kate's own eyes misted over. She willed herself not to cry. She had already fought these battles inside herself, and she wasn't going to be drawn into them again. But it was awkward and painful to watch Ann struggle. Kate wanted to put an arm around the other woman's shoulders and try to comfort her, but she imagined that Ann would simply shake it off.

Slowly Ann's sobbing subsided. She straightened up and looked into Kate's eyes. "Do you want to know why they were there when it happened?" she blurted. Kate stared at her in surprise. "The crash? You *know* why they were off course?"

"I think I do—maybe." Ann looked away, staring at some spot on the wall in the hallway. "I think Gary . . . he used to like to get in for a close look when he saw antelope out in those mountains. He used to like to take pictures. He showed some of them to me."

Kate remembered that investigators had found a charred camera in the wreckage.

"Gary used to fly for the fish and game department," Ann continued. "He said he could get so close in one of those small planes that he could almost herd the animals. I never dreamed he would try something like that with Steve in the plane. But maybe he was showing off, or . . ." Tears started to course down Ann's cheeks again. "And then after the crash, Steve still tried . . ." She buried her face in her hands, sobbing again.

The report had said the plane hit on its belly, as though coming in for a landing with the gear still up. The right wing had been torn off on impact and the left wing had been torn open. That was where the fire had started, with a ruptured fuel tank. The coroner had determined that Gary probably died on impact, even though his body was burned in the flames. But Steve had lived to get out of the passenger seat. He had been burned only on his hands; evidently he had tried to free Gary. Steve's body was found some distance from the burned wreckage. Motorists on Highway 93 had seen the smoke and alerted the sheriff's department, but when deputies reached the crash site, Steve was dead. The coroner said he had died from internal injuries.

That was one reason Kate had wanted for so long to hate Gary. She thought over and over of Steve lying on that mountainside—how long?—in pain, possibly gasping for breath, feeling life slipping away from him. Had he thought of her and the children? Had he perhaps said her name? Had he—but she had learned not to think about it.

She was surprised at what she felt now that she had every reason to hold Gary completely responsible. She could not muster the hate anymore. All the reasons, the sharp-pointed little justifications, were in place, but something had happened to her over the past few weeks, even the past few days, that had taken the hate out of her. She didn't want to spend time on it anymore.

She looked at Ann across the room, her body heaving with sobs, and only felt sorry that the other woman was suffering.

Kate crossed the room, sat down on the couch beside Ann, and put a hand on her back. Ann stiffened at her touch, sat up suddenly, and looked at Kate with tears still streaming from her eyes. "What you said about Gary was true! Don't you understand that? I wanted to tell you at Steve's funeral, but after you turned your back on me, I couldn't face you." She wiped at her tears with her fingers. "Part of me was mad at Gary too, for getting himself killed. Part of me has been mad at you all this time, thinking I had every right, and part of me has been guilty knowing *you* were right. Can you understand that?"

Kate nodded. "All of it. But being 'right' doesn't do us any good now, does it?" she answered softly.

Ann looked at her quizzically.

"Thanks for telling me about the crash," Kate said. "I suppose it eases my mind, in a way. But does it change anything for either of us?"

Slowly Ann shook her head.

"Whatever happened, I was wrong to take it out on you," Kate continued. "I hope you'll forgive me for that."

Ann looked at her for several seconds, apparently trying to decide if Kate was sincere. "OK. You're forgiven, if that makes you feel better."

"I hope it makes *you* feel better."

They sat looking at each other until Kate said: "I meant what I asked when I came here. Is there anything at all I can do for you?"

Ann glanced around the room. The fingers of her right hand brushed over the worn fabric of the couch, but Kate wasn't sure the other woman was even aware it had happened. "No—not really," Ann answered. "The insurance settlement left me out of debt. I found full-time work, but the company went belly up about eight months ago. I've been getting by on part-time jobs. We're doing all right."

Kate couldn't think of anything else to say. *"I'll call you"? "I'll be seeing you"? Unh-uh—it would sound trite and phony. We're not really friends.* She stood and walked to the door. "I'm sorry I caused you pain. I hope we can bury that part of the past," she said.

Ann nodded, but did not speak. Kate left her sitting on the couch as she let herself out.

Her legs felt rubbery as she walked down the sidewalk toward her car. Once inside, she sat limply in the seat and put her head back against the headrest. Why had this taken so much out of her, like a hard physical workout? Her hand trembled as she dug her keys out of her purse, relieved that it was over.

But it wasn't.

Something here was unfinished. She put her key into the ignition, but she couldn't start the car and drive away. It didn't feel right. She wasn't sure why. The feeling seemed to have something to do with the thought that had come to her in Ann's house: "We're not really friends." And it had something to do with Ann's fingers rubbing across the worn fabric of her couch.

What would a friend do? The thought came softly, but it was insistent. *If you really wanted to help her, what could you do for her?*

The impression that followed almost made Kate laugh out loud, and yet something told her it should not be taken lightly. The idea seemed improbable, idealistic, something that would never work.

I wonder if God ever has a good chuckle when he drops ideas like this on people. This one is way out there. It wasn't a bad idea—it seemed like a pretty good one, really. *If Ann . . . and if I . . . but no—she'd probably tell me no.*

Kate put her hand on the key again. But the thought of driving away brought back the kind of gloomy, oppressive feeling that used to hover over her on days when she withdrew into her own loneliness and inadequacy. That feeling hadn't come very much lately, not since she had started to pray regularly for God to guide her.

Slowly she withdrew the key from the ignition. *All right, I'll do it—but you'll have to help her decide.*

She got out of the car, walked slowly up to the front door, and rang the bell again.

Ann had a cleaning cloth in her hand when she answered the door. She looked surprised.

"May I come in again?" Kate asked.

Ann nodded and stood back to hold the door open. Kate stepped inside, and Ann motioned her toward the same chair in the living room.

Kate shook her head. "This probably won't take very long. Did you say you're working at part-time jobs?"

"Yes. That way I can usually be here in the afternoon when my children come home from school."

"I'm managing my father's flying service," Kate said, "and we need a good bookkeeper and office manager. I'll pay you fifteen percent more than you're making right now, and we can be flexible about the hours."

Ann looked startled. Then, slowly, she shook her head. "I appreciate what you're trying to do, Mrs. Warden. But things are, uh . . . OK. I don't need your charity."

"I'm not in a position to judge what *you* need, Ann. But I need a bookkeeper—someone with experience and maturity."

"And you're willing to pay me fifteen percent more, just like that, without having any idea what I'm making?" Ann looked dubious.

"I've checked around. I know what the top is for bookkeepers, and I'd be asking you to do more than books. You'd be handling some of the office management details that I don't have time for if I'm going to keep the flying part of the business running."

Ann looked out the window in the storm door for a moment. "And why would you trust *me*? You don't know anything about my work."

"I know that Gary told me you were good at it. He was proud of you. He said you could easily have a career in accounting if you wanted it."

Ann shook her head slowly. "You didn't really trust Gary. That's what *he* thought, and he was right, wasn't he?"

"I'm asking you to forget what I said about him back then. The Gary I knew was a lot of things—including a fairly good judge of people. I'm willing to take a chance on you based on what he told me. You're right, I don't know your work, but I'm not taking any more of a risk than if I hired somebody who answered a newspaper ad."

Ann looked into Kate's eyes for several seconds. "I'll have to think about it."

"OK. But do you think you could let me know by Monday?" Kate opened the screen door and stepped outside. "In fact, if you're interested and you feel like you could work with me, why don't you just come in Monday morning after you get your kids off to school. The girl we have part time is starting a new semester next Friday, and before she's back in school, I'd want her to show you what she's been doing."

* * *

"Right on time," Elder Martinez said, smiling as he glanced at his watch. "Everything all right?"

"Yes. Why?"

"You said when you called that there was something you had to take care of? Something to help you be ready for baptism."

"Something that should have been cleared up a long time ago. It's done." Kate glanced toward the back of the chapel, where she had left her son with Evie. "Who are those two women talking to my friend?"

"Missionaries."

Kate looked at them again, then at Elder Martinez, and shook her head. "I don't think Evie is really ready to, uh . . ."

He gave her the same engaging smile she had seen the day he came to the flight service building. "We never know unless we ask. Now, if the two of you are ready, we'll find you some baptismal clothes."

Kate realized that the ill-at-ease feeling she experienced earlier in the day had vanished, and so too had the weakness she felt in front of Ann's house. Instead, she felt energized now, eager to get on with this. She looked down at KatiLynn, who smiled and nodded.

"We're ready," Kate said.

* * *

She pulled the dress out of the closet and held it up to inspect it.

It was nice, and it flattered her figure. Basic black was useful sometimes, and with the right jewelry accents it looked good.

But she would never wear this dress again. She had worn it to the funeral, and every year since on the anniversary of her husband's death. It was the dress in which she had said good-bye to Steve. And now she knew there had been no need to say good-bye.

Kate folded the dress carefully and laid it on the chair in her bedroom. Tomorrow it would go to the thrift store.

She smiled to herself as she knelt by the bed to say her prayers.

5

Breathing hard, Bill eased down slowly and settled into his recliner. Kate lingered beside him for several seconds until he seemed to catch his breath. Then she walked across the room and sat opposite him on the couch, trying not to let concern for her father show in her face. He had started from the dining room like the healthy, vigorous man he had always been, and the effort had left him winded.

"Too much of taking it easy," Bill said. "Guess I need to get a little more exercise."

Exercise was not the answer, Kate knew. The doctor had told them this would happen; her father would be less and less able to move around, weaker and weaker. He needed open-heart surgery—but he would not agree to it. "When do you see the doctor again?" Kate asked. She knew he had refused to make another appointment after his last visit.

"Never, I hope!"

"Dad, my children need a grandfather," Kate said softly. "I want them to have one while they're growing up. If you won't—"

He cut her off with a wave of his hand. "You know how I feel about that. If I go into the hospital, I'll never come out. I'm not going to let that happen."

Tom had told her when their father came out of the hospital the first time that this would be his answer. Bill Morrow had seen his own father go to the hospital with heart problems—and die there. "Dad, the doctors have new ways to treat this now," Kate said patiently. They had been over this ground before. "The surgery could give you years—maybe decades. And Mom needs you. I need you. KatiLynn and Stevie need you." She paused. "Please, will you see the doctor? For us?"

Her father sat with his hand over his eyes for several seconds. Finally he nodded. He took his hand away so he could look at her. "Tell me about the office." It was his way of avoiding the subject of his health.

"Things are going well. Ann just finished last month's report. I'll bring it to you tomorrow." And while she was visiting, she would make sure he had called the doctor for an appointment.

"Good idea you had hiring Ann," Bill answered. He had said it before. "So, no problems? Is that Cessna you had repaired still holding up OK?"

"Everything's fine, Dad." Kate frowned. *Almost* everything.

"What?" he said.

"Remember when I told you a month and a half ago that we had a theft from a plane?"

"Yeah—a guy flew in from Wisconsin with his wife and somebody stole his radio. He causing trouble about that?"

"No—but we had another plane hit Friday night."

Bill rubbed the stubble of his beard with his hand. "Twice in less than two months? They hit anybody else out there?"

Kate shook her head. "I checked with the other flight services."

"You think somebody's got it in for us?"

"I don't know," Kate said slowly. "I've wondered, but I can't think of . . . anyway, I've talked to Harvey and asked him to watch out more carefully. He says he can't come around more than once an hour, so I called the police and asked for more patrols out our way. And I'm having a new security camera installed this week—the latest model."

Bill nodded. "Best we can do, I guess." He paused. "Are you sure Harvey *can't* come around any more than that?"

"You think he's not doing as much as he could?"

"I caught him sitting behind the airport office a couple of times when he was supposed to be on patrol. He was guzzling pop from one of those big mugs while he listened to the ball game." Bill frowned, and gazed at the picture of a jet fighter in flight on the wall. "Think I'll call tomorrow and suggest they look at another security company." He glanced at his daughter. "You mind?"

Kate shook her head. "No, of course not. It's your business."

She took pains to keep her father informed of everything to do with Morrow Flight Service—but they both knew who was running it. Bill had told her some time ago: "The business will be yours and your brother's someday, and right now it needs a manager who can be there. That's you. I hope it's not too much for you."

When she had told Tom about their father's comment, his response had been: "I'm not worried about what we're going to inherit. I'm worried about *him*." Tom had managed to arrange a transfer back to the United States—a short-term assignment at the Pentagon—and he had come to Phoenix twice in the past three months to check on their parents. After visiting the flight service offices, he had said, "It couldn't be in better hands, Kate. I hope you'll just help him feel needed—give him something to come back to."

She had assured her father that she could manage everything, and with Ann helping out now, that was true. Kate had learned how to juggle her responsibilities with Warden Avionics smoothly, and over the past six months—through the rest of the school year—both she and Ann had managed to mold their work at the Morrow office around their children's schedules. Trish or Phil, the chief mechanic, filled in for short periods when Kate and Ann both had to be gone.

Sometimes Kate brought Stevie and KatiLynn to the office after school until she could take them home to dinner. And sometimes—too often, she feared—dinner was something they picked up on the way home. She felt guilty that she enjoyed these Sunday dinners with her parents so much because she didn't have to cook.

KatiLynn came from the kitchen and stopped at her grandfather's chair to pat his arm, then walked over to the couch to sit by her mother. She was followed by her grandmother and her brother, who sat on the other side of Belle. "Grandma's going to read to us," KatiLynn announced.

Kate tried not to show surprise. At ten, her daughter often passed up story time now when Kate read to Stevie at night. But KatiLynn showed a keen sensitivity to other people's feelings, and she knew that her grandmother enjoyed reading to her grandchildren.

Belle pulled Stevie up onto her lap. She opened the book she carried, *Bible Stories,* and began to read them the story of Saul's conversion on the road to Damascus.

When she finished, KatiLynn sat silently for a moment, thinking. Then she said: "That's like Alma."

Belle looked at her granddaughter quizzically. "Who?"

"Alma, in the Book of Mormon. Our Primary teacher told us about him. An angel came and told him not to fight against the Lord. Alma fell down like he was dead, and when he woke up three days later, he told everybody he had learned that Jesus is our Savior."

Belle's lips compressed into a thin line as she closed the book. She said nothing more.

Bill picked up the conversation, changing the subject. "We're really glad you kids came for dinner. We love to have you. Did you like the roast?" He looked at KatiLynn, then Stevie.

KatiLynn nodded. Stevie made an emphatic up-and-down motion with his head. "Uh huh. And the cake." He grinned.

Bill laughed. "That's right. You ate a lot." He glanced at KatiLynn. "I don't think your sister ate enough to keep a little bird alive."

Stevie looked at his sister and laughed.

"But, Grandpa, I *did* eat," KatiLynn protested. She glared at her brother. "I *never* eat as much as *he* does."

Bill grinned at his granddaughter. "Worrying about your figure already? Trying to look good for the boys?"

"No!" KatiLynn turned red. "Who cares what they think?"

Bill laughed again. "You'll care one of these days. They'll all notice you." He glanced up at Kate. "Just like they did your mother." He looked at KatiLynn again. "In the meantime, will you still be *my* sweetheart?"

"Sure, Grandpa." But it was a bit aloof. KatiLynn was probably trying to decide, Kate realized, whether to forgive him for teasing her about boys. She was at that awkward age when she was just beginning to be aware of boys as boys, the age when a girl didn't know whether to believe that one day she might have favorable feelings toward one of those annoying creatures.

"I'll tell you what," Bill said, glancing at Stevie. "The two of you come back again next Sunday and after dinner I'll make you one of my special banana splits. Then maybe Grandma can take you to the park, or to a movie."

"Grandpa, you know we don't go to movies on Sunday," Stevie said solemnly.

"Oh, yeah. I forgot," Bill said, glancing at his wife.

Kate could see that Belle was maintaining a neutral expression only with some effort.

"Well, then, maybe Grandma could read to you again," Bill added.

Belle's expression did not change. She said nothing.

"That would be nice," Kate said to fill the silence.

In the eight months since she and KatiLynn had been baptized, this was the way it had usually been when the church or religion came up with her parents—all of them skirted the issues.

* * *

The police report was short. The thief had left little evidence behind; there would probably be no way to trace him. Kate frowned as she added the report to the insurance file. This was the third theft in three months from a plane tied down at Morrow Flight Service.

The thief had been more brazen each time. Last time, he had approached the plane from the far side, dressed in dark clothing that included a ski mask, and kept the aircraft largely between himself and the security camera. It appeared on the videotape that he was wearing gloves, and the police had found no fingerprints. The security agency that was supposed to monitor the camera had picked up what was happening only after he was inside the plane, and he was gone in under ten minutes, well before the police could arrive.

Last night he had simply sneaked up beneath the camera and blocked its lens with something before it could pick him up. The lens had been covered for a little over twenty minutes while he had removed key electronic parts from the plane's navigation system (ironically, the latest from Warden Avionics). Then he was gone—no fingerprints, minimal damage to the plane itself, no trace of what he had used to block the camera. There had been no one on the flight service property when the patrol car arrived, and when Harvey showed up five minutes later, he reported that he had seen no one else in the area.

It had to be the same man. The police said he knew his way around too well. But why us? There haven't been thefts from the other businesses around here in the past few months, and they don't have any better security than we do. Why pick on us?

When she brought in this file today, Ann had said the insurance agent was hinting that premiums could go up if security were not tightened.

But how? If a camera isn't enough, what else?

* * *

"Sister Warden—got a minute? I think I may have a way to help you with your problem."

What "problem?" And how would Rob Ellis know whether I have some kind of problem?

The elders quorum president stepped into a corner of the foyer and beckoned her to come with him. He held out a business card to her. "They were saying in priesthood executive committee that you've been having a problem with thefts at your business. I think this man could help."

They talk about things like that in . . . did he say priesthood committee meeting? But how would they know? I haven't said anything to anyone in the ward—except Chris, and she . . . but she might have told her husband, and Jerry's the . . . uh, executive secretary?

"I think I can handle it myself," Kate said, and in her mind the question came instantly: *Really? What were you thinking of doing?* It was the kind of question Steve used to ask subordinates who tried to bluff when they hadn't thought things through.

"This man can probably give you some good advice." Rob continued to hold out the card. "He's the guy a lot of high-tech firms around here turn to when they can't solve a problem internally."

Slowly Kate reached out and took the card. She glanced at the name: David R. Cutler, SafeGuard Security.

"You'll like Dave," Rob Ellis said, and smiled. "He's sharp, got a sense of humor—and he's single."

Kate started to ask if his marital status had anything to do with the effectiveness of his work, but she didn't get the chance; Rob turned and walked away.

Why do people always think they have to fix my life for me? And what makes everyone think I'm just waiting around until another man comes along? I'm married to the man I love—even if he isn't here right now. I'm going to be sealed to him.

As she walked past the garbage can in the foyer, Kate extended the business card toward it, then drew her hand back at the last second. She glanced at the card again. *All right. Maybe this man might know something that* could *help me. It's not like I have to date him just because Rob thought it was a bright idea*

* * *

"This is Dave Cutler. You called me—with a security problem?"

He sounded mellow and friendly, not curt and officious like the two security consultants she had talked with before she had the camera installed. This one seemed to feel no need to impress her. That was a good sign; people who are expert at what they do usually don't feel any need to prove it, she thought.

"Yes. I've had some thefts, and even a security camera doesn't seem to discourage the guy. Rob Ellis said you might be able to help me."

"Guy? You know it's a guy?"

"Well, ah . . . yes, or at least I'm pretty sure. He looked too big to be a woman."

"You've seen him?"

"Once, on the videotape—all dressed in black, including a ski mask."

"Umm. Pretty cocky. Sounds like an interesting challenge."

Kate got the feeling that this man liked challenges. "Last time he covered the camera lens with something while he worked," she said, "so we've only seen him once."

There was a chuckle on the other end of the line. "Boy, will he be surprised. We have some new tools that help us with people like him."

"You think you can do something then?"

"Oh, yeah. If you're interested, we can meet to talk about it."

* * *

She had no idea what to expect. He was a pleasant surprise: not tall, not exactly dark (in fact, his sandy brown hair was thinning a bit on top), but he was fairly good looking—handsome when he smiled, and that seemed to come easily for him.

But, then, why did any of that matter? This was business.

"Please make yourself comfortable," she said as she ushered him into the flight service manager's office and sat down in the chair behind the desk.

He took the chair opposite her. "How many thefts did you say you've had?"

"Three. But expensive." She pushed the folder containing the police reports and insurance forms across the desk toward him, then sat watching as he quickly scanned the documents.

When he finished reading, he looked up at her. "This guy's thorough, but he's arrogant. For some reason he wants you to know he can get past whatever you put up to stop him."

"So far, he's been right."

"Can you think of anybody who'd want to hurt you and send you a message at the same time—that he can outsmart you?"

Kate shook her head. "I've been thinking about this a lot. I can't come up with anybody."

"Well, whoever he is, his arrogance is going to work against him. If we bait him right, he'll make a mistake and we'll get him."

"You mean—set a trap?"

He leaned back in his chair and gazed into her eyes for a moment as though trying to gauge something about her. "Unless you'd like to wait for him to hit you again." He shrugged. "Or maybe that security guy you business owners pay to roll by here every couple of hours will get lucky and spot him. But does it bother you to think about setting a trap for someone who's stealing from you?"

"No, it's just . . . no. But what makes you think he'll take your bait?"

"This thief obviously knows something about your place—at least that you've got a camera, and where it's located. He knows what's valuable and how to go after it, and I'm wondering if he even has a way of knowing just *when* there's something valuable in one of the planes here. If he does, and we make it look like you've installed some new kind of security device to keep him out, I think he'll bite. It'll be a challenge to him."

"It sounds like you have a plan already."

He smiled. "I thought you'd never ask. I have an idea. Lead me to your camera, Sister Warden."

"Kate. Please call me Kate."

"All right. And all my friends call me Dave."

He followed her outside. She pointed at the security camera under the eaves of the building. The camera was situated so its wide-angle lens could cover the tie-down area where planes belonging to private pilots were chained to heavy steel loops fastened in concrete. Beyond the concrete tie-down area was the asphalt apron next to the airport's taxiway.

Dave Cutler turned in a half circle surveying the area covered by the camera. Then he stepped up directly beneath the camera, put his back against the wall of the building, and slowly turned his head in a half circle again. He unclipped the cell phone he carried on his belt, then took out his wallet, removed a business card, and held the card out to her. "I want you to go inside where you have your monitor for this system and call me at my cell phone number. I need you to help me find out just what this camera can see."

The security system monitor was under the service counter in the outer office where it could be seen from the manager's desk when the manager's door was open. Ann Keeler sat at the desk in the outer office next to the monitor. "Who is that man?" she asked when Kate walked back inside. "Another policeman, or somebody from the insurance company?"

"Dave Cutler. He's a security consultant," Kate answered as she picked up the phone on Ann's desk.

"*Whose* security?" A smile played around Ann's mouth. "Did you notice that he's good-looking?"

Kate smiled too as she punched in the cell phone number. Ann had been dating whenever she had a chance, and she couldn't resist trying to sell a friend on the idea too. "This is just business," Kate answered.

While she watched the monitor inside, David Cutler took steps in several directions from beneath the camera and had her tell him just when he was visible. Finally, he said, "OK, I think that's enough. Tell me, when they installed this camera, did they talk about any other models?"

"No—just that one. Is there something wrong with it?"

"No, not really. It's just, uh . . ."

"You think we need something different?" Kate noticed that Ann was taking an interest in the conversation. She had pulled the manual for the security system out of a drawer in her desk and was looking at the specifications. Kate hadn't known where the manual was kept; she hadn't even thought about it since the camera was installed. She had let Ann be the expert on operating the system.

"Why don't you come back outside and we'll talk," Dave said. "You can tell me how I did on my screen test."

Kate laughed. "I'll be right there." She hung up the phone.

Ann was watching her. "Maybe he's a fun guy when you get to know him."

Kate smiled and shook her head. "Strictly business."

"Well, business can be fun." Ann paused. "Is he going to put in a new system?"

"I'm not sure," Kate answered as she walked to the door. "I'll let you know."

She found him standing under the camera again. He pointed to several small pebbles placed in a rough half circle a few feet out from the wall. "Your thief had just this much space to work in when he blocked the lens." Dave looked up at the camera. "He had to know exactly where he would be seen."

"So he knows—and that means the camera's no good to us now?"

"Not exactly. But we need to make a temporary change." He glanced at his watch, then smiled at her. "What are you doing for lunch? Could we meet in an hour at the hamburger place up the street and talk about this?" He looked her up and down briefly. "Or that salad bar, if you prefer."

Had this man just checked out her figure? She had worn a pair of slacks today, belted at the waist but not tight, and a pullover top that wasn't especially form-fitting. She knew she had put on less than five pounds since she had married Steve. She worked out at home four nights a week, and Ann had told her once that she was the kind of woman who made men look twice. Still, she couldn't remember ever catching a man doing it.

It was as though he had read her mind. "In my business, I have to be able to judge people fairly well. You have the look of someone who works out regularly and tries hard to eat right, so I'll leave the choice of restaurant to you. But I have some things I need to show you, and it will be best if we don't talk about them in your office."

* * *

He opened the attaché case he had brought with him and took out a small TV camera that was encased in a heavy steel housing. He handed it across the table to Kate.

She pushed aside her empty salad plate and took the camera to examine it. "Is this better than the one I have?" she asked as she handed it back.

"Not really. But it will look like something new, and maybe more so-phisticated—a challenge. What it will do is distract our thief from these." He reached into the case and took out two small, cylindrical objects, no bigger around than large pencils, with electrical cable attached to them. "These cameras can be mounted under the eaves of your building at each end. They'll be monitored twenty-four hours a day, they'll give a full view of that side of the building, and they'll be disguised to blend in with the background. No one has ever spotted them yet."

He returned the three cameras to their case and closed it. "You'll let it be known around the office that there's a plane parked outside with something valuable in it. Then we wait to see what happens."

Kate frowned. She sat with her hands clasped in front of her on the table. "Around the office? Do you really think . . ."

Dave leaned forward, resting his arms on the table. "I think you have to face the possibility that this thief has somebody helping him—maybe somebody in your office. Does anyone there have a reason to hold something against you?"

"No," she answered slowly. "No, I can't think of anything. There was a time when Ann and I weren't on good terms—but that was all taken care of before I hired her. And there's Trish. She's a college girl who helps us around the office afternoons and three evenings a week. But she's been there three years. If she had wanted to be involved in anything like this, she could have done it long ago."

"Anyone else?"

"Well . . . maybe one of our mechanics or service people. But so far as I know, we have a good relationship with all of them. I haven't heard any complaints." She shrugged. "I can't think of a reason for anybody to single us out."

"Who knows your security system best?"

"Ann. She studied everything about it after they put it in."

"And she's your office manager?" Dave gazed at her steadily. "Do you think she could still be holding some kind of grudge you don't know about?"

Kate frowned again. *No—not Ann. She would never . . . would she? No! I'd trust her with my home, or with my children—I have trusted her with my children. She couldn't look me in the eye and do something like this.* Slowly, she shook her head. "No, I could never believe that about Ann."

Dave continued to hold her gaze for several seconds. Finally he leaned back in the cushioned seat of the booth and looked out the window. "Well, I hope for your sake you're right about all those people. Maybe your thief has some other way of getting his information. But usually in a case like this there's an inside connection."

He looked at her again. "There's only one way I know to find out for sure."

6

Reluctantly she looked away from the stark beauty of the desert landscape below and reached for her microphone button to key it, wondering why the signal from the tower was a ringing sound.

Then she opened her eyes groggily and realized that she was grasping the telephone on the nightstand beside her bed. She juggled the receiver in her hand and laid it against her ear. "Hello?"

"Sorry to wake you, Kate." The voice was David Cutler's. "We have a hit at the flying service."

"Already? It's only been three days."

"Yeah. Looks like you did a good job of planting the idea that there's something worth stealing in the plane."

"Camera equipment for a movie company—that's what I said." She hesitated. "Do you have any idea who . . ."

"No—not yet. But my people tell me we've got him on the hidden cameras. I just called the police and now I'm on my way out the door. Want to meet me?"

"Half an hour. I'll see you there."

She hung up the phone and lay still for a moment wishing she were back in that dream.

But not really. She had had the dream before, and it was a lonely one. Always she wanted to share the beauty she could see around her, and always the passenger seat was empty—no KatiLynn taking a lesson, no friend . . . no Steve.

She sighed, rolled onto her side, and got out of bed. Reality was calling. She would have to get KatiLynn and Stevie out of bed and leave them at her parents' house on the way to the airport.

* * *

Two police cars were parked in front of the Morrow Flight Service building with a truck sandwiched between them. The truck bore the logo of the security agency that business owners at the airport paid to patrol here at night. Dave must have called them too, she thought. His dark blue Ford minivan, with its SafeGuardSecurity logo on the door, was sitting next to one of the police cars.

Kate parked her Lexus next to his van, got out, and walked up the sidewalk toward the first police car. Dave and one of the officers stood talking to the man in the caged area behind the front seat of the vehicle. Kate looked in the window and gasped. *"Harvey!"*

The man in the patrol car looked away. His hands were handcuffed behind his back.

Dave nodded toward him. "Who'd know better how to beat your system than the security guard who patrols the area?"

"But why would he . . ." Kate began. She looked at the man in the car. "Why, Harvey?"

He refused to look at her.

The policeman stood with his notebook poised, listening. Harvey said nothing.

"Harvey's been pretty close-mouthed since Officer Ryan told him that anything he says can be used against him," Dave said.

A voice called out from the tie-down area: "Ryan!" It was the other officer, standing at the back corner of the building. "Did you call the crime scene people? They need to get pictures of this mess and see if they can lift any prints."

"Yeah," the police officer standing by the car called back. "They're on their way."

Harvey laughed to himself.

Officer Ryan leaned down to look in the window at him. "Think you're safe because you were wearing gloves when we caught you? Did you have them on when you swung that pipe at the camera?"

Harvey didn't answer. The police officer smiled. "We're going to check out *everything*, my man, just to see if we can pick up anything that ties in with the other break-ins here. Guys like you always foul up somewhere."

Kate looked at Dave. "What did he . . ."

"Smashed the security camera I put up back there." Dave grinned. "But he didn't spot the hidden cameras. We've got him on video trying to break into the plane, and then trying to get away from the officers when they showed up."

Officer Ryan pointed his pen at Harvey. "I'm going back there to have another look at the mess you made. You just sit tight where you are while I'm gone. Understood?" It was said affably enough, but Harvey seemed to get the message; he leaned back against the seat. Kate looked at the policeman as he walked away. He was six-foot-four, she estimated, with the kind of biceps that might be seen on an offensive lineman for the Sun Devils. He probably had had little trouble controlling Harvey.

She looked at the man in the car again, then spoke to Dave. "When you asked me about people who could be involved, he didn't even cross my mind. But I guess he's had plenty of opportunities to scout out the office."

Harvey laughed and they turned to look at him. He was smirking. "Yeah—sure. Just me, all alone."

"What's that supposed to mean?" Dave asked.

"You figure I worked this out all by myself?"

Dave studied him for a moment. "If you've got something to say, say it. You're in no position to play cat and mouse."

Harvey looked at Kate then at Dave and nodded toward the building. "Her hot friend who runs the office in there. Anyway, *she* thinks she's hot."

Kate sucked in a breath. *Ann? He's saying Ann was in on this after all?*

"Ann Keeler?" Dave asked.

Harvey nodded. "Yeah. Her."

"Why? What's in it for her? From what you just said, I 'd guess it wasn't your undying love."

Harvey hesitated, glowering at Dave. "Money." He paused, obviously thinking. "She, ah . . . she said we could split whatever I got—and she'd tell me whenever there was something good here." He glanced at Kate uncertainly, then went on. "She said she wasn't being paid anywhere near enough. . . . And she, uh, *she* came on to *me*, like if I did this maybe she might be interested in more than just the money." He glanced at Kate once more, then looked back at Dave.

"So—when and where did all this happen?" Dave asked.

"About, uh, three . . . I think, yeah, it was three months ago. I stopped in at the office one day and she asked me to meet her after work at the restaurant down the road on the other side of the fast food place—you know, the, uh . . . that—"

"The Chef's Garden?" Dave asked.

Harvey nodded. "Yeah."

"So you sat and ate one of their steaks while Ann laid out this whole idea for you?"

"Yeah. That's the way it was."

Kate turned away. She didn't like the look Harvey had given her when he finished, as though he wanted to make sure what he said hit its mark.

For money? It didn't make sense. *I'm paying Ann above the average, and she knows it. She thanked me—told me how much it helped with her son in college this year.* Slowly she shook her head.

She glanced at Harvey, who seemed to be watching her. *For him?* Ann had said more than once recently that she was lonely, and she worried out loud about whether she was attractive enough for men to ask her out. At 42, she had a few lines around her eyes, and she had begun dyeing her hair to cover strands of gray. She was thin—Ann lamented that she had no figure at all—but there seemed to be little real reason for concern about her looks. Kate looked again at Harvey, who had turned his attention to the policemen. *I don't think so. She's not that desperate. And it's not like the two of them have much in common. . . . She couldn't really . . . could she?*

Officer Ryan walked slowly back to the car making notes in his notebook. Harvey sat watching him. "Hey?" he called.

Ryan looked up at him. "What?"

"This thing wasn't all my idea. If I tell you about it, do think you can you help me out with the charges?"

"You know I can't promise anything," Ryan answered. "But if you tell me about it, I'll make sure the prosecutor knows you cooperated." His pen poised over the notebook.

"It was the woman in the office." Harvey nodded toward the building. "Ann Keeler." He looked at Kate. "Her office manager."

Ryan made a note in his book, then looked at Kate. "How do you spell that name?"

"Don't bother," Dave said. He took a step closer to the car and bent down to Harvey's level to look him in the eyes. "He's lying."

Harvey looked shocked.

"How do you know?" the policeman asked. "Why should he do that?"

"I don't know why. But I make it a point to learn something about the people in companies like this when I'm hired, and he's lying about Ann Keeler. She's clean," Dave answered. He looked into Harvey's eyes again. "The Chef's Garden doesn't serve steak, Harvey. It's a vegetarian place. You were never there with Ann, were you? You probably pumped her for information about the security system while you were in the office one day, and you're making all this up as you go along, aren't you?"

"No! It's the truth." He looked at Ryan. "It's the truth. You write down what I told you."

Dave turned to the police officer. "Look, I've had some experience with security breaches like this. Maybe you have too. Sometimes people come up with reasons to justify what they've done, or if they can't think of a reason, they try to dump it on somebody else."

Ryan nodded. "Yeah. But you know if he says somebody else was involved I've got to hear what he has to say." He looked at Harvey again.

"Ann called me," Harvey responded. "She said there was some valuable stuff in the plane."

"What kind of stuff?" Kate asked.

The police officer frowned at her. "I know this is your place, Mrs. Warden, but the questioning is my job." He turned to Harvey again. "So—what's in the plane?"

"She didn't know." Harvey shrugged. "Just something they asked her to keep an eye on—something we could probably get money for."

"That's a lie too," Kate muttered. Officer Ryan looked at her sharply. "Well, it is," Kate said louder. "Wherever he got his information, it wasn't from Ann. She knew what was supposed to be in the plane. I told her."

"'Supposed to be'?" the policeman asked.

"This was a sting," Dave explained. "There's an impressive-looking metal chest, but it's empty. It was supposed to have movie equipment in it for a film crew."

Ryan turned to look at Harvey, who had registered shock, but his face went blank when he realized the policeman was paying attention to him. His eyes narrowed as he stared at Kate.

Ryan bent down to look Harvey in the face. "That was news to you?"

Harvey looked away.

"Usually when people make up their story as they go along, they make mistakes," the policeman said to him. "I write it like they tell me. Then they get into court and the story falls apart, and a jury has to think about that when they go back in their room. Most of the time I've seen them come down hard on the liars."

Harvey tried to ignore him.

"Look at me," Ryan said. When Harvey did not move, Ryan commanded: "Hey! *Look* at me. I'm talking to you."

Slowly Harvey turned his head.

"Better," Ryan said. "Now—you were telling me about the woman who manages the office here. You wanted me to write it down. Go on." He poised the pen over his notebook again.

Harvey glanced at the notebook, looked at the policeman, and leaned back against the seat of the car. "I want to talk to a lawyer."

Ryan closed the notebook and put it in his pocket. "Yeah. That's probably a good choice for you right now."

"Harvey," Kate said, "why? Why our company? Why Ann?"

"It's usually one of those things nobody remembers later—except him," Dave said. "She turned you down for a date, Harvey? Something like that?"

Kate was shocked at the explosiveness of Harvey's reaction. The epithet he mouthed came out dripping hatred, and his face was disfigured by anger as he spoke. "Thinks she's too good for me. Had to make *sure* I knew how she felt." He mimicked Ann's words in a high-pitched voice and nasty tone. "'I can't see *us* ever going out, Harvey.' Like I'm not even good enough to talk to."

Kate remembered that Ann had been uneasy because of Harvey's persistence. *"I don't like the way he . . . I mean, he won't . . ."* Ann frowned and thought for a moment. *"It's like he's not even hearing what I'm saying—like it doesn't matter whether I want to go out with him."*

Kate had sympathized. It was hard when a man didn't know how to recognize a subtle *no*. She had agreed that Ann would probably have to make the refusal more definite if Harvey asked again. But she couldn't imagine Ann being crude about it.

Harvey sneered at Kate. "And you're just as bad as she is."

Her eyebrows went up in surprise.

"Somebody tries to be friendly with you and you haven't got the time of day." Harvey glared at her, then turned away.

When? He never . . . unless it was the day he was waiting outside when I had to rush off to pick up Stevie. But all he said to me was, "Long day?" There had been his crocodile smile, though—too big, as though he had practiced it—and that day she had felt something of the same feelings Ann had felt about him.

"Harvey, if I wasn't as friendly as you wanted me to be, was getting back at me worth this?"

He refused to look at her.

Officer Ryan leaned down to look in the window again. "Anything more to say?" Harvey ignored him too. Ryan straightened up and handed

Kate a small card. "There's my number at the station if you need to call. But a detective will be contacting you about trying to tie Harvey to those thefts you had earlier."

As they watched the patrol car drive away, Kate asked, "Is there any real chance they'll find the things Harvey stole?"

"Umm. Hard to say," Dave answered. "That aircraft navigation system might be easy to trace—if he sold it here."

"Where else . . ."

"Tucson, Nogales . . . maybe even Los Angeles. Maybe he'll help them find it if they offer him the right incentive."

"You mean some kind of deal with the court?

"A plea bargain—he gives them information and they reduce the charges."

Kate shook her head. "So he does his best to hurt us and then he gets a slap on the wrist."

"His lawyer will try to steer it that way. But if he admits the thefts, I doubt that he'll get away without jail time."

"Thanks for standing up for Ann."

"I did a little checking on her a couple of days ago. She's as straight as they come, so when Harvey started trotting out that ridiculous story, I knew better than to believe anything he said. There's no way the two of them would make a pair."

Kate started walking slowly toward her car. "Not with me either," she muttered, shaking her head. "What was he thinking?"

"What?" Dave caught up with her.

"I said if I were going to date anyone, it wouldn't be somebody like him."

"What are you going to do right now?" Dave asked as she stopped by her car.

Kate glanced at her watch. "Four o'clock? I guess I'll go try to sleep on my parents' couch for a while before I have to wake up the kids and get them ready for school."

He looked into her eyes for a moment. "But you won't, will you?"

"Won't what?"

"Sleep."

She smiled ruefully. "Probably not."

"Right now you're feeling hurt and used and probably a little bit mad, aren't you?"

He was right. She kept asking herself why—why would Harvey want that much to hurt them? And there was also anger. "Yes, I'm mad, and I won't be able to forget about this for a while—certainly not tonight."

Dave nodded. "Most of the time men and women take this differently. A lot of men want to punch somebody out, but they can't because it wouldn't be civilized, so they just let the thing eat at them. The anger may come out later when somebody does something to set them off. But women tend to make victims out of themselves. They ask questions like, 'What did I do wrong? Is there something I should have done to keep this from happening?'"

Kate laughed, but there was no humor in it. "I was just wondering if there was some way I could have seen this coming."

"No." Dave shook his head. "Don't *you* take any blame for this." He glanced in the direction of the shopping mall down the road. "Would it help to talk about it? We could stop at the convenience store down there and get something to drink."

"Well, ah . . . my children . . ." But KatiLynn and Stevie were safely sleeping, and she would probably disturb her parents again if she went back there right now. "Actually, it probably *would* help to talk."

He opened the door of her car for her. "I'll follow you."

At the drive-in market, he asked what she wanted, walked inside to buy drinks for both of them, then came back to sit in the passenger seat of her car.

Kate sipped at her drink before she asked, "Do you think Ann and I have seen the last of Harvey—or do we have to worry about his coming back to haunt us someday?"

Dave thought for a moment, then slowly shook his head. "It can be hard to say with a guy like that. If they're wacko . . . but Harvey strikes me as sharp enough not to buy any more trouble for himself, and he's already in deep. I don't think you'll see him again." He smiled at her. "If you need any more help discouraging him, I can suggest some things to do—no extra charge."

Kate smiled weakly. "Thanks. I've never had a problem like this before."

Dave's smile faded. "Seriously, if he makes any kind of trouble for you, call me. I'll be glad to help. But he incriminated himself in front of witnesses tonight. The smartest thing he could do now is stay far away from you."

75

What Dave said made sense, and his confidence was reassuring. He had been right about Harvey earlier, and sitting here talking about the situation calmly with somebody solid and rational helped her tension drain away. "I'll tell Ann what you said. I don't want her to worry about him."

"Did *you* ever make it clear to Harvey that you don't date?" Dave asked.

"Well, we never actually talked about . . ." She stopped as she replayed his sentence in her mind. *"Don't date"? How does he know whether . . .* She wasn't sure exactly why his wording bothered her. "I didn't say I don't date—not exactly. I said . . ."

"'If I *were* going to date anybody.' I wondered if it was clear to Harvey that you weren't comfortable with the idea. But if you never actually talked to him about it . . ." He thought for a moment, then slowly smiled at her. "Probably he just assumed you were dying to go out with him. Guys like him often think that way."

"Yes," she said slowly. How had her social life become the topic of conversation? "I, ah . . . I've met a few like that, mostly in the first couple of years after Steve—my husband—died. I couldn't even think about dating then. And later, when I, uh . . . well, I haven't known many single men over the past few years, except business contacts and a couple of guys my mother and her friends lined me up with." She wrinkled her nose and shook her head slightly at the memories. Dave seemed to be interested in what she was saying. Was this pertinent to the problem with Harvey—or was he just curious? "Anyway, if I'd really been into dating, a man like Harvey wouldn't have been . . ."

Dave nodded. "Not exactly your type."

She smiled. "What exactly is my type, Dave?" She hadn't been able to resist the question.

"Well, you . . . I, ah . . ."

In the dim light from the front of the store it looked like his face had reddened. It was his turn to grope for words. Kate continued to smile sweetly, waiting to see what he would say.

He tried to recover his composure quickly. "I'm sorry. I didn't realize you might not feel comfortable discussing it. I was just thinking that you're a woman with a lot of class, and Harvey, uh . . ." Dave realized he was sweating. He was used to getting directly to the point, but he had gotten in too deep this time. He was actually trying to compliment this woman. How? "I guess I meant a woman like you has a right to expect a lot more than a guy like Harvey has to offer."

Kate held her right hand out in front of her face pretending to examine her plain, well-trimmed fingernails closely, and she spoke very seriously. "Yes. Class almost oozes out of my fingertips." Then she looked at him and laughed. "I'm just a blue-jeans-and-hot-dogs kind of girl who's had some great opportunities, Dave. You make me sound like somebody out of the ordinary."

He looked into her eyes for several seconds before answering. "You really don't understand that you are, do you? You'd stand out in any crowd." He raised his cup to her, downed the last of his drink, then opened the car door. "Do yourself a favor and grab some rest after you get your kids off to school this morning. I'm sure Ann can handle the office until noon—or you wouldn't have her working there." He stepped out of the car and turned back to speak to her. "I'll call you if I learn anything more about Harvey."

He shut the door and walked away while she was still trying to decide how she should respond to his compliment.

It had been years since any man had said something like that to her.

It had also been years since she had flirted with a man.

That *was* what she had just done—wasn't it?

Embarrassing. You ought to be ashamed. You should . . . should have . . .

Should have what? Been unfriendly? And why should I be ashamed because he was kind? I didn't ask him to say what he said about me. I didn't need *him to say that.*

But there was no denying that it had felt good.

7

"For you," Ann said, covering the mouthpiece of the telephone receiver with her hand. "I think it's that man from the security company. If he's calling about their bill, tell him I have the check for you to sign right here and we'll put it in the mail today."

Kate laid the aircraft maintenance log on the front counter and put the receiver to her ear. "Hello?"

"This is Dave—Dave Cutler."

She had known his voice instantly. "Hi. Anything new?"

"Yes, the latest on Harvey. The police traced the things he stole. Harvey's been dealing with some bad dudes—gang members who were selling them south of the border. They're not happy about having the spotlight on them because of Harvey, and they have friends in the prisons here, so he'll probably try to work out a plea agreement to let him serve his time out of state. When he gets out, he'll want to stay away from Arizona for reasons of health."

"That's good news. I know it'll be a relief to Ann. And by the way, she says to tell you that your check will be in the mail today."

"Thanks, but I wasn't worrying about it." He paused. "There was another reason I called. I was wondering if an out-of-the-ordinary woman would go out with an ordinary guy like me."

"You mean—a date?"

Kate noticed that Ann smiled slightly but did not look up from the account record on the desk in front of her.

"Maybe dinner and a movie," David Cutler answered on the phone. "Friday night?"

"Dave, that's . . . it's sweet of you to ask, but I, ah, don't know whether . . ." Her hands were clammy. Despite their conversation at the convenience store two nights ago, this was not a question she had expected from him.

"If there's some problem . . ." He sounded disappointed.

"There could be," she answered slowly. "We, uh . . . that is, Ann and I were going to do some catching up on the books here. It's something we need to do right away."

Ann looked up at her, frowning, and shook her head.

Kate knew there was no good reason to turn this man down. But it had been a long time since she had dealt with the idea of dating, and there were questions about it she still had not answered for herself—or at least one big question. *After Steve?* She was planning to be sealed to the only man she had ever loved. Was there any point in dating another man if dating could possibly lead to something more than companionship?

But Dave didn't ask you to marry him—just go out with him.

Kate realized it had been several seconds since she had said anything, and David Cutler was waiting patiently on the other end of the line.

"Dave, I, ah . . . I can't be sure yet about Friday night." One part of her wanted to take the easy way out and simply tell him no, but another part of her would not. *Is going out with a man something you're never going to do again?* She wasn't prepared to answer that question at the moment. "Is it OK if I look things over here and let you know later?" she said into the phone.

"Sure," Dave said. "You have my number. You can give me a call." He didn't sound hopeful.

"Yes. I'll do that—I'll call. Good-bye." She quickly held the receiver out to Ann for her to take.

"You fibbed!" Ann grinned at her as she hung up the phone. "He must be a real toad for *you* to do that."

"No." Kate could feel the heat spreading in her face. "No, not really. He's . . . very nice. But you and I"—she glanced at the maintenance log on the counter—"talked about reconciling those maintenance records."

"*You* were the one who told me we didn't really have to do that until next week." Ann frowned again. "Is there some reason you wouldn't want to go out with him? I mean, if he's really so nice . . ."

Slowly Kate shook her head. "No. I . . . there's no reason, really." There wasn't a thing wrong with Dave Cutler that she knew about.

"Then what could it hurt? You might enjoy it. You've been to dinner with a couple of other guys since Steve died."

"Yes," Kate said, remembering. "Guys my mother and her friends lined me up with. But I didn't enjoy those dinners, and they don't really count as dates."

"Because?"

"Because with those guys there was absolutely no chance anything would ever come of it. My mother and her friends have no idea what I might be looking for in a man."

"But you do?"

"Well, I . . ." Kate hadn't really thought about this question—had deliberately avoided it, in fact. "What's the point in thinking about it? I've told you how I feel about my marriage. Now that I know I can be with Steve again . . ."

"Kate, I wish I could believe some of the things you believe. I can understand wanting to hang onto that. But even if I did believe . . . I mean, is there something in your religion that says you have to be all alone until you die?" Ann looked at her quizzically. "Do you think that's what Steve would want?"

There was the problem: in all the times since Steve's death when Kate had thought about dating—and there hadn't been very many—she had never been able to decide what *he* would want her to do. He had always said he wanted her to be happy in life. But they had been so young; they had never talked about what would happen if one of them died before they could enjoy getting old together.

After she lost Steve, she had never thought much about the need for a man's companionship—until a few months ago. Once, she had been able to push feelings of loneliness back into a dark corner of her mind. But lately there had been times when it seemed as though solitude might swallow her up, squeezing the life out of her. She hadn't talked to anyone else about those thoughts because they made her feel guilty. After all, Stevie and KatiLynn were supposed to be her life—weren't they?

"No, there's nothing in my religion that says I have to be alone," she answered slowly. "At least I don't think so. It's just, uh . . . I thought I could never find another man like Steve, so . . . so why look?"

Ann smiled. "Of course you'll never find another man like Steve. And I'll never find another man like Gary. They were both one of a kind. When I think of Gary now, I try to hold onto every wonderful thing he ever did—even the little ones. But he wasn't perfect, and it wouldn't take a clone of him to make me happy."

Kate's brow furrowed. "Well, I never thought of a clone, exactly."

"Really? You mean you never wished God would help you find another man just like Steve so you could take up life exactly where you left off when your husband died?"

The furrows in Kate's brow deepened. Ann was right; whenever re-marriage had come to mind, there had been thoughts of a man out there somewhere who could take over the hard parts of her jobs at Warden Avionics or the flying service, allowing her to play the same chief confidante and homemaker role she used to enjoy. (She ignored the little voice in the back of her mind that suggested she was learning from those "hard parts.")

"That's the way I wanted it to be," Ann continued. "For a long time, I just wanted to go back. Then I realized that life had changed for me, and if I didn't learn to accept it, I'd always be living with the leftovers of my past. Do you understand what I'm saying?"

Kate was surprised to realize that she understood perfectly. A nagging feeling in her heart transformed itself into a clear thought in her mind: with all the adjustments she had been forced to make since Steve's death, there was one thing she had refused to change—the place she held for him in her life. There was still a vacancy for him to fill, anytime he wanted to step back into it.

"Tell me the truth," Ann said. "Haven't you thought about what it would feel like to have a man put his arms around you again? Or to sit close to him and put your head on his shoulder?"

"No, I . . . not really arms . . ." But that wasn't the truth. "Well, maybe to have someone there when things are hard . . . to help when I need . . ."

"When it's hard being Mom *and* Dad?"

Kate nodded. "It would be nice for a while not to be Kate who runs the flying service, or Kate who's on the board of directors. It would be nice to be somebody's . . . to be the person that someone else just couldn't get along without." She smiled nervously. "I guess arms around me *would* be good sometimes."

Ann laughed. "Kate, you're blushing! I didn't mean to embarrass you. You're not the only one who feels that way. I know what it's like to want to spend time with somebody over seventeen, somebody who remembers the same songs and movies I do—somebody who's interested in *me*."

"But I'm ashamed of feeling that way! Right now I *have* to be Mom and Dad, and all the rest of it too. It's my job. It's just the way things are."

"And nothing else for you, forever after? You don't really believe that's right, do you?"

No, she didn't. But she had been afraid to admit it, even to herself. Go-ing out with a man like David Cutler, who didn't appear to have a thing wrong with him, would be admitting that her life *could* change—that Steve was not coming back to fill the place she was holding.

Ann picked up the telephone and held it out to her. "Go on—call him back."

Kate stared at the telephone but made no move to reach for it. "He, uh . . . he's probably gone out to lunch by now. And I'd have to look for his number."

"Kate!" Ann smiled as she turned the bill on her desk toward Kate and put her finger down just above the telephone number for David Cutler's office. "All you'd be saying yes to is a chance to enjoy yourself a little. Would that be so hard?"

There wasn't a good reason she could give Ann to say no. Slowly Kate reached out to take the phone, then punched in Dave's number.

"SafeGuard Security," Dave said when he answered.

"Oh, you . . . it's *you*," Kate stammered. She knew she was blushing again. "I thought I'd probably get your secretary."

"She's at lunch, so I'm handling the phone." He sounded hopeful. "What did you decide?"

"Friday night is OK—if you want."

"Great! That's just great." He sounded elated. "I'll pick you up at six if you'll tell me where."

She gave him her home address, he said he'd be there right at six, and they said their good-byes. Kate put down the phone, exhaled, and fanned her face.

Ann laughed. "Three days—three whole days now to think about how you're going to fix your hair . . . what you're going to wear . . . what you're going to say."

Kate rolled her eyes. "I haven't been out on a *real* date . . . well, going back before Steve, it's been eleven years!"

Ann smiled. "Listen, I'm an expert on stressing out before a date, and I can tell you it'll be useless to spend the next three days worrying. You have to tell yourself that he sees a lot to like in you just the way you are, or he wouldn't have asked you out."

"I hope he won't end up feeling like he was maneuvered into this somehow." Kate wondered if she was going to blush again. "I, ah . . . I flirted with him, sort of—the night they arrested Harvey. Dave took me out afterward for something to drink so he could talk to me and make sure I was all right—and I teased him about some things he said."

Ann laughed. "Kate! *You* flirted?"

Kate nodded. "I hope he didn't think I was doing it because I wanted him to ask me out."

Ann raised her eyebrows. "Maybe that *is* what you wanted—and you just didn't know it yet."

* * *

Kate held the dress up in front of her and examined her reflection in the full-length mirror. Then she moved the dress aside and studied the tan slacks and burgundy blouse she was already wearing.

Not *this* dress, she decided, sighing as she hung it at one end of her closet with a couple of other things she would probably never wear again. She liked the dress, but it was sleeveless, and she had learned that she would not be able to wear it after she went through the temple in a few months. She had been preparing for that temple trip almost since the day she had been baptized.

Well, then, another dress tonight?

What did "dinner" mean to Dave Cutler? A nice restaurant somewhere? Or maybe a barbecue place or sandwich shop?

Dinner and a movie, he had said. A movie probably wasn't a dress place.

Nicer slacks? She took another look at herself in the mirror on her closet door and decided that what she was wearing would have to do. There was not enough time to change again.

She checked her hair once more. Sometime after Steve's death, she had cut it shorter—just above her shoulders—because it was easier to care for. It had been that way ever since. Should she have done something different with it tonight? She hadn't tried; she just wanted to be sure it was at least nicely combed.

Snapping off the light in the bedroom, she walked out into the living room. Nothing to do now but wait. That was the hardest part.

She had tried all day to work without thinking about this evening, but it had been impossible. Finally she had left work early to pick up KatiLynn and Stevie at school and take them to her parents' house.

KatiLynn's reaction to this date had been half excitement, half curiosity. At first, she had been full of eager questions about it: Is he nice? What are you going to do? What does he look like? Last night, though, she had seemed unusually quiet. Finally, she had asked if her father was still going to be her father forever, no matter what. Of course, Kate had reassured her; nothing was going to change that—no matter what.

Stevie's feelings about the date had been clear: he had been disappointed that his mother would not be taking them out to a movie or for ice cream as she often did on Friday nights.

Maybe her children's responses were typical. But Kate realized that she had never stopped to think about their feelings before she said yes to Dave Cutler. *Should I have asked them about whether I ought to date? . . . No . . . or—maybe? . . . No, I don't think so. I'm the one who has to decide whether this is going to be part of my life again.*

Over the past three days, she had asked herself again and again whether dating was pointless. She was going to be sealed to Steve; that would not change. So could she ever permit herself to fall in love again—if that were possible? Could she ever consider remarrying?

There had been times during the past three days when she had been eager for tonight to come, to learn what it would be like to go out with someone again. That was how she felt right now—maybe. The panicky thought of grabbing her car keys and being gone before Dave arrived had crossed her mind a few minutes ago. The state of her mind, and of her stomach, seemed to change from moment to moment. At least in high school, when she had first experienced this semisweet mixture of panic and anticipation, her parents had been there to offer support.

That had been more than half a lifetime ago.

Kate jumped when she heard the car door slam in her driveway. She put a hand on her stomach and willed it to steady itself, then glanced at her watch. Two minutes to six. He was as good as his word at being prompt.

She sat waiting for the doorbell to ring. When it did, she sat still for several seconds more, then stood up slowly, walked toward the door, and stopped to take a deep breath before opening it.

She was instantly relieved to see that he was wearing slacks and a pullover sport shirt. He was holding roses wrapped in florist's paper.

"Hi," he said, almost shyly, and held the roses out to her.

"Oh, thank you. That's very thoughtful," she said, smiling. "I'd better put these in water. Come in."

"I, ah, thought you might like flowers." He followed her toward the kitchen. "Sometimes guys who want to date my oldest daughter bring her flowers." His laugh sounded tentative. "It doesn't get them anywhere. She won't be sixteen for a while yet."

Kate opened one of the top cupboards in the kitchen. Her vases were lined up on the highest shelf. She reached for a chair to stand on.

"Can I help?" Dave asked, standing on tiptoe and reaching toward the shelf.

"The large crystal one," she said.

He took the vase down for her, put it under the faucet in the sink, ran water into it, and handed it to her. "Anyway, I bet myself that you'd like roses."

"You won," she said, smiling at him again. She arranged the six roses in the vase, then carried it to the dining table and placed it carefully in the center. "Now we can go."

The car in her driveway was a surprise—not his minivan, but a small red convertible sports car with the top up. She wasn't sure how old it was, but it had been cared for lovingly.

Dave dropped his car keys and a handful of coins on the driveway while he was fumbling with them. He reddened and bent over to pick them up. She pretended to be studying her rose bushes in front of the house while he recovered and unlocked the passenger door for her.

The restaurant he chose for them was a popular one with a nostalgia theme in the decor and a waiting line in the lobby. They spent twenty minutes on a bench just inside the door making small talk about the old-time items on the wall. She pointed out an old radio on a shelf and told him about finding one just like it in the attic at her grandparents' house. He studied a newspaper clipping with a photo of the first moon landing, in 1969, and recalled seeing a historical video about it in elementary school.

The two of them didn't make eye contact very much.

Finally a hostess led them to a vacant booth and brought them menus and glasses of water.

As the hostess walked away, Kate opened her menu to study it. Reaching for his menu, Dave accidentally hit his water glass. The glass tipped—it seemed to happen in slow motion, but neither of them was quick enough to stop it—and fell on its side. Water spilled across the table toward her.

She slid to the side quickly so that the water dripped only on the cushioned seat of the booth. Dave snatched up the glass and scooped the scattered ice back into it while Kate reached for their paper napkins and blotted up the water.

"Sorry," he said, his face reddening again.

"Are you as nervous about tonight as I am?" Kate asked, making a small pile of soggy napkins on the corner of the table.

85

"No. Oh, no, it's not . . ." The flush in his face deepened. He looked her in the eyes. "Yes. This is the first time in, ah, sixteen or seventeen years that I've asked anybody out. Friends have lined me up a couple of times in the past few months, but this . . . but . . . yeah, I'm nervous. You too?"

Kate tried to make her smile reassuring. "I *was*. This is the first real date in eleven years for me, and I was on the edge of panic before you showed up at my house—ready to run." She paused. "But when you dropped your keys while we were getting into the car, I knew I wasn't the only one, and I thought if we both could just relax somehow, this would be a lot more fun."

She slid her water glass across the table toward him carefully. "Here, take mine if you want. I'm not really thirsty right now."

"Are you sure?"

"Yes."

He lifted the glass and took a long drink out of it.

She tried to suppress a laugh, but couldn't. Dave looked at her questioningly.

"If you could have seen your face when your glass started to tip over . . ."

His expression didn't change.

She straightened out what was left of her smile, hoping she hadn't hurt his feelings. "I'm sorry. It was just—"

Suddenly he made his eyes go wide and put on a look of mock terror.

Kate laughed again. "Yes—like that."

Dave laughed too. "I guess it's not the worst thing that ever happened to me on a date."

"I'm glad it was you first, and not me. I did a few embarrassing things on dates when I was younger. That was one reason I was worried tonight."

"You?" He looked skeptical. "No."

"Oh, yes—me."

"You seem like the kind of person who's always on top of everything—always in control." He leaned forward to rest his elbows on the table and slowly smiled at her. "What was the worst thing that ever happened to you on a date?

"The very worst? I don't know if I can . . . I mean, I still cringe over some of those things." Talk about them with a man she barely knew? Maybe it was a little too soon. She shook her head.

He smiled reassuringly. "I'll bet you've had worse."

Kate looked at him thoughtfully for a moment "All right. There are some I can laugh about—now."

She settled back slowly in the booth. "When I was sixteen, there was a guy I really liked who asked me out. I was still trying to decide what to wear when he showed up that night. I didn't want to leave him in the living room talking to my parents because Dad was an ex-fighter jock who worried that every guy his little girl dated was going to be like some of the pilots he'd known. So I grabbed my favorite white pullover out of the dryer and threw it on."

She laughed lightly. "We were at some burger place when I realized I had the pullover on inside out—and the tag was showing in the back! I'm sure my date probably noticed and was too polite to say anything. So I excused myself and hurried off to the restroom to put it on right. When I got back to the table and sat down again, I noticed that the chocolate ice cream stain hadn't washed out of the front. And besides, the thing had shrunk in the wash, so I had to keep tugging it down over my skirt all night, and I was sure he was looking at that stain every time I did."

Dave chuckled. "What we wouldn't give sometimes for a chance to turn the clock back about two hours."

"One of life's unforgettable moments." She smiled. "Your turn. What was the worst thing that ever happened to you on a date?

"Umm. It was probably the second time I went out with Jeanine—my wife. We were seniors in high school. The first date went pretty well, but that second time I really wanted to make an impression. I wheeled my car out of her driveway like an old pro and stopped to make sure she put on her seat belt, then I punched down hard on the accelerator—and *backed up* right into her father's truck! I'd forgotten to shift gears!"

Kate laughed, then stopped herself. "That's awful! Were you hurt?"

He smiled. "Just my pride. It only scratched the bumper of his truck, but it took out my taillight. I had to go get him to come look at what I'd done, and after he went back in the house, I could still hear him laughing through the door. He never let me forget that."

"My father the pilot taught me that any mistake you can walk away from is a blessing and a lesson for life."

"Yeah—in this case, always know which way you're going before you step on the gas." Dave sat back against the cushion in the booth and almost automatically wiped his palms on the legs of his pants under the table. But the sweatiness was gone, he realized, and so was his nervousness. This woman had put him at ease, made him feel that he didn't have to worry about being something he wasn't.

"My children can't believe I ever went through the same things they're going through," he said. "Kids never can believe their parents are real people."

"How many children do you have?" Kate asked. "You mentioned a daughter."

"Kelli. She's fifteen and a half. Ross is eleven, and Alicia is almost eight."

Kate nodded. "Your last two are about the same age as mine. KatiLynn is almost eleven. Stevie turned seven about four months ago."

"And how do they feel about Mom being out on a date?"

"Hmm—mixed feelings, I think. KatiLynn was excited for me, but she had questions about what it means. Stevie missed our Friday night out for ice cream, but I promised to make it up to them tomorrow." Kate paused. "I guess they'll get used to it." After she said it, she wondered whether he might take her last comment as an invitation to ask her out again. She hadn't really meant it to be—but the way things had gone so far, she wouldn't mind if he took it that way. This was a person she could enjoy spending time with, although there was some relief in realizing that she felt no sudden strong attraction toward him.

"And your children?" she asked. "How do they feel about Dad dating?"

"Oh, the first time, they were like yours—a lot of questions. My oldest is looking forward to the day *she* can date, and it hadn't occurred to her that people my age might do that too—especially not *Dad*." He laughed. "I hope they'll get used to it too."

"How long has their mother . . . your wife, uh . . ." *What? "Been gone?" Oh, Kate! Why didn't you think first? Maybe he's not a widower. What if it was a divorce—something ugly? Maybe he'd rather not—*

"She died two and a half years ago," Dave answered.

Kate felt relief that her question apparently hadn't opened any wounds. "It must have been hard for your children. I'm sure it was hard for you."

He glanced away only momentarily, then looked her in the eyes again. "Yes. It was long and drawn out. The two younger ones couldn't really understand what was going to happen. Kelli understood—but she hated it. She's still not completely over it, and she won't talk to me about it very much."

"What was your wife's illness? I hope I'm not prying."

"No. It was uterine cancer. By the time her doctor found out, it was too far along. The doctors did everything they could, but . . ." He shrugged. "I never could have gotten through it if I hadn't known that death isn't forever."

"Even so, it must have been like a part of *you* died."

"Yes." He paused. "Is that the way it was for you?"

She nodded. "I lost my husband five and a half years ago. My experience was the opposite of yours. Steve flew off to Las Vegas on business one morning with the company pilot. He called me at noon to tell me when he'd be home. Then a state trooper and a minister showed up that evening to tell me he wasn't ever coming back." She hesitated. "It was quicker for him—but I thought for a while that it would never be over for me."

"I'm sorry. Maybe I shouldn't have asked. Sounds like it still hurts to talk about it."

"No, not anymore. But at first KatiLynn didn't understand why Daddy couldn't come home, and I didn't have any answers for her—not even any answers for me. I was furious at God for a long time for taking away my anchor. If the missionaries hadn't found me, I'm afraid I'd be well on my way to old and bitter."

"When were you baptized?"

"Nine months ago." She paused, and smiled. "It was a blessing that the Lord helped me find a new anchor. I was shriveling up inside without the gospel. I couldn't live with the idea that death is forever."

Slowly, Dave shook his head. "We watch them slip away, or turn around suddenly and they're gone. There isn't an easy way to face losing someone, is there?"

"But you had people around who could help you."

"Yes, a lot of support. Jeanine was into everything in our ward, and a lot of people loved her. She—" Dave stopped himself before getting into something he had decided he would never do—reminisce about his wife with another woman he had just met. "I'm sure I had a lot of help you didn't have."

He smiled and picked up his menu again. "I can recommend the barbecued chicken here. The ribs are good too."

During dinner, he asked when she had gotten started in flying. She told him about learning from her father when she was a girl, about how much she enjoyed soaring above the desert and over mountains, about the peace of the open sky. Then she realized that she wasn't sure how long she had been talking about it. She laughed. "I'm probably boring you. I get carried away."

"That's OK." He sat watching her with his fork poised idly over his plate. "It's interesting to listen to you talk about something you obviously love."

"Tell me how you got into the security business. You probably didn't say to yourself when you were a little boy that you wanted to grow up to be a security consultant."

He laughed. "No—a spy."

He had gone into the army, he told her, as a junior officer in military intelligence just after he and Jeanine graduated from college and got married. It hadn't taken long to decide that a career in military intelligence could be very hard on family life, so he had left the army when his enlistment was up. He had gone to work for a security firm in Phoenix, and four years later he had been able to start his own business. He had stayed in an intelligence unit in the army reserves until Jeanine's cancer had been diagnosed. Then he had resigned his commission to spend all the time he could with her.

Kate asked him what was the most fascinating case he had ever handled in his work. He told her of several, without giving names or details. It was her turn to listen as he talked about something he obviously found worthwhile.

When they left the restaurant after dinner and walked to his car, he paused while he was unlocking the passenger door for her. "On a night like tonight, it can be nice to ride around with the top down. But it can be tough on the hairdo."

She smiled. "Let's see—what would we do if we were both eighteen and we wanted everybody to know who was in this hot little car?"

Dave laughed. "That's the way my daughter sees it. She can't wait to be seen driving around in this car after she gets her license next year. I haven't broken the news to her that she'll have to satisfy Dad that she can handle it."

"It looks like this car has been babied," Kate said as she helped him fold the top back.

"They don't make these anymore. I bought this one not long after I got married, from another officer who was going overseas and couldn't take it with him. Jeanine and I used to take it out a lot when we wanted to be alone together—just the two of us. But it's been in the garage most of the time since she got sick."

He backed out of the parking space carefully, then looked at her and grinned. "Got your seat belt on tight before I hit the gas?"

She tugged lightly on the belt stretched across her lap. "You're talking to a pilot, remember?"

Dave laughed. "I learned my lesson about showing off the first time," he said, as he pulled out of the parking lot slowly.

"What movie would you like to see?" he asked.

"I hadn't thought about picking anything. Did you have something in mind?"

He named a popular romantic comedy. "Or maybe *Sleeping Beauty*. Have you ever seen that one? It's one of those Disney classics I missed when I was a kid."

"You choose. Either one would be fine," Kate said, suppressing a smile. Evie had been right when she had speculated about this date.

"Hmm—dinner and a movie. Let's see . . . the movie won't be an action picture—some guy thing—or anything controversial. It'll be a romantic comedy—a 'chick flick'—or something completely safe, if he's as religious as you are."

Evie glanced down at her coffee cup. "That reminds me—can I get you something? Juice maybe?"

Kate shook her head. "I'm fine."

"You're sure it doesn't bother you when I drink my coffee in front of you?"

"It was hard for me to give it up at first. I used to think about it every time I passed the coffee machine at the flight service office. I finally moved that to the lounge, where I wouldn't see it anymore. But I never think about it now."

Evie took another sip from her cup. "I'm glad you said yes to him, Kate. You've been alone for a long time now."

"Not alone, exactly. I have the kids."

Evie gazed out the kitchen window into the backyard where her younger daughter was playing with KatiLynn and Stevie. "Yes. But it's not the same, is it?"

"No." Kate shook her head. "Evie, if anything happened to you, would you be jealous if Ray found someone else?"

A smile played around Evie's lips. "A little, maybe—assuming I could be up there somewhere looking down on him." She thought for a moment. "But I'd never ask him to spend the rest of his life with no one to come home to. I love him too much for that."

She walked to the sink to rinse out her empty cup, then turned and leaned back against the counter, smiling. "This is an awfully deep discussion over a first date, isn't it? Just go and enjoy yourself, Kate. You owe yourself that much even if nothing else ever comes of it."

It might be interesting to see how Dave would react to a movie like *Sleeping Beauty*, she thought. A phony—someone who had chosen the movie simply because it was safe to take her there—would probably be bored. But Dave didn't seem like that kind of man. She believed him when he said he had learned his lesson long ago; he didn't seem to do anything just to make an impression.

* * *

Kelli was sitting in the family room, staring at the television set. The sports segment of the nightly news was on. "Developing an interest in baseball?" Dave said, smiling at his daughter. "I thought you'd probably be in bed by now."

Slowly she turned to look at him. "So—how did it go?"

It was more than a question; it was almost a challenge. He wasn't sure how to answer. "We went to dinner. We went to a movie. I enjoyed it."

He sat down on the couch beside her. "We saw *Sleeping Beauty*. It made me think of . . . well, I used to dream about your mother that way after she died—that I would wake up and find her sleeping beside me, and I would kiss her and she would wake up too." He paused to glance at Jeanine's picture in the frame on the bookshelf. "I'm not sure exactly when I stopped dreaming that. It was probably when . . ." *Careful! You know how hard this hits Kelli.* "When I realized I had to go on without her."

Kelli looked at him searchingly. Her position didn't change, but something in her eyes told him that she had moved away from him. "And this . . . Kate? How was she?"

Dave's brow furrowed. "What do you mean: 'How was she?' "

"Was she fun?" It sounded like a demand.

"Yes. Yes, she was," he answered. "She's quite a woman—a pilot, successful in business—and she's nice. You'd probably like her if you met her." *WRONG! Wrong, wrong, Dave! Bad move. You know how Kelli hates to be told what to like.*

"And did she like your car?"

92

This wasn't just a question about a car, Dave realized; it was about the car she had seen her father and mother use so often. "I don't know," he answered slowly. "She didn't say."

His daughter stared at him for a few seconds more, then got up from the couch and walked toward the hallway. "I need to go to bed," she said over her shoulder.

She stopped in the doorway and turned to look at him. "Alicia cried when I tucked her in. She wanted to know why Daddy wasn't here to do it."

"Kelli?" he said to her back. But she was gone down the hallway.

Dave sighed. *She's been waiting up so she could tell me that. She's not going to make this easy for me. I wonder if it's going to be like this every time I go out? If I'll ever meet a woman she could like?*

8

Ann looked up from her work as Kate pushed through the front door. "So—how was it?"

Kate looked at her quizzically. "Fine. I just went to the salad bar down at—"

"Not lunch—Friday night. We haven't had a chance to talk about that."

Kate smiled. "It was . . . fun. I enjoyed it." In fact, she had come awake Saturday morning thinking about how enjoyable it had been. Dave Cutler had a good sense of humor and a positive approach to life. He was a gentleman, and he knew how to make a woman feel like a lady and an equal at the same time.

"He must have enjoyed it too," Ann replied, glancing toward Kate's office.

Kate walked to the door and looked in. There was a vase full of flowers on her desk—bright yellow daisies this time. Ann followed as Kate walked to the desk and reached for the card that was tucked beneath the ribbon around the vase. Kate opened it and read:

"I noticed that you had these planted in front of your house too. I hope you like them.

"Thanks for making Friday night good. I didn't know it could be so enjoyable to go out with someone again."

Ann was watching expectantly. Kate handed her the card. "When did these come?" she asked.

"Half an hour ago." Ann read the message on the card and smiled. "I hate to say I told you so, but . . ."

Kate laughed. "It was dinner and a movie—*Sleeping Beauty*."

Ann raised her eyebrows. "But this time the handsome prince found *you*."

"Well, I wouldn't go that far. This *was* just one date."

Ann laughed. "You're blushing again. Don't worry—I'm not going to meddle in your love life. I have my own to worry about. I think my handsome prince's horse went lame somewhere deep in the forest."

Kate laughed once more.

"But I think *you* need to decide how you'd feel about having a love life again," Ann added as she walked back to her desk. "I'd guess from these flowers that he thought he saw a welcome sign on the castle gate."

* * *

Kate pulled the covers up to Stevie's chin. "I'll tell you another story about Daddy tomorrow night, Sweetheart. One is enough for tonight. It's late, and you need to go to sleep." She kissed him on his forehead.

"Mom!" KatiLynn called from the kitchen. "Phone for you."

Kate turned off the light on her way out of Stevie's room, walked down the hall to her bedroom, and picked up the telephone. "Hello?"

"Hi."

It was Dave Cutler.

"Hope I'm not calling too late," he said.

"No, this is OK." It was more than OK. She had wondered if he would call again, but had pushed the thought to the back of her mind. Now she realized that she was glad to hear him.

"How do you feel about basketball?" he asked. "If you're free on Friday night, I could take the Suns up on their offer of a couple of tickets two rows behind the bench."

"*Two rows behind the bench?* I'm impressed. Who do you know?"

"I did some security work for them and they're very appreciative."

Kate smiled to herself. "You wouldn't be embarrassed if I gave the coach some advice from time to time, would you?"

Dave laughed. "Sounds like we could get along; I'm good at that too. How about six o'clock? We can go to dinner first."

"The kind of place where court shoes and blue jeans are in style?"

"Owned and operated by a certified jock—an ex-quarterback from Arizona State."

"I'll be looking forward to it."

That was true, she thought after they said good-bye and hung up. She had enjoyed going out with him.

Somewhere in her mind there was an echo of what Ann had said about dealing with a love life again. But Kate let it pass. This was only a basketball game.

* * *

He took her hand so they wouldn't be separated as they made their way toward the arena exit. "How did you like the game?" he asked.

"It's a good game any time we win." Kate laughed. "Of course, if the coach had listened to me, they wouldn't have had to go right down to the buzzer to pull it out."

Dave smiled. "Yep. That's what I was thinking all along—'Listen to Kate, listen to Kate.'" He juggled the small basketball he carried in his free hand, then dribbled it experimentally on the sidewalk.

"One of the parts I liked was when you took that ball right out of the hands of the guy behind us," Kate said.

Dave laughed. "I don't think *he* liked it." Cheerleaders had been tossing the balls, emblazoned with the team logo, into the crowd at halftime. One had arced toward them and the tall man behind them had reached out, but Dave had jumped and snatched the ball out of the air just before it touched the other man's fingertips.

He dribbled the ball on the ground twice more, then held it out to her. "Why don't you take this to home to Stevie? I never saw a seven-year-old who couldn't have some fun with a ball like this."

Kate hesitated. "What about your son? Wouldn't he enjoy it?"

"Ross has one already."

Kate took the ball from his hand. "Thank you. I'm sure Stevie will appreciate it."

"Maybe that will make up for missing his night out with mom for ice cream again this week." They walked in silence for a minute or so before he said. "Or maybe there's a better way to make it up to your children. How would you like to bring them over to my house for a barbecue Monday night? I can promise plenty of ice cream—whatever kind they like."

Kate didn't answer for several seconds. He thought she might be trying to find a tactful way to say no. Then: "That sounds fun. But do you think your children would like to come to our house? We have a pool in the backyard that they might enjoy. I could put together everything for the dinner and you could do the barbecuing. We have a nice grill." She smiled. "Steve liked to cook steaks on it. That was as outdoorsy as he got."

Was she uncomfortable, Dave wondered, about the idea of coming to his house? Or just thinking that her children would be more comfortable at home? *Doesn't make any difference to me, though, and Ross and Alicia*

96

would like the pool. Hard to know how Kelli would react. Hope she won't be a problem. "Sure, we'll be glad to come. Let me bring the steaks."

* * *

Kate walked through the living room once more, looking for anything out of place, any speck or scrap of paper on the carpet.

Why had she asked them to come here? What would have been wrong with taking KatiLynn and Stevie to Dave's house? Maybe they would have enjoyed it.

Or maybe not.

Maybe—

No more "maybe"! No more "What if?" They're going to be here in a few minutes. Dave and his children would have to see her home as it was.

If possible, she was more nervous than she had been the night he picked her up for their first date.

Why? Why am I so worried this time?

Because her children might not like Dave's children? But KatiLynn and Stevie liked making new friends. Why would they suddenly be different tonight?

Because Dave's children might not like hers? That was hardly something she could control, and Dave hadn't seemed concerned.

Because she lived in a fine home in an upscale neighborhood? There was a good chance it would be nicer than what Dave's family was used to; it was nicer than a fair percentage of the homes in Phoenix. But she had married Steve, not his home, and she couldn't be blamed because he had left her well situated when he died.

None of the rationalizations helped; she was still nervous and couldn't say why. Maybe it would have been better if she had taken Dave up on his original offer to go to his house.

Or maybe she would have been just as nervous driving there right now.

Stop it! Just make the salad. Forget about everything else. . . . Wonder if his kids like tomatoes?

She was shredding lettuce when her daughter walked into the kitchen.

"Mom, can I go over to Jennifer's?" KatiLynn smiled eagerly. "They got their new puppy, and she wants me to see it."

"KatiLynn! Not now. They'll be here any minute."

"But Mom—"

"No!"

KatiLynn looked hurt. She turned slowly and walked out of the kitchen down the hall.

Kate stood at the counter for a few seconds looking after her daughter, then followed her down the hall. She put her arms around KatiLynn and squeezed her momentarily, then let her go and looked into her eyes. "I'm sorry, Sweetheart. I was rude. I'm nervous, but I'm trying to get over it." She pointed at the grandfather clock in the living room. "Ten minutes, OK? Look at the clock in Evie's kitchen."

KatiLynn hugged her. "Thanks, Mom. I promise."

She had been gone no more than two minutes when Stevie wandered into the kitchen to ask, "When are they going to get here? I'm hungry." Kate enlisted him to help her with the salad. He was sitting on the stool beside her at the counter when the doorbell rang.

She put her hand on his shoulder and squeezed affectionately. "Do you want to answer it?"

He looked up at her thoughtfully for a moment, then grinned, showing the gap where his two upper front teeth were missing, and shook his head. "No—you."

She drew in a deep breath, then took his hand. "Let's go together."

When she opened the door, Dave stood there holding a small cooler under his left arm. A blonde-haired girl about Stevie's age stood very close to him holding onto his arm, and a dark-haired boy about Kati-Lynn's age stood next to her. Dave's teenage daughter, another blonde, stood behind them.

"The steaks are ready to cook," Dave said, holding up the cooler. "Got the grill fired up?" In his other hand he held a denim apron with brown handprints and the words "No. 1 Chef" painted on it. "I'm ready to get down to some serious barbecuing."

Kate laughed. Suddenly the nervousness she had felt about having him and his family come here seemed way out of proportion. "The grill is gas," she said, and snapped her fingers. "It'll be ready like that."

"Well, lead me to it and snap your fingers, and I'll go to work." He looked down at his younger daughter. "But first I'd like you to meet three people who mean as much to me as anybody on earth. This is Alicia," he said, smiling at the younger girl. "And Ross, her brother." He stepped back and put his right arm around his older daughter. "And this is Kelli."

"This is Stevie," Kate answered, putting her hand on his shoulder. "His big sister, KatiLynn, is next door, but she'll be home in a few minutes." She looked at Alicia, Ross, then Kelli, and smiled. "We're glad to meet you." Dave's younger daughter smiled back; her sister and brother did not.

"If you'd like to change so you can swim, and if that's OK with your dad," Kate continued, "Stevie would be glad to show you where the bathroom is."

* * *

"So, how is it?" Dave asked.

"Mmm, just right." Kate savored the last bite of her steak. "Tender, not too dry—perfect. My compliments to the chef."

He smiled. "Anytime."

Slowly she smiled too. "How are you at casseroles and soups? And do you deliver?"

He laughed and shook his head. "Anything beyond barbecue and I'm out of my league. I fix a lot of canned and packaged stuff for the kids, I'm afraid. It's a good thing Kelli and Ross are picking up cooking on their own. Every so often when I can't get home in time for supper, one of them takes pity on Alicia and fixes enough for her too."

"Well, your barbecue is too good. I've eaten more than I should. I'll have to do extra exercise tomorrow to help take it off."

"You could come running with me early in the morning," he said hopefully. "About six. I could pick you up."

She shook her head. "Sorry. I make breakfast for KatiLynn and Stevie, and I have to be at the office by 8:00."

Dave glanced at the children in the pool. "My kids usually have to settle for cold cereal and milk instead of waiting for me to fix something after I'm showered and dressed. Kelli helps me with the younger ones so we can all be ready to go on time." He paused. "Sometimes I worry about what kind of dad I am. I hate those days when I get caught up in something and don't get home for supper with my family."

Kate nodded. "There's never enough time when you're the only parent. I'm lucky. I've worked things out with Ann so we can share covering the office and still be moms when we need to be—most of the time."

Dave looked at his two youngest children, playing ball in the shallow end of the pool with KatiLynn and Stevie, and shook his head. "I just hope I'm doing right by my children."

"Oh, I'm sure you are," Kate said quickly. She recognized another single parent's need for reassurance. "They seem healthy and happy and perfectly normal."

Completely normal, she thought—just like her own.

Twice before dinner Ross had violated the one-person-at-a-time rule on the diving board while KatiLynn was taking extra time to demonstrate some of the tricks she could do. She had put him in his place; even though he chafed at letting a girl show him up, KatiLynn had made him get off the board and wait until she had finished. Once Stevie had pushed Alicia aside to climb up the ladder out of the pool, but KatiLynn had corrected him before Kate could get there, and Stevie had apologized. Kate had resolved to talk to them later about their manners. For the time being, she had told herself that at least she didn't have to worry about whether her children were outgoing enough.

Kelli had kept herself apart from the other four, at first dangling her legs in the pool while the younger ones swam, then trying out the diving board after they went away to eat. A few minutes ago, Kelli had come to the table and served herself a plate of food in silence then walked away to eat alone on the lawn under a tree. But Kate had noticed that she kept looking at the two adults when she thought they were not paying attention to her. The looks had been disapproving; Kate had noticed that too.

She wondered if Dave had sensed his daughter's feelings. If so, he hadn't shown it. He had kept an eye on his children without being too pointed about it. He had started toward the pool the second time Ross climbed on the diving board with KatiLynn, then had backed off when KatiLynn took charge of the situation. He had kept an eye out for Kelli when she was swimming alone. He had smiled at her when she came to the table, asking if she enjoyed the swimming. Kelli had only nodded.

Kate knew that Dave's relaxed approach to this situation had helped put her at ease. Soon after he had started barbecuing the meat, while they had been trading stories about their children, she had realized that she felt comfortable with him here—calm and peaceful. The tension—near panic—she had felt before his arrival had disappeared.

Apparently it had also been an enjoyable evening for him and his family—except Kelli.

Kate recognized some of Kelli's symptoms. There were a couple of fourteen- and fifteen-year-old girls in her Young Women class who behaved the same way. It had come as a surprise two and a half months ago when the bishop had called her in and asked her to be a teacher to the group. Kate had protested that she didn't know enough about the gospel yet, but the bishop had expressed confidence in her and said it was plain to him—the Spirit had told him—that she had something to offer these young women. She was sure the bishop had also known that this would be a way to accelerate her learning of the gospel, and that she would learn as much from the girls as she taught them.

At least she could remember, Kate thought, what it was like to be a girl this age—to be almost an adult physically, wanting to take on adult roles, but not quite ready for them.

With Kelli, however, there seemed to be something more to the problem. *Something's smoldering inside her. Whatever it is, when it flares up, I hope Dave's ready for it.*

After dinner, she and Dave sat on two lawn chairs next to the pool while the children played in the water. Once, as Stevie swam the width of the shallow end, Dave watched appraisingly, then walked over to the edge of the pool and squatted down to talk to him. Kate listened as Dave talked to her son about how well he swam, then coached him a bit on how he could improve the rhythm of his stroke to make it easier. Stevie tried it across the pool and back. "Good job!" Dave told him when Stevie came up again on their side, grinning.

It had seemed completely spontaneous for Dave—something that just came naturally. This was a man who genuinely liked his own children, and hers too, judging from the way he treated them.

* * *

"What are you doing this afternoon?" he asked.

"I'm not sure," Kate answered, cradling the phone on her shoulder while she rinsed her lunch dishes. "I wanted to work in my flower bed, but it's a little too hot right now. Maybe later."

"How would you like to take a drive with me?"

"Anywhere in particular?"

"Maybe down south toward Tucson. I can think of a couple of things you might enjoy. Would you let me surprise you?"

"What if we fly? You could still surprise me, but we could cover more ground."

"Hmm. No, I . . . I'm sure you're a great pilot, but I don't do well in small planes."

"Really, Dave, it's as safe as we are careful. The record of general aviation—"

"It's not that, Kate. Big ones are OK, but if a small one hits bumpy air . . ."

"Oh. Well, there aren't any guarantees, but today looks OK."

"Maybe someday when you're sure the day is perfect." He paused, then laughed lightly. "In the meantime, if we go in the sports car, I could put the top and the accelerator down and it would feel like flying."

She laughed too. "You've talked me into it. The kids are with their grandparents until I pick them up for church in the morning. How soon will you be here?"

He must have been ready for this, she thought, because he was at her house in twenty minutes. And it wasn't quite like flying—nothing else could be—but it felt free in another way. It had been a long time since she had simply dropped everything and done something just for the enjoyment of it. It felt like giving herself a gift.

"You do this often?" she asked as they headed south on Interstate 10.

"Not recently. Jeanine and I used to go exploring just for fun. We'd head south in the spring like this when it was still beginning to get warm. In the summer when it was hot we'd head north to Prescott, or Flagstaff. They're about two hours and twenty degrees away from Phoenix."

Dave talked about his wife naturally, not self-consciously or wistfully as though a part of him had been completely lost. Kate realized the gospel gave him that; he knew Jeanine was not gone, only away temporarily. Kate was coming to feel the same way whenever she thought of Steve. Sometimes she still longed to be with him, to have him hold her again, if only for a moment—but she was learning to wait, knowing that in the Lord's time, it would be.

What she had learned about the gospel so far had completely changed the way she looked at life. In the past, she had tried not to remember that life would wind down someday, as it seemed to be doing with her father. Now she could look forward to what would come afterward. There was a bit of philosophy she had read somewhere that said if you have faith in God, you have to believe there will be wonderful surprises. She only wished her mother and her father, or her brother, would let her tell them about the possibilities.

"Where are your children today?" she asked.

"At home. Kelli's watching Ross and Alicia."

"Oh. How do they feel about Dad's taking off this afternoon?" Kate wondered if she should have asked herself that question before saying yes to this.

Dave glanced her way. "Fine."

He didn't sound completely certain. "Maybe we shouldn't have—"

"Yes, we should have." He smiled at her. "They don't mind. Really. And anyway, I'm doing some things with them tonight, or at least with Ross and Alicia. I promised to drop Kelli and a couple of her friends off at a movie—if she'll go."

"What girl wouldn't want to go to a movie with friends?"

Dave smiled again. "Yeah." He shook his head. "Sometimes Kelli's a normal fifteen-year-old and sometimes she seems to feel it's her duty to fill in around the house doing the things her mom might have done—cooking, cleaning, laundry. I'm glad she's so responsible, but I don't want her to feel too tied down. I want her to enjoy being a teenager while she can."

He drove through Tucson to Davis-Monthan Air Force Base, with its row upon row of military aircraft waiting to be used again or scavenged for parts. "I thought you might enjoy this," he said. She didn't tell him she had seen it years earlier with her father and brother. The place was always interesting, and the aircraft in those rows had changed.

Dave drove into Saguaro National Park, just outside of Tucson, for a quick look at the giant saguaro cacti. "We could come back sometime when we can stay longer, if you like," he said hopefully.

Kate enjoyed the sightseeing; she had looked at these places many times before from the air, but the perspective was completely different from ground level. Maybe covering more ground, as she had suggested when he called, wasn't always as important as getting close enough to be involved. She had enjoyed the opportunity simply to relax with him this afternoon.

Just before reaching the freeway entrance that would lead back to Phoenix, he pulled the car into a parking lot and turned off the engine. "Trade places with me," he said, opening his door.

She looked dubiously at the gearshift lever on the floor, then at him. "It's been a long time since I've driven a car with gears I had to shift. I wouldn't want to . . . are you sure?"

"Kate! You fly airplanes. This will come easy for you."

He was right, she thought as she steered the car through a curve on a stretch of the interstate a few minutes later.

If it wasn't quite like flying, it was as much fun as she could remember having in a long time.

9

For the third time in ten minutes, Kate rolled into a new position in the bed, trying to get comfortable so she could sleep.

But comfort wasn't really the problem.

She opened her eyes and stared up at the ceiling in the dark.

The fireside tonight had been a good one. The speaker, a local institute teacher, had talked about how many blessings there were in the gospel for every individual. It was true. Her life was better, her thoughts and her heart were more at peace since she had listened to the message of the missionaries and been baptized.

In fact, there were too many blessings to list right now—like counting so many spiritual sheep. Maybe that was why she couldn't go to sleep.

Or maybe there was another reason.

The spoken message at tonight's fireside had been plain: life can be good even when you don't have a companion.

It was the unspoken message that kept her awake—a thought that seemed to hover just in the background during the speaker's remarks: life could be even better *with* a companion.

That was a thought Kate had managed to push to the back of her mind for the past six years, and even recently as she had begun going out with Dave. But tonight's fireside had made it clear that she could no longer ignore the possibility of remarriage. There was, as she had told Ann, nothing in the Church's teachings that required her to be alone for the rest of this life. In fact, while the objective wasn't plainly stated, everything about Church activities for single members seemed to encourage finding potential mates.

It was obvious that Dave was becoming more comfortable with the idea of remarriage, while she was still reconciling herself to the simple need for companionship. If companionship was her only reason for dating Dave, she probably wasn't being fair to him.

And maybe not to herself. She knew so few single men—at least men who could be considered marriage material—and she had only dated one. How could she know yet whether she was ready to share her life with someone—anyone—again?

After Steve's death, she had thrown herself into caring for her children and providing direction for Warden Avionics. When she had stepped out of the chief executive role at Warden, she had told herself that now she would have plenty of time to be a mother and to do some of the other things she wanted to do with her life. But meeting her challenges as a parent and as an individual had turned out to be much more than a question of finding adequate time. The decisions she had to make and the problems she had to handle as a single parent were getting harder as her children got older. And some of the things she had always wanted to make part of her life—travel, plays, the symphony—did not seem nearly so attractive without someone to share them.

Even with the promise of Steve in her eternal future, was she prepared to go through the rest of this life—perhaps forty or fifty years—alone?

She *wasn't* alone! She had KatiLynn and Stevie.

For now. In ten or fifteen years, though . . .

Kate felt tears coming, and shut her eyes to squeeze them away. She refused to feel sorry for herself. Both before Steve and after, she had felt self-sufficient. She could be that way now, for as long as she needed to be.

In her heart, she struggled with questions about remarriage that she could not answer. She was not sure anyone had answers. At the moment, her biggest question was this: If she married again after she was sealed to Steve, would she somehow be unfaithful to him—at least in his eyes? Even if she came to know there was nothing wrong with marrying again, could she really fall in love with another man after Steve? Would it be fair to marry someone if she didn't feel that same kind of love?

She felt guilty thinking about how much she still loved Steve and at the same time how much she wanted not to be alone.

She felt guilty about Dave, tonight.

He had taken her hand when they walked out of the fireside, and not just so they wouldn't be separated. It said he wanted to be with her. It had felt . . . nice. Natural. She had enjoyed it.

Kate turned into another position and tried to push her pillow into a comfortable shape.

Dave was a good man—but someone to marry? She did not know him that well yet. How could she know if Dave might be the right one . . . or if maybe someone else . . . how would she know without meeting other single LDS men?

One of the announcements at tonight's fireside had been about a singles dance at a stake center across town next Saturday. Dave had said he would like to invite her, but his daughter Kelli had a piano recital Saturday night.

It had been a long time since Kate had been dancing.

* * *

"You're new here, aren't you?"

Kate turned to look at the red-haired woman who sat down next to her. "Yes. How did you . . ."

The other woman smiled, and glanced at a thin man wearing boots who stood several inches taller than the other dancers. "Billy surprised you when he dipped you low on that last dance and then swung you around. I could tell you were wondering whether you really should have gotten yourself into this."

Kate smiled too. "Yes. Does he always, uh . . . *whoop* like that during the music?"

The other woman laughed. "Only the country songs. That's Billy. He likes to check out all the new girls right away. He'll come and ask you to dance again the next time there's a country number. It's OK to say no if you don't want to. He doesn't get his feelings hurt easily."

"You know him."

"Since we were in high school. He's forty-two years old and he wears a hairpiece now, but every time there's a dance he comes to kick up his heels the same way he did back then. That's Billy too."

"Do you come to these dances all the time?"

The other woman nodded. "Just because I like to dance."

That much had been obvious. Kate had watched this woman out on the floor earlier. She was attractive and she danced well. She made any man with her look good.

Kate extended her hand. "My name is Kate."

The other woman shook it lightly. "Helen." She smiled. "I have to warn you, the good ones go fast here."

"What?"

106

"The men," Helen said. "The good ones go fast—if that's what you're after."

Kate glanced around the room. "Well, I haven't met very many of them yet. I've danced a couple of times with Billy, and that's once more than with anyone else. Is he one of the good ones, or, uh . . ."

"There's nothing wrong with Billy, if you love camping and hunting and getting off in the mountains somewhere on horseback. His first wife didn't. And I guess they had other problems too—I've never asked."

"But surely out of all the men here, there must be some . . ."

"Oh, yes," Helen answered. "Nick, over there, is one of the good ones." She nodded toward a man dancing with a woman in the middle of the floor. "But I think they're the next thing to engaged." She looked at a man across the room who was holding hands with the woman next to him. "And Karl. And there are some others."

Helen frowned. "But if you come here often enough, you'll meet guys like Greg. He's not here tonight. If you meet him sometime and he wants to take you somewhere after the dance, don't go."

Kate raised her eyebrows. "He, ah . . . why?"

"A friend of mine went with him once. He started asking her some fairly personal questions, about why she wasn't married yet, and she told him it wasn't any of his business. When they came to her street, he just passed it up and kept driving. He wouldn't turn around and go back. He told her they hadn't had enough time to talk. So she got out of his car at a stoplight and went to a store and called a taxi. Nothing happened, but . . ." Helen left the thought hanging.

Kate frowned too. "Why don't they keep guys like him out of here?"

"Oh, they would—the leaders, the people who chaperone these dances—if they knew. But my friend didn't want to talk about it—didn't want any trouble. She doesn't come here anymore, and I just quietly pass the word when I have a chance."

"How can you ever know?" Kate asked. "I mean, how can you tell if someone's a good guy, or if he's one who . . ."

Helen thought for a moment. "It's hard to say. I guess you develop a kind of sense for it. If he only talks about himself . . . if he ignores what you say, or if he tells you that he wants to dance with you and acts like it's not up to you to decide. . . . Maybe he brings you punch and a cookie and tells you he knows you want them. . . . I don't know—you just have to learn to feel it."

Kate thought for a moment. "But you keep coming back?"

"Oh, don't get me wrong. There really are some good guys here," Helen said. She laughed. "I just haven't found *mine* yet." Her smile faded. "I've learned if I don't expect much I won't be disappointed."

The tune that had just started was another country and western number. Kate hadn't noticed that Billy was standing there until he spoke. "Would you like to dance again, little lady?"

Kate wondered if he remembered her name. She glanced uncertainly at Helen, then back at him. "Well, I . . . I, ah, don't know how to line dance, but I guess there's always a first time."

Helen smiled at him. "Be nice, Billy. Go easy on her until she gets the hang of it."

"Shoot, Helen, you know me. I'm as gentle as an old bronc out to pasture." Billy smiled broadly and winked.

Kate resisted the temptation to roll her eyes. *Well, you wanted to meet new people.*

* * *

Dave leaned back in his swivel chair inside the tiny cubicle that served as his office at home—a converted storage room—and shut the door. He thought Kelli's door down the hall was closed, but just in case, he wanted to keep this call private.

He dialed the number and waited. When he heard Kate say hello, it seemed like some of the day's heaviness dropped away.

"Hi," he said. "How are you doing?"

"Fine, Dave." She sounded cheerful, he thought. "How are you?"

"Better now that I'm talking to you. I was wondering if you'd like to go to the fireside Sunday night?"

"Well, I, ah . . . I'm already going—with someone."

His eyebrows went up in surprise, but he tried not to give away the feeling when he spoke into the phone. "Oh, I, uh . . . I should have called earlier."

"That wouldn't have . . . I mean, he asked me last week—at the singles dance. You couldn't go that night, and after the fireside I was thinking that it might be fun to know some of those people, so . . . ."

"It's all right, Kate, you don't have to explain to me."

But he needed an explanation. Had he done something that made her sorry she dated him?

He had wondered if he should be going to some of those dances himself. But why would anyone want to go to a dance alone? The

108

dancing was enjoyable enough—if you already had a partner. The *dances* were the problem. The way he felt about them hadn't really changed since junior high school. If you saw somebody you wanted to dance with, then you had to walk all the way across the floor wondering if she would turn you down with everyone else watching. Or if she turned out to be somebody you didn't want to dance with more than once, could you handle that without making her feel bad? At almost 39, he felt like he had reverted to teenage awkwardness in trying to deal with single women his own age.

He had been so *comfortable* with Jeanine.

He tried to think of what Kate was probably feeling. Before he had gone out with her, he hadn't realized that he was lonely. Now he had begun to feel sometimes that he was incomplete. He felt it most at times like this, at night when the children's needs had been met and he was left alone. Did Kate feel that loneliness too?

"Dave?"

It had been several seconds since he had said anything. "Sorry. I was just thinking," he answered. "Thinking about, ah . . . anyway, you made some new friends at the dance?"

"Yes. There was Helen Cameron—she's from Mesa—and some other people she introduced me to." Kate paused. "I think you know the man who asked me to go to the fireside. He said he knows you. Hal Seward?"

"Yeah. Hal's in another ward in my stake."

"Yes. Well, he asked, and, ah . . ."

It sounded like this was uncomfortable for her. *Well, it isn't easy for me either! I'm the one going down in flames here.*

"Maybe another time?" he said.

"Of course." Kate sounded relieved.

"Then I'll call you when, uh . . . I'll call you."

"I hope so."

Neither of them seemed to know how to handle good-bye. For a few seconds after they said the words, he held onto the telephone, until he heard the *click* of hers hanging up.

When would he call her again? Did she *really* want him to?

She had sounded like she meant it.

But it might take a while to work up his courage.

Why?

Because she had chosen to go out with someone else, and that must mean he hadn't measured up in some way. Or it might mean that she

109

had gone out with him in the first place just because she wanted to expand her circle of friends and he was a start. Either way, he wasn't sure he wanted to know the truth.

What does Hal Seward have that I don't have?

The quick answer was: no children at home. Could that be it?

But Kate seemed to like children. She was devoted to her own, and she had been good to Ross and Alicia when they had visited her house for the barbecue. She had gone out of her way trying to reach Kelli.

Hal was a couple of years younger, had a full head of hair, and was a little taller and thinner. But he was no Mr. Universe either, and he was quiet—not very outgoing. He had a solid career as an accountant. He and his wife had had no children; she had left him for a man with male model good looks, someone she had met at the bank where she worked.

Dave sighed. It was no good making comparisons. If the answer were in the comparison, *he* probably wouldn't see it because he was too close to the problem. And anyway, there was no accounting for the intuition of women; they seemed to have some mysterious ability to sense or know things about men, reasons for their choices, that *he* could never fathom.

He leaned back in the chair once more, put his feet up on the corner of the desk, and stared at the framed picture of Jeanine on top of his filing cabinet. She had told him that he was too young to be alone for the rest of his life, and a couple of weeks before she died, she had pleaded with him to promise that he would eventually find someone else so the children would not be without a mother. He had promised—halfheartedly. He had ducked that promise so far. He hadn't even wanted to think about it.

But now people he trusted—his bishop, his stake president, even Jeanine's father—had begun to suggest that he ought to find another companion.

Maybe it was time to work on expanding his own circle of friends.

Maybe he needed to think about going to more of those singles activities, whether he liked the idea or not. But it would take some time to work up to that—especially if there was a chance that Kate might be there, with someone else.

It would be almost like being back in junior high, on the sidelines again.

* * *

Stevie came running to greet her before Kate had time to shut her parents' front door. "Hi, Mom!" he said, wrapping his arms around her waist in a hug. "We're watching *Peter Pan*. Want to see it with us?"

Kate glanced at her watch. "It's almost bedtime. I've got to get you home."

"Please, Mom? It's almost over. *Please?*"

Kate smiled at him. "All right. You go on watching the movie while I talk to your grandmother for a few minutes."

Stevie dashed out of the room ahead of her. She followed him down the hall to the TV room. He and KatiLynn were seated on the floor in front of the television watching the movie. Belle sat in her recliner chair, a TV tray beside her. On it was a plate, empty except for cookie crumbs, and a book of Bible stories.

Belle gestured toward the book. "I was going to read them some stories, but they wanted to see the movie first."

"Maybe there'll be time for a short one as soon as the movie's over," Kate answered, smiling at her mother. The book contained stories of the Savior's life—simple, suitable for children, but short on knowledge about the full purpose of His mission on earth. Kate knew her mother still worried that her grandchildren were not learning the right things about Jesus in their church. Since Belle's reading of these stories seemed to strengthen the bond between grandmother and grandchildren, Kate did nothing to discourage it; she simply tried to fill in the gaps in knowledge for her children later. "Where's Dad?" she asked.

"Gone to bed. He was so tired he . . ." Belle frowned as she glanced toward the bedroom. "He was exhausted."

She smiled at KatiLynn and Stevie's backs. "So I got to entertain my grandchildren." She looked up at Kate. "How was the, uh . . . the program?" her mother asked. "What did you call it?"

"A fireside. It was fine." Kate frowned for a moment, then mustered a smile for her mother. "Very enjoyable." The speaker had talked about temple ordinances and what they meant for the dead. Kate knew she still couldn't discuss that subject with her mother. The last time she had tried, Belle had pointedly steered the discussion to something else.

Her mother smiled slightly. "And the man you went with?"

"He was nice. He's a good man." It was true, Kate thought. The fireside had been enjoyable, and Hal had been . . . nice. If he asked her out again, she would probably go with him. If he never asked, she wouldn't feel a loss.

"And this man was a Mormon too?" Belle's face was expressionless.

"Yes, he was." Her mother already knew the answer to the question, and Kate didn't need to guess why she had asked it. They had talked about this before.

Belle smiled brightly. "Well, if you're interested in meeting some other nice men, I know of two. My friend Yvonne has a son just a little older than you who's not married. And Mary Randall has a son your age who's never been married. I've met him. He's charming. He's—"

"The one who lived with a woman for six years, then left her, but it was all her fault, and now he's ready to settle down. And Yvonne's son is the one who's been married twice, isn't he?" Kate's face felt hot. She hadn't meant to let irritation come out in her tone.

"You don't have to talk down to me!" her mother snapped. She looked away. "Maybe I've mentioned them before. If I did, it's only because I have your best interests at heart."

"Mother, why don't you let *me* decide—"

Kate stopped herself as Belle turned away, anger in her face. Out of the corner of her eye Kate could see that KatiLynn had stopped paying attention to the movie and was watching this exchange between her mother and grandmother.

Keeping her voice low and even, Kate began again. "I'm sorry, Mom." She reached out to put her hand on top of Belle's. "I didn't mean to be rude." She paused. "There's a question I hope you'll answer for me. I've been wondering about it for a long time, and I need an answer." She grasped her mother's hand lightly, hoping Belle wouldn't pull it away. "Why is it you don't like members of my church?"

Belle looked at her. "I never said that."

"But you don't, do you?"

Slowly Belle shook her head.

"Why? I can't remember that you've ever known any Latter-day Saints until I joined the Church."

"There was one. A long time ago."

"One? Just *one*, and you—"

Belle's look cut her off. Kate tried to keep her voice neutral as she continued. "All right, I'm sure you had good reason. I wish you'd tell me about it."

Her mother was silent for so long that Kate wondered if she was going to reply. Belle smiled at KatiLynn and waited until her granddaughter lost interest in their conversation and turned to watch the TV again. Then she spoke.

"He went with my friend Margie when we were in high school. He was from one of those *good*"—she made the word into an epithet—"Mormon families over in Mesa, prominent people, the kind that are always into everything and everyone makes a fuss over." Belle turned to look at her daughter again. "He got Margie in trouble, and then he didn't want to do the right thing by her; he wouldn't marry her. And his parents wouldn't make him. They blamed Margie. But I knew—" Belle clenched her fist on the arm of her chair—"I *knew* whose fault it was. I knew how he was with girls. He tried to get something going with me behind Margie's back while he was dating her. I was sorry later that I didn't tell her before he . . . before *she* . . ."

Belle unclenched her fist and stabbed at the arm of the chair with her finger for emphasis as she spoke. "And his . . . his minister—what do they call that?"

"Bishop?"

"Yes. His bishop blamed her, and all the rest of them blamed her, because he couldn't go off to be a missionary in Argentina, or somewhere, but I knew—*I* knew—whose fault it really was." Belle looked at Kate as though challenging her to disprove it.

Kate sighed. "Well, it doesn't sound like he deserved to be a missionary. Did Margie love him?"

"Yes. Even after. She cried for him a long time."

"So he didn't exactly force her to—"

"No! No you don't! You're not going to blame her too. She *loved* him, and he only *wanted* her. He used her."

"Yes, you're right about him, Mom. All I'm saying is that it usually takes two to—"

"I don't care. It was *him*. And I don't trust *any* of them."

"Including me?"

Belle looked startled. "No. That's not what . . ." She looked into her daughter's eyes for several seconds. "I mean I don't trust any of those Mormon men. If you're going to marry again, I wish you could find a good Catholic, or even a Protestant. I know you could find one who'd be good to you."

Kate returned her mother's gaze. Slowly, she shook her head. "I tried good Catholics and Protestants for several years before I met Steve, remember? There's no shortage of guys like Margie's boyfriend—with or without religion."

"I'm not naive, Kate. I know that. But there are good ones out there if you're willing to look for them."

Kate didn't answer. Any response would involve explaining why she was interested only in a man with Latter-day Saint values, and she didn't think her mother would listen just now.

"I've wondered what might have happened with some of the men you dated," Belle mused. "You know, it was only four years ago when Arthur finally got married, and if—"

"If I'd kept going with Arthur, Mom, I might have ended up like your friend Margie when I was nineteen."

"No! I can't believe—"

"Yes! Arthur, the one you liked so much—Arthur, the altar boy. He was pressuring me to do what he wanted. He said the two of us were right for each other, but we weren't ready for marriage yet and we could always get married later. When I finally broke up with him, you didn't ask me why. You just kept telling *me* I'd made a mistake."

Belle looked stunned. "Dear, I never meant—"

"I didn't hold that against you. Mom. You didn't know. But Arthur wasn't the only one. There were other guys I met in college—Catholic, Protestant, one Jewish guy that I really liked. I thought he was my good friend, until he started telling me one night how it wasn't just my mind he appreciated."

Belle sat silently, looking at her daughter, for several seconds. "I wish I had known about those. You could have talked to me about—"

"Really, Mom? I was never sure. Sometimes I thought I was just supposed to do what *you* wanted me to do."

It was obvious instantly that she had hurt her mother's feelings. That wasn't what Kate had wanted, but because of the way this discussion had gone, she had not been able to withhold the truth anymore. She squeezed Belle's hand. "It doesn't matter now. I love you. I really do."

Belle stared at the far wall. Then, after several seconds of silence: "Well, Mormon men could be just like those others."

"Some could," Kate conceded. "I met one like that at the dance last week. I certainly wouldn't have let him drive me home." She paused. "But most of the members of the Church I know—men and women—are good people trying their best to do what God wants. I've seen that in the way they live."

Belle's expression did not change.

"There's more to this, isn't there, Mom? Who I go out with isn't what this is all about—at least not in my mind."

"What do you mean?"

"Something happened between us when I was baptized—something I don't understand. There's a barrier that didn't exist before, and I want it down." Kate could feel tears forming in her eyes, and she knew she wouldn't be able to stop them. "What is it, Mom? What's wrong?"

Belle didn't answer for a time. Finally she looked at her daughter and Kate could see that there were tears in her mother's eyes too. "Maybe it was because you started trying to make me a Mormon as soon as you were baptized—as if I weren't good enough anymore."

Kate shook her head. "I never meant it that way. I'm sorry if it seemed so. You're a wonderful mother to me. You always have been."

The tears began to slide down Belle's cheeks. "You started telling me all that stuff about marriage forever, and, uh . . . and didn't I want to be with your dad again? And with him so sick! That hurt."

"I'm sorry, Mom."

"It isn't going to be like that after we die, Kate—at least not the way Father Hailey explains it to me. I'm sorry, I just can't believe some of the things you do, and you've made me feel like I'm not living up to your expectations somehow. But I never will be able to believe those things."

Kate sat down on the arm of her mother's chair. "I love you deeply, Mom. I've been trying to share something with you because I love you so much. I thought it was a wonderful gift. But if you want me to stop, I'll stop."

Belle nodded her head once. "I want you to stop."

"All right. And I want you to stop trying to unmake me."

Belle raised her eyebrows questioningly.

"You've fought me since I first told you I was going to be baptized. You've seemed like you were frustrated because you couldn't get it through my head that I was wrong."

"Kate, I—"

"You've acted like you couldn't trust my judgment anymore, as a person or as a mother." Kate nodded toward the Bible storybook. "You assume that you have to teach my kids about Jesus because you're afraid I can't or won't do it. But you know Stevie's heard those stories before because he can tell them to you. Where do you think he learned them? At home and at church. That's what my religion is all about, Mom—knowing Jesus Christ."

Belle was silent again, but after several seconds she nodded.

"I think I'm a *good* mother," Kate said. "I'm trying my best, and I want—"

"I never questioned that, dear. You *are* a good mother," Belle said, keeping her voice low. "You're doing a fine job for someone who has to raise your children alone."

"Then will you stop trying to unmake my children too? Will you trust me to make decisions for them? You may not believe what I believe, but I learned for myself that it's true. I know my children need it in their lives, and I think *I* have the responsibility to decide that."

"Yes, you do." Belle paused. She reached out her arm and drew her daughter to her. "I *have* tried to work against you sometimes. I promise you, it won't happen again."

Slowly Kate leaned her head on her mother's shoulder.

"Kate, I know *you're* sure of where you're going," Belle said. "You always have been, ever since you were a little girl."

Kate raised her head and wiped away her tears with her fingers. "I'm sorry about your dress. I got you wet."

Belle smiled. "It dries out just fine."

KatiLynn was standing beside them, looking concerned. Kate tried to smile. "It's all right, sweetheart. Everything's fine."

KatiLynn looked puzzled. "What were you and Grandma talking about?"

"About how much we love each other," Belle answered, squeezing her daughter's shoulder.

* * *

Very enjoyable. That was what she had told her mother about the fireside. And it was true; she had enjoyed the program.

It was what happened after the fireside that she was thinking about as she lay staring up at the ceiling once more.

She had been leaving the meetinghouse, in conversation with Hal, when she had glanced at the people ahead of them and thought she recognized the back of David Cutler's head. She had tried to keep an eye on him while listening to Hal. Then the man in front of them had turned to speak to someone and she had been sure—it *was* Dave.

He was with a woman.

Or maybe he wasn't with the woman—but he had been talking to her.

The two of them had walked around the corner of the building as Kate and Hal walked toward Hal's car at the curb. The last Kate had been able to see of Dave, he had been walking across the parking lot—with the woman.

Well, why couldn't he go to the fireside with someone else? That's what *she* had done. He had a right to do the same thing, didn't he?

Without being too obvious, she had tried to watch for Dave's car in the parking lot as Hal drove away. She had been surprised when she had seen it—the dark minivan with the SafeGuard Security sign on the side. She had not been able to see whether there was anyone in the passenger seat.

Why had seeing Dave with someone else made her feel depressed?

Why did it make her feel good that he had not been driving the two-seater sports car?

10

Ann looked up from her desk and smiled as Kate walked into the building. "Couldn't resist trying out the new plane, could you?"

Kate laughed. "It's been a long time since I've flown a twin that nice."

Ann's smile faded as she nodded toward the flight service manager's office. "You have a visitor," she said softly.

Kate raised her eyebrows in a question.

Ann shrugged and shook her head slightly.

Walking toward the door of her office, Kate saw the flowers first—on her desk, a spray of red and yellow roses. *Dave?* Her pulse quickened momentarily, until she realized it could not be him or Ann would have said so. The warm feeling inside began to fade as quickly as it had come. Then who?

It was a shock to see the man seated in front of her desk: "Kenji!"

Kenji Nakamura turned to smile at her, stood, and held out his hand tentatively. "Kate. It's good to see you."

She sidestepped his outstretched hand, gave him a quick hug, then stepped back. "It's good to see *you*. It's been too long since I've heard from you—almost a year, I think"

He seemed momentarily surprised by the warmth of her greeting; Kate wondered if she should have been more restrained. But it seemed to please him; his smile widened. "A little more than a year—but you make me glad I came. It won't be so long next time."

"You probably didn't come all this way for a social call, did you?"

His smile faded. "I confess, there was more than one reason."

Kate leaned over to sniff the flowers. "Well, it was sweet of you to bring these."

"They're a peace offering, in a way."

"Oh?" Kate sat back against the edge of her desk and Kenji sat down again in the chair.

"I'm afraid I'm not bringing good news," he said. "Because of our friendship, I thought I should tell you in person." Then he sat looking at her, seemingly trying to decide how to go on.

"Let me see," she ventured. "Nakamura Electronics is finally going to start building its own avionics systems?"

He nodded. "How did you guess?"

"I think we both suspected it would happen one day, didn't we?" She looked at him speculatively for a moment. "Your father's decision?"

"Yes."

"And he's planning to farm the work out in Taiwan or Singapore?"

Kenji sighed. "Maybe eventually—production only. But in the beginning, the design and production will all be done in Japan, no matter what it costs."

"Even in Japan, you won't be able to build better quality than what Warden offers."

He stared out the window behind her desk and shook his head again. "No. But we hope to equal it." He looked back at Kate. "Have I ever told you about my father?"

"Only a little about the way he runs his business."

Kenji leaned back in the chair. "He was just coming into his teens when World War II ended. His older brother had died as a *kamikaze* pilot, and my father hated Americans at first—he was afraid of what he had heard they would do to our country. Then he found out it was a lie, and after a while some of the GIs became his friends.

"My father was from the farm country outside of Tokyo, and by the time he was eighteen, he had a business going, supplying vegetables to American bases. But when some of the American occupation forces pulled out, his business came close to failing, and he had to find something else to do. He'd also been selling a few electronic items to the GIs, and that was the beginning of Nakamura Electronics."

Kenji glanced at the small stereo system on the credenza behind Kate's desk; it was a product of one of the Nakamura subsidiaries. "Americans made him rich buying our electronic products, and he knows that, but I think he determined in his own mind that he would never be entirely dependent on the Americans for anything again." He paused, and sighed once more. "So, we're going to be building our own avionics equipment. I still believe it's not our best move, and I will regret it because of what it means for the relationship with your company—and you."

"Warden Avionics may not be able to put the money into this that you will, Kenji, but the company isn't going to roll over and play dead. We'll find another way to market our products in Asia."

Kenji nodded. He stared out the window again.

"So, will we at least be friendly competitors?" Kate asked.

He turned and slowly smiled his broadest smile. "I was hoping for that, Kate. In fact, would you let me take you to dinner tonight—for friendship's sake?"

She hesitated before answering. "That's a very kind invitation, Kenji." She paused, wondering how to say this tactfully. "Is Lily traveling with you this time?"

He looked out the window once more and stared into the distance for several seconds before speaking. When he finally turned to look at her again, there was a sadness in his eyes she had never seen before. "I'm afraid I wasn't very good about letting people know, but Lily . . . I lost her. She died late last summer."

"Oh, Kenji! No!" Kate stood with her mouth open for several seconds, trying to think of what to say. Nothing but questions came to mind. "She was so young. What happened?"

Kenji massaged his temple lightly with the fingers of his right hand; Kate wasn't sure he was even aware of the gesture. "It was one of those nights when I had to work very late at the office, so I stayed in our apartment in Tokyo. Lily . . . she fell down the stairs, in our country house. They said it looked like the heel of her shoe caught on . . . anyway, the maid found her that way the next morning." He had stopped massaging his temple and was staring at the floor. "The doctor told me that if somebody had been there—if she had gotten help right away . . . but then she would probably have been a quadriplegic. That would have been like prison for Lily."

When he looked up again, Kate could see the pain in his eyes. "I haven't thought about it for a while. I try not to. At the time, I felt like the work that kept me in Tokyo that night was important, and now I can't remember what it was. If I had gone home . . ."

"Don't, Kenji. Don't do that to yourself," Kate said softly. "It doesn't help. I know."

"For the first six months, I was just existing. I should have let some old friends know what had happened, but it was all I could do to get through a day. I thought I could never live without her. Then over the next few months, I learned to face the fact that I had to go on alone. That was probably the hardest part." He paused. "It's only the past couple of months that I've decided I need to try to live life and not just walk through it. I think that's what Lily would want me to do."

Kate nodded. "I'm sure she would. But oh, Kenji, what a loss! She was a lovely woman. Are you all right now?"

"Yes, I am, Kate—now. Thank you for asking. You *are* a good friend." He smiled at her again. "That's why I feel I owe you more than just bringing the bad news in person. So—dinner tonight?"

Perhaps some of her experiences could help Kenji if she shared them, Kate thought. But on a school night, she might have trouble finding a sitter, and lately her mother had her hands full with her father. Maybe Evie? "I'd love to, if my neighbor can keep KatiLynn and Stevie for me. What time would you like me to be ready, or should I meet you somewhere?"

"I'll pick you up. Seven?"

* * *

"No wine for the lady," he told the steward, and smiled at Kate. "Would you like something else?"

She thought of a favorite soft drink, but somehow it didn't seem to belong in a crystal goblet. "No, thank you, water will be fine."

There was silver on the table, with china, and linen napkins. The restaurant was one of the finest in Phoenix. Kenji had picked her up in a limousine with a driver. She felt no need for pretense with him because they were friends, but she was glad she had remembered that the heir to Nakamura Electronics knew how to enjoy the finer things of life. The black dress she had chosen for the evening, with a matched pearl necklace and earring set, had last been out of her closet for a formal dinner with officers of Warden Avionics and their spouses.

Their conversation on the way to the restaurant had been mostly about business—his company's growing presence in Western Europe, his upcoming trip to Eastern Europe and the Middle East to build business contacts, the day-to-day decisions for the company that were now in his hands. Once they arrived at the restaurant, he had been very attentive, wanting to be sure that she enjoyed everything about the evening.

Kenji was a genial and charming host. But their conversation was largely superficial, about the cuisine, the atmosphere of the place, the spring weather in Phoenix as compared to Tokyo. Finally, in a lull before dessert, Kate asked him what she had been wondering. "How are you really, Kenji? I hear you telling me how busy you are. Is that a way of keeping loneliness at a distance? I know I used my work that way for a while."

The question seemed to embarrass him. She hoped she had not been too blunt. Kenji put down his fork and sat back in his chair. "You're right, of course, Kate. I've been talking too much about my work, and it's kept me from telling you what I really wanted to say." He paused. "But there was a point. All of it—all the work—isn't much to come home to." He sat looking at her for so long that she wondered if there was something she was supposed to say in answer. But finally he smiled, a bit shyly, she thought. "Lately I've been wondering if, uh . . ." He leaned forward and reached across the table to touch her hand with the tips of his fingers. "If there's any possibility that the two of us could ever be more than friends."

The words were stunning. The idea would never have occurred to her, even though Kenji was a fine man. But he had obviously thought this out well. He was the kind of man who would never have brought it up if he hadn't.

"You're the reason I came to Phoenix," he said. "I've realized that I need a woman like you in my life. You have many of the same qualities Lily had, and some wonderful ones of your own. I've been trying to think of a way to ask you if you could ever see yourself being part of my life."

Kate struggled for a response. "Kenji, I . . . you're . . ."

He held up his hand to stop her. "I know this is unexpected, Kate. I haven't done any of the things a man normally does before he asks that kind of question. I don't want you to answer me right now. Please don't try. You'll need to think." He took hold of her fingers again and held them lightly in his hand. "But will you . . . could you possibly think about that?"

"You know . . . there are so many things—the children, my father's business. Warden Avionics would be a conflict for me."

"Yes, I know. You would have much to decide. And I have no experience as a father, but I know you are a good mother. I am willing to let you teach me about being a parent. I believe I could provide more than adequately for your children's needs. I'd like you to think about what the two of us could do together—what we could be. Will you?"

"Well . . . yes, Kenji, of course I will." What could she say? He deserved to be taken seriously; Kenji was too good a man to hurt. And maybe his proposal deserved serious thought. "But . . . but I'll need time."

He squeezed her hand lightly. "Yes. I'll be coming back to Phoenix in about a month or a month and a half. Do you think we could talk again?"

She said yes, still in a daze. The rest of dinner passed in a blur. When he took her home in the limousine, he sat beside her this time, instead of sitting opposite her, but he said nothing. Kate wondered if it had been this way with Lily—if they simply had some kind of quiet communion between them, and that was what he expected. She wasn't sure a relationship could ever be that way for her.

When the car stopped in front of her house, Kenji reached for his briefcase in the corner of the back seat and took out two small packages. "I am sorry that I didn't have the chance to visit with KatiLynn and Stevie, but I brought something for each of them," he said. "Two of the newest Nakamura products—a portable music player for her and a pocket game console for him." He smiled as he held them out to her.

Kate was surprised again, and a bit nonplussed. The gifts were not inexpensive. She had never wanted the things that money could buy to come too easily to KatiLynn and Stevie. Even though she might never have to worry about providing for them, she did not want them to grow up feeling like children of privilege. When they were old enough, she wanted them to work as she had when she was young and learn how to spend their own money wisely.

Something of her feelings must have shown in her face. Kenji's smile faded. "I hope I haven't done something wrong?"

"No. No, of course not. You're a very generous man." She managed a smile as she took the packages from his hands. She would have to talk with KatiLynn and Stevie about Kenji when she had had more time to think. They would have a lot to talk about.

The limousine driver opened the door for her, and Kate stepped out. Kenji leaned out to speak to her. "I won't be calling right away, Kate. I want to give you all the time you need to think, and I don't want to pressure you in any way. But I'll be thinking about you, and if you want to call me, I'll be hoping to hear from you."

"Yes." She didn't know what else to say. She watched the limousine move away down the street before she turned to walk up her driveway. Then she remembered the children and turned toward Evie's house.

* * *

"Mom! I said if X equals nine and Y equals seven, does that mean X times Y is sixty-three?"

Kate poured the chocolate chips into the cookie dough and began to stir. "I'm sorry, Sweetheart, I was thinking about something else. But you know the answer to this. Nine times seven is sixty-three, and if X is just another way of saying nine and Y is just another way of saying seven, then the answer must be . . . fifty-six, right?"

KatiLynn grinned. "No! Sixty-three."

"See? You can do this. You don't have to ask me the answers. Do you have any more?"

"No, that was the last one." KatiLynn reached for her book bag, across the kitchen table. "Can I have a couple of those cookies in my lunch tomorrow?"

"Yes. I'm hurrying so maybe you and Stevie can have one right out of the oven before you go to bed."

KatiLynn pulled her knees up under her chin, locked her arms around them, and sat perched on her chair at the table. "Whenever I take homemade cookies in my lunch, Jenny always says, 'How can you stand to eat *those?*' and she takes her sandwich cookie apart and licks the frosting off, and then she eats both pieces." She grinned again. "So I always take a little bite of my cookie and eat it really slow, and then I say, 'Ummm, how can *you* stand to eat *those?*' Then we each give a little piece of cookie to the people around us and let them vote. Your cookies always win."

Kate laughed. "Run get your pajamas on and maybe I can read you and Stevie a story before bed."

"That's OK, Mom, I have a book from school to read," KatiLynn answered. "But you can read to Stevie." She gathered up her backpack and walked out of the kitchen.

KatiLynn was becoming more independent in many ways, Kate reflected. Her daughter was beginning to slip out of girlhood without even realizing what was happening to her.

What would life be like when her daughter and her son were both grown and gone?

And in the meantime would she be able to handle them both as teenagers?

Right now it was the "grown and gone" part that worried her more. Making cookies tonight hadn't been entirely selfless. This was one of those nights when she had felt the need to dispel her own loneliness, so she had taken the opportunity to do something with KatiLynn while her daughter was studying. But her mind had wandered even while KatiLynn had talked to her from time to time.

She had not told her children yet about her conversation with Kenji. She was not sure how to explain what had happened. She was not sure whether to tell them of his request until she had decided how she felt about it herself. In fact, she had told no one about it—not Evie, or Ann, or her parents. The morning afterward, she could hardly make it seem real. But it had occupied her mind much of the time since Wednesday night.

In some ways, marrying Kenji would be like marrying Steve again. In Kenji's case, she could be an influential consort to one of the world's more powerful men in business. She would never lack for anything financially; that alone would be enough to make some women say yes, certain they could learn to love him or live very comfortably in the attempt. He was not only wealthy, he was also a man of strong character. Kate had no doubt she would feel secure in his devotion and affection.

But what would be the cost? Could her newfound faith survive in a country where Church meetings would be in a language she did not understand? How would KatiLynn and Stevie fare in a society where they were *gaijin*—foreigners? Who would care for them if Kenji expected her to travel with him on business?

His proposal had made that seem likely. "Think about what the two of us could do together." It had sounded almost like a merger. Or an acquisition? Could Kenji possibly be thinking of it that way?

No—not owning *her*, not buying her, any more than he had done so with Lily. Kenji had shown true devotion and respect for his wife. More likely, Kate thought, what he was offering her now was an expression of what he felt for her. He had also said to think about "what we could be." In his own eyes, perhaps, he was offering to share all the things and opportunities the world held for him. Seen in those terms, it was a generous offer. She felt flattered and touched that Kenji would think of her that way. A woman could learn to love a man like him, probably—or at least be deeply grateful to him.

But considering the possibilities in his proposal did little to dispel the loneliness she had been feeling tonight.

Before going out with Dave Cutler that first time, she had never felt this loneliness—or at least she had never recognized it. What had made the difference?

"Who's the man you're going out with tonight?" KatiLynn sat on the bed watching her mother put on makeup.

"His name is George—George Ryan. I met him at the fireside last week."

KatiLynn watched in silence for several seconds. "Are you going to get married again, Mom?"

Kate stopped with the lipstick halfway to her mouth and looked at her daughter in the mirror. It was a fair question, and a logical one. It deserved an answer. But Kate wasn't sure she had one. "I don't know, Sweetheart. I really haven't thought about marriage that much." In all honesty, she might have added that she had deliberately avoided thinking that far ahead. "Does it bother you when I go out?"

KatiLynn smiled slightly and shook her head. "No. I just wondered what you were, uh . . . why you're doing it."

Kate outlined her lips with the lipstick then pressed them together while she tried to think of a good answer. "It's just nice to have friends like . . . friends who are men."

"Like boyfriends?"

"No . . . not exactly. Friends—you know, like the ones you have your own age."

KatiLynn thought about that for a moment. "You mean like the boys at school, and at church?" She frowned. "They're just . . . there. It's not like I know any one that I . . ."

Kate turned to look at her daughter. "Someday you will—someone who makes you happy and cares about you because you're trying to be the best person you could possibly be. When you marry him in the temple, you'll make those forever promises I told you about."

"Is that the way it was with you and Daddy?"

Kate walked over to sit by her daughter on the bed. "Yes. I jumped at the chance to spend the rest of my life with him. If we had known about the temple, I'm sure we would have wanted to promise each other forever."

"So if you find another man now who loves you that way, will you marry him?" KatiLynn's eyes seemed to be searching her mother's.

"I don't know." Kate held her daughter's gaze. "I might never find another man that I could love like your daddy, so maybe I'll never have to answer that question."

"Do you want to, Mom? Find a man you could love like that?"

Kate looked at her own reflection in the mirror while she thought for a moment. The woman in the reflection didn't have an answer either. She looked into her daughter's eyes again. "I don't know—and I'm not sure *whether I'm ready to find out." She put an arm around KatiLynn. "But I promise that if I ever do find someone like that, it will never change the way I love you and Stevie."*

She knew her answer hadn't left KatiLynn completely satisfied—but there hadn't been anything else she could say.

George, her date that night, had been nice too—nice like Hal. And that was all.

Not counting Kenji, she had gone out with three different men since she had last dated Dave, and each time it had been enjoyable—pleasant.

But each time, she had wondered what it might have been like with Dave.

Why was she using him as the measure?

Maybe because he was the only man she had ever dated, except Steve, who made her feel that he cared more about her than he cared about the impression he was making on her.

Maybe because he made her laugh often, and easily.

Maybe because inside the father and successful businessman that everyone else saw there was a man who liked to go fast with the top down when she was with him.

She wished Dave would ask her out again.

But what if he didn't?

Maybe *she* could ask *him*.

No.

Why not? Women do that now. Ann's done it. What's wrong with it, really?

Kate shook her head. *No.* She would not chase a man. She had always hated seeing other women chase men.

But you don't have to throw yourself at him. You don't even have to ask him out to a dance or a movie. You could ask him over for dinner again. You told KatiLynn you wanted to have "friends." Can't you have a friend over for dinner?

Kate spooned the last of the chocolate chip cookie dough onto the cookie sheet and slid it into the oven.

"Mom?" It was Stevie, standing in the doorway in his pajamas, holding one of his favorite books. Lately, they were adventure stories. A couple of years ago, he had wanted her to read *Where the Wild Things Are* for him every night. Some nights she had called him her wild boy, and he had grinned his gap-toothed grin and clawed at the air with his hands while he made roaring noises like Max in the story. It was as close to rowdy as Stevie ever got.

He had his father's thoughtful, deliberate manner. Sometimes she would see him quietly pondering, and then he would get a paper and pencil or some sticks or clay and begin to make something, and she knew that when it was finished it would be what it had been destined before his hands ever touched the materials. If he had to improvise along the way, he would somehow manage to keep his original design and make it better. Steve would have seen a bright future for his son in the family business.

KatiLynn would take a pencil or crayon and draw some simple, beautiful thing, then do a creative variation on it, and then another. Stevie would ponder for a few minutes and draw some intricate thing he saw in his mind—exactly that, and nothing more. Two different, intelligent ways to approach things—but both worked.

Kate was proud of her children, and she knew Steve would be, too. Would another man ever be able to feel that way about them? Kenji had said he would be willing to learn about being a father, but could he do it fast enough to meet KatiLynn and Stevie's needs? Would he be there for them enough? Dave had already shown he could care about KatiLynn and Stevie. But if it became necessary, would a widower in his position be able to meet the needs of his own children and someone else's at the same time?

Kate forgot about her questions as she read Stevie his story, then talked with him and KatiLynn while they waited around for warm cookies from the oven.

It was after they were asleep, when she sat down in her bedroom to read for a few minutes, that she thought of Dave Cutler again. Why hadn't he called her? Had he decided that he didn't really care about going out with her again? Or had he backed away because she had gone out with Hal?

Why did men do that? Why did a man think that a woman shouldn't have the chance to go out with anyone but him?

Or could Dave have thought that in her eyes he didn't measure up to other men somehow? That certainly wasn't the truth.

What would he say, she wondered, if she did ask him over for dinner again?

There was only one way to find out. She glanced at the clock on her nightstand: ten after ten. Would it be too late to call? She stared at the opposite wall, wondering if she dared.

The best way to handle this was the approach Ann had taught her—don't think, just do it.

She put down her book and reached for her purse. The business card with his home number on it was still in her wallet. She picked up her telephone and willed herself to punch in the number without taking time to think it over.

While the telephone was ringing, she almost lost her nerve. *I could just hang up before he answers. But if he has caller ID, he'd know I—.* He came on the line before she had time to think it out. First she heard the sound of the TV news in the background, and then he said, "Cutlers'."

"Dave, this is Kate Warden."

The TV suddenly went silent. "Oh, hi! How are you?" He sounded surprised, almost shocked.

"I'm fine. But I thought you promised me another good backyard dinner," she said, trying to make this conversation light. "And I haven't heard from you." *Careful. Don't sound like you're interrogating him!* She could feel herself blushing.

"Oh. I, ah . . . I thought maybe you'd . . . I thought you were probably pretty busy."

"Not that busy." *Try to sound a little warmer.* "Not too busy to work in a good cookout." *Too much? Am I sounding like a flirt now?*

"Really?" He sounded surprised again, but also pleased.

When he didn't say anything more, Kate took the next step. "Yes, I was hoping I could get you to barbecue this time."

"I . . . sure, I'd be glad to."

Why had he hesitated, she wondered? "Good. When can you come over?"

"Well, ah . . . how would it be if you came over to our house this time?"

"Of course, if that would be better." *I thought he enjoyed coming to our house. Wonder if there was some problem with his children?*

"It's just that I have trouble getting Kelli to go anywhere with the family these days," Dave said, "so if you could come here . . ."

"Sure. That's not a problem."

"And I think I'll ask Kelli to make the salad, if you don't mind. She's really pretty good at it, and I know she'd like to feel that she helped out."

So there *had* been a problem with Kelli. She was the woman of the home in some ways, and she probably didn't like the idea of some other woman intruding on that role. "That will be fine, Dave. Can I bring the ice cream this time?"

"OK. Whatever your family likes, we'll like. How about Monday night, 6:30?"

"All right. You'll have to tell me where you live."

He dictated his address, in the north part of Mesa, then added: "We don't have a pool, but we have a trampoline in the backyard and Ross has some video games your kids might like."

"I'm sure they'll have a good time. We'll see you then."

"Kate?"

"Yes?"

"I'll be looking forward to it."

So will I, Kate thought after they said good-bye and she hung up the phone. *I just hope KatiLynn and Stevie will feel the same way when I tell them about it.*

* * *

"Mom, he won't let me have a turn." KatiLynn glanced over her shoulder at Ross, jumping on the trampoline. "He won't let any of us have a turn."

Kate put an arm around her daughter. "I'm sorry, Sweetheart. He really should, shouldn't he? But I don't know what I can do about it."

"Well, it isn't fair! He's just showing off. Why do boys always have to do that?"

"I don't know. Sometimes they just do. I know you'll want to remember this if they come to our house again so you can show him how to take turns fairly when you're diving."

KatiLynn nodded. Then she frowned. "Well, when they were over at our house before, I was just trying to show him . . . I mean, in the pool I thought he needed . . ." She looked at Ross for a moment, then nodded again. "OK."

Dave stepped out the back door of the house, glanced toward the trampoline, then walked over and gestured to his son. Ross stopped bouncing and bent down to listen. It was obvious that he wasn't happy about what his father said, but he climbed down from the trampoline. Dave boosted Stevie up onto it.

Kate squeezed her daughter around the shoulders. "Looks like the problem may be solved." She smiled. "I won't be surprised if the boys go off to play video games in a little while. Then you and Alicia can have the trampoline all to yourselves."

Dave smiled at KatiLynn as he walked toward them. "Your turn's coming right up. Think you can do some of the things on the trampoline that you did on the diving board?"

KatiLynn looked uncertainly at her mother, then at him. "Maybe. It's not exactly the same thing."

Kate gave her a small push toward the trampoline. "Go show us. But be careful."

Dave looked at Kate questioningly as her daughter walked away. "I thought she'd want another shot at the trampoline."

Kate suppressed a smile as KatiLynn glanced back at them. "She does. We were just having a talk about the importance of taking turns, and I was reminding her about all the time she spent showing her tricks on the diving board when you and your family came to our house."

Dave laughed softly. "I guess we owe it to your kids to come back to their home turf next time." He picked up the wire brush used to scrape off the barbecue grill.

"'Next time' can be anytime you like." Kate smiled at him. "Thanks for dinner. It was delicious."

Dave put down the brush and took her hand, then sat down on the bench at the redwood picnic table and patted the place beside him. "I can clean up later. This is a good time for a little relaxation."

He held her hand as they sat and watched KatiLynn bounce on the trampoline. KatiLynn tried a couple of backdrops and a front flip off her knees. She bounced for a while seemingly trying to decide something, then suddenly went into a front flip, managing to stay upright at the end. She looked at her mother and grinned.

Dave stood. "Come on," he said, pulling Kate by the hand. "Let's show them that old people can do that too."

"Jump on the trampoline?" Kate looked at him in surprise. "It's been years—since high school. And my hair . . ."

Dave smiled. "Your hair will be fine. You always manage to look good, no matter what you're doing. And you're in jeans, so you're dressed for it. Come on."

Dave went first. He bounced a bit to warm up, then tried a few flips, to the delight of his son and younger daughter. After he had bounced for a few minutes, he stopped and reached out his hand to help Kate up. "Your turn."

She bounced experimentally for half a minute, trying to get the feel for a trampoline again. She had enjoyed this once upon a time. She thought she could remember how to drop to her seat and come up again. When that worked, she bounced a few more times, tried a backdrop, and made that work too. "All right, Mom!" Stevie called. KatiLynn clapped. Kate stopped, smiled for them, and did a quick bow. Then she started bouncing again, tried a couple of knee flips, and worked up to a front flip for a finish.

"Very good," Dave called, applauding.

Kate laughed. "If you mean it's a good thing I didn't hurt myself after all these years, you're right." She climbed down from the trampoline and put her hand on Alicia's shoulder. "Next?"

Alicia obviously enjoyed the trampoline. She bounced high to warm up, did a front flip, and then a back flip as she had seen her older brother do. All of them clapped and cheered for her.

As they watched her bounce, Kate noticed that Kelli came out of the house to gather up the food and condiments on the picnic table and carry them inside. Two or three minutes later, she came back to gather up their paper plates, the silverware they had used, and the platter that had held the steaks.

Kate leaned toward Dave. "I think I ought to offer to help Kelli clean up."

Dave looked over his shoulder at the house, staring at the back door for several seconds as though trying to see inside. Then he nodded. "Sure, go ahead and ask her."

When Kate stepped into the kitchen, Kelli was standing at the sink rinsing the salad bowl before putting it into the dishwasher.

"I wouldn't want to get in your way, but I'll be glad to help you if I can," Kate said, taking a position a couple of feet away at the counter.

Kelli ignored her, picked up the silverware, and began rinsing it piece by piece. Kate stood in silence, watching. Kelli turned away to sort the silverware into slots in the dishwasher rack. The platter that had held the steaks was still sitting on the counter, so Kate picked it up and began rinsing it in the sink. When Kelli turned again and saw what Kate was doing, she snatched the platter out of the sink, shoved it into the dishwasher rack, and slammed the door of the dishwasher.

She turned and glared at Kate. "I saw you holding hands with my dad."

It was an accusation. Kate wasn't sure how to respond.

The silence stretched out between them awkwardly. Kelli backed up against the sink, putting her hands on the edge of the counter behind her. The look of defiance in her eyes was unmistakable. "We don't need a mother!" She almost spat out the words. "We're doing fine just the way we are."

The implication in Kelli's words seemed clear. Kate did not respond to the girl's challenge. "I'm sure no one could ever replace your mother," she said softly.

Kelli laughed harshly. "But you want to try, don't you?"

"No," Kate said, still softly. "I'm sure your Heavenly Father picked out exactly the right mother for you. She'll always be an important part of your life. You should treasure her memory."

Kate's response was obviously not what Kelli had expected. The girl's lip quivered and tears began to slide down her cheeks.

"I don't know what it's like to lose a parent," Kate continued, "but I do know what it's like to lose someone you love." She paused. "If you'd ever like to talk about—"

"You leave my dad alone!" Kelli sobbed. She wiped at the tears furiously with her fingers. She looked past Kate, toward the back door, then ran from the kitchen out the doorway that led down the hall toward her bedroom.

Kate turned to look at the back door too. Dave was standing outside looking through the window in the storm door.

As he stepped inside, he glanced down the hallway where Kelli had fled. "What, ah . . . what's happening?"

Kate smiled slightly. "A little woman-to-woman talk."

His eyebrow went up. "Oh? What did she say?"

Kate didn't know how much to tell him; she didn't want to put a wedge of any kind between father and daughter. "I think she wants to know exactly what my intentions are toward her dad."

Slowly he reddened. "Was it something like 'Stay away'?"

Kate said nothing.

Dave started toward the doorway into the hall. "I think I'd better go have a talk with her."

Kate reached out and took hold of his arm. "No—no, please. I don't want to tell you how to deal with your daughter, but right now probably wouldn't be a good time."

He stopped and looked at her questioningly. The color in his face began to subside. "I think I need to teach her how to treat guests in this house."

"You're right. And I know it's up to you to decide how to do that. But maybe it's a lesson for another day. Right now she probably needs to be sure of your love. I'd guess that she's missing her mother a lot—and wondering whether you're forgetting her."

"Forget Jeanine? I could never—" Dave stopped, obviously not certain what to say to her about his wife.

"I know," Kate replied. "You shouldn't. I'll never forget Steve, either."

"But I have the rest of my life to live," Dave said. "And one day my kids will be gone."

"Yes." Kate stared down at the floor for several seconds. "I hadn't really thought that way about my own future until you asked me out the first time. After I said yes, I wondered if I should have talked to my children about how they felt—about how they would feel if I . . ." But she didn't want to mention marriage just now. "I realized that in the end it would have to be my decision about what I do with the rest of my life. I'll always be their mother—I'll always want to be—but I have to go on being Kate, too."

She looked up at Dave. "In a way I feel guilty whenever I think about what *I* want out of life. But I don't think I'm supposed to live only for my children."

"Yeah. I understand. I love my kids. I want to see them through a mission, getting married in the temple, being on their own. But it might be tough to do those things all alone. And afterward, what?"

They stood looking at each other across the kitchen until they both spoke at the same time:

"Kate, you're the first—"

"Dave, I want you to know—"

They both laughed self-consciously. Dave nodded toward her. "You first."

Kate stared out the window beyond him. "I feel like a part of me has been drifting since Steve died—and I didn't even realize that until you asked me out. I liked going out again, and I think that scared me. I knew if I started dating I might be faced with deciding sometime whether I would commit my future to life with someone else. I panicked a little bit. I told myself I didn't know anything about single men my age, I didn't know any others in the Church, I needed to . . ."

She looked him in the eyes again. "That's why I went out with Hal, and a couple of other men you don't know. It wasn't that I didn't enjoy going out with you—I enjoyed it very much. It's just that I thought I had to know some other LDS men socially."

Kate realized she was fingering the small gold chain she wore around her neck. She put her hands at her sides and resisted the urge to wipe her damp palms on her jeans. "Is this making sense? I just wanted you to know that I didn't look for the chance go out with those other men because of anything about you. It was me—my need to know . . . I mean, after almost six years of being a widow, I was finally dealing with the fact that I'm free to date again."

He thought about what she had said for a moment, then nodded. "Thanks for telling me. Sometimes men wonder . . . well, *I* wondered if I said something that wasn't quite right . . . or if I did something . . ."

Kate smiled and shook her head.

Dave glanced toward the doorway again. "I apologize for my daughter. Right now, she probably wouldn't like *any* woman I went out with. She'll have to get over that—and she will, in time." He sighed. "I love my kids. I want them to be happy. But I can't let them—any one of them—tell me . . . I mean, I'm going to live with whatever I decide about the future for a lot longer than they will. I want to be happy too. Is it wrong for me to think about that?"

"No," Kate said softly. "I don't think so."

"It's been hard for me to deal with the thought of getting married again—even after I promised Jeanine." He gazed at nothing in particular out in the hallway. "I don't know whether I'd dare ask any other woman to take on my kids." There was a pause. "If the bishop hadn't talked to me . . . and then my stake president . . . I probably wouldn't have asked anyone out yet."

Dave looked at her and smiled. "Kate, could we start over?"

"What do you mean?"

"It seems like we've both struggled with the idea of dating. I don't know what could develop between us. Maybe we won't be anything more than friends. And maybe that's OK—at least we can help each other out a little." He grinned. "For now, I'd enjoy working on the dating thing together. If you would too . . . well, are you free next Saturday night?"

She smiled back. "I happen to have an opening on my calendar."

Kate didn't know where this might lead either. Marriage? It was far too early to think in those terms—especially with a man whose daughter obviously despised her. But Kate realized that she had just given herself permission to enjoy life fully again, and it felt good.

11

Dave glanced at a poster by the door as they walked out of the theater complex. "So, what did you think of the movie?"

"I liked it. But we didn't have to see another romantic comedy. I mean, if you'd like to see something else . . ."

"Oh, no," he said solemnly. "I live for movies like these. I can't get enough of *An Affair to Remember*. I've been thinking I'd really like to see *Sleepless in Seattle* and *Steel Magnolias* again. I—"

"Stop it!" Kate said, laughing.

He grinned. "So you think you're ready for a real guy flick like *The Dirty Dozen*, or some Clint Eastwood film?"

"I could risk it, if that's what you like."

"I like a few of those. But a lot of them have too much bang-bang or too much flesh." He thought for a moment. "Maybe we should make popcorn at my house next time and watch one of my old Humphrey Bogart classics—you know, *The Maltese Falcon* or *Key Largo*." He chuckled. "Jeanine always said I identified with those strong, protective types."

There was good reason for that, Kate thought. "Jeanine probably loved that about you, didn't she?"

Dave nodded.

"But I'll bet Kelli doesn't appreciate it very much."

Dave looked at her in surprise, as though he wondered how she could know so much about his daughter. "Noooo, she doesn't want protecting, thank you. She tells me she needs to make her own choices—and her own mistakes."

Kate stopped next to a rack of clothes on the sidewalk outside of a shop that catered to teens. "This would look really cute on Kelli," she said, holding up a pullover top.

Dave took hold of the edges and spread it out so he could examine it. "That's nice," he said. "I think it would go with a skirt and a couple of pairs of pants she has."

Kate held the shirt in front of herself. "I'm a little taller, but I think it would fit her. This could be part of a nice dad-and-daughter moment when you let her know how much you appreciate everything she's doing at home."

Dave thought it over. "Yeah. I'd like to try that."

He paid for the shirt and they walked away. "Kelli will be pleased to know you picked this out for her."

Kate shook her head. "I think you ought to keep that between us. I don't think she'd appreciate it if she knew I had anything to do with it."

Dave frowned. "I'm sorry about her attitude. I wish I knew what to do about that. I keep hoping she'll learn to be civil to you."

"I keep trying to tell myself it's not just me," Kate replied. "I keep thinking she's trying to make a statement about your having another woman in your life after her mother—*any* woman."

They came to his car in the mall parking lot and he fished in his pocket for his keys. "I try to make it easy for her to talk to me. I just want to be there when she needs me. I wish I could make her believe—"

Kate wondered at first where the ringing was coming from, but Dave grabbed the cell phone off his belt so smoothly that she realized he must be used to these interruptions. He glanced at the number on its display screen, then put the phone to his ear. "Hi. Is everything OK there?"

His eyes widened slightly and he looked at Kate. "When?" He listened for a moment, his eyes never leaving Kate, and asked: "Which hospital?" He listened again, then: "All right. I might be late getting home. Love you."

He snapped the phone closed. "What?" she asked anxiously.

"KatiLynn called my house looking for you. She's with your parents' neighbors, the Murphys. Your mother had to take your father to the hospital. His heart."

* * *

Her father had never looked so gray. He lay back against the pillow with his eyes closed. Asleep? Unconscious? "How is he?" she said softly to her mother. Belle was seated in a chair next to the bed holding her husband's hand, just as she had been the last time Kate saw them here.

"Stable," her mother answered, dry-eyed. But it was obvious from her red, puffy eyes that she had been crying earlier.

Bill opened his own eyes. "I'm OK, Sweetheart." It was almost a whisper. "They're taking good care of me. Everything's fine." He managed a weak smile.

137

"He has to have surgery," his wife said. "It can't wait any longer."

Belle looked inquiringly at Dave, who stood at the foot of the bed, and Kate realized that her father was staring at him too. "This is Dave—David Cutler," she said. But how to explain him? As her date? Her security consultant? That wasn't important enough to worry about right now. "How soon?" she asked her mother.

"Right now—tonight."

Kate took hold of her father's other hand. Bill looked at his wife, at his daughter, then gazed at Dave for several seconds before he closed his eyes and relaxed against the pillow. Dave walked around to stand next to Kate. Almost instinctively she reached for his hand and held onto it too.

They were standing that way a few minutes later when an orderly in scrubs and a surgical cap stepped into the room. "We're ready for Mister Morrow now," he said.

As the orderly began to maneuver the wheeled bed toward the door, Bill gave his daughter's hand a squeeze. He smiled up at her. "Kate, I want you always to remember how much I love you."

She understood what he meant. If he didn't come out of the surgery, he wanted her to remember these last words from him. "You can tell me that again tomorrow, Dad. You'll be out of here in a few days, and in a couple of weeks when you feel up to it, we'll go flying."

She hoped she was right about his future and he was wrong.

* * *

Kate looked up from her desk as Dave tapped lightly on the open door with his knuckles. "How is your father today? The hospital wouldn't tell me anything when I called this morning."

She smiled. "Groggy, and cranky about being in the hospital. I think that's a good sign. The doctor said everything went very well. It's thoughtful of you to ask. Did you come by just for that?"

"I was hoping everything would be all right with him. And I wondered if you might need a listening ear today." He moved a chair next to her desk so he could sit closer to her. "What time did you get home this morning?"

"About 3:30. Do I look that bad?"

"No—never." He reached across the corner of the desk to take her hand. "But I'm sure it had to be a long night. Considering the way he looked when they took him away, you had to be worried."

She leaned closer so she could look him in the eyes. "Dave, something happened last night—something I haven't really been able to share with anybody else. My mother was too worried to understand when I tried to explain it, and I don't think my brother got it either when I tried to tell him about it this morning."

Belle crossed herself, then stood up from the cushioned rail behind a bench where she had been kneeling in the hospital's meditation chapel. Carefully she sat down again beside Kate.

It was the third time since they had come in here that Belle had been on her knees praying. Kate had knelt beside her the first time, saying her own prayer, and she had continued to pray in her heart all the time she had been here.

She took her mother's hand and squeezed it. "He's going to be all right. I know it."

Belle nodded. "I'd like to believe that too. God has been good to me. He's—" Her voice cracked, and she paused, then turned to look at her daughter. "He's given me a lot of good things in life. Thank you for being here for me tonight."

"Always, Mom. And I mean what I said—Dad's going to be all right. I know it." Should she explain? Or would it start another disagreement over religion? But this was no time to hesitate in sharing what she knew. "I know because the Spirit—the Holy Ghost—told me. Dad's going to get well," she said, holding her mother's gaze.

Belle looked surprised at first, and then her face showed a mixture of curiosity and relief. "I'm glad you can be so sure," she said slowly. She turned toward the front of the chapel, gazing at the far wall with its small image of Christ on the cross, and sat back against the bench.

Kate faced forward too, closed her eyes, and leaned her head back against the wall, thinking about the assurance she had received. That peaceful, calm feeling had come in answer to her first prayer when she knelt here. It still warmed her. She had simply continued praying that everything would go well during the surgery.

But . . . was it possible she might have misunderstood the answer? She had felt strongly that everything would be all right. Did that really mean her father would live to leave this hospital? Kate frowned. Could it have meant things would be all right however they turned out for him? Maybe it meant that the Lord would take Bill Morrow to himself too, like Steve, and—

No. That wasn't what she had prayed for, and she had felt an assurance that her prayer would be answered.

She whispered the words so softly that no one but Him would hear. "Father, You know I'm new to this, and maybe I don't understand things very well sometimes, but I believe in You, and I believe I felt an answer. I told my mother I know things will be all right for Dad. Please tell me if he—"

The peaceful, strong assurance came to her once more.

"Thank you," Kate breathed.

Her father would walk out of here, and he would be here years longer, for her and his grandchildren. She knew it.

Dave could see tears glistening in her eyes. He took her hand between both of his. "And what did your brother say when you told him about that?"

"Tom was a little like Mom—he was glad *I* could feel that kind of comfort. It's been so long since we really talked about anything important that I don't know what he believes in." She frowned. "He's seen too much of war. I think he feels like God doesn't pay much attention to one little person—like we're on our own."

She opened her desk drawer and pulled out a tissue to dab at her eyes. "Dave, I'm still new to asking Heavenly Father about things and knowing I can get an answer. Do you get answers sometimes? I mean, does this happen often when people believe, or was what happened last night just, ah . . ."

She was groping for words, Dave thought. "Sometimes I get answers," he said. "Maybe when we're living right it can happen more often, if we just pay attention." He paused. "I've had answers like yours. When Jeanine was sick, I . . . we both got the same answer. It wasn't the one we wanted, and I fought against it for a while. Jeanine accepted it better than I did. But I realized later that it allowed us to get ready."

He could see pain in Kate's eyes. "Oh, Dave, I'm so sorry," she said. "It must have been so hard for you, and now here I am telling you how I've been blessed. I didn't mean to make you remember—"

"What I'm saying is that I was blessed too. I didn't understand that very well at the time. But the Lord was giving me strength when I needed it—strength for what I would have to go through."

Kate looked into his eyes for several seconds. "I didn't understand either, after Steve died. I think the Lord tried to help me sometimes when I was hurting so much, and I didn't understand that He was there.

I wish I'd known what I know now. Maybe those times could have been more like last night."

Both of them turned at the sound of a tapping on the door. Ann stood in the doorway. "You have a call, Kate. It's your brother."

Dave stood to leave, but Kate motioned him to stay as she picked up her telephone. He heard her side of the brief conversation. "Hi. You're . . . All right, we can arrange that. . . . No, stay where you are. I'll pick you up outside the terminal in about twenty-five minutes."

She hung up the phone. "I'm sorry, Dave. My brother's at the airport. He wants to see Dad and meet with the doctors." She stepped to the door. "Ann, I have to go pick up Tom, and then go to the hospital with him. Can you close up tonight?"

"I can't stay. I'm sorry. Sherry's in a choir program at the high school, and I promised her I'd be there."

Kate frowned. "And Trish won't be here today. Are we expecting anyone tonight? Maybe you could close up early."

Ann shook her head. "No, we have one person flying out about six-thirty and one coming in from San Diego—some business executive, I think. He called to ask if anyone would be here between seven and eight tonight."

"I'll stay for you," Dave volunteered.

Kate looked surprised. "But you couldn't. Your work . . ."

He smiled. "I'm the boss, remember? I can do what I want—if you think I could handle things here. Anyway, Ann will be here until five"—he looked at Ann and she nodded—"so she could show me what to do before she leaves."

"Thank you!" Kate picked up her purse beside the desk and stepped past him on her way out of her office. Then she turned around and surprised him with a peck on the cheek. "Thank you. You're a lifesaver today." She started for the front door. "I hate to ask Evie to keep my kids again, but I'll call her on the way and ask her if she can pick up KatiLynn and Stevie when she picks up her daughter at the school bus." Then she stopped with her hand on door and turned back toward Dave. "You can't stay here! Your children—"

"I'll pick them up and bring them here, if that's all right. If they have homework, they can do it here just as well as at home."

"But they'll need dinner."

"I'll order in pizza, OK?"

"Make yourself at home."

"Would you like me to pick up your kids too and bring them here? We can have a pizza party while we wait for you."

Kate thought for a moment. "Great idea. Bring a video." She pointed toward the television set in the waiting area. "Ann can show you where the player is." She started to open her purse. "Let me give you some money."

"Go!" He waved her toward the door. "Just go be with your family."

"Go on," Ann echoed. "We'll take care of things here."

* * *

It was an oriental print on a wall in the hospital that made her think of Kenji.

The painting he had sent her lay on the dining room table at home, where she had left it yesterday afternoon. Artistically, it was exquisite. It depicted a simple scene: a Japanese home with tall pine trees flanking it and a waterfall behind it. True to his word, Kenji had not written anything asking her for an answer to his question. In fact, there had been no message with the painting at all—only an eight-by-ten photograph of a similar home flanked by tall trees. She guessed that it had to be his country home, the one he had built for Lily. It appeared as though he had not worried about cost in making the home exactly the way he wanted it. She suspected the same was true of the painting; it did not look like the ordinary tourist goods seen in shops in San Francisco or Los Angeles. Everything about it exuded quality, including the lacquered frame.

It was a thoughtful gift, and a gentle reminder; he had said he would be thinking of her. What kind of response, if any, should she give to Kenji for the gift?

She still wondered what kind of response to give to the question he had asked her.

There was another reason she had thought of Kenji. He had told her that his own father had undergone open-heart surgery and was now in good health.

Kenji lived not far from his aged father. If she were living in Japan too, and something happened to her father, or her mother, she certainly wouldn't be able to get home to Phoenix as quickly as Tom had come from Virginia. No doubt Kenji could afford to spare no expense in getting her here, but would it be at the last minute—or perhaps too late? And if she were thousands of miles away while her parents were aging and

142

her children were growing up—well, what value could anyone put on lost time with loved ones?

Maybe it was only seeing her father confined to a hospital bed that made her think this way. But these things would have to be considered before she could answer Kenji.

There was something else, maybe more important, she would have to consider too. It was the fact that since she had left the painting lying on the table yesterday, she had not thought of Kenji. She did not miss him when he was not here, even though she had fond thoughts of him when he came to mind—thoughts of a friend whose company she enjoyed. And that was all.

She had thoughts of friendship for Dave too. But there was something more.

She was looking forward to seeing him, she thought as she drove back to the flight service offices.

Maybe she was simply feeling good because things were going well with her father?

No. Somehow things would be better because she would be seeing Dave.

It was a few minutes before eight when she parked in front of the office. Dave looked up in surprise and then smiled as she stepped through the door. "You're back early."

"Hi, Mom!" Stevie called. He stood looking over Ross's shoulder as Ross did something on Ann's computer. KatiLynn sat at Dave's left on the couch in the waiting area; his daughter Alicia sat on the other side with her father's arm around her. KatiLynn stood and walked over to hug her mother. "How's Grandpa?"

"He's doing well tonight, Sweetheart. How have things been here?"

"Fine. My homework's all done," she said, pointing to her stack of books and papers on the end table next to the couch.

"And we had time for a tic-tic-toe tournament before the video," Dave said. "Guess who's the champion." He pointed at KatiLynn.

She smiled and did a small bow. "Ta-da."

Ross looked up from the computer screen long enough to roll his eyes.

Dave gestured toward the computer. "Stevie showed us that you have a flight simulator game. The boys have been taking turns. I hope that's OK."

"Of course." Kate looked at Stevie and Ross. "How are you doing?"

Stevie grinned. "I flew the twin this time."

Ross looked up at her without smiling. "Can you fly all those planes out there?" he asked, pointing in the direction of the door that led to the tie-down area. The question sounded faintly like a challenge.

"Yes. I'd be glad to tell you about them—if you want."

Ross didn't answer. He looked down at the computer monitor and went back to playing the game. Kate walked around behind the desk to look over his shoulder. He was taking his turn at trying to fly the on-screen version of a twin-engine airplane like the one tied down outside. She started to offer some suggestions, but he seemed bent on ignoring her, so she said nothing.

"How are things at the hospital?" Dave asked.

She walked around the service counter toward the couch in the waiting area. "Good, really. They made us leave so Dad could get some rest."

"I'm sorry your daddy is sick," Alicia said shyly. "Is he going to be all right?"

Kate smiled at her. "He'll be fine—and thank you for asking." She laughed as she looked at Dave. "Dad's doing well enough to harass the nurses. I think that's one reason they wanted him to go to sleep."

"We saved you some pizza and some pop." He pointed at the box and the two-liter bottle on the counter. "Hungry?"

"Yes." She glanced toward her darkened office. "But I probably ought to see whether Ann left anything I need to do."

Dave shook his head. "She said to tell you she finished everything before she left."

All the other rooms were dark too, Kate noticed. "Kelli didn't come with you?"

"She didn't stay. It was 'so-o-o boring.'" Dave made quote marks in the air with his fingers. "She needed to do some research at the library for a project, so she called a friend with a driver's license and a car to pick her up. I'll go by the library for her when we leave. Is it OK if we finish watching *Beauty and the Beast*? It's almost over."

"You can stay as long as you like. I can't leave until the pilot from San Diego comes in."

She put a piece of pizza on one of the paper napkins and walked around the corner to the small nook that held a refrigerator, microwave, and soft drink machine.

From where she stood while her pizza was warming, she could see Ross seated at the computer with Stevie and KatiLynn looking over his shoulders. KatiLynn watched the screen for several seconds, then said, "You'd better pull up before—"

It was too late. An alarm sounded from the computer, and then a voice intoned, "The flight was unsuccessful. The aircraft has crashed."

Ross punched at a key on the keyboard. He turned to glare at KatiLynn as though it were her fault things had gone wrong.

"My turn," Stevie said cheerfully. Ross turned to look at him, started to speak, then glanced at Kate and thought better of it. Slowly he got out of the chair to let Stevie sit. He stood directly behind the chair so that KatiLynn had to move away to the side. She looked at Ross momentarily, then walked away toward the couch in the waiting area.

The *ding* of the timer announced that Kate's pizza was ready. She went to sit by Dave on the couch while she ate. KatiLynn came to sit beside her, so Kate moved slightly toward Dave to make room.

KatiLynn leaned toward her and asked quietly, "Mom, can we go visit Grandpa tomorrow?"

"I think so. I'll ask the people at the hospital if it's OK."

Dave leaned toward her on the other side and said softly, "If they can visit him, it might be good for everyone. When Jeanine was in the hospital, I took the kids to see her every time I could. I think it helped them, but I know it helped Jeanine." He lowered his voice to a whisper. "We played tic-tac-toe tonight because KatiLynn was thinking about your dad. I guess that's one of the games he plays with her."

When Kate finished eating her pizza, Dave reached over to take hold of her hand.

The girls were caught up again in the movie, but Kate found herself thinking about the sensitivity Dave had shown toward her and her children today. He was a man of strength in areas where many men were lacking. He would never move in the same circles as Kenji Nakamura, but he could focus on her and the world she lived in without looking beyond them for wider worlds to conquer. She felt at ease around him, but it was more than simply being comfortable. She felt at peace.

When the movie ended, Dave squeezed his daughter around the shoulders. "What do you think, Ally? Did you like it—for the two hundredth time?" He winked at Kate.

"Daddy!" Alicia protested. "Not two hundred!" She smiled shyly at Kate. "It's my favorite story."

"It used to be KatiLynn's too." Kate put an arm around her daughter. "She's a little like the girl in the story—at least she's always liked books that way."

KatiLynn leaned forward to look at Alicia. "I have some things that go with the movie—a book, and some paper dolls. You could have them, if you want."

Alicia looked at her father as though to ask if she could accept. He looked at KatiLynn. "Are you sure?"

"Yes. I don't use them anymore."

The drone of an aircraft on the runway caught Kate's ears first, and then everyone turned toward the sound as the engine noise grew louder outside. "That'll probably be the flight from San Diego," she said.

"Sounds like our cue to leave," Dave answered.

"You don't have to."

He glanced at his watch. "Yeah. We need to pick Kelli up at the library a little after nine."

He helped Alicia gather her things and shepherded his children to the front door, then followed them outside. Kate stepped outside with them.

"You two go get in the van," Dave said, handing Ross the keys. "I'll be right there."

"Thanks for helping me out today," Kate said. "That was way above and beyond."

"Thanks for letting me." He took one step closer and stood looking into her eyes.

Her back was against the door. She knew what Dave was going to do next. Was that why he had sent Ross and Alicia ahead to the car? She could have moved away—but she didn't.

He leaned forward and kissed her lightly on the lips. Then he backed away, looking into her eyes again—waiting for a response? She wasn't sure how to respond, so she said nothing.

Finally, he smiled at her. "You missed when you did that this afternoon." He paused, still looking into her eyes. "I'll call you—tomorrow."

It almost sounded like a question. "OK. Tomorrow." She smiled back at him. She did not know what else to say.

He moved as though to step close to her again, and then they heard male voices inside the office. Kate realized it had been some time since the engine sounds in back of the building died.

"Tomorrow," Dave said again, and turned to walk to his van.

She stood for a moment with her hand on the door handle, wondering if she should feel guilty about what had just happened.

Was it wrong—maybe disloyal to Steve?

Was it wrong that she had let it happen? That she had enjoyed it?

12

"When are they going to start your father on exercise?" Dave asked.

"They already have, just a little bit, but the doctor told him they'll probably step up the pace after his checkup Monday. In a couple of weeks, they hope to have him out walking around the park."

"Maybe I'll go walk with him so I can ask all the things I've wanted to know about you that you haven't told me," Dave said. He steered her expertly past a couple whose style of dancing demanded that others on the floor give them plenty of space.

"You could ask *me*," she said, smiling. "I'm not trying to keep secrets from you." She felt light and graceful in Dave's arms, as though somehow he made her that way, and being at this singles dance with him was a welcome bit of relaxation after the events of the past two weeks.

He spun her around and dipped her low to the floor as the music ended. Kate laughed as he pulled her up again. "Why didn't you tell me you could dance like this? Now I know why Helen wants to dance with you."

"Helen asked *you*?"

"When I was in the ladies' room. She said, 'Would you mind terribly asking Dave if he'd save one dance for me? It's not often I get to dance with anybody that good.' "

"I enjoy dancing. It's the *dances* I don't like. This is fun, with you. But if people come to these looking for . . . for companionship, or maybe something more . . ." He grimaced. "You might come to a lot of these before reality lives up to expectations."

"Where *did* you learn to dance like this?" Kate asked.

"I was on the ballroom dance team for two years in college. My partner and I won a couple of competitions."

"That wasn't Jeanine?"

"No—but she was very understanding about it. I took a dance class one semester just because I needed a credit, and the teacher talked me into trying out for the team."

"You're a very interesting man, David Cutler. The more I know about you, the more impressed I am." Kate linked her arm tightly through his. "I think Helen has her eye on you. You're one of the 'good ones' she told me about."

Dave glanced toward Helen, dancing with someone else to the tune that had just started. "She'd make some man a wonderful wife."

"But not you?" Kate teased.

He shook his head. "Look at her—not a hair out of place, and the dress looks like it came out of a Neiman-Marcus catalog. She needs a man to match her style—somebody who likes to go out socially the way she does, not a guy who's struggling to raise three kids while he keeps a business going. Helen and I would be like a . . . like . . . your crystal vase with a dandelion in it!"

Kate laughed. "Don't sell yourself so short." She looked at him speculatively for a moment. "Did you sell yourself short the night you came here and I was with Hal?"

Dave hoped surprise didn't show too plainly on his face. How was this woman able to see into his mind so easily sometimes? "Well, I . . . when I saw the two of you together, and I thought about everything Hal has to offer . . ."

"Hal is a fine man," Kate said. "He'll make some lucky woman a wonderful wife."

Dave looked at her quizzically. Kate laughed again. "His house is much neater and better organized than mine," she explained. "We went there for a few minutes so he could let me taste a special fruit drink he makes. His recipe books are all lined up on a shelf in the kitchen where he can consult them whenever he needs them, and his spices are all neatly put away in one of those little racks in the cupboard. At my house I've got just one beat-up old cookbook my mother gave me when I moved away from home after college. The front of it is scorched because I laid it on top of a burner on the stove one day. And almost anything beyond salt and pepper is exotic for me." She shook her head. "I don't think Hal and I would fit together very well."

Two dances later, they were standing on the sidelines waiting for the music to start again when Helen walked by. "Hello, Dave. Hi, Kate." She smiled at Dave.

He looked at Kate, wondering how she had felt about Helen's request. Kate smiled at him weakly. "Go ahead. I'll wait right here."

He turned to Helen. "Would you like to dance?"

"Of course. I'd love it!"

Kate watched them through the next two numbers. They were very good together. She had to admire the way they moved in unison, as though each knew what the other was going to do next. She had never in her life thought about being that good at dancing—but it had never mattered before.

It had been a long time—years—since she had felt what she was feeling right now. Jealousy?

She reminded herself of what Dave had said: he and Helen were not a match. She reminded herself that she and Dave had not made any kind of promises to each other. But none of that mattered. She couldn't help wishing that she were the one in his arms at the moment.

"You've gone out with him three times in the past two weeks," Evie said. "But you haven't told me anything about him."

"There's not much to tell, really." It was partly true. Even though she had tried to spend time with her father almost every day for the past two weeks, she had also been able to accept one lunch invitation from Dave and he had taken her to dinner two Friday nights in a row. But as good a friend as Evie was, Kate did not feel she could share much about Dave. She was not sure yet where their relationship was going.

"Well, you must like him," Evie said, and smiled over the top of her cup. "Has he kissed you yet?"

Kate blushed. He had kissed her again last Friday night when he brought her home, and this time he had lingered at it. She had enjoyed it this time too.

Evie laughed. "Kate! That's wonderful. I'm happy for you."

Kate looked at her in surprise. "You don't think I'm being . . . disloyal? I mean, you were Steve's friends . . ."

Evie raised her eyebrows. "We're your friends too, and I've watched you for years trying to go it alone. I don't think that's what Steve would have wanted."

"But—I still love him."

"He was a great guy. I hope you can always hold that in your heart." Evie paused. "Does that mean there could never be room for anyone else?"

149

Kate had not known the answer to that question when Evie asked it, and she was no more certain of an answer now. But there was no denying what she felt when she saw another woman in Dave's arms.

Kate did her best during the next number to show him how much she enjoyed dancing with him. It was another cha cha, but with his help she was beginning to learn how to do it.

When the music ended, he glanced at his watch. "Do you think your kids would let you stay out past ten tonight? Because if they would, I'd really like to take you out for ice cream."

Kate laughed. "I think Mom won't mind keeping them a little longer. If I eat a *small* cone, it will be all right."

At the ice cream shop, he bought two cones, and as they walked out the door, he said, "There's a nice park a couple of blocks down the street where we could sit and enjoy these."

The park was empty. They left his car near the entrance and walked into the park between two rows of tall oleander bushes flanking the sidewalk. Just beyond the bushes, they found a bench where they could sit.

"How do you think your kids would feel about a backyard dinner at our place again?" Kate asked.

"Hmm." He thought for a moment. "Well, you know I can't predict how Kelli will react. But I think Ross and Alicia would enjoy your pool. Home evening Monday night?"

"With their favorite kind of ice cream for the treat. What should I get?"

Dave grinned. "It's my turn to choose. Make it rocky road. They'll like it."

When they finished their ice cream, he stood and held out his hand to her. "I suppose I'd better take you home. I don't want to keep you out past the mom curfew."

He held her hand as they walked back up the sidewalk toward his car.

They had nearly reached the parking lot when a stocky figure stepped into their path from behind the last oleander bush.

He was no taller than Dave, but his chest was broad and the shoulders and arms that his tank top did not cover were very well muscled. The light behind him illuminated his sandy hair, but his face was in shadow. The folding knife he held in his hand was probably just like the ones some men wear in sheaths on their belts, but to Kate the blade looked enormous.

"We were just going to our car," Dave said evenly. "If you don't mind—"

"The nice little red job out there?" The young man's teeth stood out from the shadow on his face as he bared them in a grin. "Why don't you just give me the keys? Give me your wallet too."

"Look, I've only got a couple of bucks left in my wallet. This really isn't worth the trouble it—"

"Shut up and give me the keys and the wallet." The younger man took one step closer and pointed the knife toward Dave's belly.

"OK," Dave said, trying to sound soothing, non-threatening. "I'll give you all the money I've got, and then if you'll just let the lady and me—"

The other man cut him off with an obscenity. "Quit stalling! Now!"

With his left hand, Dave reached slowly toward his hip pocket. He shifted his body to put himself between the other man and Kate. As he reached for the wallet, he went into a slight crouch, balanced on the balls of his feet, ready to move quickly if he had to. "All right. Don't do anything you'll regret. I'm—"

When the man swung the knife, Dave reacted instantly, twisting, trying to parry with his left hand, trying to get out of the way—but he wasn't fast enough. The knife slashed into his left side just above the hip. Kate sucked in a breath and jumped backward as Dave fell to his right and lay on the sidewalk, moaning.

The other man's face was in the light now. He was a boy, really—no more than eighteen or nineteen. He bent toward Dave and extended the hand that held the knife.

"Leave him alone!" Kate commanded.

Slowly the young man looked up at her. His stare was undoubtedly meant to be threatening. "Shut up," he said. Then he bent toward Dave again, his eyes on the bulge in his victim's hip pocket.

"Get away from him!" Kate ordered. She wanted to scream for help, but the three of them were alone in the park.

The young man straightened up and stared at her again. Then he looked at her left wrist. "Nice watch, lady. Cost a lot of money?"

It probably had. Steve hadn't been reluctant to buy the best when he had bought her gifts. She glanced down at the watch on her arm. Whatever it cost, it wasn't worth getting either of them hurt. But it might offer a way to draw this man away from Dave. Kate took one step backward.

The man pointed his knife in her direction. "Give it to me. Now."

"No." She took another step backward. She noticed that Dave, still lying on the ground, was watching her intently. Slowly, almost imperceptibly, he shook his head. But somehow she had to draw the attention of the man with the knife away from him.

The man stepped around Dave and took one more short step toward her. He was perhaps three strides away. His wrist moved and he waggled the knife up and down in his fingers as though testing the balance. "I'm not playing games. The watch."

"Why don't you come and take it?" She didn't wait for his answer. She turned and started to run toward the center of the park.

"Kate—no!" Dave shouted.

Dave probably thought she couldn't outrun the younger man. He was right, and she was counting on the younger man to believe the same thing. The skirt she wore allowed her complete freedom of movement, but the young man's stride would be much longer. She heard his feet on the sidewalk behind her. She took four steps, then stopped and pivoted suddenly, hoping she could remember what her brother had taught her and hoping the young man would be where she wanted him to be. He was—two steps behind, lunging after her with the knife. She stepped to his left—the side away from the blade he held—planted her foot, and swung her left fist, putting all her weight behind it, aiming for his throat. His eyes went wide in surprise at the last instant, and he tried to halt his charge, but too late. Her fist hit him squarely in the Adam's apple. She brought her right arm into position to push him as he passed her, hoping to make him go down.

But she didn't get the chance. Suddenly he slammed down face first on the sidewalk. Dave had tackled him around the ankles and yanked him backward. The young man lay still momentarily, then began to writhe in pain, gasping for breath and gagging.

Dave was on him immediately, twisting the arm that held the knife behind the man's back and bending the man's wrist until he opened his fingers and let the knife fall to the ground.

Dave yanked the man's left arm up to meet his right arm in back. "Take off my belt," he said to Kate, "so we can tie him up."

Kate knelt beside him, reached for his belt buckle, then stopped. Blood was staining Dave's shirt at his waist on the left side and it was beginning to spread. "You're hurt. You need a doctor."

"It's not as bad as it looks. Hurry, and then we can take care of that."

Kate removed Dave's belt and laid the cell phone that had been clipped to it on the ground. Then she began to wind the belt around the young man's wrists. "Make it as tight as you can," Dave said. When she finished and cinched the belt tight using the buckle, Dave nodded. "It'll take some work to get out of that."

Carefully Dave moved off of him and tugged at the man's shoulders to roll him over. Kate pushed at the man's hip. When they had him on his back, Dave loosened the man's belt with his right hand, tugged it loose, and handed it to Kate. "Now his ankles."

Still gasping, the man struggled as though to get up. Dave put his left knee on the man's chest, picked up the knife from the ground, and held it where the man could see it. The man stopped struggling and Kate began to wind his belt around his ankles.

The young man was bleeding badly from a cut above his left eyebrow, and his cheek was oozing blood from a bad scrape. When he raised his head to see what Kate was doing, blood ran into his eyes. They went wide in panic and he turned to look at Dave. "Bleeding," he croaked.

Dave touched his own side gingerly and looked down at the red wetness on his fingertips. "Yeah."

"Wasn't gonna . . . hurt . . . the lady," the man gasped out.

"Liar! Keep your mouth shut," Dave snapped. Anger was plain on his face.

Kate cinched the belt tight around the young man's ankles and backed away from him.

Dave stood very slowly and backed away too.

"Bleeding," the man muttered again, and noisily sucked in a breath.

"Keep your head tilted back and lay still," Dave answered. "That might keep you from losing too much blood." His tone was anything but sympathetic. He touched his hand to his side again; the palm was red when he took it away. He sat down on the ground about ten feet away from the other man.

Kate picked up Dave's cell phone and dialed 911. When the dispatcher answered, Kate said, "We need help immediately. My friend's been stabbed, and he's bleeding."

"What is the address?"

Kate gave her the name of the park. "By the west entrance. Please send an ambulance. Hurry!" She heard the dispatcher call out a paramedic unit. Then the dispatcher asked: "How bad is your friend's injury?"

"I don't know. It's hard to tell. It's . . ." She looked closely at Dave's side; his fingers covered the wound. "He's bleeding a lot."

Dave shook his head "It's not a stab wound. It's only a slash." He reached into his back pocket for his handkerchief.

"The other man's bleeding too," Kate said to the dispatcher. "He's—"

"The other man?" she answered. "There were two people attacked?"

"No, this is the man who did it. We're holding him. He's—"

"*You're* holding him? Wait a minute." Kate heard the dispatcher call a patrol car and direct it to the park. Then she came back on the line. "We'll have a couple of officers there in about two minutes."

"The other man is tied up." Kate glanced at him and noticed that he was watching her. "If he tries to get up, he'll probably pass out. He's losing blood and he may have a concussion." Actually, it looked like the man's bleeding had slowed down. But he didn't need to know that.

Kate walked over to where Dave was sitting on the sidewalk. "I've got to help my friend, so I'm going to put the phone down."

"Please leave the line open until the officers get there."

Kate heard a siren in the distance. She knelt at Dave's side and put the phone on the ground. Dave started to shift his position so he could face her, then winced with pain and sat still instead. The handkerchief he had pressed to his side was turning red. "Do you want to lay down and let me hold that?" Kate asked. "Maybe I could put more pressure on it."

Dave glanced at the other man. "No, I've got it. Just don't go anywhere."

The siren was louder now. The other man rolled to his side and moved as though trying to get up again. "Don't do anything stupid," Dave said to him. "All they'll have to do is follow the trail of blood until they find you passed out somewhere."

The man continued trying to get to his knees, wavered, then toppled onto his side again and lay still, breathing hoarsely.

Kate moved to Dave's right side and sat down next to him.

With his free hand, he reached for hers. "You scared me when you started to run away," he said. "I thought at first it was crazy. Where did you learn to go for the throat like that?"

"From Tom, when I was in college. I had a couple of night classes, and he didn't think it was safe for me to be walking around campus late at night by myself, so he taught me some basic self-defense."

Dave nodded toward the man on the ground. "I was sure he would catch you, and if you fought him . . ."

"*I* was afraid he was going to use that knife on you again. I had to keep him from doing it. I thought he had hurt you badly. You shocked me when you took him down like that."

"Part high school wrestling, part hand-to-hand combat training. I was playing hurt, waiting for him to get closer so I could surprise him." He paused. "You were protecting *me*?"

She nodded. "I had to. You wouldn't have gotten hurt if you hadn't been trying to protect me."

Kate leaned her head on his shoulder. "I *had* to," she repeated. "I couldn't let anything happen to you."

* * *

"Stay there and I'll come around to help you," she said.

"I'm all right," Dave answered as he slowly turned to the side and put his feet out of the car.

"I know—you said that at the park and at the hospital. But stay there and let me help you anyway." Kate shut the driver's door and hurried around to the passenger side of his car.

He was easing to a standing position. "I'm OK—really."

"The doctor said you shouldn't put any strain on those stitches."

"I know—no exercise, no stretching, no lifting. And be very careful about having a good laugh." He put on a mock scowl. "No kidding around, Kate. I've had enough of cut-ups."

She laughed. "Behave yourself."

He walked to the front door and fished in his pocket for his house key. "Do you want to come in for a minute?"

"Long enough to be sure you're all right before I leave."

He stood looking at her, toying with the key in his hand. "Thanks for hanging in there with me tonight." Slowly he leaned forward and kissed her mouth, lightly at first and then more firmly. She returned it.

When Dave broke it off, they stood looking into each other's eyes again. And then the moment passed.

Not since Jeanine, Dave thought. *I haven't felt like doing that with anyone since Jeanine. And now, when I'm around Kate . . .*

She was married, Kate remembered—*was* married, used to be married . . . would be married forever once she was sealed to Steve in the temple. *What would Steve think?* That question whispered itself softly in the back of her mind each time Dave put an arm around her, or held her hand—or kissed her.

Besides, Dave's children were close by—just beyond the door.

Kate put her arms around him at shoulder level and hugged him lightly, careful not to press against his left side. "I'm just glad you weren't any closer to that knife."

Dave unlocked the front door and eased it open. Kate followed him into the living room and shut the door behind them. "Are you going to tell your kids tonight?" she asked softly.

"No, they don't need to know until tomorrow. I don't want to wake them up."

"Tell us what?" Kelli's voice came from the corner of the room, which lit up suddenly as she switched on the reading lamp next to Dave's recliner, where she had been curled up. "Where have you been?"

"Oh, Kelli!" Dave turned carefully toward her. "I'm sorry it's so late. We were—"

"I'm sorry you were too busy to call." Kelli glared at Kate as she crossed the room to stand in front of her father. "Alicia made herself sick crying. We were—*she* was worried about you. She kept asking me, 'What if Daddy doesn't come home? What will we do?' I couldn't get her to stop crying, and she finally threw up before she went to sleep. I think she might have a fever."

Dave turned toward the hallway and walked slowly to the girls' room. Kelli followed, and so did Kate.

The bedroom had two twin beds with a nightstand between them. The bed on the left, with a stuffed monkey lying on the pillow and two movie posters on the wall above it, was apparently Kelli's. Alicia lay asleep in the bed on the right. Dave sat down carefully on the edge of it and snapped on the lamp on the nightstand. Alicia stirred, opened her eyes to look at him, then reached out her hands to take hold of his right arm. She clung to him.

He shifted carefully so he could reach out with his left hand to stroke her forehead gently. "How are you feeling, Sweetheart?"

Tears welled up in Alicia's eyes and her lower lip quivered. "Not very good."

Dave let his hand rest on her forehead for a moment, frowned, then looked at Kate and Kelli, watching from the doorway, and shook his head slightly.

Kate raised her eyebrows. "Do you have a thermometer?"

"In the bathroom. Medicine cabinet."

Kate cleaned the thermometer with a cotton ball soaked in alcohol, then brought it back to the bedroom and knelt by the bed. Alicia still clung to her father's arm. Kate smiled at her. "Shall we find out if you have a fever?" Alicia opened her mouth and let Kate slide the thermometer under her tongue.

156

Kate brushed the blonde hair back from Alicia's face with her fingers. What could she say to take away some of the fear she saw in this child's eyes? "Were you worried about your daddy?"

The little girl nodded.

Dave had dropped his left hand to his lap and straightened up to avoid putting strain on his left side. Kate stroked Alicia's forehead lightly. "Heavenly Father watches over your dad for you. He knows how much you need him right now."

Alicia thought about what Kate had said for a moment, then nodded.

"Did you ask Him to protect your daddy when you said your prayers?"

Again, Alicia nodded.

"He heard you. Heavenly Father always hears you."

Dave squeezed his daughter's hand. She smiled at him.

"Sometimes I get scared," Kate said. "When I'm flying and there's a storm up ahead, I wonder if I can get around it. Or sometimes if KatiLynn or Stevie aren't home by the time they're supposed to be, I worry about them. Do you get scared that way?"

Alicia looked at her father, then nodded once more.

"When I'm afraid like that, I pray to Heavenly Father. He helps the fear go away and helps me feel peaceful inside. Have you ever had that happen?"

Alicia frowned and shook her head.

"I know Heavenly Father listens when you ask Him to help. Do you think you could remember to pray the next time you're worried about your daddy?"

Alicia nodded. Kate put her hand on top of the girl's hand, which was still grasping Dave's arm, and squeezed it. Alicia looked into her eyes for several seconds, then let go of her father's arm with one of her hands and put it on top of Kate's hand. She lay holding onto both of the adults.

Ordinarily, Kate thought, she might feel a bit out of place trying to comfort someone else's child. Undoubtedly Alicia's mother would have known exactly what to say. But then ordinarily Alicia's mother would also be here tomorrow morning and every other morning to help reinforce the lesson about prayer. Kate felt the pull of her own children right now; she needed to go pick them up. But if there was any way a mother—even someone else's—could help this child for the moment, she had to do it.

She took the thermometer out of Alicia's mouth and held it up to the light so she could read it. "Hmm—no fever. That's good. Is your tummy feeling any better?"

Alicia smiled weakly. "A little."

Kate glanced at her watch: a quarter to one. But maybe . . . "Do you need anything to eat? Or drink?"

"No. Kelli gave me some water after I threw up."

Kate glanced in Kelli's direction. The older girl should have been relieved that her sister was feeling better. But that wasn't what Kate saw in her face. There was anger, and defiance.

Why?

Dave put Alicia's hand into his left hand, lying in his lap, and stroked his younger daughter's forehead again with his right. "Do you think you can go back to sleep now, Ally? I'll stay right here until you do, and then I'll be right there in my bedroom."

Alicia nodded.

"That's my princess. Remember?" Dave began to hum "Some Day My Prince Will Come," from Walt Disney's *Snow White*. Alicia smiled and closed her eyes.

"I'll put this thermometer away," Kate said. She walked to the bedroom doorway and squeezed past Kelli. "Excuse me."

"I hate you!" Kelli hissed softly as Kate passed. "You pretend you care, but it doesn't matter to you if you keep my dad from being with his kids when they need him. I hate you."

Kate stopped to look at her, stunned.

Kelli stared at her coldly, then turned away to watch her father and her sister.

Mechanically, Kate walked to the bathroom to put the thermometer back in its place. When she turned to walk out again, her mind was in such turmoil that she couldn't remember if she had actually put the thermometer into the medicine cabinet and had to check to be sure.

She stood looking at the girl leaning against the doorjamb of the bedroom. Insolence—pure insolence! Was it jealousy that had made her say something so spiteful? Was she so threatened by the idea that her father might find another woman that she had to destroy a relationship before it could get started?

Or was Kelli right? Kate had worried about leaving her own children again tonight—the second night this week—even though they were with her mother. Did she have a right to do that so she could enjoy herself? And was she wrong to take Dave away from his children?

She wasn't sure. But she didn't think it was wrong for her and Dave to enjoy being together. And this self-centered young girl didn't seem so concerned about her father's well-being as she did about having her way.

Kate walked up the hallway and took hold of Kelli's arm.

Kelli glared at her. "Let go of me!" she whispered.

Kate turned the girl so her back was against the wall, just outside the door. "Your father's hurt," she said flatly. "A man with a knife cut him. He has stitches in his side."

Kelli gasped and looked over her shoulder at her father's shirt, noticing for the first time the tear just above the belt line and the dark stain around it. She looked at Kate again. "Why didn't you . . ."

"Tell you?" Kate whispered. "In front of your little sister? Right now?" She nodded toward Dave. "Someone needs to check his stitches before he goes to bed and make sure they aren't bleeding too much. Do you think you could help with that, or do you want me to stay and take care of it?"

"Dad?" Kelli said.

He turned to look at her.

She walked across the room, knelt beside him, and put her head down on his knee, careful not to touch his side. "Dad! Are you all right?"

He glanced at Kate, then looked back at his daughter. "Yeah, sure, Kell. I'm OK." He rested his left hand on her head while he continued to run the fingers of his right hand lightly across Alicia's forehead.

Kate left them that way. She walked out of the house, went to his car for the bag of medical supplies they had given him at the hospital, put them just inside the front door of the house, then stepped outside and shut the door.

It was cool in the early morning now. Why was she sweating? In fact, she was trembling.

Maybe what she had just done to Kelli was cruel. She had let a self-centered fifteen-year-old bring out the worst in her at the moment. But a part of her did not care.

She would have to repent of that.

Later.

Numbly, she reached into the pocket of her skirt for Dave's keys. Drive the car home, he had said. Bring it back in the morning.

While she and Dave had waited at the hospital for a doctor to take care of him, she had gone over their experience at the park again and again in her mind trying to decide what it meant for her—and for the two of them.

She had been willing to put herself between him and the knife, without even thinking of the possible cost to her, or to her children.

It was time to admit that he meant more to her than simple companionship.

And yet, could he ever be more than a sometime companion if she had to compete with his daughter?

Thinking things through at the hospital, Kate had to acknowledge that she was feeling the need for a man in her life again. Perhaps that was why the thought of having Dave taken away suddenly, like Steve, had terrified her tonight.

And yet she had barely begun to sort out how deep her feelings were for him.

She might never get the chance to do that, if Dave's daughter had her way.

Kate wondered if she could ever be completely his—or any other man's—with her feelings for Steve lingering in the background.

She realized she was sitting behind the wheel of his sports car, and she could not remember unlocking the door and getting in. Her hand shook as she tried to put the key into the ignition switch. Tears came to her eyes. She tried to will them to stop, but she could not.

Why now? Why not in the park, after that man . . . or when the police came . . . or at the hospital, when they were stitching him up?

Driving here from the hospital, she had felt gratitude and exhilaration that they had been protected, that they had escaped serious injury, or worse. Now she was struggling, not knowing whether to respond to the relief of their escape in the park, the clarity of her realization at the hospital, or the ugliness of the confrontation just now.

She felt like crying.

Or laughing.

Or screaming.

13

"How did you get my car home so early?" Dave asked. "I didn't even hear you."

Kate cradled the telephone on her shoulder while she put the last of the Saturday morning breakfast dishes in the sink. "I called a cab last night. Your keys are on the bookcase in your living room."

"*Why?* Why didn't you just take my car?"

"I, uh . . . I didn't want to disturb you early this morning." The truth was that she hadn't wanted to risk another confrontation with Kelli by going back to his house.

"Is something wrong, Kate?" He sounded puzzled.

"No."

"Good. Then how about dinner tonight? Last night didn't turn out so well."

"I don't think so. We . . . maybe that's not a good idea."

"Why not?" He sounded puzzled again.

"Well, we've already been out two nights this week—left our kids all alone . . ."

There was silence for several seconds, and when he spoke Kate could hear anger in his voice. "Kelli said something to you last night, didn't she? What was it?"

"She may be right—I *have* been taking you away from your family. And I've been away from mine too. Maybe we need to think about that."

"Kate, I can't tell you what's best between you and your kids, but I know mine aren't really suffering. I could try to be there every waking minute for them because their mother is gone—but that would be overprotective. I give them all the love I know how to give. I'm doing everything I can." He sounded frustrated.

"I know—it isn't easy. I have the same problem you do; my children feel like I'm gone too much." Stevie's "Aw, Mom" had become automatic whenever she told them she was going out.

"But your kids aren't like Kelli, are they?" Dave asked. "I can't imagine KatiLynn giving you the kind of grief Kelli gives me."

Actually, the questions from KatiLynn this morning had been pointed. First it was, "Why were you out so late?" Then when she had heard the story of last night—without some of the more frightening details—there had been alarm and something of a challenge in her voice: "Are you going out again tonight?"

But that was not Kate's first reason for turning down his dinner invitation. "Dave, I don't know if I can fight your daughter over being with you. I don't think I should. I don't want to make her an enemy, and I don't want to create problems for you."

"I don't see how *you* could ever make anyone an enemy. And why don't you let me worry about any problems for me?"

He was right in one way, Kate thought; as long as there was no real commitment between them, it was not her problem to resolve. "But I still think we shouldn't go out again tonight. Maybe sometime next week—some night other than Friday. Is that OK with you?"

He sighed. "I guess it has to be."

"Disappointed?"

"Yes."

"Me too. Really. Would you call me? Please?"

"Yeah. Sure." He paused. "Would every day be OK? I *need* to talk to you, Kate."

She smiled to herself. "I'd like that."

"And every evening?"

She laughed. "I'll look forward to it."

The thought stayed with her after they said their good-byes. Not only would she look forward to his calls, she would have a struggle waiting until next week to see him. She had come to enjoy his company very much.

No—it was more than that. She *needed* his company, the way he said he needed to talk to her.

Why couldn't Kelli understand? Or KatiLynn? Especially KatiLynn, who had seemed excited at first when her mother started dating.

She hadn't seemed excited about it this morning.

"If I go out tonight, I'll leave you with Grandma and Grandpa. You like staying with them, don't you?"

162

KatiLynn speared the last bite of her breakfast with her fork. "Uh huh." She examined the wedge of blueberry pancake—her favorite—closely, then put it back down on her plate. "But it's been every Friday night now, and now Saturday night too." She sat looking into her mother's eyes.

Kate put down her fork and returned her daughter's gaze. "Is it bothering you that I'm dating Dave?"

"No." KatiLynn looked down at the table. "Maybe."

"I thought you liked him?"

Her daughter nodded. "He's nice."

"But?"

KatiLynn looked up at her again. "It's not him. We don't get to do anything with you anymore."

"We went to the movie last Saturday, and the park before—"

"Just with you. It was always just us on Friday nights, or on Saturday when we went to the movies—you and me and Stevie. Now a lot of the time you're out with Dave."

"Sweetheart, it would have been like that sometimes if your father had lived. You may not remember it, but he and I used to leave you with Grandma and Grandpa while we went out together. When people are married, they do that to help their relationship because they love each other. Your father and I did that, and you'll do that too someday."

"But you're not married to Dave."

"If I were—or if I married someone else—would you be afraid that I couldn't love you anymore? That will never happen. No one could ever make me stop loving you."

"Mom, whenever you take us anywhere now, there's always Dave, and Alicia and Ross too."

It wasn't completely true. Kate made an effort to spend time with just KatiLynn and Stevie at least once a week, and to do special things with them like fixing their favorite breakfast this morning. But she wasn't going to argue that point because it sounded like the real issue might be something else. "Is it his children? I know Ross does things that aren't very nice sometimes. He's—"

"He's mean!"

There was an element of truth in what her daughter said. "Yes, sometimes he has been," Kate conceded. But there was another side to the story. How to handle this? "Do you think maybe you've said things sometimes that could have hurt his feelings or made him mad?"

Her daughter frowned and turned to gaze out the window.

"KatiLynn, I know you try very hard not to be mean to people. But are there times when you feel like you just have to let him know he's not your boss? Or that he's not as hot as he thinks he is?"

"Boys are so . . ." KatiLynn wrinkled her nose in exasperation as she looked at her mother again. *"So* dumb *sometimes!"*

Kate smiled. "They're just boys. Your Uncle Tom used to do some of the same things to me when we were young. It wouldn't be much different if Ross were your older brother."

"Well, he's not *older, and he's* not *my brother!"*

Kate reached out to touch her daughter's hand. "I know that. I'll try to make sure he's not mean to you whenever they're around."

KatiLynn's look suggested that she doubted her mother would have any influence with Dave's son.

"Will you try to be patient? Boys usually grow out of that kind of behavior, at least by the time they're thirteen or fourteen."

"How long does it take girls to grow out of it?" KatiLynn asked.

She meant Kelli.

Kelli was even more of a problem for KatiLynn than Ross. Dave's son was guilty of pushing ahead of KatiLynn and Stevie on the trampoline, of a deliberate bump sometimes, of mocking laughter. Kelli's actions were more subtle, but probably more damaging: cutting barbs at the opportune moment, snide remarks calculated to make KatiLynn feel small and childish. Ross simply seemed to follow the lead of his older sister in the way he treated KatiLynn.

Kelli's hostility was not directed primarily at KatiLynn, of course. Dave's older daughter made no secret of the disdain she felt for her father's "girlfriend." Kate knew it was a constant source of frustration for Dave. *And I don't know how much more of it I can take.*

Yet Kelli showed no animosity toward Stevie. In fact, she had been oddly tender with him at times. The girl was a puzzle.

That puzzle stayed with Kate until she arrived at her office. Then the stack of flight service maintenance records that she and Ann had set aside for this Saturday morning took her mind off of Dave or his family.

Until 11:15.

She heard Ann, in the outer office, laugh and say, "Wow! Valentine's Day was weeks ago. Where did you get—" Ann stopped as though someone had cut her off.

"Is she in there?" Kate could barely make out the words, but it was Dave's voice.

As she walked to the door to look out, she was met by a large spray of red roses in a vase that Dave held in his hands. He stepped into the office, shut the door behind him, and put the roses on her desk.

She opened her mouth to speak, but he put his fingers on her lips to stop her.

"Don't say anything, Kate." He smiled at her. "Please don't say anything. Just listen."

He took hold of her hands. "I love you. I can't say just when it happened, but I've fallen in love with you. I need you in my life." He put his arms around her and kissed her, keeping his lips on hers for a long time.

She simply let him hold her at first, trying not to admit to herself how much she wanted this. But she could not make herself deny what she felt. Slowly she put her arms around Dave, pressed her hands against his back, and clung to him.

When he finally broke off the kiss, he put her head against his chest and gently stroked her hair. "I had to tell you that I want to live the rest of my life with you. Whatever problems there might be, we can work them out if you feel about me the way I feel about you."

She stood still, enjoying his arms around her, enjoying the warmth and strength of him. But finally she tilted her head back to look into his eyes. "Dave, I don't know if—"

"Shh. Not now." He kissed her again. She wondered momentarily if the two of them should be doing this here, now—or ever. But this was not a time for thinking. She pressed her lips against his and was sorry again when he ended the kiss. She laid her head on his chest once more.

He squeezed her tightly. "Don't say you don't know if the two of us could have a future together. You kissed me back, so I know you feel something too."

Kate nodded. "But we need to talk."

"I know. Not now. I'm not asking for an answer from you right now. Just think it over. I have, and I know I need you in my life."

She stood back to look into his eyes, and as she let him go, she accidentally brushed her hand across the bandage on the knife cut he had received last night. He winced slightly.

"Oh, Dave, I'm sorry! Is it—"

"It's all right." He put his fingers over her lips again and smiled. "Just think about what I said. We'll talk about it in a day or two." He turned and walked out of her office.

As she watched him go, Kate remembered again that she had been willing to face that knife last night. She could no longer ignore the reason. *I couldn't bear the thought of seeing him get hurt.*

She had been ducking the question of whether she could love David Cutler by keeping their relationship in the "just good friends" category in her mind. But no longer. Somehow she and Dave had become much more than friends in what seemed like only a few dates. Of course, there had also been a few family dinners, and jogging or walking together several times in the early morning. Kate wasn't sure just when the change had taken place in her own heart, but now the thought of spending the rest of her life without him seemed depressing. He was tender and kind toward her. He made her happy when she was with him. He was a good father, and the kind of man who guided his life by the right stars morally. He brought a peace into her life that she had not known for a long time.

For nearly six years, she had longed for the opportunity to be with Steve again—and now that she knew it was possible, there was Dave. When they were apart, she sometimes felt confused about her feelings, but when they were together, her feelings for him blocked out other considerations.

And there were plenty of other things to consider—his children, for example. Could she possibly handle them? Could she ask her own daughter and son to deal with Kelli and Ross?

And how would she ever explain to Steve someday that there had been another man in her life?

Or maybe Steve would know all along. How would he feel about that? Since she planned to be sealed to him for eternity, would it be wrong somehow—unfaithful in a way—to marry another man in this life and share herself with him?

Was that something she could talk to the bishop about?

Ann peered through the office doorway. "The flowers are beautiful—very impressive." She grinned. "Must have been quite a date last night."

Kate smiled weakly. "Definitely out of the ordinary. We ended up in the hospital emergency room."

Ann's eyebrows arched. Her mouth opened, but she didn't say anything.

"A man with a knife tried to rob us in a park," Kate explained. "Dave got cut, but the other guy is in worse shape."

"You mean Dave just took him on?" Anne frowned slightly. "That's brave. *Really* brave. But what if he hadn't been able to . . ." She left the sentence hanging.

"Dave was trying to cooperate and calm the guy down so no one would get hurt," Kate answered. "The man cut him anyway. But I think he didn't expect both of us to fight back."

"You mean *you* . . ." Ann's eyes went wide. "I don't know if I'd have been able to do anything at all in a situation like that. I'd have been terrified."

"You'd have done something if you'd been in my place. I had to keep him from using that knife on Dave again." Kate briefly laid out the sequence of events in the park.

Ann shook her head. "You were both very lucky."

"Blessed, I think."

Ann glanced at the roses. "And the flowers . . ."

"Don't have anything at all to do with last night. They're because . . . because, um, I told him this morning that I was wondering whether we ought to be going out so much."

"Why? What did he do wrong?"

"Nothing. He's a wonderful man. I'm happy when I'm with him."

"Kate, you *sound* like a woman in love," Ann said uncertainly.

"Yes. Yes, I do, don't I?"

Ann smiled, but the smile changed to a puzzled look as tears began to slide down Kate's cheeks. "What's wrong?"

"His daughter hates me!"

Ann frowned. "Oh. *Oh*." She thought for a moment. "I see your problem."

Kate nodded. "That's not the hardest part." She wiped the tears from her cheeks. "I've never stopped loving Steve. How can I be in love with two men at the same time?"

* * *

Dave took the dish Kelli handed him and put it into the dishwasher. "Thanks for all your help. Have I told you lately how much I appreciate all you do around here?" He leaned over and kissed her on the cheek.

She smiled and reddened slightly. "Thanks, Daddy."

"You've taken on a lot of responsibility—more than anyone should have to carry at your age. I'm sorry it's been so hard on you since your mom died."

"I don't mind." She kept her eyes on the sink and handed him the next dish.

They worked in silence for several minutes, Kelli rinsing the dishes and her father placing them in the dishwasher.

"I wish I could make things easier for you," he said finally.

"It's OK, Daddy, really. I can handle it," Kelli answered.

She *will* handle it, Dave thought. His older daughter never gave up on anything she determined in her own mind to do, and she had assigned herself certain roles in the home in her mother's absence. *Wish she'd ease up on herself.*

"I know you can handle it," he said. "But I don't want you to cheat yourself out of some of the things you'll only do while you're young. I want you to have time to do things with your friends."

Kelli glanced at him curiously. "I do those things. I went to the library with Callie and Lisa Tuesday night."

"Yes, to study. But I wouldn't mind if you take time to do some of the other things you'd probably like to do with friends."

Kelli frowned. "Why are you telling me this?"

"Because you need things like that in your life at your age. Everybody does. I've watched Ross and Alicia lately, and KatiLynn and Stevie when they're around, all doing the usual kid things. But you don't give yourself much of a chance to do the normal high school things. Sometimes I think you're growing up too fast."

Kelli's frown deepened and her eyes narrowed. "This is about *her* somehow, isn't it?"

"Who?" Dave said, surprised.

"Your *girlfriend.*"

"No. This is about you," Dave said evenly. "Kate doesn't have . . . what made you think Kate could possibly have anything to do with this?"

"Because *everything* is about her anymore!"

"Kell, I want you to listen to me and believe what I tell you. Kate cares about you. She told me when we were at the hospital that I ought to call you so you wouldn't worry, but I didn't want to wake you. It's my fault you didn't know until we got home. And Kate has nothing to do with what I'm talking to you about right now. *I'm* your father, and *I'm* the one who's watching you wear yourself out sometimes. I've been thinking that I can do more to take some of the pressure off of you. If your mother were here, *she'd* tell you that she wouldn't want you trying to take on so much."

"Why? Haven't I been doing a good job?"

"Yes, you have. I just told you that, and—"

"And Mom *isn't* here, is she?" It was angry, and bitter.

Dave tried very hard not to respond to his daughter's tone. "That's not my fault, and it's not yours. It's not anybody's. We all have to go on until we can be with Mom again. In the meantime, I'd like to have—"

"You'd like to have your girlfriend take Mom's place! Well, she never will! She never could."

Dave pressed on patiently. "What I'd like is to have a loving relationship with each of my children that lets them grow up at a normal rate. I'm trying to tell you that I appreciate everything you've done to help and I couldn't have asked for more. I *wouldn't* have asked for more. I don't want you to feel like you have to be the cook, the cleaner, and the mother too."

"Well, Kate will never be the mother here!" Kelli's voice had risen to just below the level of a shout. Dave hoped it didn't carry down the hall; Ross and Alicia were supposed to be sleeping.

"And if she ever moves into this house with us," Kelli continued defiantly, "I'm out of here as soon as I can find a place to go!" She balled up the dishrag and threw it into the sink, then turned and ran out of the room. Dave heard the door to the girls' bedroom slam shut and the lock click into place.

He sighed, fished the dishrag out of the sink, and began wiping cheese sauce out of a saucepan.

Once upon a time there had been a little girl who liked to crawl into his lap and have him tell her stories in which she was the beautiful princess that the handsome prince came to rescue. Where had that little girl gone?

14

The restaurant was well known locally, a steakhouse called Frank's, and the vehicles in the parking lot were an indicator of its clientele; they ranged from hefty pickup trucks with ranch dirt on the side panels to upscale SUVs and a Mercedes sedan.

Kate maneuvered her car into a spot near the door, then waited as Kenji got out and walked around to the driver's door to open it for her. When he had called to tell her the day he would be arriving, he had seemed pleased when she said be glad to make dinner arrangements. But he had seemed uncertain about the arrangements today when she told him she would pick him up at his hotel and there would be no need to dress formally.

His version of informal was a sport jacket and no tie with his white shirt. She wore a dressy pair of pants and a nice blouse—but nothing too fancy. Her choice of clothing and of the restaurant had been deliberate.

Frank, the owner, greeted them personally. He looked at her a second time, glanced briefly at Kenji, then looked back at her. "It's been a long time. It's good to see you again, Mrs. . . . Warden, isn't it?"

She smiled at the man. "My husband and I used to come here often—but I haven't gone out for dinner a lot since he died."

"I remember. The plane crash. I never had a chance to say I'm sorry for your loss—but welcome back." He looked at Kenji uncertainly. "Would you like a table, or a booth?"

Kate spoke before Kenji could. "A booth would be nice." She turned to Kenji. "Will that be all right?" In Japan, a woman probably would not speak for the president of Nakamura Electronics. She hoped she had not made him feel uncomfortable.

Nothing in his face indicated he was disturbed by her assertiveness. "Yes, a booth, if that's what you'd like."

They followed Frank to a corner booth. When they were seated and Frank had walked away, Kenji looked around the room. "I remember this place," he said, smiling at her. "Steve brought me here once for lunch. The best steaks in Arizona, he said. I think he was right."

They talked about his business while they waited to order and then to be served. If he was eager for an answer to the question he had left with her, it was not obvious. Kenji was the rare combination of a dynamic personality and a man of patience.

Kate had given a great deal of thought to her answer. But she left it to him to bring up the subject.

He waited until they were in the middle of dinner, less likely to be disturbed by the server. "I hope I've given you enough time to think about the question I asked you."

"Yes. Yes, I've thought about it a lot." She put down her fork and sat back against the cushion of the booth. "I'm deeply touched that you would think of me that way, Kenji. You're one of the finest men I know. Any woman would be lucky to have you for a husband." She paused. "But I . . . you and I . . ." She had worked through this moment a dozen times in her mind, had almost rehearsed what she would say, but now, looking him in the eyes, it was harder than she had imagined. "The two of us . . ."

Kenji shook his head and smiled sadly. "There's no need to go on, Kate. I think I recognize the sound of 'no' when I hear it."

They looked into each other's eyes for several seconds, until Kate said finally, "It's important to me for you to understand why."

He nodded. "Go on."

"Please believe what I said. Any woman would be lucky to have you for a husband. But some things have happened in my life that would make remarriage more complicated for me."

His brow wrinkled questioningly.

"Do you know what a Mormon is?" she asked.

"Yes, of course. It's an American religion. They have one of their temples in Hawaii—a beautiful place. I saw it when I was a boy."

"There's one in Tokyo too, and Fukuoka. I'm a Mormon, Kenji—a member of The Church of Jesus Christ of Latter-day Saints. I was baptized almost eleven months ago."

He smiled slightly. "Your religion wouldn't be a problem, Kate. I told you about Lily's faith. She was a practicing Catholic, and it was never a problem between us."

Kate thought for a moment. "What do *you* believe about God, Kenji?"

"I thought I knew that, when I was younger, but now . . ." He shrugged. "I'm not sure. Lily believed that God is our Father. I don't *know* what God is, but I can't believe that we're the highest form of life—at least, I hope not."

"Mormons have some things in common with Catholics," Kate said. "We both believe that God is our Father. He is eternal, and in our church we believe that as His children—the spirits He created—we're eternal too."

Kenji smiled. "You could be right, Kate. I could live with that idea."

"There's more," she said carefully. "Because we're eternal, we can be married for eternity." She gave the idea a moment to sink in before she went on. "That means Steve and I can be husband and wife forever. I'm going to have that ceremony done for us, in one of the Church's temples."

Kenji frowned. "And that means you could never get married again?"

"No—not exactly. But it means that after this life is over, I'll be Steve's wife, for always."

"My friend Steve was a generous man, a very kind man," Kenji said slowly. "He told me the last time we talked that the thing that made him happiest was to see his wife and children happy. I know if he were here, he'd be watching out for you as best he could." He paused. "But Steve *isn't* here now. And you would always have the best I can offer to help you be happy."

"It's thoughtful of you to feel protective of me, Kenji. But if I get married again in this life, the man will have to understand that I will be Steve's in the end. Lately when I've thought about remarriage . . . well, I'm still not sure how I feel about it, and I'm not sure how Steve will . . . how he would feel about it."

Kenji studied her face for a moment. "There's another man in your life right now, isn't there?"

"Yes." *Perceptive. That's one of Kenji's strengths.* Kate felt herself start to blush. *But why should I be embarrassed?*

"A member of your church?"

She nodded.

"Well, I suppose I feel a little better about that—I think. At least I can feel better about losing out to a real person, not just an idea." He paused. "Is he a good man? One who could take care of you the way Steve would?"

"Yes." It wasn't that simple, really. Dave did not have all of Steve's strengths, all of Steve's drive, but he was strong in areas where Steve had not been. He was more well-rounded. She had thought about this a lot. But Kenji did not need to hear the comparison.

"Tell me more about him. Has he been married before, in the way you talked about—forever?"

Kate nodded. "His wife died about three years ago."

"Then you would believe that she is waiting for him?"

"Yes, that's true."

"This man loves you deeply—the way Steve did? And you love him?"

The question took her off guard; she had not yet put the answer into words for anyone else. "I, uh . . ." Kate was sure she was blushing this time. "Well, I've never actually said that to him."

"Why not? What would stop you from being happy with this man for the next thirty or forty years?"

"Steve. I still love Steve too, so . . ."

"If you're right about Steve still being alive out there somewhere—if you really believe that—do you think he'd want you to stay alone? I don't think I'd want Lily to be all alone."

"Well, no, you wouldn't, and maybe Steve . . . but it isn't so simple, Kenji. I mean, have you *really* thought about what it would be like to live with another woman—me, or anyone else? Are you ready to give yourself completely to another woman the way you did to Lily—so completely that she would never have to wonder if you were thinking of your first love?"

He thought it over. "Umm—I see what you mean. And for a woman that could be even more difficult, couldn't it?"

Kate nodded.

They sat in silence for several seconds. Then Kate said, "I have to ask this. Is what you've felt for me really love? Or is it more a feeling of needing to be close to someone?"

He looked away for a moment, thinking, and she knew the answer before he spoke. "I admire you, Kate. I respect you. You're a beautiful and intelligent woman. I'm sure I would learn to love you."

She smiled at him, saying nothing. He studied her face. "But that isn't what *you'd* need, is it?"

Slowly Kate shook her head. "You told me once to be true to my own judgment. You should be true to your own heart in this, Kenji. Find a woman that you can't wait to go home to—someone who has your heart along with your admiration." She paused. "Have you looked at home? Aren't there any women around you that you want to know better?"

His lips formed a thin smile. "My father has talked to me about this several times. I should marry again, a traditional Japanese woman—one who would be silent, support me in the home, and leave my career to me. But women like that don't really make me want to know them better. Steve once told me I'm a man of two cultures; I need the kinds of things Lily had to offer. She spoke up when she thought I needed to hear something. She was a strong woman, a good partner."

"Perhaps you might find a younger woman—one who could also give you children?"

"At my age? Many men my age are grandfathers."

Kate laughed. "I think you'd make a wonderful father. You wouldn't be afraid to try it, would you?"

"I, uh . . ." He laughed nervously. It was one of the few times Kate had seen Kenji Nakamura at a loss for words. "I suppose not. I hadn't thought about that. And there are many younger women who are not afraid to speak up the way Lily did."

"How would your father feel about grandchildren?"

"I'm not sure." Kenji thought for a moment. "He's never said anything about it—I think he doesn't want to hurt me—but I know he would be proud to have a grandson to follow in the company some day."

"Or a granddaughter?"

"He would be pleased. And I would want her to grow up to be just like you, Kate."

She laughed again. "You don't know how stubborn or difficult I can be sometimes. Did Steve ever tell you about *that*?" Her smile faded. "But it means a lot to me that you think of me the way you do. If I had never found the Church, or if I had never met Dave . . ." She left the thought hanging.

He smiled ruefully. "So—only friendly competitors then?"

"Friends, Kenji. Always friends. Please don't stop calling me or letting me hear from you. I'll want to know when you find happiness with someone."

"I'm not sure I'm up to starting a search, Kate—at least not yet." He hesitated. "I *am* sad that you could not see your way clear to, ah . . . but I'm happy for you that you have found someone."

"Actually, he found me, and it's far from a sure thing. We would have some problems to overcome." Her brow furrowed. "His children . . . well, his daughter hates me."

"*Hates* you? It's hard for me to imagine anyone could feel that way about you. Why?"

"Because I'm not her mother. Her mother died—went away and left her. His oldest daughter and his son have gotten used to life without their mother. I'm an intruder."

"But if this man is all you say he is, could you not work out the problems?"

"Maybe. We've talked about it."

Kenji thought for several seconds. "I wish you well, Kate. I honestly mean that. But if things don't work out for the two of you . . ."

"Thank you, Kenji. I value your friendship." It was the nicest way she knew to indicate that friends were all they would ever be.

* * *

She had driven Kenji back to his hotel, said good–bye as warmly as she felt she could, asked him again to keep in touch, and left him with a farewell wave as he walked into the hotel.

This morning, she found herself hoping that Kenji would be able to find happiness, but she felt no particular sense of loss or regret that it would not be with her. It seemed ironic that he had been ready to make her his wife, but they had ended up talking about the place of other men in her life.

She had never been one to spend much time analyzing her own feelings—until recently. Now it seemed she spent a lot of time trying to sort out how she felt about two men she loved.

All the good things she had told Kenji about Dave were true, and more.

And all the good things Kenji had said about Steve were true too. She closed her eyes and let the warmth of remembering him flow through her.

A tear slipped out of the corner of her eye. She brushed it away.

Why does this have to be so hard, so . . . so . . . impossible! How could she choose between Steve and Dave?

Was it truly that kind of choice? Would she somehow be abandoning Steve if she married Dave for the rest of this life?

Did Steve know what she was doing day by day, hour by hour?

Would he be jealous of another man's arms around her?

That's silly! People up there don't have feelings like that . . . do they? And maybe he would never think . . . maybe there's no one really worrying about this but me.

I've been wanting to make my promises to Steve in the temple, and nothing's changed about that just because I found Dave. But could I still be true to Steve if I . . .

Steve's not here! Not for years. And I wasn't looking for love.

Other people get married again—other women—so why would it be wrong for me to . . .

More tears came. One thing she knew: she could not let go of Steve—she would *never* let go of Steve, even if it meant living alone for the rest of this life. Even if it meant that she would never again have the man she loved lean close at a party and whisper that he couldn't wait to be alone with her. Even if it meant that she would never again go to bed snuggled against him and wake to find his arm draped across her shoulders. She would endure.

And yet—she *needed* to see Dave, tonight, to talk to him, to have him hold her hand. She didn't want to spend the evening alone. She reached for the telephone on the desk.

Alone? KatiLynn and Stevie will be there.

Kate drew her hand back.

KatiLynn and Stevie. She could do something with them. That could cure the loneliness she felt. They had always been her cure before, and she really shouldn't go off and leave them again tonight.

But she knew in her heart that another impromptu pizza-and-video party, another movie-and-ice-cream night with KatiLynn and Stevie would not erase what she was feeling.

Maybe there was a compromise.

She picked up the phone and dialed the number of Dave's private line in his office. She could hear someone talking in the background when he answered. He seemed surprised to hear her voice when she spoke. "Is everything OK?" he asked.

"Fine," she answered. "Fine, I just wondered . . . well, when I talked about not leaving our children alone so often, I wasn't thinking that maybe we could *all* get together again—you, and I, and our kids."

"I like that idea—but if you're thinking about tonight, Kelli would have a problem."

"Oh. Well, I understand that you wouldn't want to go off and leave her, so—"

"I mean she's got a Young Women activity. But Ross and Alicia could come with me. If you can think of something that four kids ten or under could do while we spend some time together . . ."

"I'm sure I can." Kate was ashamed of the momentary relief she felt when Dave said Kelli would not be there. *I can't give up on her—but it would be nice to have peace tonight.* "What if we meet you at the park near your house about six?" she said. "I can bring pizza and salad." She would stop somewhere and buy them.

"Sounds good. I'll bring drinks and ice cream. And thanks for thinking of this."

"I'll be looking forward to it. But I'd better let you go. I know you've got someone with you."

"Yeah." He paused only briefly, then went on as though he didn't care who heard him. "I'm glad you called. I've been thinking about you—a lot."

His words made her heart feel good and made her feel guilty at the same time. Would she simply be using him this evening to drive away her own loneliness?

No! That's not true! I love him.

Then why couldn't she give him the answer she knew he wanted—the answer she longed to give him?

* * *

Kate flipped on the motion sensor light before she stepped out the door of the flight service building. She paused before pulling the door shut behind her, checking to be sure there was no one in the shadows beyond the bushes to her left or behind the wrought iron furniture on the patio to her right.

Ordinarily, she made sure one of the mechanics was working a late shift on nights when she or Ann had to close the office, but tonight the last mechanic had left at 8:00 and she had been alone, locked inside, for nearly two hours. She hated feeling the need to be so cautious about her own safety. But when she had first consulted Dave about the security problem at the flight service, he had indoctrinated her in the importance of personal protection, even in the seemingly safe confines of her own building. Their experience in the park a short time ago had reinforced his lessons.

Walking toward her car, parked near a light, she glanced at the clear space she could see underneath it, then checked the outline of its shadow to be sure there was no evidence of anyone hiding there. She got into the vehicle quickly, locked it, and started the engine.

As she drove past the fence along the edge of the parking lot, an image to her right registered in her mind: someone leaning against the chain link mesh, looking toward the building. Kate frowned. *Glad I got away quickly.*

The figure turned toward her car as she drove through the gate. *Strange—not a man. It's a woman . . . or a girl.* And there was something about the skirt she wore . . . something that reminded . . .

Kelli!

The tires of her car screeched briefly on the pavement as Kate put on the brakes. The brake lights illuminated the girl's figure when Kate shifted into reverse. It *was* Dave's daughter. Kate backed up and parked next to her by the fence, pushed the button to lower the passenger side window, and turned off the engine. "Kelli? Is something . . . are you all right?"

Kelli seemed to think it over for a moment before she nodded. "Yes. I just . . . I wondered if I could use your phone?"

"You need a ride? I can take you home."

"No! Uh, no, I have a friend with a car, and . . . well, she can take me home. I just need to call her."

Kate knew she could limit this encounter to two minutes by loaning Kelli her cell phone. That would avoid any possibility of unpleasantness between them. But the mother in her would not let her do it. Obviously there was more to this situation. "OK—sure," Kate said. "But let's wait inside until your friend comes." She put up the window, got out and locked her car, then motioned for Kelli to follow as she headed toward the building. "Come with me."

Kate unlocked the door to the flight service building and stood back to let the girl enter. Shock registered in her mind at what she smelled as Kelli slipped past. Kate had not smelled that sickly sweet odor in a long time—but it was unforgettable. And it was wildly at odds with everything she knew about Kelli.

She locked the front door behind them. Kelli stood just inside the building lobby. Kate looked her up and down slowly. "Before you use the phone, I think we better do something about that knee." A streak of dried blood ran from Kelli's right knee down her shin.

Kelli glanced down at her leg. "Oh. I, uh . . . I fell on, uh . . . on the road, while I was walking."

Kate looked into her eyes for several seconds without speaking. Then: "Why don't you sit down on the couch? I have some alcohol and bandages in the supply cabinet."

Kelli eased down on the couch in the waiting area and watched warily while Kate got the supplies out of the cabinet, then moistened a square of gauze with alcohol. When Kate blotted her knee with the gauze, Kelli sucked in a breath sharply and squeezed her eyes tightly shut but said nothing.

Kate wiped the dried blood off of Kelli's shin. "You're a long way from home, and a long way from the school out here." Kelli opened her eyes to look into Kate's, but her face remained expressionless; she was deliberately trying to keep it that way, Kate thought. There was apprehension in the girl's eyes—fear. Of what? "We need to put something on this knee to protect it," Kate said, reaching for another bandage from the box. Again, Kelli was silent.

Obviously, the girl did not want to talk about why she was so far from home or what had happened. What Kate knew of Dave's daughter, coupled with what she had just smelled, suggested that Kelli had found herself in a situation she was not prepared to handle.

She probably needed to deal with what she was feeling right now, to talk about it with someone she trusted—someone who could listen without getting angry. And she would probably be afraid of her father's reaction. *I know what it's like. I could help. But she wouldn't talk to me if I asked her about it. We don't have that kind of relationship. What could I possibly say that would make her—*

But maybe there was a way to open the door without asking directly. Kate followed the idea that came to mind.

"I knew a girl who ended up on foot out in the country one night when she was sixteen," she began as she reached for the roll of tape. "There was a guy she wanted to go with who asked her out a couple of times. The second time, he took her out for something to drink. They hung around a fast food place for a while, just talking, and then he took her riding out toward the edge of town." She glanced up at Kelli. The girl was looking wary this time. Kate went back to her work, measuring and cutting a strip of tape as she talked. "When they got out where there weren't very many houses, he turned off on a little side road and parked. Then he started to move over to her side of the car"—she glanced up momentarily at Kelli, who was gazing over her head into the distance, frowning—"and when he got real close, he put his arm around her. She was pretty uncomfortable with that—trapped against the door—but she didn't know what to do."

Kate paused while she put the first strip of tape on the gauze. Kelli was still silent, evidently waiting for her to go on. "He started to run his fingers up and down her arm. And then . . . then he touched her leg with his fingers."

Kate glanced up once more. The look in the girl's eyes this time told her that she had guessed correctly. She went back to cutting and applying the second piece of tape. "This guy started talking about how they were all alone, how no one would ever know what they did." She paused. "It ended up with her fighting him off. Finally, when he saw that she wasn't going to do what he wanted, he opened the door and pushed her out."

A drop of water fell onto Kate's wrist, and then another. She looked up. Tears were sliding down Kelli's cheeks. Slowly Kate stood, then sat down on the couch next to Dave's daughter. "Want to tell me about it?" she said softly.

Kelli sobbed a couple of times and wiped at her eyes with her fingers. "How did you know?"

"Experience. He left me where he pushed me out of the car, and I had to walk until I found a house where they'd let me call my dad."

Kelli fought tears as she gazed into Kate's eyes, comprehending. "I was so scared. I think I was glad when he pushed *me* out of the car. I fell on my knee, and on my hands—except I had my notebook in this hand." She held up her spiral-bound notebook in her left hand; scratches marred the book's paper cover. She held out her right hand, palm up; there were deep scratches on the heel of it.

"And did he . . . did he do anything else to you?" Kate asked.

"No!" Kelli shook her head vigorously. "Not anything like . . . no. He called me a name, and he slapped me in the face." She turned her head so Kate could look at her left cheek. There was a red mark on it. Kate reached out and touched it carefully. Kelli winced and turned her head away.

"You may have a bruise tomorrow," Kate said.

Kelli's tears had stopped. She stared at the opposite wall.

"I think we need to let your father know," Kate said slowly.

"No! Don't tell my dad. Please? I didn't want him to know because . . . because . . ."

"He didn't know you were out with this boy?"

Slowly, Kelli nodded her head. "No, he didn't. I went to the library with my friend—the one who has the car. I told Dad she would bring me home."

180

Kate glanced at her watch: 10:15. "Would he be expecting you home before now? The library probably closed at 9:00, didn't it?"

Kelli nodded.

"I think we have to call him, before he calls your friend—or the police.'

Kelli moaned. "He'll ground me forever. I won't be able to date until I'm twenty-four!"

Kate smiled. "He might be mad, but I don't think he'd do that to you, Kelli. He loves you, more than you can understand right now."

"Parents always say that."

There was no real anger or bitterness in the girl's words; that was a good sign, Kate thought. "Right now, your dad's probably feeling a little sick inside, wondering if something's happened to you. He'll be grateful just to know nothing's wrong with you. Really, you need to call—and then I'll take you home."

Kelli looked down at the floor, wiping at her eyes once more. "He'll be mad because I didn't tell him the truth. He'll be hurt."

"Maybe. But I know he has a lot of confidence in you and he wants to trust you. The two of you can work on that together."

"I don't even know why I agreed to go anywhere with *him*—with that guy," Kelli muttered. She continued to stare down at the carpet.

"Because you thought he saw you as someone special." Kate paused. "You deserve someone who knows that you really are."

Kelli looked up at her again. "Will *you* call my dad—please?"

Kate picked up the phone on Ann's desk and dialed Dave's number. He answered on the second ring. She could hear the anxiety in his voice: "Hello?"

"Dave, it's Kate. I have—"

"Kate? Oh—you surprised me. I was hoping . . . uh, I was *expecting*—"

"Kelli?"

"Yes. How did you know?"

"She's here with me."

There was silence on the other end of the line for three or four seconds. "*Here?* Where?"

"At my office."

"How did she . . ."

"I'll let her tell you that. I'll have her home in a few minutes. OK?"

"Yeah—sure." Kate could hear the relief in his voice. She said good-bye and hung up.

Kelli stood up resignedly.

"How far did you walk to get here?" Kate asked.

"I don't know—half a mile maybe. He left me in a subdivision down the road. I guess I could have walked back to the mall to find a phone." She paused. "But it's farther, and I needed someone to . . . I needed . . ." Tears slid down her cheeks again. "I was really scared, and I thought if you were in your office . . ."

Slowly, Kate put an arm around the girl. Kelli stiffened momentarily, then relaxed and let Kate pull her closer. She held the girl that way for several seconds before she let go and stepped back to look into Kelli's eyes. The anger she had so often seen there was gone, at least for now. "Let's get you home."

They rode in silence for about ten minutes, with Kelli gazing out of the windshield. Finally she turned to Kate and asked: "What happened—with the guy?"

"What?"

"The one who pushed you out of his car."

Kate thought for a moment. Looking back on it, she couldn't suppress a smile, then a small laugh.

Kelli looked at her quizzically.

"I punched him out. At school," Kate said. "I found out he was telling lies about me—bragging about what never happened. I walked up to him in the hall when he was standing with a group of friends and yelled at him. I said, 'Say it, Jason—say it in front of me. Let me hear it.' He just stood there looking at me with some silly smirk like he didn't know what to do. I was so mad that I made a fist and hit him in the face. He fell down. I don't think I knocked him down—he was too much bigger—but I took him by surprise. And while he was lying on the floor I stood there screaming at him: 'Tell them you're a liar, Jason. Tell your friends.' He didn't say anything, so I just turned my back and walked away. I went in the bathroom and cried."

Kelli sat watching her as she drove. "And what happened to you? I mean, did your friends . . ."

"Some of the girls I *thought* were my friends dropped me. And I didn't date for a while; some of the guys stayed away from me. But there were other people I found who were ready to be my friends—girls who helped me get over it, who made me feel like I was somebody worth caring about. And there were guys—*good* guys. One of them became a close friend. He took me out to dinner or dances a few times in high school, and we used to have a lot of fun together at the university here until he went away to MIT."

Kelli gazed out of the windshield in silence again.

Kate went on. "I guess it didn't seem like a happy ending at the time. But what happened was right for me in the end. A couple of those girls were like sisters to me for a while. We're still good friends."

She didn't know Dave's daughter well enough to guess what was going on in her mind. It had been a shock that this girl had turned to her, and Kate had responded as she would to any young woman in need. Now she searched for a way to keep the communication going, but no words came to mind, and Kelli said nothing more.

Kate parked in the driveway at Dave's house and he opened the front door before they reached it. He looked Kelli over carefully as she stepped inside, glancing down at her bandaged knee. "Are you all right?" he asked, his brow furrowed.

"Yes, Daddy," she answered. "But there's something I have to tell you."

Dave looked questioningly at Kate as she followed his daughter through the door. She shook her head slightly and nodded toward Kelli's back.

Kelli turned to face him. They stood in a tight little grouping just inside the door, Dave waiting for his daughter to speak. Kelli glanced at Kate. Kate smiled encouragingly but said nothing. It was Kelli who needed to tell the story.

The girl retreated to the couch across the room, where she sat down and placed her notebook carefully beside her. Dave followed and sat on the other side of her. Kate settled in the recliner opposite them.

Kelli stared down at the floor for several seconds. "I lied, Daddy." She looked up at her father. "Well, I did something that wasn't honest. I'm sorry."

Dave nodded. "Go on, Kell. Whatever it is, we can work it out. I'm just glad you're OK." He glanced down at her knee. "What happened?"

Kelli told the story briefly without sparing herself or trying to make excuses. Kate admired her honesty. The girl's eyes searched her father's face as she spoke. She seemed to be trying to read his feelings.

Kate could see that Dave was angry. It was in the set of his jaw and the tenseness of his body, as though he were ready to react to some sudden threat. Kelli undoubtedly sensed his anger too, and probably worried that it was directed at her. But Dave kept looking away from his daughter momentarily, staring into space, and Kate could tell his anger was focused elsewhere. She guessed that he was thinking about what he would do if he had the boy within reach right now.

Kelli finished telling about walking to the flying service offices, then stopped talking and waited for her father to respond. He looked into her eyes for several seconds. "Is that . . . all?" he asked.

The girl looked as though she were confused; she had told the whole story. She hadn't understood what her father was really asking, Kate thought. "He hit her across the face, but he didn't do anything else to her," she said.

Kelli turned her head slightly so her father could see the spot on her cheek that was turning into a bruise. Dave looked closely at it. He reached out slowly to put his arms around his daughter and pull her close to him. "I'm glad you're OK, Sweetheart."

Then he sat back, holding his daughter by her shoulders and looking into her eyes. "But I don't understand why you would go anywhere with a boy like that."

"Daddy, I thought he . . . I mean, he didn't seem like . . ." Slowly, Kelli shook her head, and shrugged. She turned to look at Kate helplessly. There was an appeal in the look.

"Dave, a girl can't always know what's in a guy's mind," Kate explained. He turned to look at her. "And when you're a sophomore, and the senior guy that *everybody* wants to date pays attention to *you* . . ." She smiled at Kelli. "I'd have felt lucky—and important."

"Kelli *is* important. She's important to me." He looked at his daughter. "And important in our family."

"But when a daughter is becoming a woman, she hopes one day she'll be the most important person in the life of another man. And when a young woman's just beginning to learn about men . . . well, she finds out that some of them are good at hiding what they *really* are. You're strong and trustworthy, Dave, and until now, you've been almost everything your daughter knew about men. Tonight she met another kind. It's a shock, and it hurts."

Dave looked into his daughter's eyes again. He put an arm around her neck and pulled her close once more, pressing her head against his chest. "I'm sorry, Kell—sorry this happened to you."

Tears ran down Kelli's cheeks, wetting his shirt. "I'm sorry too, Daddy. I thought I knew . . . but I . . ."

He held Kelli close to him until she sat up straight, wiping at her eyes. "Who is he?" Dave asked.

"Daddy, don't—please. . . . I mean, if I . . . if he says it didn't happen, nobody's going to believe *me*."

"*I* believe you. Kate believes you. I'll bet there are a lot of others. The police will—"

"Daddy! I couldn't! If they . . . do you think they could possibly *arrest* him?"

"What he did was a crime, Kell—assault, at least." He paused. "And I'll bet there are other girls who would believe you—girls who already know from experience what he's like."

"You won't be the last," Kate said softly. "Not with a guy like him."

Kelli moaned. "I don't think I could—" She looked at Kate and left the sentence unfinished. She said nothing for several seconds, gazing into Kate's eyes. Then she sighed. "All right. I didn't really want anyone else to know about this, I didn't want to talk to anybody about it. . . . But I guess if I have to . . . I mean, if it will help . . . and if *he* doesn't have to be there . . ."

"We can talk about all that in the morning," Dave answered. "Right now, I think you need to get your sleep."

Kelli frowned. "Daddy, whatever you're going to do to me, I wish you'd tell me now. I don't want to have to wait and worry about it."

"Kell, I can't think of a thing I could do that would teach you more than you've learned tonight. Can you?"

Kelli seemed to relax as she thought about his question. "No. I guess I can't." She smiled hesitantly.

"Look, I've learned something too," Dave said. "I won't always be able to protect you the way I want to. You're going to have to learn how to take care of yourself. But there are a lot of things I can still teach you, and we need to talk about ways for me to do that. I promise to listen to you if you'll listen to me."

Kelli put her arm around his neck and lingered just a moment hugging him. "I'm glad you're my dad." She stood and picked up her notebook to walk to her room, but she stopped just as she reached the hallway and turned to face Kate. "Thanks for . . . ah . . ."

Kate smiled at her. "I'm glad I could help."

Kelli smiled back briefly—it was the first time the girl had ever smiled at her—then walked away down the hallway and they heard the door to her bedroom close.

"Is there anything more I should know?" Dave asked.

"I don't think so. Anyway, you know everything I know."

"Thanks for being there for her."

"I almost wasn't. If a couple of small things hadn't kept me in the office . . ."

"Kelli needed you tonight, and someone knew that."

Kate nodded. Then she glanced at her watch. It was almost 11:00. "Speaking of someone needing me, I've got to go pick up my kids." She stood and moved to the door.

"Just a minute," Dave said. He walked across the room, took her in his arms, and kissed her. Kate couldn't help responding. She enjoyed it when he kissed her. But she broke it off too soon—before he was ready.

Dave stepped back and looked at her questioningly. "Is something wrong?"

"No. No," Kate said, giving him a quick smile that was meant to be reassuring. "It's just that my mother will be wondering what happened to me. She worries when I'm late. Mothers never get over that." She opened the door. "Call me tomorrow," she said as she stepped outside.

If there really wasn't anything wrong, Kate thought as she drove toward her parents' house, then why had she felt the need just now to get away?

Maybe because for the first time, it looked like everything might be right for her and Dave.

Maybe there's a chance now that things can work out between Kelli and me. . . . Or maybe tomorrow by the light of day she'll be back to her surly little self. Who knows? . . . But there's a chance. And if things work out . . .

If things worked out with Kelli, if she and Kelli could somehow peacefully coexist in the same vicinity, then Dave would want an answer to his question.

He'll want me to tell him the two of us can have a life together.

That's what had scared her when Dave had kissed her just now and she had enjoyed it so much, feeling the need to have his arms around her.

She knew now that she hadn't been completely honest with herself all the times when she had blamed Kelli for being the barrier to their happiness.

She could not explain it, even to herself, but she still did not feel ready to give Dave his answer.

15

To: *kenjin@nakamura.com*
Last night I looked at the beautiful painting you sent me and wondered how you are. I hope you are happy and life is going well for you. Are you feeling more comfortable with the idea of socializing again? I hate to think of your being so alone.

You are a good friend, Kenji. I wish only the best for you.

Kate's fingers paused on the keyboard. Should she tell him the rest of what was on her mind?

Well, it shouldn't hurt; she thought there was enough trust between them.

I have prayed for you, that you will be happy and that when you're ready you'll find another love to warm you the way Lily's did.

When you have a moment, please send me a note to let me know how things are going for you.

To: *kate@morrowflight.com*
That is a very beautiful wish for a friend, Kate. I hope I am worthy of it.

Please forgive my delay in answering. I have been away on a business trip in Europe and Southeast Asia. (I have sent some little gifts for you and your children. I hope they arrive safely.)

I saw in Europe advertisements for Warden Avionics' newest system. The company will truly be a good competitor. Some of my hosts asked me what Nakamura Electronics has to offer that is comparable. It is a hard question to answer right now.

Yes, socializing was part of the trip. My hosts in England, France, Germany, and Singapore took pains to see that I had companionship. I met some beautiful women and some fine women—not always the same.

Of course none shines like Lily did. Or like you do.

I have been thinking about everything you told me when I visited you, and I understand now that I have not been doing Lily honor by refusing to look for anyone new. Marriage was a delight with Lily, and so I believe that if I find the right woman it could be again. But there is nothing happening in that area so far, or I would tell you.

How are KatiLynn and Stevie? Please give them my regards.

And how is your friendship with the man from your church?

To: kenjin@nakamura.com

I'm sorry I haven't gotten back to you sooner, Kenji. Your message came on Saturday, when I was not in the office, and then I was sick on Monday with something I caught from Stevie. But that is past now.

You will probably soon be seeing ads for Warden Avionics equipment in Asia, too, but of course you have a head start there. It will be interesting to see how we can do in that market.

KatiLynn and Stevie are doing fine. She is discovering fashion, and the puzzle of boys—and she hasn't even started sixth grade yet! I don't know if I'm ready for this.

Thank you so much for the gifts you sent. That photograph was a find! Lindbergh's plane in Paris—you knew I'd like that. It's hanging in the office where I can look at it often. KatiLynn treasures the pendant (I hope it wasn't too expensive!) and Stevie keeps finding things he can "fix" with the Swiss army knife. They will be sending you notes to say thanks for themselves.

It must be a great comfort to you, Kenji, to treasure your memories of Lily. But you mustn't compare another woman to her. It isn't fair to either of them. I have roses growing in front of my house and also daisies. I love them both for different reasons, and I would not want to give up either one of them. When you find another woman to love, she may delight you in completely different ways than Lily.

David Cutler is a wonderful man and so was Steve, but they are very different. It does not matter to Dave whether his company outdoes all others so long as he runs his business with integrity and he's able to support his family. But he is patient and strong sometimes in ways that Steve was not. I've found many things to love in him just as I did in Steve. I wish I could resolve in my own mind the problem of loving two different men.

I know that Lily is and always will be a part of you. I think that is the highest kind of honor. I believe she would be happy about that.

I'm told that in Japan a career for a businessman can be all consuming. But I hope you will find time for things that bring you joy in this life, Kenji. Happiness is my wish for you.

To: kate@morrowflight.com
Happiness also is my wish for you, Kate. If I were the kind to visit a shrine, I would leave a prayer that you will reach out and grasp your own happiness. Right now, it almost seems that you are not allowing yourself to take hold of it.

After I read your last message, I wondered what you would do if you had to move to a smaller place where you could no longer grow both kinds of flowers. I suppose you would not stop loving the roses even though you could not grow them. But would you love the daisies less because you could not grow roses? Would the thought of planting roses again someday keep you from enjoying the daisies now? I cannot understand how the value of one flower for you would depend on your feelings about another.

As for my social life, I think I may have found a flower—not a Lily, but still beautiful. She works in my own company. One of my managers pointed her out, very respectfully, as we Japanese do when talking to a supervisor. Mayumi has many of the same fine qualities as Lily, and many of the qualities you have, and also many of her own. She is not afraid to tell me what she likes or to tell me no, tactfully, if she believes I am wrong. I like that. And yet she would please my father. She grew up in a traditional home and has very strong feelings about home being the most important part of life. I find that very attractive about her.

She practices your religion. I didn't know that until the third time we had been out together.

She is also a very good artist. She gave me a sketch of myself that I think is very well done, although it flatters me. She gave me a pen-and-ink drawing of what she says is the most beautiful place she knows. I believe it is your temple in Tokyo. She said if I could see the inside of it sometime, I would understand what she means.

If something more happens, I will let you know.

Kate's brow furrowed in thought. How would this Japanese woman respond to the attention from Kenji Nakamura, owner of the company she worked for, a rich and powerful man? Was she younger? Perhaps, but it seemed as though she was mature enough to hold her own with him. Despite his wealth and power, could she see into the heart of Kenji the man?

What of the Church? Did she have hope that she could persuade Kenji somehow to make the gospel part of his life? Would she fall in love with him and face the pain of knowing that they could not be married for eternity? Would she be willing to take a chance on "someday"?

Kate knew that even if she could talk with the woman, she would not be able to give her answers. She hoped Mayumi was the kind of person who relied on counsel from her Heavenly Father. Silently, Kate said a prayer for the Japanese sister she might never know.

Her own problem, she felt, was different. The flower analogy that Kenji had turned back on her did not hold up in her case—at least not completely. She still intended to be sealed to Steve in the temple, but it had occurred to her—more than once—that she could choose to be sealed to Dave instead. That choice would not be changeable with another growing season.

A man could be sealed to more than one woman for eternity—but only if the second woman had never been sealed to anyone else. So if she were sealed to Steve and then married Dave and they lived out their natural lives together, he would lose the opportunity to be sealed to another wife.

She had mentioned that to him once. He had laughed lightly and said, "Well, that settles it, then—back to prowling the singles dances!"

When he had realized that she was looking for a serious response, he had taken her hand, put it to his lips, and kissed her fingers lightly. "We have to deal with us, Kate, not some hypothetical situation. It's not just any available woman I want to spend the rest of my life with—it's you. If that means five years or fifty, it's what I want. It just feels right."

But would it be right for her, after she made those promises to Steve in her heart?

The bishop had indicated that she might be worrying unnecessarily.

"Those covenants I want to make in the temple, the promises I want to make to Steve—those mean everything to me. I could never do anything that would even come close to breaking them."

"Sister Warden, there are a lot of couples who marry for time only, in the temple, after they've both been sealed to someone else and then widowed. I know several of them myself. The Brethren wouldn't permit that if it were wrong."

Kate nodded. "I understand. But Steve . . ."

"You're still worried about how your first husband might feel when you meet him again?" The bishop frowned. "Was he a jealous man?"

"No, not the way some . . . I mean, he trusted me. We trusted each other completely." She thought for a moment, and smiled, remembering. "But there were a couple of times—once on our honeymoon, and once later—when he caught other guys flirting with me, and he let them know pretty clearly that I was taken."

The bishop chuckled.

Kate looked at him quizzically.

"I was just thinking back," he said, "remembering when Linda and I were married, while we were in college. Every guy who saw her on campus would look at her once, then look again."

Kate nodded. The bishop's wife was still strikingly good looking, in her late forties, after five children.

"There were times back then . . ." He smiled ruefully. "Well, I let a couple of guys know in pretty strong terms that she wasn't available."

He leaned back in his chair for a moment looking at her. "But have you ever thought that your husband might want someone to care for you right now—someone to keep you from spending the rest of this life alone? Perhaps he may even approve of Dave."

Kate's brow furrowed. "Steve knew I could take care of myself. I don't think he would ever feel . . . well, I . . . I just wish I could be sure somehow."

"I have a friend who was a widow like you. She married again after her children were mostly grown. Her husband had been sealed to his first wife in the temple too. I don't think I've ever seen a couple who love each other more. They say, 'Maybe we'll live in neighboring kingdoms someday.' They look forward to introducing each other to their spouses. They think the four of them could be good friends."

The bishop was smiling. Kate smiled uncertainly. He seemed to sense that she wasn't sure the example would apply to her.

"There was more to it than finding out they could love again," the bishop continued. "They have each other for comfort and support. They're finishing this journey together, however long it may be."

He leaned forward, resting his arms on the desk, and looked her in the eyes. "I want you to understand that I'm not telling you I think you should marry Dave. I don't know what you should do. I think the Lord wants you to make that decision. I'm only telling you that as far as the Church is concerned, you'd be doing nothing wrong. In fact, it could be a good thing—for both of you. And I don't think you should automatically assume that Steve would be uncomfortable with the idea.

Maybe he would want someone with you for the time being. After all, where he is right now, his perspective on this experience may be very different from ours."

Kate had believed him. In her mind she had believed that there would be nothing wrong, in the eyes of the Church, with marrying Dave. But in her heart it was a different matter.

Her marriage to Steve had not been perfect, but she had loved him unreservedly, with all her heart, and she was sure that as long as he had lived he had felt the same about her. He had been romantic and at the same time he had been practical about love the way he had been about other things he did in life—he found what worked for him and he put everything into it.

Could she do less for him?

KatiLynn had asked a number of times lately about her father. How had Kate known that she loved him? How had he shown that he loved her? How had she felt inside when she lost him? But Kate feared that her daughter's real question might not have been spoken: "How could you fall in love with another man if you truly, deeply loved my father?"

Or maybe that question wasn't really in her daughter's heart at all.

Maybe it was only in her own.

* * *

The scene could have been an old Norman Rockwell painting—a young girl standing in front of a mirror trying to fix her hair in a more sophisticated style. Kate smiled as she walked past in the hall. Sometimes she wasn't sure whether to feel anticipation or anxiety at these early signs of her daughter's inevitable move toward womanhood. The signs were showing up more frequently.

She stopped and went back to stand in the doorway of her daughter's bedroom.

KatiLynn stood sideways looking at the mirror out of the corner of her eye, straining to see at least part of the back of her head as she tried to weave her hair into a French braid. She was struggling with it.

"That would look very pretty on you, Sweetheart," Kate said. "When did you learn to do that kind of braiding?"

"Last night. Kelli showed me." KatiLynn wrinkled her nose at her image. "I think I need to grow my hair longer—maybe down past my shoulders."

"*Kelli?* Kelli taught you?"

"Last night while you and Dave went to get the videos and ice cream.' She frowned into the mirror. "Can you help me for a minute?"

Kate moved into place behind her daughter and began weaving strands of hair into the French braid pattern. She looked into KatiLynn's eyes in the mirror. "I'm a little surprised that Kelli would . . . I mean, I didn't know you and Kelli were on such good terms."

"She was nice to me, Mom. She's never been like that before."

She looked at Kelli from time to time as the older girl braided her long blonde hair. Katilynn tried not to stare; she could never be sure how Kelli was going to react to her.

Kelli glanced her way once and caught her looking. KatiLynn quickly turned back to the television, waiting for Kelli's usual cutting comment. It didn't come. Instead, Kelli said, "Your hair could look really cute braided like this."

KatiLynn turned toward her, surprised.

"Want me to show you how?" Kelli asked as she put the finishing touches on her own braid.

KatiLynn thought it over warily for several seconds. The offer seemed to be sincere. Slowly, she nodded.

Kelli walked into the bathroom and came back with her hand mirror. She gave it to KatiLynn and sat down on the carpet behind her. "I'll tell you what I'm doing. Try to watch."

Kelli began to weave strands of KatiLynn's hair into a small, tight pattern. KatiLynn was concentrating on what the older girl was doing when Ross walked into the family room. He watched for half a minute, then looked KatiLynn in the eyes as he spoke. "It doesn't matter what you do to it, it's still going to be ugly."

"Shut up, Ross!" Kelli snapped. "If you can't say anything nice, don't say anything."

"Why are you doing that for her?" he flared at his sister. "You told me you hated her!"

KatiLynn stiffened. Kelli held her braided hair in place. "I never said I hated . . . I didn't mean that."

"You said no house would ever be big enough for them and us. You said their mom just wants Dad and she doesn't care about us. You said we don't need a new mother around here."

"Shut up, Ross!"

KatiLynn moved as though to get up. Kelli put one hand on her shoulder and gently held her in place. She leaned forward and to the side so KatiLynn could see her face. "You have nice hair and it's going to look good this way. And you have pretty eyes. Great complexion, too. In about four years, every boy my brother knows will think you're really hot."

She looked up at her brother. "If you're going to stay here and watch TV with us, you can't talk like that."

Kelli leaned back and started over on the braiding. "I was wrong, Ross. You need a mother—even if you don't know it right now. Alicia needs a mother." Kelli paused, and when she spoke again she sounded like she might be close to crying. "Maybe I need a mother too."

"No, we don't," Ross said angrily. "I'm going back to my video game, and everybody can just leave me alone. Alicia and her brother"—he gestured toward KatiLynn—"have had their turns. It's all mine now."

"Don't be mean to anyone," his sister warned.

He turned and started out of the room.

"R.J.?" Kelli said to his back.

Ross turned on his heel and came striding back to stand over her, glowering. "Don't you call me that! Only Mom can—only Mom called me that."

"Please—listen to me," Kelli said. Her tone was conciliatory. "Since Mom died, when have you seen Dad really happy?"

"I . . . I don't know."

"Yes, you do. Tell me."

Ross's expression softened. "Since he and Kate . . . and a little before that, maybe . . . well, since then, anyway."

"Yes. And I don't want to take that away from him. Do you?"

Ross stood looking at his sister without answering.

"What we've been doing is wrong," Kelli said. "Think about it."

His look said that he wasn't going to do anything his sister suggested just now. Ross turned and walked out of the room.

Kelli went on with the braiding. In a minute or two, she leaned close to KatiLynn's ear and spoke softly. "Remember last week when Dad brought us over to your place to swim and I yelled at you not to talk to my brother the way you did?"

"Yeah. And, uh . . . your dad got mad. I'm sorry you got in trouble."

"I was mad because Ross told me you called him a . . . a bad name." Kelli lowered her voice to a whisper and said the word in KatiLynn's ear. "Did you call him that? You can tell me the truth."

"NO!" KatiLynn tried to turn to look Kelli in the eye, but Kelli had too firm a hold on her hair. "I'd never call anybody anything like that!" She hesitated. "Maybe I said . . . well, I think I called him a creep, but he was—"

"Being a creep?" Kelli sighed. "I thought it was something like that. He's good at it—being a little creep—when he wants to be. I, ah . . . I hope I haven't helped make him that way."

"Mom, why are boys so mean?" KatiLynn asked, wrinkling her nose.

"They're not always mean. I told you, they grow out of it—most of them. It just takes them a while to learn how to behave with girls."

"Do you think Ross will grow out of it? He's like . . . he's so mad all the time."

KatiLynn was right. Ross seemed to be carrying around a lot of anger. Why—because it was just part of his personality? Or because he missed his mother and didn't know how to express it? Because in dying she had gone off and left him? Kate didn't have an answer. She sighed. "I hope he'll get over it, for his family's sake—and his." She paused. "Sometimes young people have to find out who they really are before they can be happy with themselves—or anyone else."

KatiLynn watched her for a time without speaking. Then: "Were you unhappy, Mom?"

Kate looked into her daughter's eyes in the mirror. "When?"

"Before you met Dave, like Kelli said about her dad. You know—how he's happier since he started going out with you. Are you happier now too?"

Kate's fingers stopped their braiding motions. "I was never really unhappy. It will make me happy to know I'm married to your father for always. And you and Stevie make me happy. I need both of you very much."

"I know. I believe that. But do you ever . . . I mean, if you couldn't go with Dave any more, would you be unhappy?"

"I don't know."

Actually, she did know, and her daughter looked dubious about the reply. KatiLynn deserved a better answer. But the feelings involved seemed too complicated to explain to a child.

"You said you need me and Stevie. Do you need Dave too?" Kati-Lynn asked.

There was no ducking this question. And maybe, Kate thought, she ought to have more confidence in her daughter; maybe a girl who was almost eleven could handle some things at a more grown-up level. "I love Dave, if that's what you're asking. But I'm not sure yet what's going to happen between the two of us."

KatiLynn thought for a moment about what her mother had said. "I think he loves his kids the way you love me and Stevie. I think he's a good dad." She paused. "Remember how you told me I'd find someone someday and get married? And Stevie too? Then you'd be alone. I don't want you to be alone, Mom."

Kate blinked against the tears that wanted to come, and went back to braiding her daughter's hair. After she finished, she busied herself with other things and tried not to think about the implications of their conversation. But when she finally got into bed, it was another night to lie staring up at the ceiling.

Did she *need* Dave? Yes.

Would she be unhappy if she couldn't go out with him anymore? She couldn't even bear to think about it.

But there were other things—important things—to consider beyond the needs of the two of them.

This afternoon her daughter had given her permission to marry Dave. Had KatiLynn done it simply because she didn't want her mother to be alone someday? Or did she really like Dave herself? Sometimes it was hard to tell. There had been no conflict between the two of them, and KatiLynn seemed to enjoy the things Dave did with them, but she had never gone out of her way to say she liked him. Stevie liked him—that was obvious. He liked it when Dave played ball with the younger children, or played with all of them in the swimming pool.

How would KatiLynn and Stevie deal with being part of a blended family? Suddenly there would be five children, not two.

And how, Kate wondered, would she handle it herself? In all of her experiences with Dave's family so far, she had been concerned about getting along with the three individuals who were his children. This was the first time she had thought at any length about suddenly being a mother of five. Did she have it in her to meet the needs of that many children at once? Or even to meet the needs of any one of the three she did not know as well as her own? How, for example, could she handle Ross when she had so little experience with boys his age?

It was past 1:30 in the morning when she finally drifted off to sleep.

* * *

KatiLynn arced into the air above the pool in a passable swan dive, then dropped cleanly into the water. Kate wondered momentarily if she had a budding diver or gymnast in the family. She and Dave clapped from their chaise lounges near the shallow end and Dave cheered, "Nine point five! Two years from now at the Olympics." Kelli, seated in a beach chair on the other side of Dave, clapped politely.

KatiLynn smiled in their direction—at Dave?—as she moved away from the center of the pool.

She had barely cleared the area when Ross was on the diving board. He raced to the end, bounced high a couple of times, gulped in air, and went into a suicide version of a front flip, arms flailing out from his sides, legs far apart. Somehow it worked. He entered the water feet first.

When he bobbed to the surface, everyone clapped enthusiastically. Alicia cheered, "Yay, R.J., yay, R.J.," and Kelli whistled shrilly between her fingers. "See? I told you you could do it," she called to her brother.

Ross reddened, whether because of the attention or because of the nickname his little sister used, Kate was not sure.

As he swam toward the side of the pool in the deep end where KatiLynn clung to the ladder, she said to him, "That was good, Ross. If you keep doing it, you'll get better."

He gave her an I-don't-care-what-you-think look, grabbed the ladder, and pushed past her to get out of the pool.

Dave frowned slightly, but said nothing.

Ross's disdain for Kate and her family had been less than subtle today, even though it was by his choice that he and his family were here. His father had asked him if he wanted to celebrate his birthday with a picnic at a park or a backyard barbecue at Kate's house—she had volunteered the use of the pool again—and the idea of swimming had seemed to appeal to him.

Things had gone fairly well so far, Kate thought. Ross had taken turns on the diving board without pushing anyone out of the way. He had deliberately kept Stevie at a distance—but he had treated his younger sister the same. He had gone out of his way to show disgust over the dab of potato salad his older sister had served him, a salad Kate had made—but then "E-e-e-u, yuck!" was not uncommon when eleven-year-olds wanted to express their distaste for something.

His birthday, May 16, came near the end of the school year, making him one of the younger students in his fifth-grade class. KatiLynn's birthday, however, came on August 7, shortly before the beginning of the school year, and Ross had pointed out at least twice today that she would probably always be "the *baby* of your class." He had tried a couple of wild, dangerous tricks off the diving board, loudly daring KatiLynn, "Let's see you do *that!*" After the second one, Dave had quietly spoken to him about his behavior, and Ross had said no more than two words to anyone since then.

Kelli stood and reached for her father's empty paper plate and plastic utensils. "Let me take those for you, Daddy." She walked around to Kate's chair. "Could I . . . do you want me to take yours too?"

Kate smiled at her. "Thank you."

"I'll just put these in the garbage in the kitchen, if you don't mind. If you want me to bring out some plates for the cake . . ."

"That would be nice. They're on the kitchen counter."

Kelli had not been talkative today, but she had been polite and helpful and had brought a chair to sit by the adults while the younger children played in the pool. No doubt she would be much more outgoing among friends her own age. Her walk showed an easy, natural grace, Kate noticed as the girl moved toward the kitchen, and Kelli looked good in the modest, one-piece swimsuit she wore. Of course boys would find her attractive.

Kate pulled the beach cover-up she wore down to her knees.

She had thought for a long time before wearing her swimsuit this afternoon. She had stood in front of the full-length mirror in her bedroom evaluating the front view, the side view, and, over her shoulder as best she could, the view from the back. KatiLynn had walked past the doorway once, grinned at her, and said, "You look great, Mom." Kate had smiled back—but she didn't believe it. She wasn't overweight, but she thought the suit felt tighter somehow in the hips than she remembered, and her stomach didn't look flat to her the way it once had. At last, sighing, she had thrown the beach shift over her suit and determined to go swimming. She wasn't going to pass up the fun with her children.

Once in the pool, playing dodgeball and keep-away with everyone, she had forgotten to worry about how she looked—until just now, when she had watched Kelli walking into the house.

I'm comparing myself with a fifteen-year-old. That's ridiculous.

Why didn't the thought make her feel better?

Maybe she was being too hard on herself. But it had not been lost on her while they were all in the pool that Dave's legs and chest were well muscled and his stomach was still fairly firm. Kate wondered what he thought when he looked at her. She resolved to be more diligent about getting exercise every day.

Dave turned toward her and moved his hand as though he were about to touch her on the knee, then seemed to think better of it. He took hold of her hand instead. "I think I'll go in and see if everything is OK with Kelli. I'll take in the rest of the food," he said, squeezing her hand as he stood. He gathered up the condiments and hamburger buns, leaving only the birthday cake on the serving table near the shallow end of the pool. "You're the lifeguard," he called as he walked toward the house.

Kate realized she hadn't been paying attention to the children in the pool. KatiLynn was at the shallow end playing with Stevie and Alicia. Ross was sitting on the side at the deep end dangling his legs in the water, throwing something into the pool. It registered in Kate's mind that a few minutes ago she had seen Ross kneeling by the flower garden at the back of the yard and she had wondered fleetingly what he was doing there. Now she saw a small pile of marble-sized pebbles beside him on the pool deck. He was skipping them across the water, trying to see how far he could make them go before they sank.

Sometimes when she watched other people's children, and even her own, do heedless, foolish things, she wondered what they were thinking—or if they were thinking at all. And sometimes as a parent, she reacted without taking time to weigh the words. "Ross, don't do that, please. We don't put rocks or other trash in the pool." It came out sounding like a warning sign at a public swimming pool. Kate winced internally.

Ross glanced at her over his shoulder, picked up another pebble, skipped it across the water, and watched it sink in the deep end. "Your pool guy will get them out," he answered sullenly.

Kate was shocked at his audacity. She didn't hesitate with her retort. "We don't *have* a pool guy. *I* clean it out—and I don't have a lot of time to spend on that. If some of those rocks get through to the pump, it will cost a lot of money to fix it. So please don't put any more of them in the pool!"

Ross didn't answer. He stared down into the water, his arms at his sides, hands braced on the edge of the pool.

Kate turned to look at the other children. They had been standing still listening to the exchange between her and Ross, but now Alicia went back to bobbing in her float ring as KatiLynn pulled her through the shallows.

"Watch, Mom," Stevie called. He went head first into the water, put his hands flat on the bottom, and pushed his body straight up into a handstand. After a few seconds, he slowly slid down and forward, and Kate clapped for him as he surfaced.

Out of the corner of her eye, she saw the splashes of another pebble skipping across the deep end of the pool.

"Ross, I asked you not to do that!"

His answer was muttered, but still she heard it clearly: "I don't care. You're not my mom."

The other children were watching again as Kate rose from the chaise and strode toward Ross. He watched her come, a mixture of defiance and apprehension on his face.

She stopped beside him, scooped up his pile of pebbles, and flung them at the flower garden, then turned her back on him and walked away.

She lowered herself carefully onto the chaise lounge again and tried not to look at the boy at the far end of the pool. "That was a good handstand, Stevie," she said, then turned to Alicia and added as brightly as she could, "Show me how you can swim."

Alicia smiled for her and began to dog paddle across the shallow end.

At the edge of her field of vision, Kate saw Ross's arm whip sideways across his body, saw another splash in the water. "Ow!" KatiLynn yelped from where she clung to the far edge of the pool about halfway up the side. She twisted around in the water, her hand going to her bare back between her shoulder blades. Kate saw the black speck of a pebble sinking beside her daughter. KatiLynn looked pleadingly at her mother, pain in her eyes.

Kate stood and walked to the edge of the pool. "Are you going to be all right, Sweetheart?" she asked her daughter. Hesitantly, KatiLynn nodded.

Kate started slowly toward Ross with no idea what she was going to do when she got there this time.

Ross scrambled out of the pool and stood facing her defiantly, arms rigid at his sides, hands clenched into fists.

Kate stopped five feet from him. "I told you not to throw any more rocks. Why did you do that?" she asked evenly. "You could have hurt KatiLynn badly."

"I don't have to do what you tell me," Ross hissed at her. "You're not my mother." The next word out of his mouth was not hissed, but clear and distinct—a filthy name.

KatiLynn gasped.

"Ross!" Alicia protested. "You shouldn't say that! You know what Dad told us."

The boy continued to look at Kate defiantly. She felt her cheeks burning. But her steady gaze was finally too much for him; he looked down at the ground.

Alicia moved to the side of the pool and looked up at her brother. "You know that's a bad word. When we heard it on television, Dad told us we should never say it to anybody."

"Say what?" Dave asked.

Kate turned to see that he had just come out of the house, with Kelli close behind him, her hands full of paper plates and plastic forks.

"Say what, Ross?" Dave repeated with a firmness that indicated he expected an answer.

Ross stood glaring at his father but said nothing.

Dave looked at KatiLynn, who obviously had been a witness, but she looked away. He looked at Kate. Her brow was furrowed, her lips compressed into a thin line. She simply shook her head slightly.

Dave turned to Alicia, who had tears in her eyes now. "What was it?" he asked softly.

She looked down at the water before speaking. "A word we heard on TV once. You told us it was a bad name." She looked up at her father. "He said it to Kate."

Dave looked wonderingly at his son. "You . . . you called Kate a dirty name?" His voice had risen. He began to advance on Ross. The boy looked surprised and began to back away.

Dave looked into Kate's eyes as he passed her. She said nothing, gave no sign of assent, but what he saw there seemed to tell him what he needed to know.

Dave took three quick steps and caught Ross by the arm to keep him from retreating farther. "You . . . I can't believe you would say something like . . ." He glanced at Kate and shook his head. There was a deep red flush in his face. She had never seen him look so upset.

Holding onto Ross's arm, Dave walked the boy toward Kate. "You need to apologize—just for starters. Right now."

The boy's look told Kate he was feeling anything but apologetic. As his father stopped him in front of her, Ross jerked his arm free of Dave's grasp and bolted. In his rush to get away, Ross ran straight into the serving table at the end of the pool. The table began to tip and he stumbled behind it, shoving it forward. Kate moved to grab the table but missed. The birthday cake began to slide, slowly at first, and then as the table tipped farther, dropped to the ground in a ruined heap of devil's food cake and thick white frosting.

Ross fell over the table, missing the cake but landing hard on the patio. He lay stunned for a moment before he moved.

Dave stepped around the table and bent over his son. Ross had a scrape on his left elbow from the patio stone, but no other apparent injury. His father lifted him to his feet. Dave's face was ashen now. "Are you all right?" he asked very deliberately.

Ross watched his father's face apprehensively. "Yeah—I guess."

"Good. Now go wait for us in the van."

"I can't. It's, uh . . . it's locked." Dave looked around for the duffel bag with his jeans in it, where he had left his keys. "And it's too hot," Ross added hastily.

"Then you wait for us on the grass beside the car. You don't go *any-where*. And you don't touch another thing here. Are we clear on that?"

Ross nodded and headed toward the driveway, around the corner of the house.

Kelli knelt on the patio and began scooping chunks of the cake onto a paper plate. Tears ran down her cheeks. Kate understood; Dave had told her how lovingly his older daughter had made and decorated this cake for her brother. Kate knelt too and put a hand on Kelli's arm. "It was a beautiful cake. And don't worry about that. I can do it later."

"I'll clean it up," Dave said. "Please, Kell, can you help Alicia get her things together?"

Dave put the table upright then began using one paper plate to scoop chunks of cake onto another. "What set this off?" he asked Kate. She thought for a moment before answering. "Maybe I was too hard on him, Dave. I think I didn't handle the problem very well. If—"

"I can't believe that, Kate. But what was the problem?"

"He, uh . . . he was throwing rocks into the pool and I asked him to stop."

"He hit KatiLynn with a rock," Alicia added as Kelli put a towel around her.

"With a *rock?* Where?" Dave asked.

KatiLynn turned her back so he could see it. There was a large red welt below her right shoulder blade.

Dave breathed in slowly. "It looks like my son and I have a lot to talk about." He shook his head. "I'm sorry, Kate. I thought everything would work out well this time."

"It's all right. This wasn't your fault."

"Still, it seems like every time . . ."

"Alicia and I had fun," Kelli said. Dave and Kate turned to watch as she wrapped her little sister tightly in the towel. Kelli still had tears in her eyes. "Didn't we?" she said to her sister.

"Yes," Alicia answered. She hugged Kate around the waist before heading off toward their car. "Thank you," Kelli said softly as she followed after her sister.

Dave stood looking at Kate across the table. He walked around to her side and took her in his arms. "I'm truly sorry for my son's behavior." She thought he was going to kiss her on the lips, but he glanced at KatiLynn and Stevie and gave her a peck on the cheek instead.

Kate managed a smile. "Stop worrying about it. And call me later."

She watched as he walked away, then turned to busy herself with the cleanup so she wouldn't have to think about what had just happened.

She caught Stevie scooping up a gob of the ruined cake with his fingers and putting it into his mouth. He saw her watching as he licked his fingers. His smile was completely guileless. "It's good cake."

Kate smiled, then laughed in spite of herself, and wondered how she could do that when she was on the verge of tears. She knelt to put one arm around her son and held out the other arm beckoning for KatiLynn to come to them. "I love you both so much. I'm glad you're not like . . . I'm glad I have the two of you."

16

"Where was he when they found him?" Kate asked.

"Almost at the cemetery," Dave answered.

"At 1:30 in the morning?"

"Yeah." Dave veered automatically around a small rough patch in the grass and increased his pace to stay beside her.

"His mother's grave," Kate said. She slowed to a walk, breathing deeply.

Dave matched his stride to hers. "Yeah. He almost made it. He wouldn't give the police my name at first—just hers. He cried when they wouldn't take him to the cemetery. But he doesn't know they told me that." Dave walked a few paces before he spoke again. "It was a shock to me when they called. I thought he was asleep down the hall."

They had been running for nearly half an hour. Sweat rolled off his face. The wet spot on the front of his T-shirt covered much of his chest. Kate's back was soaked; sweat ran down her face too. Her cheeks were flushed, and some of the hair she had not pulled back into a ponytail frizzed out to the sides of her head.

Even that way she was beautiful, he thought. He studied her face. She did not look at him. "Something wrong?" he asked finally.

She walked a ways before answering. "Nothing, really. I'm just glad Ross is OK. Poor little guy."

"What do you mean?"

"Holding it in all this time—about his mother."

"Holding what in?"

"All that anger. About his mother."

Dave frowned. "His *mother?*"

"Yes. Sometimes when people die, the ones who are left behind can carry anger around for a long time. They feel like they've been robbed of something important. It feels so unfair! And they may feel abandoned.

At one level, they know the person couldn't help dying, but at another they may feel like the person went off and left them. I know—I felt that way sometimes after Steve died, when I was alone with two little children." Kate paused. "That was before I knew about the gospel."

Dave thought it over for several seconds. He couldn't remember feeling that way after Jeanine died. Had Kate actually studied this subject, or was she just practicing armchair psychology? "I don't think Ross would feel that way," he responded.

Kate glanced at him. "Don't you? Twice yesterday, he told me, 'You're not my mother.' And where was he going last night? I'm afraid he misses her and he needs her—needs to know that she still loves him. Maybe he needs to be able to tell her somehow that he still loves her."

"But if he's angry about *her,* why would he take it out on you?"

"On his birthday when his mother wasn't there, and he was with someone he doesn't want to be his mother? I was a handy target." She walked in silence for a ways before she looked at him and continued. "The problem is, I'm afraid I'd always be the handy target." She paused again, then went on. "Early this morning I had a nightmare about Ross coming after *me* with a rock—a big one the size of your fist."

"It was only a dream, Kate. Ross is about to be an adolescent, and maybe I need to learn how to handle him right, but I think he'll grow out of this."

"It may not be as simple as growing out of this. It may take time for him to understand his own feelings. Right now he seems to need to know that he's important to you, and that he's still tied to you and Jeanine. I'm afraid I could be in the way."

Dave stopped walking and took her arm so that she stopped too. "Kate, what is it you're trying to tell me?"

"That I'm afraid I could come between you and your children—just by being there."

"I don't think that would happen. Things are going well between you and Kelli, and Alicia loves you. Ross is sorry about what happened yesterday. You read the note I brought you."

It had been written on lined paper torn out of a notebook, in Ross's handwriting. It read: *"I'm sorry I was so angry with you yesterday. I'm sorry I called you an ugly name. Please forgive me. It was an unworthy thing to do."* Those didn't seem like words an eleven-year-old would use. "Was the note his idea—or yours?" Kate asked.

"Well—he agreed that it was a good idea."

"I'm afraid Ross might not really feel that way deep inside, and the next time something comes up between us—"

"He knows there'd better not be a next time like the last one!"

Kate looked into his eyes for several seconds before answering, and when she spoke, he had the feeling she was trying to be patient with him. "Dave, we're normal people with our share of normal differences. You can't force him to think like you, or me. Things *will* come up." She gazed off across the park for a moment. "I might be OK for Alicia right now because she needs a mommy. And there's peace between Kelli and me for the moment, but she's coming up on times when she'll need to make more and more of her own decisions. What if I'm not up to helping her—or if we disagree? I'm afraid I might never measure up to what she remembers of her mother." She looked at Dave again. "And I'm afraid of putting you in a position where you might have to side with me against your daughter or your son."

"Kate, have you noticed how many times you've said 'I'm afraid' in this conversation? Are you letting fear stand in the way of choosing the right thing for your future? I think we could work out any problems. We've got the Lord and the gospel to help us, and you'd be better at working with my kids than you know."

"Are you sure of that?" she asked softly. "In your heart, are you sure of what would be the right thing for my future—or for ours?"

When he did not answer immediately, she turned and began to walk toward her car in the parking lot.

Dave walked beside her. "There's something else bothering you," he said.

"Oh?" She glanced coolly at him. "Are you into mind-reading today?"

He ignored the challenge in her tone. "No. But I haven't heard you discouraged like this very often. You usually don't run from challenges. You take them on and beat them. So I think there must be more to this than what you're telling me."

"How do you know so much about what I'm thinking?" She stopped by her car and turned to face him. "What makes you think you can . . . who do you think you . . ." She stood frowning at him, seemingly at a loss for words.

"Okay, tell me there's nothing else to this," Dave said, "and then we'll talk about my kids. I think we can find ways to handle any problems you see with them."

Kate leaned back against the car, folded her arms across her chest, and stared down at a lump of asphalt in the pavement that had oozed out during the summer's heat. He leaned against the front fender patiently waiting for her to speak first. When words finally came out, she did not look up at him. "All right. I've been wondering if you and I are really right for each other after all. I love you. But maybe this trouble between me and your children is one of the warning signs that this can't really work out. Maybe I could never really compete with Jeanine. Maybe I'll never really be able to let go of Steve. Maybe . . ." She shrugged. Then she looked up at him. "Maybe we're fooling ourselves."

"Is that what this is about? You're wondering if I can *really* let go of Jeanine? Because you're afraid you can't really let go of Steve."

"All right!" Her voice rose. "I still love Steve. It's been six years and sometimes I still miss him. I feel like I need to be sealed to my children's father. I *want* it that way. I'll probably never stop loving him. Can you live with that?"

"Of course. I'll never stop loving Jeanine. I'm not going to try, even if we get married. But I can love you too, with everything I've got to give. Can *you* live with *that?*"

"Dave! Haven't you ever wondered how Jeanine might feel knowing that you found someone else you could love—knowing that you were *living* with someone else? Haven't you ever wondered how that would affect your relationship when you see her again?"

"No, I don't have to wonder. I told you she made me promise that as soon as I could deal with it, I'd look for somebody I could love so I wouldn't be alone—somebody she'd like too. I found you."

Kate didn't respond or look his way. Her eyes seemed fixed on some point in the distance.

Finally he said, "You're worried that when you meet Steve again, he won't see it the way Jeanine did, aren't you?"

"Yes. When I married him, it was with all my heart, and for always in my mind, even though I didn't know anything about eternal marriage. I told him how I felt, and he said that's all he could ever ask of me."

Dave hesitated before asking the next question. He wasn't sure he was ready to push for an answer. "Do you love *me*, Kate?"

"Yes, I just told you that. You know I—"

"I know what you've *told* me. But do you really believe it yourself, deep inside? I can't help but wonder if—"

She stopped him by taking his face between her hands and kissing him. She made it last for a long time. It surprised him. Usually she waited for him to take the lead. There were only a couple of other joggers in the park this morning, but she had never done anything like this in public before.

When she let him go, she looked into his eyes and said, "Yes, I really, really love you."

"You're sure? In your heart? I mean . . ."

"Yes. That's why this is so hard for me." Dave could see tears in her eyes.

"I love you," she continued. "And I know what I want to do about that. But I . . . but . . . I've only loved one other man like this, and when I'm sealed to him in the temple, that will make it complete. I'll be his for eternity. So if I love someone else too, and if I marry him, what does that mean? Did I fool myself about Steve—didn't I know what I *really* wanted? Will Steve feel like I wasn't faithful? There are so many things I don't know, Dave. I don't know what I should feel now. I don't know what to do."

"You're the only one who can decide." He waited several seconds for her to say something, then turned and started walking slowly toward his car.

She followed. "Please tell me what to do, Dave. I don't know the answer."

"I can't tell you what to do, Kate. Nobody on this earth could—"

He stopped walking suddenly, and she stopped too, looking at him questioningly.

"You're waiting for Steve's permission, aren't you?" he said. "You're wanting *him* to tell you what to do!"

She looked surprised. "No, I . . . why would I . . ." She gazed off across the park thoughtfully.

Dave shook his head. "You're going to wait a long time."

"Dave, you don't understand! When I was baptized, I looked forward to making my covenant with Steve in the temple. I *know* Steve wants that too. I know that he knows what I'm doing sometimes. I almost feel like he knows what I'm thinking. You don't understand how that—"

"I *do* understand. I'm sure Jeanine knows what's going on with me and our family sometimes—especially with her children. She'll know that the covenant I made with her is just as firm as it ever was. But Kate, right now you and I are on our own in *this* life."

Dave put his arms around her, held her close to him for a moment, then kissed her tenderly. "I love you deeply. I want to spend the rest of my life here with you. But I don't think I could do it with Steve looking over my shoulder all the time. And I don't think I can go on living with the way things are now—just seeing you whenever we're able to get together." He kissed her lightly on the lips once more. "Someone needs to decide whether we can be together *all* the time—and I think it will have to be you."

There were tears in her eyes now. "You know it's not that simple. There are a lot of things we need to be sure of. The kids—"

"I know—could our kids get along? I think they could. They're normal, they'd probably fight sometimes. But I have faith in them—KatiLynn and Stevie too. They could learn to handle living together."

He touched her cheek gently with his hand, then pulled it away. "The only real question is the one you're not facing—are the two of us going to be together for as long as we have in this life, or are we each going to go it alone?"

Kate made no effort to wipe away the tears that would not stop. "Dave, I don't know—"

He put his finger to her lips. "Somehow you've got to find out."

Dave let go of her, unlocked the door of his car, and opened it. "Please call me if you decide anything—one way or the other."

Tears dripped onto the soggy spot on the front of her shirt. "Please don't, Dave. Please don't do this to me. I can't—"

"Yes, you can. You have to." He wanted to hold her in his arms and tell her he didn't mean what he had said, that it was all right, that things could go on just as they were. But things *couldn't* go on just as they were. He *had* meant what he said, and it was obvious that things between them had to change somehow—one way or the other. He leaned forward and kissed her tenderly again. "This will be hard for me too. I have to face trying to figure what to do with the rest of my life if you decide . . ." He looked into her eyes for several seconds. "Well, anyway, you need to decide what you want. I hope you'll call me just as soon as you know."

Dave kissed her once more, pressing her close to him and lingering on her lips. Then he let her go, got into his car, started it, and drove away.

Kate walked to her car, got in, shut the door, and leaned against the steering wheel sobbing.

She was angry with him for saying how much he loved her then abandoning her. How could he go off and leave her like that? How could he say she was the one who would finally have to decide what would happen to their relationship?

It was frustrating. It was unnerving.

In fact, it was frightening, because she knew he was right.

* * *

Bill Morrow was leaning over a picnic table, stretching the muscles of his calves, when he realized there was someone standing beside him. He turned to look at the man, a stranger dressed in a tee shirt, Bermuda shorts, and running shoes.

No—not a stranger.

"You're . . ."

"Dave. Dave Cutler." The man extended his hand.

Bill shook it tentatively. "You came to the hospital with Kate. And I've seen you a couple of times when you dropped her off to pick up the kids." He paused. "She hasn't told us a lot about you."

Dave smiled. "And a man can't be too careful about who goes out with his only daughter. What do you want to know?"

Bill laughed in spite of himself. He wasn't sure how to feel about this man. The guy seemed likable enough. But Belle had strong feelings about their daughter's "boyfriend." It might be best not to get too friendly with this Mormon.

Bill turned and started walking along the grass at the edge of the park. The other man walked beside him. "Do you mind if I walk with you?"

Bill glanced at the man and shook his head. "No. It's everybody's park."

They walked almost to the end of the park before Dave said, "I was hoping I would find Kate here. She told me she walks with you some mornings."

"Yeah—but not this morning. She had a meeting over at the Warden offices."

"Oh."

They walked in silence for several seconds more while Bill tried to figure out what might be going on in the other man's mind. Why had he shown up here today?

"So Kate's been pretty busy?" Dave asked. "I, ah, didn't hear from her for a couple of days, so I tried to reach her by phone and couldn't get an answer."

Kate had caller ID and voice messaging, Bill knew. If she had wanted to answer, she would have.

"We had a disagreement a few days ago," Dave continued.

"A fight?" Bill chuckled. "It usually takes two, but I know my daughter can be pretty firm about things when she's made up her mind."

"Not a fight, exactly. Just a disagreement." Dave glanced at him. "And you hit on the problem—she can't make up her mind."

Bill's eyebrows went up. "That might be a first."

"I was waiting for her to make a decision about, ah . . . something important, and call me. But I decided that maybe I was too wrapped up in what *I* wanted when we talked about it. Maybe I didn't take her feelings seriously enough."

Bill shook his head slowly. "One more guy learns a lesson the hard way." He glanced sideways at the other man. "So—how do I fit into this? What do you want from me?"

"So there's one thing I'd like to know from you, and I think you're the kind of man who'll tell me honestly if I ask."

"Shoot."

"I get the feeling you and your wife may not approve of me. Did I do something to offend you?"

Bill shook his head. "Not me."

"But Kate's mother doesn't like me?"

Bill glanced sideways at the other man and walked a ways before answering. "I wouldn't say that, exactly."

"Is it my religion?"

"Yeah—I think that's it."

"Can you tell me why she feels that way, and is there anything I can do about it?"

"She had a bad experience with Mormons when she was younger. I don't know if there's anything anyone could do to change the way she feels now."

"And you? How do you feel?"

"Me? I don't much care what religion a man is if he lives a good life. I judge more by what he does than by the building he walks into on Sunday morning."

Bill wished he knew more about this man. Kate trusted him, and she had good judgment. That was an important point in Dave Cutler's favor. But Bill knew his daughter needed a strong man. Was this one strong enough?

They had walked nearly the length of the park again before Bill spoke. "You know, maybe there is something you could do that would please my wife. We love having the grandkids over to visit with us. Sometimes Sunday afternoon is all we have with them. My wife thought maybe we could take them to the movies, or the kiddy arcade, or someplace they'd really enjoy. But Kate doesn't seem to want us to do that. Do you think you could talk to her about it—maybe get her to loosen up a little for Grandma and Grandpa?"

Dave was silent for several seconds. Then: "Well, I suppose . . ." He looked sideways at Bill as though trying to read his face. Bill kept it expressionless.

Dave faced forward again. "I suppose KatiLynn and Stevie are old enough to make some choices like that on their own. I don't know if you've asked them what *they* want. But if Kate has asked you not to offer them the choice, then as a parent I'd have to back her up. It seems to me you raised *your* daughter to know good principles and live by them. I'd think you'd be proud that she's doing it."

Bill laughed heartily. "You're OK, Cutler. And you put me in *my* place."

Dave's brow furrowed. "Was that some kind of test?"

"You passed. I wouldn't think much of a man who'd compromise his principles to please somebody else. My daughter needs a *strong* man—a man who lives by what he believes. After Steve, I didn't know whether she could find one to measure up. But since she's been going out with you, it seems like she's found something she needed in her life. I'm glad to see it."

"She didn't say anything to you about our discussion the other day?"

"No." Bill frowned. "But these past two weeks or so I've felt like she's under a lot of pressure. I'm planning to take some of it off of her. The doctor says I can start going back to the office. That'll give her more time to be a mom again."

Bill studied the other man's profile for a moment as they walked. "So you had a discussion, she left you standing, and now you're looking for a way to patch things up?"

"Actually, I was the one who left. I told her she needed to decide if Steve was the only man she could ever live with. I've told her I'd like for the two of us to spend the rest of this life together—but that will be up to her."

Bill had been wanting to ask another Mormon about something Kate had said, and Belle wasn't here to look daggers at him if he brought it up. "You really believe in this eternal marriage idea she's told us about?"

Dave looked Bill's way as he answered. "Yes. I know it's true."

"How?"

Dave seemed to be considering carefully what he should say.

"Sorry," Bill added. "I didn't mean to ask about something that may be none of my business."

"I know because of my wife, Jeanine," Dave answered. "I don't talk about it a lot, but she's been there sometimes to help me with our kids."

"You've seen—"

"No. She's just *there*. You'd have to feel it to understand. Thoughts come, almost like words she'd say to me—what she'd tell me to do for the kids. I know God has let her be there to share ideas."

Bill was not sure how to respond. Something inside—something he couldn't put a name to—told him this man knew what he was talking about. And maybe this eternal marriage idea didn't agree with what priests and ministers taught, but it was what ought to happen if God really loved His children the way all the churches said. He would want that with Belle.

He glanced at Dave again. "You're willing to let Kate be Steve's someday as long as she spends the next thirty or forty years with you?"

"Yeah. I want to marry her. I'm in love with her. I can't explain exactly how that works because I still love my first wife—but I'm in love with your daughter." He looked at Bill. "What I want most is what's best for Kate. It's up to her to decide what that is." He paused. "But I believe spending our lives together would be good for both of us."

"You'd get my vote, for what that's worth. Belle . . . well, I have to live with my wife, so I probably won't bring this conversation up with her. But I don't think you have to worry about her influencing Kate." Slowly, he shook his head. "If you're the best thing for my daughter, she'll come to that decision on her own. I doubt there's much anybody else could do to convince her one way or the other."

* * *

Kate hesitated with her hand raised to knock on the door. She felt uncertain about coming here. She wasn't at all sure how she might be received.

But finally she tapped tentatively.

It was Ross who opened the door. He looked at her in surprise. Then his brows knitted.

"I brought back these dishes," Kate said. She held out the cake plate and cake server they had left at her house after the birthday party. She had expected that Dave would pick them up the next time he stopped by or brought her home from a date. But of course he had not come to her house since their conversation in the park.

Slowly, Ross reached out and took the plate in one hand and the serving knife in the other, carefully, as though she might suddenly grab him and drag him outside. Then he stood looking at her.

"May I come in?" Kate asked.

"My dad's not here," Ross answered.

"That's all right. I thought you and I might talk a little."

The look Ross gave her was somewhere between questioning and glowering. "Talk about what?"

"We haven't been on very good terms. I thought maybe we could talk about that."

"Why?"

"I think we could do better, if we try."

Ross seemed to be weighing something in his mind. Then: "I don't know if I can talk to you."

"Really?" She tried to smile. "It might help."

He gazed down at the ground intently, as though he were studying something there—perhaps her shoes. "I don't think we . . . I mean, when I talk to you, I get in trouble, so . . . " He looked up at her again and said nothing for several seconds. Finally, he began to close the door slowly. "I'll tell my dad you were here."

Kate opened her mouth to speak, but no words would come out. She watched as the boy slowly shut the door, staring into her eyes until the crack became too narrow. She heard the lock click softly into place. She stood looking at the varnished wood of the door for several seconds. Then she turned and walked away.

In her car, she sat thinking for a while before starting it and backing out into the street. She had shifted gears and was ready to drive away when the door of Dave's house opened and Alicia came running out to the driveway. Kelli peered out the door behind her. Alicia stood in the driveway waving. Kate tried to smile at her as she waved back. Then she took her foot off the brake and let her car begin to move.

Dave came driving up the street from the other direction just as she was pulling away from his house. He stopped his minivan, rolled down his window as she approached, and leaned out ready to talk to her. She slowed her car to a crawl, tried to smile for him, then waved through her window and drove on.

Dave's smile faded as she passed. He watched over his shoulder as she came to the cross street, turned right, and disappeared behind the house that sat on the corner.

Should he go after her?

He backed into a neighbor's driveway, changed gears, and started to accelerate out of the driveway in the direction Kate had gone. But something stopped him.

Obviously, she hadn't felt like talking. If he caught up with her, he would not know how to change that. He could only tell her again that he loved her, and beg her to make a decision—one way or the other.

And what if she had come here just now to tell him that she *had* made a decision? What if she had decided finally that things could never work between them? Did she pass him up because she didn't want to have that discussion sitting here in the street?

He knew he didn't want to face a *no* right now. First he needed to think about what he might say to persuade her, if it were possible, that they could work out any problems together.

Slowly he let his van roll across the street into his own driveway. He turned off the engine, locked the car, and walked to his front door.

It was Kelli's raised voice he heard when he opened the door. "What were you thinking, Ross? Honestly! Why would you tell her something like that? You're hopeless!"

Dave shut the door behind him. His three children, standing in the hallway just beyond the living room, turned their heads to look at him. Kelli stood almost toe to toe with Ross, whose hands were clenched into fists at his sides. Alicia, tears in her eyes, hugged Kelli around the waist from behind. "Kelli?" Dave said.

She looked away.

"I can't think of a good reason to talk to your brother that way."

Kelli looked him in the eyes again. "Kate was here. He was rude to her. He wouldn't even let her in."

Dave studied his son's face, trying to determine what was behind the anger he saw. "Kell," he said carefully, "I promised you a driving lesson in the high school parking lot this afternoon. Can you be ready in half an hour?"

His daughter understood. She put an arm around Alicia and led her toward their bedroom.

Dave sat down in the nearest chair and beckoned to his son. "Ross, come in here please. I think we need to talk."

Ross lingered in the hallway for a moment, then walked warily across the room and sat on the edge of the sofa opposite his father.

"Want to tell me about it?" Dave asked softly.

Ross shrugged. "She brought back the dishes we left at her house. I told her you'd be back later."

Dave leaned forward in his chair. "I'm sure there was something—" He stopped when he realized Kelli was standing in the entrance to the living room.

She walked toward Ross. "I came to tell you I'm sorry for what I said to you. It was a bad thing to do. You're not hopeless." She put one knee down on the carpet so she could be on his level. "Kate was trying to be your friend. Couldn't you try too instead of talking to her that way?" She waited for an answer, but her brother looked down at the floor and said nothing. Finally, Kelli stood, glanced at her father, and walked out of the room.

"Talking to her what way, Ross?" Dave asked.

The boy continued to look down at the floor. His words came out in a rush. "She brought the dishes back, and I took them, and then she said maybe the two of us could talk, and I said why, and she said maybe we could do better than we have been, and I didn't know if we could." He looked up, read the expression on his father's face, and plunged ahead even more nervously. "Dad, I told her I didn't know if I could talk to her. . . . I didn't know what we could . . . and besides, you told me if I talked to her again, I'd better . . ." His voice trailed off as he watched his father's face.

Dave let out a breath slowly. He would not permit anger to take over again. "Son, do you think maybe she was trying to say she was sorry for the way things have gone between you? Do you think she was trying to make it easier for you to be friends?"

"Dad!" There was anguish in Ross's voice. "I don't know if we can *be* friends."

Dave raised his eyebrows. "Why not?"

"Because . . . because—why would she want to be friends with me?"

"Do you think she might care about you?"

"Yeah, sure! She cares about *you*, not about me. She only says she cares about me because it makes you feel good. And you care more about . . . anyway, if I talk to her, I get in trouble, and if I don't talk to her, I get in trouble. Whenever I'm around her I get in trouble!" Ross jumped up from the sofa and ran out of the living room. Seconds later, the door to his bedroom slammed shut.

Dave slumped in his chair, hand over his eyes. It masked the tears that blurred his vision.

He didn't have emotional highs or lows very often. Jeanine had said he was too even-tempered, that it just wasn't in him to be giddy with joy or to rage in anger or cry in grief. He might feel those things inside, but he usually kept them under control.

Usually.

Today was one of those rare hurting times when frustration and disappointment came out in tears. Quickly he wiped them from his eyes. Kelli would be coming out for her driving lesson soon. He couldn't let his daughters see him cry. They needed him to be strong, didn't they? If he couldn't offer them strength, what else did he have to offer?

He might need all the strength he could find within himself if his life continued to go the way it had for the past few days.

Maybe Kate was right. Maybe the two of them were not meant to be together.

Maybe he had wanted it so badly that he had been fooling himself.

17

Kate gazed out at the planes in the tie-down area. Which one, if she went flying today? The new twin was a very nice aircraft, smooth handling, easy to fly. The single-engine Cessna had always been a favorite of hers. Or the trainer . . .

No good. It's not working. Just thinking about flying usually makes me feel better. Why not now?

Sighing, she turned and walked toward the building and the work that was waiting. Her father would be here in an hour to continue their review of the current status of Morrow Flight Service. They had been at it for the past four days. On Monday, he would officially be the manager once more and she would revert to part-time helper.

Ann looked up from her desk and smiled as Kate pushed the front door open. The flowers on Ann's desk caught Kate's eye immediately.

Dave! Did he . . . it would be wonderful if he decided that he needed to see me. But he hasn't called or come by since . . .

Not since she had left his house in tears after Ross turned her away.

But now, flowers! She turned up the card attached to the vase to read it.

It was addressed to Ann. Kate let go of the card immediately—but not before she noticed the name signed at the bottom: "Rich."

"Oh. I thought maybe Dave . . . ah . . ." Kate felt herself blushing. *There's no way to get out of this gracefully.* "I'm sorry, Ann. Rich is the man you told me about, isn't he? You met him at . . ."

Ann brightened. "At the gym. He took me out to dinner and a movie last Saturday." She glanced down at the flowers. "These came this morning—and then he called to ask if I'm free tomorrow night."

The bouquet was a modest size, Kate thought—smaller than the last one Dave had sent to her. And she regretted instantly the self-centeredness of that thought. She made herself smile. "So, are you free tomorrow night?"

"Of course." Ann smiled broadly.

"Things are going well with him so far?"

"Yes. He's a nice guy. I like him a lot."

"I hope everything works out the way you want it," Kate said as she walked away toward her office.

She was studying some papers she had picked up from the Federal Aviation Administration when Ann walked through her door a few minutes later. "Here are the maintenance logs," she said, putting them on the desk.

She stood hesitantly for a moment looking at Kate. "Is everything all right? You didn't seem very happy this morning. And for the past few days—"

"I haven't seemed like myself?" Kate interrupted.

"Well, yes. I wondered—"

"You, and my father, and my daughter." Kate sighed. "I'm just fine, thank you." There was a finality about it she hadn't intended—a tone that said, "Don't ask."

Ann opened her mouth as if to say something more, then seemed to think better of it. She turned and walked out of the office.

Why, Kate? Why were you so prickly with her? She's concerned about you. That's the way a friend feels. You should be grateful that Ann and your father and KatiLynn care so much.

Last night it had been KatiLynn who sensed that something was wrong. She hadn't brought it up directly; instead, she had tried to do all the things that ordinarily cheered her mother up. When those had not worked, KatiLynn had simply wrapped her in a hug and said, "I love you, Mom," before going off to bed.

Two days ago it had been her father. Bill had been blunt.

"Lately you're just going through the motions, Kate. You're behaving a little like you did after you lost Steve. You need to get off the fence and move one way or the other."

She gave him a puzzled look. "What does that mean, Dad? I'm just fine."

"Sure, Kate—fine." He smiled at her the way he always had when she was a little girl and he was trying to console her. "You're pining—almost mourning. You need to decide whether you can't live without Dave Cutler or you're going to tell him good-bye and move on. Your children need you to decide. He needs you to decide."

"I've been trying to be what the children need, Dad. I've tried not to let them feel—" Kate stopped as her mind replayed the last thing he had said. *"You've talked to him, haven't you?"*

"Yeah. He showed up at the park one morning last week when I was walking. He hoped to find you there. You weren't answering his calls."

"What did you talk about?"

"Not much, really. He was wondering if your mother and I were working against him. I told him I wasn't, but it probably wouldn't make any difference anyway because this is a decision you're going to make for yourself." Her father reached out to take her hand; his large hands easily covered hers. *"Kate, let yourself be happy. Whatever decision does that for you, I'll support it, and I know your mother will too."*

Kate blinked away tears. *"Thanks, Dad. I need all the help I can get. There's not really any way for me to be sure whether Dave and I . . . it's just so hard to know! Some days I'm desperate for it to work out. But when I think about everything—his children, how I feel about Steve . . ."*

"Well, I know what's not making you happy—letting things go on the way they are. If you're sure it could never work out between you and Dave, then maybe you need to cut him loose. You might be doing him a favor and freeing yourself at the same time."

She had been trying not to face this decision. But her father was right—she could not go on drifting, hoping some heaven-sent solution would drop into her lap. She would have to make a choice.

Her father had simply been trying to help her the best way he knew how. And so had Ann. *You weren't very happy for her, the way a friend would be. And there was no need to be so curt. Why did you do that?*

The question—*Why?*—would not go away. Kate tried to concentrate on the maintenance records, but she could not. She kept thinking about a recent Relief Society lesson on receiving graciously from others and giving generously of ourselves.

After about ten minutes, she put down her pencil, stood, and walked out to Ann's desk. Ann looked up in surprise. Kate pulled a chair over to the desk and sat down. "I'm sorry. I've been self-centered and rude, and you've been kinder than I deserved. Forgive me?"

Ann gazed at her for a moment before answering. "It's about Dave, isn't it?"

"No, not exactly. It's—" Kate stopped. It *was* about Dave. No matter how she tried to tell herself it was about other things too, it was about Dave. Slowly, she nodded.

"It must be hard," Ann said, "if you're still having trouble deciding how you feel about him. But—"

"There's the problem—I'm not having trouble deciding how *I* feel about Dave. It's how his kids feel about *me*. And I still can't help wondering how Steve would feel about him." Kate blinked away tears again.

"I can't help you there," Ann said slowly. "I wish I could, but I'm afraid there's no one on earth who . . . Kate, I know you pray. I think you need answers no one here can give."

No one on earth. It was an echo of Dave's words the last time they spoke.

Kate put her hand on top of Ann's. "I just wanted you to know that I appreciate your concern, and your friendship." She glanced at the flowers on the desk. "I'm taking you to lunch today so I can hear all about Rich—if you want to share."

Ann smiled. "Of course I do."

"We'll go to the pie place down the street. You can have your favorite while you tell me what's going on."

Ann touched her flat stomach. "No pie today. I'll be seeing him at the gym tonight."

Kate laughed. "All right—salad and a few croutons, and you can tell me all the things that make this man worth sacrificing for."

* * *

She lay in bed staring up at the ceiling that was no more than a lighter shade of the dark.

In one way she envied Ann, for whom the decision would be much easier. Ann had loved Gary, but in her mind he was lost forever, perhaps never to know of her again. If things went as she hoped now with Rich, there would be no reason not to spend the rest of her days happily married to him.

It was not nearly so simple in her own case, Kate thought. It might be easy for others to make judgments about the situation on general principles, but she was dealing with real people—two men, both very much alive for her. There was an emotional barrier she had not been able to cross because someday she would be with Steve again. How would he feel if she had spent decades with Dave here on earth—*decades*—while she and Steve had had only five years? But never mind someday: how would he feel a few weeks or months from now if he could see that she was happily married to another man? She had loved Steve so much—still

221

loved him so much—she ached at the thought of doing anything that could possibly hurt him.

She loved Dave too much to go on hurting him, and it seemed her indecision was doing that.

It was certainly hurting her.

Her reluctance to remarry might easily have crumbled if it weren't for his children. If as a mother she couldn't accept Ross like a son, if she could not meet Kelli's needs, then the marriage could not succeed. In the end, all of the children would suffer.

It seemed that no matter what she decided, someone would be hurt.

She sighed. *Heavenly Father, please help me. I need knowledge—I need something—that I don't have. Please help me, in the name of Jesus Christ, amen.*

She lay as she had before, staring up toward the ceiling. Nothing changed inside of her. There was no answer.

It had been the same when she had prayed about this tonight before going to bed. It had been the same this morning when she had prayed before starting her day. It had been the same last night.

Kate threw back the sheet, got out of bed, and went to the window, where she could see a sliver of light between the curtains. She pulled them open and looked out. Somewhere above the house a veiled moon lit the backyard, casting weak, angular shadows of the jungle gym and swings on the other side of the swimming pool. She and Steve had talked about buying a swing set for the children before he died, but they had never gotten around to it. Kate had picked it out alone and assembled it herself after it was delivered. That had been five years ago, when Katilynn was just five. Now her daughter was beginning to outgrow the swings. Stevie and Alicia had been the ones to enjoy them a couple of weeks ago during Ross's birthday party.

She stood at the window for a long time, it seemed, keeping her mind blank except for the scene in front of her. She was tired of thinking about the decision that needed to be made. Somehow it was comforting that there was light, however faint, out there in the darkness.

Leaving the curtains open, she turned back to the bed. But instead of dropping into it, she felt impressed to kneel beside it once more.

Dear Heavenly Father, I don't know what to do, and I need Your . . . I need Thy help.

She had grown up without a personal God that she could pray to, and despite a year's experience, it still seemed awkward sometimes to pour out problems to Him in her own plain words. If He already understood her hopes and her desires, what was the point of trying to explain them to Him? But she needed His help right now as much as she had ever needed it in her life, and if He truly had a Father's heart, He would not be displeased by hearing her feelings once more.

You—Thou knowest how important this decision is to me, and I feel that it shouldn't be put off any longer. Is that right?

She felt a small stirring inside, like the beginning of the feeling that had come into her heart at other times when she was sure she had received an answer.

But it is a very difficult decision, and I don't think I'm wise enough to make it by myself. Please tell me whether I should marry Dave.

The small feeling of reassurance faded, replaced by a leaden one, and she felt as though she had just spoken to an empty room. Evidently that had been the wrong request.

Father, is this a decision I must make all by myself?

Something in her heart rejected that possibility. All she had learned about God, all she had studied in the scriptures and the prophets' teachings told her that He wouldn't leave her completely alone when she truly needed Him.

But if her questions were not getting responses, was there something she was overlooking?

Kate spoke softly. "Heavenly Father, if this is the kind of decision I'm supposed to make for myself, but with Thy help, the way it was when I asked about Thy Church, then—"

The feeling came very strongly this time, almost as it had on the day when she prayed about the truth of what the missionaries had taught her. This time too, she felt as though something had opened up inside of her, as though light were pouring in. An impression that had been only a half-acknowledged thought in her mind became fully formed and instantly clear in her heart: her Father wanted to help her, was ready to help her—when *she* was fully ready to commit herself to a choice. Of course He could easily tell her what to do, but the gift of agency was so important to Him that He would not override it. When she decided what she truly wanted to do, then He would confirm that decision if it were right. Expressing her deep, true feelings to Him was a way to be sure that *she* was committed to follow where He might lead.

Her heart was flooded with the certainty that He cared deeply about what she did with her life. Her eyes were flooded with tears.

Kate remained on her knees in silence for a minute or two before she finished her prayer, whispering again. "Father, please guide my thoughts as I deal with this choice in my own mind. Please help me see things clearly so that I can make the right decision, in the name of Jesus Christ, amen."

She got off her knees, climbed back into bed, and lay staring at the ceiling again. The last thing she felt before drifting off to sleep was the impression that her thinking so far had been too narrow, that she was not seeing all the possible effects of a marriage on lives beyond hers and Dave's.

* * *

The sun was halfway through its morning trajectory in the sky when she lifted off the runway in the twin. As she climbed out over the city, she brought the plane to a heading that would take her toward the arid mountain ranges to the west.

Her mother had been surprised when Kate had telephoned to ask if she could bring KatiLynn and Stevie over to spend Saturday. "I thought you weren't working today," Belle had said. "Your father is out at the airport."

"I need to go out there too," Kate had answered, unable to explain the urgency she felt.

"Is something wrong?" Belle had asked when Kate stopped at her house with the children.

"No, I . . ." Kate gazed off into the distance. "No, I need to go flying . . . to, uh . . ."

Her mother had smiled. "Just to think?"

"Yes."

Belle had laughed. "You and your father. He can't explain to me exactly what happens up there, but he'll go flying when he's been thinking about a problem and then come back with answers." Her mother had given her a hug. "I hope you find the answers you need."

Her mother's intuition was startling. Kate felt sure somehow that answers awaited her up here today. That was why she had resisted KatiLynn and Stevie's pleas to go flying with her, promising them another time instead. Today she needed to be alone.

A part of her was afraid to face this—afraid of dealing with the changes that answers might bring, afraid that she needed to think about the problem longer. But there wasn't any facet of it that she hadn't already turned over in her mind again and again.

It was decision time.

That thought made her stomach knot up. In her mind she heard the same chorus of questions to which there seemed to be no sure answers. Could she handle the emotional needs of five children? Could she give herself to a man who was not Steve, and feel comfortable about it? Could she reach the level of strong emotional interdependence that Dave had apparently enjoyed with Jeanine? That kind of relationship was something she and Steve had still been developing.

And the hardest question today: did she have the right to ask her own children to run emotional risk—mostly the risk of Ross—so she could enjoy whatever happiness she might have with Dave? The feeling that had come to her just before she dropped off to sleep last night seemed to be a reminder to consider the difficulties for the children. If she spread herself too thin trying suddenly to care for all five . . . if Dave were forced to be the referee between her and his son . . . if Ross took his anger out on KatiLynn and Stevie . . . if she had to choose between the needs of Dave's children and the needs of her own . . .

It had been two weeks since she had seen Dave.

Seven days ago—last Saturday afternoon—an express delivery courier had knocked on her door and handed her a small package. Inside was an exquisitely formed, clear crystal rose. The note with it said simply, "Thinking of you—every minute. I love you deeply. Dave."

KatiLynn had found her sitting in the living room, holding the rose in her hand, tears sliding down her cheeks and falling on the carpet. "Oh, Mom! It's beautiful. From Dave?" Kate had nodded and handed her the note. After reading it, KatiLynn had settled beside her on the couch, put her head on her mother's shoulder, and asked, "Are you going to call him?"

"I don't know, Sweetheart. Should I?"

KatiLynn had hesitated before answering. "I want you to be happy, Mom."

Except for that, KatiLynn had said nothing at all about Dave during the past two weeks. But she had been visibly relieved on Friday, before the rose was delivered, when she had learned that they would not be with Dave's family that night.

Stevie had mentioned once in the past two weeks that he had liked playing catch with Dave. He had also mentioned once that it had been fun having Alicia play games with him in the pool—but he had asked at the same time why Ross did not like him.

Dave had called four days ago, while she was at the Warden Avionics offices, and left a message: Ross had offered an apology of sorts for his behavior when she visited their house. He had been mad, he told his father, but he was not sure why; it was not her fault. "I guess you were right when you said he's carrying around a lot of anger," Dave added. It sounded as though he wanted to say more—but his message simply ended.

When she thought about marriage, it seemed more and more that whatever happiness she could gain with Dave might be at the expense of her children. Her responsibility to them would be eternal. She did not know if she could ask them to make the sacrifices that might be required. It seemed she was the one who needed to make the sacrifice instead.

She hurt inside whenever she thought about it.

Kate was turning all the questions over in her mind when she glanced down at the freeway far below. She could see the truck stop that marked the beginning of the road where she had landed the night she and Steve had been stranded out here. She realized that her flight plan today had not been haphazard; somewhere in her mind, or some part of her, she had been planning—*needing*—to come here.

She banked left forty-five degrees and flew southwest for three or four minutes, then put the plane into a wide turn that would bring it in line with that road headed north. She began a slow descent until she was no more than one hundred feet above the graded roadway.

Could she spot the place where she had taken off the morning after her father had repaired the plane? The question was only a matter of interest; it would be foolhardy to try to set this low-winged twin down on the roadway below. The bushes on the left would pose a threat that they hadn't for the high-winged Cessna when she landed here before.

She came to the spot where she thought she had lifted off of the ground that morning in the Cessna and, just as she had that day, climbed and banked right toward Phoenix to the east.

On that earlier morning, she had looked down on a desert landscape marked by shaded gullies and mountain ridges trailing shadows that obscured some of the rough spots in the terrain. She remembered also the day after Steve's funeral when she had flown across this landscape again, wishing that she could lose herself in one of those black pools of shadow.

Now, in midmorning sunlight, the desert landscape held no secrets. She could see almost every bit of it perfectly illuminated to the horizon.

It was stark, forbidding—but here and there she could see traces of green clinging to life along meandering washes that had a trickle of water running in their sandy beds.

The morning after the funeral when she had flown out here, she had decided she would live, for her children. Today, too, the choice seemed clear: she would live for her children. She owed it to KatiLynn and Stevie to provide for them emotionally in ways they could not provide for themselves. If she let them down now, it might never be possible to make up for the love and care she missed giving them at this stage of their lives.

And as for her own needs . . .

Kate sighed. As for her, it hurt not to see Dave. It had been all she could do several times in the past few days not to call him. But she knew that if she saw him, coming to a decision on her own might be impossible. The longer she went without seeing him, the less she seemed to hurt inside—most of the time. There were times, like last night, when she retreated to her bedroom to sob into her pillow behind the closed door. She would get over it—eventually.

She had thought once—one of those despairing times when she had been crying into her pillow—that perhaps she should be sealed to Dave. After all, Steve was part of her past, before she knew about eternal marriage. For her, Dave was now. But she had felt guilty immediately for the thought and had shoved it far back in her mind. Later, little by little, she had been able to deal with the idea. She had come to know that for reasons she might only understand sometime far in the future, it was right in the eternal scheme of things to do what she had planned from the day of her baptism—to be sealed to Steve. That had never seemed plainer than this morning when she awoke.

This past Saturday had marked a year since she was baptized. Four months ago, she had been planning to go to the temple on the very day, if she could, to be sealed to her husband. Now she had let the date pass. That had not been fair to him. She was sure Steve was waiting for opportunities that baptism and sealing would open to him.

Despite all her questions and her own desires, Kate thought she understood now which decision she had to make—which decision she needed to put before her Heavenly Father.

"Steve, I wish you were here," she said softly. "I wish I could tell you about this face to face. I hope you know what I'm thinking. I'll be true to you all my life. I could never knowingly do anything to make you love me less."

Her prayer was not spoken. *Heavenly Father, I've come to a decision. I hope you will . . . thou will . . . wilt tell me if it is right. I love David Cutler deeply. I want all the happiness that is possible for him and his family. But it looks like my being part of his family might not bring happiness—and maybe it would hurt my children too. I can't let that happen. For Dave's sake, and for KatiLynn and Stevie, I will let him go. You—Thou gave me a fine husband. I will be sealed to Steve and feel blessed that I am his. I thank Thee for that. In the name of Jesus Christ, amen.*

She waited. There was a small feeling of relief at having chosen, and a feeling of her Father's constant love. But there was not the feeling of complete peace she had hoped for. She waited longer, basking a bit in the lingering reassurance of His love. The feeling of confirmation she was expecting did not come.

After her prayer in the moonlight by her bed last night, she had felt confident that a sure answer would come today. Kate sighed softly. She had *not* felt that this would be easy. Things this important rarely were easy.

She called in her position to air traffic control, then added a course change. She would be heading south. *At least for a while—while I think.* Her hands on the yoke and her feet on the pedals made adjustments almost automatically to keep the plane in trim.

"Dear Heavenly Father," she whispered, "I'm grateful for Thy love, and grateful for Thy willingness to help me. It seems that maybe I haven't arrived at the right answer yet, or maybe there's something I still haven't understood. I want to do what Thou . . . wantest?—what You want me to do. Is there something more—"

You can marry him, Kate, and still be true to me. You don't have to choose between us. I know you love me. I know your heart. There's a lot of good you could do for him and his family.

Steve! Startled, she held her hands and feet locked in their positions as she turned to look momentarily at the seat next to her. It was empty. But it *was* Steve! It had been his voice she had heard in her mind. And it had been the kind of trusting, loving thing he would say to her.

She looked again at the passenger seat. She saw nothing. But she knew he was there—close enough to touch her, the way it had been in Hawaii on their honeymoon when she had flown their rented plane from island to island.

No voice spoke out loud. But thoughts flowed into her mind, rapidly forming into words in her own internal vocabulary. Some impressions came faster than she could form them into words, but still she understood at a level she could not explain. She felt Steve's continuing confidence in her, along with her Heavenly Father's. She understood that Steve trusted her to do the right thing, that he was happy about the way she was teaching KatiLynn and Stevie, and that she could be given the strength and wisdom to go on doing it as they got older. Last, there was the strong impression that it would be right for her and Dave to share all the happiness they could find together—that they could offer great strength to each other, making the rest of this lifetime more rewarding for both of them.

Then it stopped.

How long had it lasted? Maybe thirty seconds? As much as two or three minutes? More likely the first, but the impressions were so profound that it seemed they had gone on for a long time.

The strong feeling of peace and surety she had sought stayed with her as the plane flew on, her hands and feet making automatic adjustments to the controls. Kate basked in the feeling, her eyes fixed on the horizon. She tried to keep the sense of Steve's presence with her as long as possible, but when she turned to look at the seat beside her again—had it been perhaps five minutes?—she knew he was no longer there. But the feeling that she was in her Father's care lingered, along with some words she had read that Jesus said to His disciples: "I will not leave you comfortless."

The experience had been so powerful that Kate almost felt like crying. But she could not; she was simply too filled with happiness for the emotion to come out in tears.

And she could not wait to share what she had learned with Dave. She hoped it would make him as happy as it did her.

She called in another position change and turned east again, toward Phoenix.

"Heavenly Father," she said aloud, "thank You for answering my prayer. I don't have enough words to say how it feels. Thou knowest. Thank you—I mean, I thank Thee for letting Steve be the one to share these answers with me. And if there is anything more I should know, please tell me."

The last sentence had been a sincere expression from her heart. Still, she was surprised when the feeling of another presence in the seat beside her came again almost immediately.

Steve! He was back. What more would he—
No—not Steve.
It was someone else.

18

Bill Morrow strolled across the tarmac toward his daughter, who had just finished a post-flight inspection of the twin and was striding toward the office. He had not seen that confident stride for some time.

"You look happy today," he called as she approached.

Kate laughed. "More than just happy." She stopped next to him, took hold of his arm, leaned close, and kissed his cheek.

Bill stood back to look at her. "I don't think I've seen you this full of life in months."

"Maybe years. I've found out . . ." She looked into her father's eyes, then hugged him and held him close for several seconds before letting him go. "I'll tell you later. You and Mom—tonight. There's something I have to do first." She let go of him and started to walk toward the building, then turned back to ask, "Do you know if the trainer's available this afternoon?"

"The Cessna? Yeah. Why?"

"I may be giving a flying lesson in a few minutes."

Ann looked up and smiled as Kate came through the back door from the shop. "Your Saturday off and all you can do is spend it here? This place is in your blood."

"Best thing I could have done," Kate said. She pulled up the nearby chair and sat next to Ann's desk. "The best thing I've done in a long time."

"Oh?" Ann stopped typing and turned to face her expectantly. "More fun than usual today?"

"More than fun. Wonderful. Enlightening. I don't even know how to tell you."

Ann raised an eyebrow. Kate didn't answer the implied question. "Do you still have Dave's home number on your phone list?" she asked.

"Yes." Ann tapped the keys on her computer keyboard to call up the file. "Ready?"

"Would you call him for me, please? Tell him I have a security problem and ask him how soon he can get here."

Ann frowned. "Is something missing again? I haven't heard—"

"Tell him *I* have a security problem—and he's the only one who can help me with it." Kate smiled. "Ask him if he can come right away."

Ann looked at her questioningly for a moment. Then slowly she smiled too. "Is there anything I should know?"

Kate laughed. "As soon as there is, I'll tell you." She stood up quickly and moved her chair back to its original position. "While you're calling him, I'm going to go see if there's anything I can do with my hair and makeup."

She was finishing a preflight check of the trainer half an hour later when Dave came walking across the tie-down area toward the plane. She looked up from what she was doing and smiled at him. "Hi."

"Hi," he said. "Ann told me you have a security problem. Another theft?"

"No." She nodded toward the plane. "Climb in. Let's take a ride while I tell you about it."

He leaned against the fuselage of the plane and looked at her skeptically. "I told you once, I'm not big on small planes."

"You also told me once that you'd go flying with me sometime when the day was just right." She gave him her most inviting smile. "I promise you, there'll never be a better day than today."

Dave thought about her words for a moment, then walked around behind the plane, climbed in the other door, and took the passenger's seat.

He sat uneasily, she noticed, even after he belted himself in. As she taxied the plane toward the runway, he found a way to brace one arm against the door, and he held onto his seat with the other hand while she took off. Except for brief glances her way, he stared straight ahead out of the window as they climbed above Phoenix.

She had picked a heading that took them out away from the city where there was no other air traffic. Dave seemed to relax a bit as they climbed smoothly above the suburbs. He turned to look at her. "So far so good," he said, smiling. His smile seemed almost shy. "But maybe it's just because you're a good pilot."

She shook her head. "Days like this make up for the rough ones."

"You haven't called me," he said. "I tried to call you."

"I'm sorry, Dave. You deserved answers to your calls, and I wasn't very kind. I've missed you, more than I can tell you. But I've felt so much like

I'm not up to being what you and your children need. I was afraid—"
She smiled. "I said it again, didn't I?"

He sat looking at her, but said nothing.

"I have an answer now—if you still want one from me."

"Why wouldn't I, Kate? I still love you." He looked out the window. "I just hope you haven't got me up here in this airplane so I can't get away when you, ah . . ."

She leveled the Cessna off at a good cruising altitude well away from the city. "See that control yoke in front of you? Take hold of it."

He looked at her dubiously.

"Go ahead." She smiled encouragingly.

Carefully he took hold of the yoke in front of him.

As soon as he had a grip on it, Kate took her hands off of the one in front of her.

Dave's arms went rigid, locking the yoke he held into a fixed position. "What are you doing? You know I don't know anything about flying."

"Take it easy—we're doing it together. You handle the yoke and I'll guide you. I'll take care of the pedals. Keep an eye on the horizon to make sure we stay level." She pointed out the window to his right. "Look out at your wings from time to time to make sure they haven't dipped."

Dave checked the horizon, then glanced out to his right. He relaxed his grip on the yoke enough that she could see the blood come back into his fingers. He held the yoke in silence for several seconds staring straight ahead out the window. Then he glanced at her and at the wing beyond her before turning to gaze at the horizon again. "This flying lesson is part of your answer?"

"I learned something very important today that I didn't understand before." She reached out to touch his forearm. The muscles in it were rigid. She stroked it lightly. "I've been used to flying alone. I understood today that we could do it together and be better at it than the sum of one plus one, if we have the Lord's help."

He glanced her way again. "I tried to tell you that you didn't have enough confidence in yourself."

"I didn't have enough confidence in *us*, Dave. The Lord taught me something today about how love works. Maybe you grew up knowing it already because you understood that marriage is eternal. But Steve and I didn't know it, and the Lord helped me see it today."

He glanced her way once more. "What are you trying to tell me?"

"I learned that I can go on loving Steve and also love another wonderful man who, uh . . . who told me he wants to share the rest of his life with me."

Dave turned to look at her for several seconds. Then he realized he was neglecting his flying. He glanced out each window and looked straight ahead once more.

"The left wing has dipped a bit. Turn the yoke a little toward your right," Kate said. He looked at the wing, then the horizon and watched as the wings came level. "That's good," she said, checking the instruments on the panel in front of them. "Just hold us steady."

"You got the answer you were wanting, didn't you?" he asked. "From Steve?"

"The Lord was kind enough to let Steve bring it to me, yes."

"You saw him up here?"

She shook her head. "No. But he was here. I just *knew*."

"And?"

"What do you mean?"

"The answer?"

She put her hand lightly on his arm again. "That I can share this life with you and still be true to Steve in the ways that are most important to him. That it's OK if I love you for all the good things you are, and that we can do each other a lot of good. That between us we can do a lot of good for the kids—yours and mine."

"I've missed KatiLynn and Stevie," Dave said, looking her way once more. "I've been learning to love them. You think Steve approves of that?"

"I know he does. I think he's glad for all you could teach them."

She gazed out the front window watching the horizon. "I learned that I've been focusing too much on the problems and not enough on the good things that could happen for the kids. KatiLynn and Stevie need a dad. There are ways I could help Kelli while she's turning into a woman, and I could help Alicia too. I saw myself doing some mom things for them. And I learned . . ."

When Kate didn't speak for several seconds, Dave turned to look at her quickly. Tears were sliding down her cheeks. She was staring out the front window. When she finally spoke again, he could see out of the corner of his eye that she had turned to look at him. "I saw myself doing some things to help Ross. I saw him a little older—the kind of young man he could be. I learned that he needs someone around, a woman, who can help him learn to relate to other women." Kate paused. "I . . . I *wanted* to love him, in ways I didn't know I could."

Dave's brow furrowed. He glanced her way so he could look into her eyes for a moment. "You learned all this from Steve?"

She shook her head. "From Jeanine."

"*Jeanine?* You saw . . ."

"No—I didn't *see* anyone. I didn't hear anyone—at least not out loud. But there were two . . . two *people* up here with me. One of them was Steve. I think the other one had to be Jeanine. She cared a lot about the children—all five of them. And I think she . . ." Kate felt herself beginning to blush, but she was not going to hold anything back from him. "She doesn't seem to mind if you and I—if we get married."

Dave smiled broadly. "I told you she'd like you. I knew we could all be friends."

Kate laughed. "Would you like me to take back the flying now?"

"I thought you'd never ask." The moment her hands touched the yoke in front of her, he let his go.

"Dave, there's something that came out of this I need to share with Ross—soon. I think I'm supposed to talk to him about what it's like to lose someone you love and feel abandoned. I need to help him realize his mother still cares about him very much—that she's still there. But I don't know how to go about it."

"Kate, I took him to the cemetery last weekend, just the two of us, to his mother's grave, and we talked about what it is to say good-bye—at least for now." He turned to look at her again. "I think Ross will listen to you when he feels how much you care about him. We just have to find a way to put the two of you together."

"Do you think he'd like to learn to fly?"

"I think he'd love it."

Dave leaned back in his seat and watched her for several seconds as she handled the controls. Finally, he said, "I think I'd like to kiss the pilot."

Kate laughed. "I'll bet you say that to all the girl pilots you know." She touched two fingers to her lips, then reached across to touch them to his. "That'll have to do for now."

She called in their position again and reported that they would be coming to a heading of two hundred seventy degrees—west. She added that she would be practicing stall recovery with a student.

"What does that mean?" Dave asked.

She grinned at him. "Do you like roller coasters?"

He looked out the window. "Well, yeah—but those are attached to solid ground. They have something under them."

"So do we—a whole ocean of air. Let me show you how well we can ride it. Put your hands on the yoke again." When he hesitated, she said, "Come on. We'll do it together."

He took hold of the yoke. "Think of that as the face of a clock," Kate said. "Your right hand is at 3:00 and your left is at 9:00. Move your right hand to about 4:30. I'll tell you when to move it back." He did as she said. The plane went into a bank to the right. She waited until just before the compass reading reached 270, then said, "All right, turn the yoke to the left until we're level again."

When he had brought the airplane back to level flight, she said, "Now, this is the part where we work together and trust a lot. It's been a while since I've had to work with someone else on the most important things in life. Do you trust me?"

He glanced at her and nodded.

"Keep your hands on the yoke so you can feel what's happening, but let me do the work." Kate pulled the yoke back and the plane went into a climb, steeper and steeper. The yoke began to shudder and then suddenly there was a loud buzzing sound. Dave looked at her in alarm. "What's that?"

"Stall warning. It's normal," she answered. Suddenly the nose dropped over, and Dave gasped in surprise. Then he laughed as he felt the momentary sensation of weightlessness just before the plane went into a dive like the downhill run of a roller coaster.

Kate cut back on the throttle and pulled the plane out of the dive. "Are you OK?" she asked, glancing his way.

He smiled at her. "You do that often?"

"Sometimes when I'm especially happy. You should have been up here with me earlier today after I got those answers."

"Well, I'm happy." He grinned, and pulled back lightly on the yoke. "Let's do it again. I like it."

She pushed the plane upward into a stall. This time Dave laughed all the way down. It was infectious; she did too.

She began a wide figure eight, then brought the plane into a narrower one and a third one that was even narrower. "Feel the rhythm? When you get into it, it's almost like dancing."

Dave laughed once more. "I like it. I'll dance with you anytime, anywhere," he said. "By the way, if we keep going this direction do we get to the beach?"

"Next stop on our tour itinerary would be Disneyland, Hollywood, and points west."

"I know a great restaurant at the marina."

"Sounds wonderful. But I promised my mother I'd take the kids home for dinner tonight."

"Another time, then. Maybe we'll take the kids along."

"I could borrow a plane that would let us make a day of it. But for now you'd better turn us around."

While they were turning, Kate called air traffic control and reported that they would be inbound to Phoenix Deer Valley airport.

When they were headed east again and the plane was in level flight, Dave took his hands off the yoke to let Kate take over. "As soon as we're on the ground, you can expect me to kiss you the way I've been wanting for the past two weeks," he said.

Kate increased their airspeed. "Promise?"

Dave sat watching her as they flew. Finally he reached out his left hand and put it on top of her right one on the yoke. "Kate, will you marry me?"

She looked into his eyes and smiled for a moment before giving her attention to the horizon again. "You know my answer to that."

"Say it for me?"

"Oh, yes, Dave. Thank you for being patient with me. I love you."

He moved his hand to the back of her neck and caressed it lightly. Startled by the memory that came to mind, she stiffened momentarily, then relaxed immediately.

Dave took his hand away. "Did I do something wrong?"

"No." She reached for his hand and put it back where it had been. "I like that. Sometimes Steve used to do it when we were flying."

Dave massaged her neck lightly. "I told you once that I didn't think I could live with you if I had to feel like Steve was always looking over my shoulder," he said slowly.

"I think I can promise you that there will only be two people in this marriage."

Dave leaned back in his seat and gazed out at the desert landscape for a moment while he continued to caress her neck. Then he looked at her again. "You should have been born with wings. If anyone could have known how to use them, it would be you."

Kate laughed. "I have a feeling we were all born here to learn to fly. I'll spend the rest of my life helping you if you'll help me."